Mari Hannah is a multi-award-winning author, whose authentic voice is no happy accident. A former probation officer, she lives in rural Northumberland with her partner, an ex-murder detective. Mari turned to script-writing when her career was cut short following an assault on duty. Her debut, *The Murder Wall*, (adapted from a script she developed with the BBC) won her the Polari First Book Prize. Its follow-up, *Settled Blood*, picked up a Northern Writers' Award. Mari's body of work won her the CWA Dagger in the Library 2017, an incredible honour to receive so early in her career. In 2019, she was voted DIVA Wordsmith of the Year. In 2020, she won Capital Crime International Crime Writing Festival's Crime Book of the Year for *Without a Trace*. Her Kate Daniels series is in development with Sprout Pictures and Atlantic Nomad.

Also by Mari Hannah

BLACK FELL

Stone and Oliver Series

Book 4

MARI HANNAH

ORION

First published in Great Britain in 2023 by Orion Fiction,
an imprint of The Orion Publishing Group Ltd.,
Carmelite House, 50 Victoria Embankment
London EC4Y 0DZ

An Hachette UK Company

1 3 5 7 9 10 8 6 4 2

A CIP catalogue record for this book is
available from the British Library.

ISBN (Paperback) 978 1 4091 9241 1
ISBN (eBook) 978 1 4091 9242 8

Typeset by Input Data Services Ltd, Somerset

Printed and bound in Great Britain by Clays Ltd, Elcograf S.p.A.

www.orionbooks.co.uk

For Mo

Prologue

The rush of euphoria didn't last. The feeling of disconnect was strong this time. He could hear the sea crashing to shore on the shingle beach in front of his parental home in Iceland. The house of horror. Impossible. The place had been derelict for years, though that didn't stop the walls closing in on him now. A pair of hateful eyes arrived in his head, his father's motor-mouth in full working order. Accusations. Recriminations. Yelling at his mother over stuff she had or hadn't done, beating her senseless if she spoke back.

The ruthless moron showed no mercy.

He was beyond tears now, but the images wouldn't budge. The flashback was the worst ever, accompanied by a vivid soundtrack. He covered his ears, trying to shut out her screams, cowering on the cold ground with his hands over his head to fend off imaginary blows. They seemed as real as when his younger self would run and hide under the stairs until the silence came.

Drenched in sweat, he shivered.

It was chilly close to the shoreline. The slap-slap of water against the retaining wall of the reservoir soothed him, but not for long. His head lolled to one side, eyes struggling to adjust to the darkness, mouth parched from too much Brennivin he'd consumed on the flight over. *The Black Death* some called it. Mixed with drugs, it was a lethal cocktail.

If only.

The hypodermic broke the skin.

Take the plunge.

What are you waiting for?

He had no clue, even less as to how he'd arrived here to-night, only a vague recollection of stumbling through the dark

– a metaphor for his life. Suicidal thoughts were no stranger. He'd tried before, but was found and taken to A&E. The tosser should've minded his own business and left him to it. He'd get it done this time.

His thumb hovered.

Empty the syringe.

Do it now.

One press and your pain will be over.

Those walls will collapse, one brick at a time.

He rolled onto his back and was met by a million stars against the night sky, a sight so beautiful it made him weep. If he were to die tonight there was no better view. A rare moment of clarity. The sound rushing through his ears wasn't the Atlantic Ocean. It was the power of a stiff easterly through a forest of conifers – nothing to be scared of – and yet, beneath the tree canopy, everything appeared still.

Too still.

Unsettling.

He turned his head to one side, a pinprick of light appearing through the trees in the distance, closing on him . . . thirty metres . . . twenty . . . ten . . . closer and closer still. The light shot off to his left like a comet, then vanished. What the fuck? He blinked, looked again, harder this time. He could've sworn he'd seen movement but there was nothing there. A trick of the light, an addled mind.

Get a grip.

No, there it was again.

There *was* something.

He not only heard it. He saw it. Moving rapidly through the trees. Hard to tell if it was human or animal, probably a deer come to check out a stranger in distress, or was it something more sinister? That was a possibility, even here – especially here. It wouldn't surprise him if it was someone with a score to settle. He had enemies.

This could turn ugly.

Hauling himself into a sitting position, ripping out the needle, he strained to focus on the narrow path in front of him. A memory stirred, arriving like a disjointed movie sequence: a party getting out of hand; a roaring flame; pissed-off faces; a fight. Hard eyes. Harsh words. The glint of a long curved blade. That was it. Drugs had fried his brain to a mush of confusion and amnesia.

Pity it hadn't extended to his childhood.

For a split second, he was back in that house, a pool of red slime creeping across the floor. It triggered a panic attack, a shameful reminder that he'd done nothing to stop it. He was not to blame. They all said so. Then he remembered that he was in the UK and why. He'd come with good intentions, to make recompense for a deed he was deeply ashamed of. He never knew her name, though he'd never forgotten her face.

Fate had brought them together.

Tanked up on booze, he'd blown his last chance of redemption. She wouldn't listen. To her, he was as much a monster as his old man whose face came out of nowhere, a whispered curse spooking him further: *One fucking word from you and I will kill her. And when I'm done, I'll kill you too. Now stop your snivelling and get to bed.*

Like his five-year-old self, he felt warm liquid spread out between his legs, every tree in his eyeline morphing into a familiar and terrifying psychopath waiting to strike. More whispering. Same voice. A slew of insults coming at him from every direction, each one louder and more intimidating than the one before.

Run and I will find you.

It will not end well.

He was out.

He was here.

Move, move!

Out in the open he was a sitting duck, a target pinned to his chest. Grabbing his knife, with superhuman effort he managed to haul himself upright, the drive to protect himself overriding all else. The thought sounded ridiculous in his head. For as long as he could remember, all he'd longed for was to rock himself off. His choice. No one else's. Now he desperately wanted to live.

1

The number was on speed dial. Detective Chief Inspector David Stone lifted his mobile to his ear, listening as it rang out at the other end, urging Frankie Oliver to pick up. He'd keep it simple. A call from Control. An unidentified victim. At this ungodly hour, that's all his second-in-command needed to know. He had no intention of telling her that he'd been up half the night and was wide awake, cooking breakfast, when the call came in. She'd jump to the conclusion that he was still experiencing night sweats, reliving the murder of a close colleague, or that he had company, someone he'd met since transferring from the capital to his home force, retreating to the place where he grew up – a fresh start.

One of those was right.

As excuses go, he never talked about the first and had no time for the second.

'Oliver.' Frankie's voice was deeper than normal, coming from that labyrinthine space we all disappear to when the lights go out; a place of safety in the dark waters of nothingness for the lucky ones, a world of frightening images and unresolved conflict for others. 'Whoever you are, bugger off,' she said. 'I'm state zero.' She meant off duty. 'David, is that you?'

'Who else were you expecting at five a.m.?' He flipped his eggs. 'Shake yourself, Frank. We're on . . .'

She yawned. 'Go back to bed, guv. You're not the on-call SIO this weekend.'

'I am now, which means you are too, so get a move on.' He waited a beat, allowing her a moment to come round, himself enough time to slap the eggs onto buttered bread, adding another slice on top. He bit into the sandwich and tried her again. 'Frank, are you properly awake?'

'Barely. What've we got?'

He swallowed what was in his mouth. 'A body floating in the drink.'

'Again?' It came out like a whine.

Frankie would be imagining the River Tyne, a drunk floating in the water, an unexplained death. She'd be asking herself had the victim fallen or were they pushed? Probably concluding that it would come to nothing, a waste of time and MIT resources, a regular occurrence they could do nothing about. David could hear her shifting around now, dragging herself from a warm bed, not yet ready to greet the day.

He could relate.

Another yawn. 'Location?'

'Kielder Water.'

'Someone fall off *The Osprey* ferry?'

'Not funny. I'll collect you in half an hour. Unless the victim managed to fold themselves into a barrel and roll into the reservoir unaided, we have a murder on our hands.'

Frankie looked out through the windshield, eyes scanning a blanket of mist hanging over Northern Europe's largest man-made reservoir. The water stretched out to the west for as far as she could see. It was what she couldn't see that worried her. No sign of first responders, CSI vans or police vehicles in the south car park. No crime scene tape or personnel. No sign of life full stop, early morning fog preventing a view of the north shore.

David had been uncharacteristically quiet on the journey west. He'd given her little detail, beyond the fact that the barrel containing the corpse had been dragged from the water and broken into by an Icelandic tourist skinny-dipping at dawn. The thought of that pursuit, now or at any time of the year, made her shiver. The water was damned cold, even in a wet-suit. She'd learned to sail there with her father.

'I'll bet you twenty quid that this is a wind-up,' she said.

6

'Too many happy pills. I can't be doing with pagans, ancient rituals and traditions. It may not happen down south, but the summer solstice is notorious for crank callers up here. It brings out the weirdness in people. I mean, Icelanders believe in elves, right? You've got to admit, that's pretty flaky.'

'It sounded legit to me.'

Touchy – unlike him.

'The caller was badly shaken.'

Frankie kept her thoughts to herself.

David dropped a gear, turning off the C road, a winding ribbon of grey tarmac that cut through Kielder Forest, a gateway to Scotland for some. The scenic route. David seemed preoccupied. Curious. He'd shown no sign of it when he left the MIR last night. Quite the opposite. He was in high spirits, heading to party, time to let his hair down. A few laughs, a few beers on someone else's tab. She wondered if he was pissed off that she hadn't gone too, a birthday date with an old school friend taking precedence. Somehow, she didn't think so. If not that, then what had brought about such a dramatic change in his mood? She'd have a word with the lads when she returned to base, see if they could shed light on it.

'You all right?' She had to ask.

'Fine. Why?'

'Seriously? Take a look in the mirror. I've seen better-looking dead people.'

'Yeah, well I didn't get much sleep.'

'Self-inflicted doesn't qualify. You'll get no sympathy from me.'

'I don't remember asking for any.'

'What's wrong? You had two lemonades last night? You *know* you can only handle one.'

'Hilarious, Frank. You should do stand-up. My mind is on the job, which is where yours should be.'

A few moments passed without either of them speaking. Fine, have it your own way, Frankie thought, but didn't say.

She broke the silence with a work-related question. 'Was the finder male or female?'

A monosyllabic reply. 'Male.'

'And the victim?'

'Undetermined.'

She gave him the side-eye. 'What does that mean?'

'Let's wait and see, eh? The finder only saw a skull before legging it.'

'A skull?'

'That's how he described it.'

Frankie waited for more. It didn't come. 'Was it something I said, or did you get out of bed the wrong side?'

'Ignore me. I'm knackered, that's all.'

An hour and a half ago, he'd driven out to the coast to collect her from her apartment to save them taking two cars. She was waiting outside, on tenterhooks, her only thought to get to the crime scene as quickly as possible. He'd said little on the journey. Most probably didn't want to prejudice her opinion before reaching their destination. That way, she'd view the body in isolation, with no preconceived ideas that might jeopardise the first few hours of a new enquiry.

Under a vast sky, they crossed Kielder Dam, heading north towards Hawkhope, a place they were both familiar with. It occurred to her that the recovery spot – the point at which the barrel was removed from the water – may not be a crime scene, merely a deposition site. Either way, they were to meet first responders at the location given by control room personnel, ordinarily a peaceful haven for deer and other wildlife, no place for death and destruction. Crime was zero here, violence practically unheard of. Till now.

2

At the north end of the dam, ignoring the entrance to the car park, David took a right fork towards an access road, authorised only to forestry vehicles. He braked suddenly, nearly putting Frankie through the windscreen. She shot forward, the seat belt digging into her shoulder. A warning would have been nice.

No apology.

With his right hand on the steering wheel, his left arm resting on the back of his seat, he reversed at speed, a short detour. In the car park, four vehicles stood empty, facing a vast expanse of water. Next to them, an angler was standing at the rear of a rusting van, taking a moment to appreciate the view. He was not the focus of David's attention. His eyes were fixed on two identical Range Rovers, blood red with black contrasting roofs, parked side by side at the back of a toilet block, separated from other vehicles.

'Glasgow plates,' he said.

'Correct . . .' In her peripheral vision, Frankie caught site of a backpacker heading off at a pace, camera in hand. By the time she'd jumped out of the car, leaving the door wide open, he'd disappeared into the trees. She pulled out her mobile and made a call. 'Mike 2151. I'm dealing with the body up at Kielder. Can you pass a message to those on scene? I just saw a young guy heading their way.'

Control: 'He won't get far, Sarge. Officers have been deployed at various locations. They've been given instructions to take the details of anyone they come across and turn them back—'

'That's reassuring. Might I suggest a sign to alert the public that the Lakeside Way is closed until further notice?'

The controller agreed to pass the message on.

Frankie asked, 'You wouldn't happen to know if anyone took a note of the vehicles parked at Hawkhope when they arrived?'

'Affirmative.'

'Roger that.'

Hanging up, Frankie approached the angler. He was now bent over, rooting around in the rear of his van, a folding chair strapped across his shoulder, reminding her of her grandfather. Unable to stand for long periods on arthritic pins, he had a chair just like it. He loved to fish. Since she was a kid, he'd taken her along for company at weekends and school holidays. A nice memory.

'Sir, can I have a word?'

No answer.

She repeated the request.

'Aye. Be with you in a minute.' The accent was distinctly Northumbrian.

She watched his hands closely, unsure what to expect. In this area, some people were licensed to carry firearms. She was about to alert David when the man found what he was looking for, stood upright and swung round to face her. He was mid-sixties, short and stocky, a mop of grey hair poking out from beneath a flat cap. He was wearing hearing aids, she noticed.

She held up ID. 'I'm Detective Sergeant Oliver.' She nodded at the fishing gear. 'You coming or going?'

'Coming . . .' The angler leaned two rods against his vehicle, put down the bag, apologising for keeping her waiting. 'I have a weekend permit if you'd like to see it.'

'That's not why I'm here.' She thumbed over her shoulder. 'You may have noticed the patrol car as you drove in?'

'Hard not to. Blue lights is not something we see around here much.' He pushed his specs up onto the bridge of his nose, the better to see her. 'The name's Ron . . . Ronald, Harbottle. Has there been an accident?'

Frankie sidestepped the question. 'Has anyone spoken to you this morning, sir?'

'Only you. I arrived seconds before you did. Saw you drive in.'

'Well, you might consider a new pitch today. The area is currently being sealed off. I'd hate for you to get settled and then have to move you on.'

'Thanks for the warning.'

'I have another . . .' She admonished him with a raised eyebrow, a nod towards the wheels of his van. 'Do yourself a favour and get a new set of tyres. Those are illegal.'

He blushed. 'I only live down the road, flower.'

She didn't take offence. Like pet, flower was a term of endearment in these parts, not a put-down. 'Mr Harbottle, most accidents occur within spitting distance of home. Bald tyres are lethal. Trust me. I've scraped more than my share of body parts off public highways since I became a police officer. I'd hate for the next one to be yours.'

'I'll get them sorted.'

The twinkle in his eye was all it took to dissuade her from making an issue of it. 'Promise?'

'You bet.'

'Then I haven't seen them.'

'That's very kind.'

'On your way then.'

Relieved to have got off lightly, the old man threw his fishing gear in his vehicle and drove off to find another pitch. Frankie watched him cross the dam before turning her attention to the twin Range Rovers.

Peering in through the windows of the first one she came to, she noticed sweet wrappers, empty crisp packets and squashed beer cans abandoned in the footwell; on the rear seat, a discarded jumper, a clean pair of heavy-duty walking boots. Nothing unusual. The second vehicle was more revealing, a Hertz rental document on the dash in the name of Kristján Kristjánsson.

Icelandic?

Maybe.

Capturing the image on her phone, and another of both registration plates, a job she hoped someone else had already done, she returned to the car and gave David the low-down, including the name on the rental document.

'Nice of him to stick around,' he said.

'He's the one called it in?'

'The very same.' Handing her his mobile, David invited her to check out the audio link sent through by control room personnel, then drove out of the car park, retaking the un-authorised road, ignoring the No Entry sign. A red-and-white barrier, normally locked, was open, a uniformed officer stand-ing guard, his patrol car pulled off the road, lights flashing. Winding his window down, Stone identified himself as the SIO. 'Where is everyone?'

'Belling peninsula, sir.'

'Don't let anyone else through.'

The copper waved him on.

The scent of coniferous resin got stronger as they ven-tured further into the forest. Accessing the audio link Stone had given her, Frankie listened. Kristjánsson spoke excellent English. There was desperation in his voice. He stumbled over his words trying to describe what he'd found. He sounded young. Loaded too, she speculated, if he could afford to hire such a high-end vehicle. The lad was trying to console some-one sobbing in the background. A girl. This was no crackpot celebrating the sun's zenith. It was a distressed visitor to the county who probably wished he'd stayed at home.

3

The sun broke through as David parked the car. He got out and walked down a narrow path as directed by an officer in a standard-issue high-vis jacket, Frankie trailing along behind. The walk lifted the SIO's spirits, the fresh air clearing his head as he picked his way forward, the ground beneath his feet rough and uneven, tree roots poking through in places, overhanging branches making the route more difficult.

'David, look!' Frankie pointed skyward. A magnificent bird of prey was circling overhead, wings fully extended, riding the air current, sharp eyes fixed to the surface of the water beneath. 'Isn't he wonderful?'

'He's hunting for breakfast.'

'Wish I was. Put it this way, a bacon butty wouldn't go amiss. I should have brought one from home.'

'Yeah, you should. What kind of bagman are you?'

'A rubbish one . . .' Frankie grimaced. There was no chance of finding anything to eat around here this early in the day. Stone probably missed the Met with an eatery on every corner. 'When we see what's what, I'll get one of the uniforms to nip into Falstone and collect some grub. My shout.'

'I'm not hungry.'

'You're always hungry.'

'Not with a fry-up in my belly.' David laughed, in a better place now. 'It's called thinking ahead. You should try it some time.'

Kristján pushed his hands deep into the pockets of his shorts. His view was like the set of a TV cop show: crime scene tape; police vehicles and personnel; men and women in forensic suits crawling all over the place; about as far removed as it was possible to be from his idea of holiday heaven. Twenty minutes ago, a youngish woman had arrived in a private car, carrying a leather bag. A medical examiner, he assumed. She'd not spoken to him or any of his friends. Having identified herself to the cops, she'd disappeared behind a canvas privacy screen that had been erected close to the water's edge.

She was still in there.

Surrounded by law enforcement from a foreign force, Kristján felt uncomfortable. Taking on the responsibility as designated spokesperson for his group this morning, as he had done last night, was something he didn't want. He set off to join the others, picking his way through the trees with a sense of foreboding.

At the end of the path, Stone stopped at the edge of a clearing, a campsite where five small tents were arranged in a close-knit semicircle, all of them bottle green. Good camouflage in an area such as this. Beyond the encampment, the scenery was jaw-dropping, the sun reflecting off the water in places where the mist had lifted. Where it hadn't, the water was gun-metal grey, a thin, delicate cloud suspended in mid-air above it.

David turned, scanning the scene.

Bags, walking shoes and litter mostly. Must have been quite a party. Beside the remains of a campfire, swimming trunks and towels hung on a makeshift clothes horse made of sticks. He counted nine Icelandic kids sitting on a felled tree trunk, stripped of its bark. Some were preoccupied with their mobiles, others eyeing the detectives. Two uniformed officers, one male, one female, assigned to look after the tourists were doing their best to engage them in conversation. The kids were bored, keen to be on their way.

That wouldn't happen until they were questioned.

David was wondering which one was Kristjánsson when a tall male emerged through the trees, around six two, blond, athletic build, ice-blue eyes, a serious expression on his face. He dropped his head as the SIO caught his eye.

'Hello, Kristján,' David whispered.

'You're talking to yourself again,' Frankie said.

'Just weighing up our audience.' They played this game often.

'OK, which one is he?'

'Light blue shorts, navy T-shirt, I'd bet my pension on it.'

'Looks a bit shifty, don't you think?'

'He has no business being here. Wild camping is prohibited outside designated backpacking sites, as is swimming and setting fires, three rules that seem to have passed him by.'

'Have you forgotten your youth? Hardly hanging offences, are they?'

'You were the one said he looks shifty, Frank. I'm just offering an explanation as to why that might be. Ever seen a forest fire? There are millions of trees here. Imagine if they went up in flames.'

Before she could think of an answer, the most senior officer on site sauntered over towards her. Jardin had a supremely toned physique, three stripes on his epaulettes. On account of his prowess on the force footy team he had an unforgettable nickname. Smiling warmly, Frankie thumbed to her right.

'This is my guv'nor, DCI Stone.'

The man in uniform proffered a hand. 'Jardine, sir.'

'Bex to his friends, guv. He takes a mean free-kick.'

David said, 'Keep an eye on this lot till we get back.'

'Sir.'

'Where's the body?'

Jardine pointed through the trees, the way Kristjánsson had arrived. 'Walk west. Keep to the path, then bear left. The pathologist is there already.'

4

Home Office pathologist Beth Collingwood emerged from behind a white screen, a volley of camera shots going on behind her. Removing her nitrile gloves, pulling a mask clear of her face, the cap from her head, she acknowledged the murder detectives with a smile and an upward tip of her chin. She was a small woman, hair streaked with purple highlights. To look at her, you'd never know that she was at the very top of her profession, revered by everyone on the force, with qualifications that would make most academics' eyes bleed.

Hers were sharp, her expression difficult to read.

'Guv . . .' Frankie drew David's attention to a deep gouge in the ground at the water's edge where a heavy object had been dragged ashore. The channel ended where the CSI screen began. 'The container can't have been in the water long,' she said. 'At this time of year, it would have been spotted before now. In an hour or two, this place will be swarming – and not just with midges. It's a mecca for tree huggers.'

'You have something against environmentalists?'

'Just telling it like it is . . .' Frankie didn't move her head, only her eyes. 'Did you leave your sense of humour at home? You know I don't do prickly before eleven a.m.'.

'No squabbling, you two.' Beth was used to their banter. It was what kept the detectives sane. 'You should be happy on this glorious morning.' She extended her arm, inviting them to take in the magnificent view neither seemed to have noticed. 'Not a bad place to start your working day, is it?'

'Yeah, shame we're not on a jolly,' Frankie bit back. 'Last time I was here, I was snoozing on a blanket, not a million miles from this very spot. A good book, a cold flask of Pimm's, pork pies and my mum's homemade brownies in a picnic basket.' She tipped her head toward her boss. 'If that were the case today, Mr Grumpy might even crack a smile.'

Collingwood laughed.

David didn't.

He moved away.

'What's up with him?' Beth asked Frankie. 'Even at this early hour, he usually has his head in gear. I get the impression that the unfolding narrative isn't the only thing on his mind. Any ideas?'

A shrug. 'I've given up trying to second-guess what's happening on planet Stone.'

Beth waited for more.

Frankie held her tongue, less puzzled by her guv'nor's mood. He'd encouraged her to speak her mind. To ignore his rank. Maybe she'd overstepped the mark in front of the pathologist. DS Jane Vincent was the reason he couldn't sleep, his motivation for taking a demotion to return to the north-east when he was the golden boy in the Met. He hid his grief most days. When he couldn't, Frankie backed off, allowing him time and space to get over it. He was better now than when they first met, though not yet over it.

The murder of a loved one never left you.

Frankie liked and trusted Beth implicitly, but her guv'nor's business, professional or personal, wasn't open for discussion. He was strong and dependable, yet vulnerable at the same time; sensitive and apt to retreat into a cave she knew little of. He deserved her loyalty. 'We're supposed to have the weekend off,' she said by way of explanation.

'Ah, maybe he had plans—'

'He never has plans.'

'Harsh.'

'But true. Actually, that's not fair. David and Ben have taken up golf recently, a bit of male bonding going on there, I reckon. It'll be good for them to spend more time together.' Ben was David's nephew, a young man he'd taken in, acting as surrogate father to the lad at her suggestion. His father, David's brother, had died in a car crash, a dark time for both of them. Frankie changed the subject, a glance at the crime scene tent. 'I take it the skull is human?'

Collingwood answered with a nod.

'Male or female?'

'Oh, please . . .' Beth gave her a pointed look, faking irritation. 'As a formidable DS, you know better than to ask for an educated guess as this stage of an enquiry.'

'Oh, go on. Can't you make an exception, just the once?' Stone asked as he walked towards them. 'As you heard so eloquently from my 2ic, I need cheering up this morning.'

Beth hesitated. 'If you quote me—'

'He won't,' Frankie cut in.

David gave a three-fingered salute. 'Scout's honour.'

A smile from Beth – she liked him.

Frankie? This morning, David wasn't so sure.

Collingwood caved. 'I can only see a skull covered in soil deposits, so I can't say for certain, though I'm ninety-nine per cent sure the victim is male. If that changes, I'll let you know.'

David was aware that the ridge along the brow was more prominent in males than in females.

'You won't want to hear this,' Beth added, 'but from what I saw, there's no muscle or tissue left on the bones. Skeletonisation took place some time ago.'

'How long?' Frankie asked.

'Decomposition is determined by environmental factors. Depends on whether the body was left out in the open air, in water, in shade or full sun, if it was buried in sand or soil and dug up later. Just because it turned up here in a sealed barrel, you can't assume it hasn't been in the ground. I suspect it has . . .' Her grimace was as good as an apology. 'In which case, the only given here is we're talking years, not months – more than a decade, possibly several.'

Frankie locked eyes with David.

He didn't comment.

His attention was on the woods where ghostly figures in forensic suits were combing the area looking for anything of evidentiary value. Given what Beth had told them, on this occasion they were not seeking a murder weapon. The best they could hope for was the print of a tyre or shoe, a fag end or piece of gum discarded by whoever dumped the container. This case was complicated and he was struggling to get his head around it. How had the body in the barrel arrived in this place? Who'd put it there and why Kielder?

A protracted enquiry was on the cards.

'David?' Beth spoke again. 'I'd like to have the body moved to the morgue in its container. That way, if any of the skeleton is intact, it'll stay that way. If I try to extract it here . . . Well, without going into the whys and wherefores, I'd rather not, if it's all the same to you.'

He eyed the canvas screen behind her. 'Mind if I take a look?'

'Be my guest, for all the good it'll do you.'

5

The oak barrel looked vintage, the type with metal hoops traditionally used by distilleries and wine merchants. It lay on its side, a jagged gash around eight inches long and six across at one end. Frankie crouched down beside it. Using her Maglite torch, she peered in. Beth was right in her description. A dirty skull was all the detective could see: a forehead, eye sockets, adult teeth, the jawbone slightly ajar, giving the appearance that the man in there – if it was a man – was laughing.

Or screaming.

She stood up, handing David the torch. 'No wonder Kristjánsson was spooked.'

He took her place, taking a few moments to examine the perforation in the wooden casket. As with every case, their questions would fall into the categories of: who, what, why, when and how? Cause of death was up to Beth. Given the time lapse since, they all knew identification could take a while, discovering how the body ended up at the reservoir even longer. Only then could they turn their thoughts to potential offenders, motive, opportunity, method and means.

Having seen enough, David exited the screen.

Collingwood hadn't moved an inch.

He rolled his eyes. 'I assume you're done here?'

'Yes. OK to get it shifted?'

'I'm in your hands.'

'You never want to be in my hands,' she joked.

'How long till you start the PM?'

'I'll take care of my side of it today. Can't estimate when I might get hold of an anthropologist. I'll update you as soon as I hear.'

A nod from David.

As Beth stepped away to make the necessary arrangements, a text pinged on his mobile. He accessed the screen, then put the phone away as Frankie arrived at his shoulder.

'That barrel is old, guv. It must've taken some force to punch a hole in it. There's no sign of a tool being used, an axe for example.'

'Speak to Kristjánsson, find out what he used to smash it open and whether anyone witnessed him do it.'

Beth turned, held up a finger and spoke into her mobile. 'Hold the line, I need a quick word with the SIO.' She covered the handset. 'I'm told your boy used a rock, David. It was photographed and bagged. His camera too, and a wet towel. They were lying on the ground when I got here.'

'That's good to know.' He thanked her.

'So, what's the plan?' Frankie said.

David hesitated. She wasn't going to like what he said next. 'Grab Kristjánsson and his party. Get the interviews underway. I'll head off and get the ball rolling—'

'That's beneath your paygrade, isn't it? Can't you call Abbott? It's his job to set up the incident room and put the team on alert.' When David didn't shift his position, she spread her arms, affronted. 'That's it, I'm on my own?'

'You're good for it.'

'Boss, you heard Beth. Until she's completed the post-mortem, we have zero to go on. We're hardly on the clock – and those kids aren't going to take us anywhere with this one, are they?'

'They still need questioning.'

'What's the rush?'

'All of them, Frank. If we don't do it now, what's to stop them hopping on a plane out of here.'

She wasn't buying his explanation. 'Fine, I get it. You want me out of your hair.'

'That's not the case.'

'No?'

'Bright wants to see me.'

'What for?'

'Don't know, didn't ask.'

'I listened to the local news this morning. There was nothing going on that would involve us, nothing as important as a murder investigation anyway.'

'If the head of CID says jump, you ask how high.'

'I know that,' she said. 'Only there are ten of them and one of me. I'll need help.'

'I'll send someone with a bacon butty, how's that?'

Her shoulders dropped.

He laughed. 'Now whose sense of humour has gone AWOL? Look, there's no point dragging those kids any further than we have to. Hexham nick will do nicely. I'll have Abbott meet you there. You've heard of car share, right? When you're done, cadge a lift with him. We'll regroup at Middle Earth.' It was the nickname for Middle Engine Lane, Northern Area Command HQ, their base. 'I want names, addresses, travel plans and copies of passports, minimum. You know what to do.'

6

Kristján looked up as the Senior Investigating Officer reached the encampment, then walked off at a fast pace in the direction of the Lakeside Way, leaving the female cop he'd arrived with, standing alone, a face like thunder. She watched him disappear through the trees, hands on hips. As if sensing Kristján's gaze, she turned and made her way towards him. He'd taken steps to get rid of certain items, anything and everything British police might view as suspicious. He'd have to be careful now.

Whatever Bright wanted with David, Frankie had no time to dwell on it. She had to keep the area locked down, supervise the removal of the body, instruct uniformed officers to hang fire until further notice, wait for the Crime Scene Manager to give her a nod that his crew were done. The list was endless.

She sighed.

When CSIs were finished, and only then, would the footpath reopen to the public. As for house-to-house, she was screwed. There was bugger all in terms of property close by. She'd get Jardine and his crew to concentrate on nearby villages: Yarrow, Falstone, Kielder, isolated homes dotted around the countryside and any outbuildings, lodges etcetera.

A pointless exercise.

Houses grouped together were often so small they didn't even rate as hamlets. Asking for details of strangers hanging about was laughable in an area visited by tourists from across the globe. In her opinion, a media appeal was unlikely to bear fruit either. CCTV? Forget it. Detectives would have to unravel this case without the benefit of modern technology.

Depressing.

As she made off in the direction of the students an object glinting on the ground caught her eye. She bent over to pick it up: a new tent peg. Bagging the item, she slipped it into her jacket pocket, then looked up. The lad David had identified as Kristjánsson was watching her.

'Kristján?'

A nod.

'My name is Frankie Oliver. I'm a police officer. Can I walk you to where you were when you found the barrel? Nothing for you to worry about. I'll need to take a formal statement from each member of your party. This will be done at a police station nearby. Before we go, I'd like to ask you a few questions while it's fresh in your memory.'

Kristján was wary. Why here? Why separate him from his friends? The answer was obvious. Divide and conquer. That's how the police operated. She led the way. He hesitated. She turned, catching his reluctance before he could hide it. He followed. What else could he do? As they walked, she put his mind at rest, telling him she was sorry that his trip has been interrupted, that finding a body must've been a dreadful experience.

She didn't know the half of it.

He felt compelled to tell her that he was innocent of any wrongdoing, that he was simply a bystander. Wrong time, wrong place . . .

'I had nothing to do with that body—'

'Relax, Kristján. No one is accusing you of anything. The remains are old. You're not under suspicion. Do you understand?'

A nod – she must see that he did.

'When we've completed the interviews, you'll be free to leave.'

He hoped that would be soon.

*

Kristján seemed nice. Quietly spoken. Polite and articulate. Frankie noticed a recent scratch on his left cheek. She expected him to show relief that he was being treated as a witness and not a suspect. He looked anxious. Delayed shock, in all probability. He was half-man, half-boy. Right now, the boy was winning. He was pale, and deeply troubled. He didn't look at her, rather looked through her. He seemed socially awkward. Living where he did, he probably didn't meet many strangers, let alone cops. There was crime in Iceland but very few murders.

Sounded like a cool place to live.

The lad reminded Frankie of David's nephew, Ben. She sat down on a log, outside of the police cordon, well away from the corpse in the barrel, inviting him to do likewise. She decided to go easy on the foreigner, keep it friendly, build rapport. 'Will you go home or continue with your holiday?'

'Depends what the others say. This place gives me the creeps.'

'That's perfectly understandable. Are you from Reykjavík?'

'Ísafjörður, in the north.'

'Never heard of it . . . and probably couldn't pronounce it.' She threw him a wide smile. 'Geography was never my strongest subject. I'm ashamed to say that your capital city is the only place I know in your country. I visited once, on a school trip, and would love to return.' She wasn't making small talk. The country known as 'the land of fire and ice' appealed.

'You should,' Kristján said.

'My job keeps me busy. A social life isn't always possible. One day, perhaps.'

'The rest of Iceland is beautiful but remote. There's nothing there for me. I moved to Reykjavík to study at the university. My father wasn't happy.'

'Are they ever?' Frankie rolled her eyes. 'My father was a cop, grandfather too. They weren't too keen on me joining up.

I guess you could say it's in my DNA. That or the Olivers have no imagination.'

The lad smiled. 'You like it?'

'Like' wasn't the right word.

'I'm good at it,' she said.

7

Kristján's dream trip had turned into a nightmare. It had been quite a journey from Iceland, the route south from Scotland taking him longer than scheduled due to roadworks, a detour that had taken him out of his way. He'd got very lost.

He was even more lost now.

Taking a pen and pad from her pocket, Frankie readied herself to make notes, asking him to walk her through how he'd come across the barrel in as much detail as he was able. He glanced over his shoulder, anxious to check on Eva. After the events of the morning, exhaustion had set in. For her too, he imagined. She was so upset by the discovery, and the fight that took place afterwards. Her brother had taken her back to the campsite.

They hadn't spoken since.

Frankie waited. Kristján had gone someplace else. Wherever he was, it was causing him a great deal of anxiety. She felt sorry for him and wondered if she should call his parents. He hadn't heard a word she'd said in the past few minutes. He turned to look at her, apologised for not paying attention . . .

'I was miles away,' he said.

'Welcome back.' She smiled. 'These things are always difficult to talk about. Doubly so if you're in a foreign land with no support. The sooner we start, the sooner we finish. Are you up for it?'

'Yes, sorry. Ask your questions.'

'How long have you been camping here?'

'We arrived last night.'

'What time was this?'

'Is it important?'

Frankie answered his question with one of her own. 'Is there a reason you don't want to tell me?'

'No.' Kristján rubbed at his forehead. It was important, of course it was. The detective would want to know everything about his trip. Everything about him too in all probability. He'd hate her to think that he was being evasive. A half-glance in her direction. 'Our flight got into Glasgow shortly after two. We took our hire cars and headed south, stopping to eat on the way. We arrived at around seven o'clock, left the cars at Hawkhope and walked the rest of the way.'

'You'd planned the trip beforehand?'

'Online, down to the last detail . . . or so we thought.'

'Impressive. I'm more of a "go with the flow"-type traveller.'

'You get a lot more from everything if you plan. As a group, we'd done our homework. We picked a spot with a south-facing view. When we got here, we set up camp, had something to eat, sat around talking for a few hours, then went to bed.'

'Is that all?'

'There's nothing else to do here after dark.'

'Yeah, daft question. You lit a fire, I noticed.'

'We were very careful.' He dropped his head, then looked up. 'We were planning to move on this morning. I woke at dawn, grabbed a camera from my rucksack and went for a walk. I wanted to explore what I hadn't seen before nightfall. Landscape photography is my passion. I took some photos, then stripped off and had a swim. I'd just got out of the water when Eva arrived.'

'Friend or girlfriend?'

Kristján hesitated, keen to get his story straight. After his foray into the woods in the small hours, Eva arrived, cold and tense as she crept into his tent beside him, tears in her eyes. He'd pulled her into an embrace, asking her what was wrong. She wouldn't answer. He'd told her not to worry. A new day always brought peace. He remained awake until she fell asleep. They hadn't woken warm and safe in each other's arms as he expected. She was gone when he opened his eyes.

The next voice he heard wasn't hers.

'Kristján?'

He jumped, turning his head. 'What?'

'Are you and Eva more than friends?'

He shook his head, changing the subject. 'I didn't expect to see her up so early. She said she couldn't sleep. I couldn't either.' He didn't mention their clandestine meeting during the night. Best keep things simple.

'What happened after your dip?'

'I asked her if she was going in, told her the water was warm by Icelandic standards—'

'Remind me never to swim in Iceland.'

'If you visit again, try the Blue Lagoon.'

'Yeah, I heard it's fantastic. Did Eva swim too?'

'No.'

Frankie wondered if Eva was the girl hiding in the trees, trying to earwig their conversation. She'd been there a couple of minutes already, a pretty girl, about five two, skinny, a blond ponytail. She had little on for so early in the morning: jeans shorts, a light grey hoody, falling off one shoulder, flipflops on bronzed feet. If it was her, she could wait. Frankie would speak to her at the station. For now, she kept her focus on Kristján.

'You're all students?'

'Some, not all. Postgrad.'

'What were you studying?'

'Life and Environmental Sciences.'

'What about Eva?'

'She's at college still. Wants to be a doctor.'

'Clever girl.' Time to open up the discussion. 'Do you have a job too?'

'Me? No, why?'

'Travelling isn't cheap.'

'My grandfather left me some money.'

'Nice. You rang the police shortly after dawn?'

'Yes, Eva and I were standing on the bankside where the screen is now.' He pointed toward the crime scene tent. 'She spotted a barrel floating in the water. I found a branch and went to investigate. I pushed it to the edge. She helped me drag it ashore and was curious to see what was inside. I smashed it open and that was when we saw the skeleton. Is it real?'

Frankie nodded. There was something off about this lad she couldn't get a handle on. His leg was shaking. Realising that she'd clocked this, he moved his hand to his knee. He couldn't control it. This strange body language niggled at her as she continued to talk to him. 'How long before you phoned it in?'

'I did it right away.'

'Did you make any other calls?'

'Not personally. I can't vouch for anyone else.'

'I'm sorry, you're not going to like this. Your camera cannot be returned until we examine it. Did you take any pictures?'

'Of the body? No. Why would I?'

'People do.'

'Not me.' He was angry at the suggestion.

'What about on your mobile?'

'I didn't have it with me.'

'Did Eva?'

'No, yes, I think so. Yes, she did, I used it to call the police. Then all hell broke loose. The others heard her scream. Her brother didn't wait to find out why. He just laid into me, knocked me flying. She was hysterical, trying to get him off me.'

Frankie was intrigued. 'Why would he do that?'

'Eva and I were the only two here. It was an easy mistake to make. I was comforting her. She was scared, trying to pull away from me. As he ran towards us, I guess he misread the situation. He's very protective of her.'

Frankie pointed at his injured cheek. 'That looks sore.'

Kristján covered the broken skin with his left hand. 'It's nothing.'

'Does this brother have a name?' Frankie waited a beat.

'Look, I told you, it was an innocent mistake. I don't want him to get in trouble.'

'Kristján, if you don't want to report an assault that's your business. I need his name.'

'Aron.'

'Jakobsson?' It was important to be sure.

Kristján answered with a nod.

Frankie wrote the name down, mentally walking her way through his verbal statement, imagining him entering the water, guiding the barrel onto dry land, punching a hole in the side, recoiling as he caught sight of the remains. The fight afterwards. Maybe this explained his nervousness, his inability to concentrate when she began asking questions. The girl in the woods moved away, prompting the detective to ask, 'You haven't been totally honest with me, have you?'

He didn't answer.

'There's nothing more you want to tell me?'

He shook his head. 'I told you everything.'

Frankie raised an eyebrow. 'Except Eva's not just a friend, is she?'

8

Stone swiped his ID to access HQ and took the stairs two at a time to Bright's office, curious to know why he'd been summoned so early in the day. It was too soon to be the Kielder case, though the head of CID had his finger on the pulse of the MIT and would know of it. The first thing he did when he opened his eyes was to view the list of overnight incidents.

David silenced his mobile as he arrived at a door marked: Detective Chief Superintendent Philip Bright. He knocked and waited, a muffled instruction to enter reaching him through the door.

Turning the handle, he pushed it open.

Bright was immaculate, as always: smart suit, sharp eyes, switched on. He was a male version of David's former Met commander, Detective Superintendent Sinead Friel. Behind green smiley eyes, the woman who'd taught him everything he knew was a formidable presence. Cross her and your career was over. Bright was equally discerning. Fortunately, in both instances, David got along with them.

'You wanted to see me, sir?'

'Yes.' Bright put down his fountain pen, leaned back in his chair, studying his visitor.

Having come straight from a crime scene, David suspected that he might not measure up. His shoes were dusty and he hadn't had time to shave. The stubble on his chin began to itch. 'Excuse the state of me, guv.'

Bright waved away his apology. 'I'm aware of your early call-out.' He pointed to a chair, inviting David to take the weight off. 'I'm due at the airport in a couple of hours. What I have to say won't take long.'

David sat down, eyeing two folders on the desk in front

of him. He didn't need to read upside down to know what they were. The one on top was Frankie's personnel record, a document brimming with commendations and compliments. The one he couldn't see would be Abbott's, another DS with an impressive track record.

He nodded toward the files. 'Are they what I think they are, sir?'

'Good and bad news, yes.'

David's stomach took a dive. Dick Abbott had been trying for the next rank for years and been knocked back. This was Frankie's first attempt. David wanted to see his detective sergeants rewarded for their efforts. Both had passed their inspector's exam. 'Good and bad news' was confirmation that only one of them had made it through their promotion board, but which one?

Frankie ushered the Icelandic visitors into the waiting room at Hexham police station and went in search of the backup David had promised to send. She checked in with the front desk and was told that DS Dick Abbott and DC Raymond (Mitch) Mitchell were already there, two of her colleagues from the Murder Investigation Team. She found them in the bait room, scoffing breakfast, with a likely story that a local officer was still busy allocating interview rooms in which to conduct their enquiries.

Dumping a box of flight documents and passports on the Formica table, Frankie leaned over, grabbing half a sausage sandwich from Mitch's plate. She sat down, stuffing it into her mouth before he could object. He pushed his coffee towards her, strong and black, just the way she liked it and got up to fetch another.

'What's the score then, Sarge?' he said as he retook his seat.

Frankie slid a handwritten list across the table, containing ten names that were hard to get her Geordie tongue around, especially with her mouth full. She'd scribbled them down while waiting for a patrol car to pick her up, and another to ferry the witnesses to Hawkhope to collect their vehicles.

Control had sent a couple of Traffic cars to escort them to the station, one of which was driven by Tango 7003, Inspector Andrea McGovern, Frankie's sister's civil partner for the past ten years, a senior accident investigator who'd responded to the radio and happened to be in the area with nothing urgent on.

Mitch studied the list.

'Get copies for each of us,' Frankie said, licking a splodge of brown sauce from her lower lip, wiping it off with the back of her hand. She was keen to get started and return to base. 'I'll take the top three names: Kristján, Eva and her brother, Aron. Mitch, you take the next three. Dick, the bottom four are yours.' She put a hand on her stomach. 'I'm stuffed. You guys ready to roll?'

9

The Icelandic tourists were cooperative, their individual accounts corroborating one another, as anticipated. The interviews hadn't taken long. Frankie organised a lift for Mitch to Middle Earth, leaving him to copy their documents and see the Icelanders on their way, before leaving with Abbott.

As he drove out through Hexham's West End, she relaxed into her seat, a thought niggling at her. She swivelled her body to face him. 'Did you get a chance to talk to Kristjánsson like I asked?'

'Shit! I forgot all about it. Sorry, was it important?'

'Not really. We're not holding him and yet he was jumpy around me—'

'The boy has sense.'

Frankie punched his arm. 'I'm serious. He nearly flipped when I told him I was good at what I do.' She took in his smirk. 'I wasn't bragging. You know that's not my style. It was a throwaway comment, a response to him asking if I liked my job. I have a feeling he's holding back. It's been bothering me and I can't shake it off.'

Dick turned left, heading downhill. 'Maybe you're too old to mix it with the young 'uns—'

'Hey! I might not have kids, but I know a worried face when I see one. I just can't make sense of his nervousness and thought you might.' As they crossed the River Tyne, Frankie yawned, raising her arms to massage her aching neck, glancing across the carriageway to what was known locally as the bridge end service station. 'Fancy a Starbucks?'

'Too right.'

Frankie checked out the café through the window. There were

hardly any customers. Having ordered to go, most were sitting in their cars, keen to eat, drink and be on their way. An outside seating area was empty, the table furthest away drenched in sunshine.

'We're going to be locked indoors for the rest of the day,' she said. 'Let's sit out.'

'Suits me. What do you want?'

'Double espresso.'

'Anything to eat?'

'No, thanks.'

As he walked away, Frankie slipped on her sunglasses and sat down, checking her text messages. Nothing that couldn't wait. A couple of minutes later, Dick reappeared and sat down, lifting a caramel frappuccino to his lips, pushing hers across the table. 'So, are you going to tell me what we're doing here?'

'Am I that transparent?'

'You are today.'

Frankie crossed her arms, eyeing him across the table. 'Any idea what's going on at HQ? It's unlike the boss to piss off at the beginning of a murder investigation. He left the crime scene without a word to the witness who found the barrel. It seemed to me that he couldn't get out of there fast enough.'

'I may have heard rumours.'

'About what?'

'The results are out.' He meant from the promotion board.

'That's early . . .' Unable to read his expression, Frankie had to work hard to keep her cool. 'I was told the twenty-eighth.'

A redhead arrived before he could respond. Dick stood up. They hugged, started chatting, a couple of old friends by the sounds of it – and maybe more. Frankie was grateful for a moment to herself. *The results are out*. Was that why David was in a strop this morning, why he'd said so little on the way to Kielder? Had he left her to it in order to return to the MIR and give Dick the good news, leaving her clueless?

She felt betrayal, then instant guilt.

It was disingenuous even to think that of him. David was a good boss, a decent guy who played fair with everyone, even the prigs they dealt with day after long day. He'd hardly leave her in the dark. If she'd failed her board, wouldn't he tell her the bad news before congratulating Dick? It was unlikely, if not impossible, for two detective sergeants from the same unit to get the nod, which meant that he'd got through and she hadn't.

Frankie was distraught.

She was sure she'd done enough.

The redhead kissed Dick, made her excuses and disappeared inside the coffee shop. He sat down again. With his back to the sun, he'd only see his refection in Frankie's dark lenses, not her emotional turmoil. Congratulations followed, her tone suggesting she was happy for him, and she was, even though secretly she wanted him to crash and burn.

'I'm really proud of you,' she said.

'Relax, I've heard nowt. I thought you might have.'

'No, not a thing.'

10

Engrossed in her own thoughts, Frankie took little notice of the route along the way. Her eyes were now fixed like glue to the tarmac, the colour of which matched her mood. All she could think of as she stared out the windscreen was what her father would say if she hadn't passed her board. Operationally, she'd done what was required. She had the acumen, leadership qualities and management bollocks that would take her to the next rank. She'd come top in her inspector's exam and her old man had coached her on how to conduct herself at the final hurdle.

You'll ace it, Frances.

The fact that he'd used her Sunday name was proof that he was nervous of the outcome. These boards didn't always favour the brave or reward the best candidates. Frankie knew a highly qualified female officer who'd been blackballed because some shitbag had marked her file with a comment that called into question a room-mate who also happened to be female. Homophobic bastard. Political correctness and equality were written into every policy document. What occurred in practice was a very different thing.

'You said you'd heard rumours.' She kept her eyes front. 'About who?'

'Maddison got through.'

'Well qualified then.'

Dick's mouth fell open. 'That tosser?'

'I was being ironic, divvy. The brass love him. He couldn't get any further up their arses if he tried.'

'Well, the self-satisfied prig is lauding it up at Central this morning, telling anyone who'll listen. You know how he loves to gloat. It boils my piss that someone so clueless is on his way up, while you and I are at the sharp end, putting in the hard yards and getting nowt for it. I wouldn't care, but he's got four years in. Four! Can you believe that? What does he know?'

'You're asking the wrong question,' Frankie said. 'If he made it through, it's not what, but *who* he knows—'

'Yeah, well I'll tell you what he doesn't know: the definition of law enforcement, for a start. He couldn't find his way out of a paper bag, let alone investigate a murder. And I'll tell you something else: your old man would've kicked him into touch on his first week.' Dick and her old man had known each other forever. 'Whoever heard of a copper called Hugo, anyhow?'

Frankie couldn't raise a smile. 'Who else passed?'

'Gina Crawford from the marine unit. Good call, if you ask me.'

'Agreed, she must be buzzing. Anyone else?'

'Moses, though that's to be confirmed. A civvy told him she'd seen his name on the official list while tidying up in the Super's office. Tidying up being the euphemism for snooping, in case you didn't catch it.'

'Priceless!' Frankie snorted. 'My old man always said, if you want to know anything, ask the cleaner.' She sighed. 'Well, that's that then. For your information, I'll be wearing a slapped-arse face tonight, so keep your distance. If you were hoping for commiserations drinks in the police club after work, forget it. I'd end up lamping someone who looks at me the wrong way. If it's all the same to you, I'll drown my sorrows alone.'

'What's with the negativity? You'll be fine. The boss is impressed with you. You've had some great collars.'

'With your help. You and I both know that's not how it works. Anyone who thinks that a meritocracy exists in the police service is delusional. Strings are pulled, good officers passed over in favour of those with the right connections. Happens every day. We either walk or suck it up and move on.'

'Let's not jump the gun, eh?' Dick's expression was gloomy,

but he hadn't given up hope altogether, unlike Frankie. 'We might still be in with a shout.'

'You think so?' She wasn't convinced.

'If the worst comes to the worst, there's always next year.'

'Er . . .' Her eyes widened. 'When have I *ever* displayed patience?'

'Follow my lead,' he said soberly. 'I'm making a career of it.'

Frankie felt his disappointment as if it were her own. The arseholes making the decisions had probably made up their minds that he only wanted the promotion to enhance his commutation and retirement pension. She tried to lift him from despair in the only way she knew how.

Reaching up, she flipped the sun-visor down, sliding open the vanity mirror, peering at her reflection, turning her head this way and that.

He gave her an odd look, asked what she was doing.

She checked her watch. 'We're ten minutes out. Thought I might practise my I'm-not-too-disappointed face, like the also-rans at the BAFTAS. I'll have it down to a T by the time we get there.'

He laughed and so did she.

Minutes later, they were in a better place when her phone rang.

Frankie took the call. 'All done, Mitch?'

'Sarge, we messed up.' He was almost hyperventilating, his voice breaking as he continued the dialogue . . . 'A call came through for you from Jardine. There's a second body at Kielder, found a short distance from the first. This one has skin.'

11

'Shit!' Frankie hung up. 'I can't get through to Kristjánsson and the boss is still not answering.' She tried Eva's number. Her phone was also switched off. When Abbott glanced into the passenger seat, she gave him the death stare. 'Can't this rollerskate go any faster?'

They were heading in the direction of the reservoir, a C road, a blue light but no siren available in Dick's private vehicle. She texted Stone: **There's been a development. Call me.** Next, she called Control, putting a marker on the two Range Rovers. If they were seen they would be stopped.

Frankie threw her mobile on the dash. Stone would go ballistic when he heard that the Icelandic visitors were no longer helping with enquiries. He'd expect them to be in a cell.

Abbott spoke up. 'You think it's the kids we interviewed?'

'Hey! With your intelligence, you should be on *Mastermind*.'

In spite of the gravity of the situation, Abbott grinned.

Frankie added, 'I can't see it being a coincidence. Mitch said the guy was dragged from the water less than a few hundred metres from their campsite.'

Movement in her peripheral vision.

'Watch out!'

She looked on in horror as a slow-moving tractor nosed out from the field to the right of the road, a tall hedge obscuring it from Abbott's view. Giant tyres emerged directly in front of them. Off the pace, Abbott swung the wheel one way, then the other, like they were moving through a chicane, avoiding the heavy machinery by a whisker.

Frankie blew out a breath, wishing David was in control with his advanced driving skills. 'This is the sticks,' she warned. 'Keep your eyes peeled. I'd like to get there in one piece.'

'Make your mind up. Fast or slow?'

Frankie ignored the sarcasm, an image of Kristjánsson flooding her thoughts as the speedo climbed, sixty-five, seventy . . . seventy-five. She'd known that he'd been less than honest, though it never occurred to her that it might involve something serious or fatal.

At Kielder, Dick depressed the brake too hard, kicking up dust on the dirt road. Frankie told him to grab a forensic kit and cover up. She was out of the car before the vehicle came to a halt. Andrea and Mitchell were waiting, grim expressions on their faces. The Traffic Officer had obviously driven him to Kielder. Ignoring them, Frankie made her way past Jardine and his crew to a point where she could view the body at a safe distance.

A young man she guessed was early to mid-twenties was lying on the ground, wearing dirty jeans and worn trainers, his upper clothing covered in bits of plants and other debris. There was soil on one side of his face, a bulge in the right-hand pocket of his jeans, track marks, old and new, on his arms.

She studied the scene, trying to make sense of what it was telling her. There were no obvious signs of a scuffle, no tent pitched nearby to suggest he was rough camping, though to the west of where she was standing was an odd, cone-shaped stone building that looked like a Gaelic cairn stood close to the water's edge. Its wooden door was ajar, pushed inwards.

Had he been sheltering there?

Questions were piling up.

Had he tripped and fallen in, drifting some distance from where he'd entered the water? Was there was a connection to the first victim? Could the man on the ground have thrown the barrel into the reservoir and got into difficulty? Only a fool would swim fully clothed and with shoes on.

She called out to Jardine. 'Who found him?'

'Cooper.'

The officer he was pointing at was pale, angular features, dark eyes, furrowed brow. Frankie gave him the once-over. Sensing her interest, he ran a hand through short spiky hair, dropping his head, avoiding her gaze, like a child hiding behind his hands, too young to realise that you could see them even if they couldn't see you.

Frankie addressed Jardine. 'You realise we have serious contamination issues here?'

'You could say that.'

'Well, there's no other major incident team available. Abbott and I will have to deal. Organise an outer cordon. Tell your crew to move behind it and keep away from that.' She pointed to the cone-shaped structure. 'Know what it is?'

'A wave chamber,' Jardine said. 'When you close the door, the floor appears to turn liquid and the walls echo the sound of the waves outside. My kids love it.'

'Anyone been inside today?'

Jardine shook his head.

'That's the right answer.' Frankie beckoned Cooper over. 'Talk to me.'

He shifted his weight from one foot to the other, took a deep breath.

'C'mon, man. We haven't got all day.'

'Sorry, Sarge. When you left for Hexham, we were clearing up, removing crime scene tape and whatnot. I needed a cr—' He blushed. 'I was caught short, Sarge.'

Frankie shook her head. 'Never volunteer for an observation stint, Cooper. You need to be potty-trained.'

Cooper had no idea if she was joking or being serious. 'The public loos were too far away. I knew I wouldn't make it to Hawkhope—'

Raising a hand, Frankie decided to help him out. 'So, you went to find a convenient spot to take a dump and that's when you found him?'

A nod. 'Face down in the water.'

'Finally!'

'I thought he might still be alive and dragged him out. I'm so sorry if that wasn't the right thing to do.'

'It was exactly the right thing to do. Preservation of life takes priority, always.' Jardine's crew were moving away. 'Come with me, Cooper.' They moved towards Jardine, Frankie issuing more instructions. 'Bex, I need a new search team out here: dog section, support group, CSIs, the lot. A pathologist too. Anyone but Collingwood. Make the calls and stand down.'

'Everyone you asked for is already on their way.' Jardine gave her a disparaging look. 'In uniform doesn't equal dim, Frank.'

'Did I say that? I'm busy, mate. I don't have time to stroke your ego. If your feelings are that sensitive, you're in the wrong job. We have to do this right. If I didn't ask, Stone would can me in a heartbeat. Are we clear?'

'Crystal.'

'What's the ETA for a Crime Scene Manager?'

'At least an hour, possibly two—'

'You're kidding!'

'No need for you to hang around,' Jardine said. 'When they give the all-clear, I'll call you.'

'I'm going nowhere.'

'Thought you said you wanted to do it right.'

'We just handed ten foreign nationals their passports. Last night, they were camping yards from here. Right now, I don't have that luxury.'

'Your funeral.'

12

Dick arrived in forensic kit, carrying a bag containing more of it. He gave Jardine the thousand-yard stare. 'Everything OK here? You look like you need a mediator.'

'No, we're cool.' Frankie made light of it.

Jardine didn't follow her lead. He glared at Dick.

Frankie added, 'Bex has kindly agreed to lend me some tread plates.'

Without speaking, he sloped off in the direction of his vehicle.

Dick watched him go. 'What's his problem?'

'Search me.'

'If he's giving you grief, just say the word.'

'He's not. And if he was, I don't need you to fight my battles. Any news from the boss?'

'Not when I left the car. No texts or missed calls – from anyone.'

'Sod him them . . . he can't say I didn't try.'

Frankie checked her mobile again. A weak signal was still a signal. Still nothing. She thought of ringing Bright directly, then had second thoughts. It might be misconstrued as going over David's head and that wasn't on.

Dick was waiting for her input.

'I'm sticking my neck out here,' she said. 'You're not exactly a clean skin but as near as damn it. You weren't at the barrel scene. If I can find someone else to search the IP's pockets, that's good enough for me.' Given the fact the injured party was fresh and not crawling with maggots, it occurred to her that Jardine's crew might have beaten her to it. Had there been any decomposition, they would have run a mile. Keeping the thought to herself, she focused on Abbott. 'Sound like a plan?'

'Fine by me.'

Frankie caught Jardine's scowl, as miffed as he was a moment ago. She moved towards him, offering an olive branch. 'Hey, I wasn't getting at you before. I have a job to do, that's all. Think of it as a halftime talk and let's draw a line under it, eh? I can't do this on my own, Bex. I need your help.'

He didn't respond.

She'd made things ten times worse by making a joke of it. *C'est la vie*. 'Has anyone searched the victim's clothing?'

Jardine shook his head.

'Is anyone here now who wasn't here earlier?'

'Couldn't tell you, not a hundred per cent.'

She gave him hard eyes. 'Could you ask, or would you like me to do that for you?'

He raised his voice, addressing his crew collectively with an angry, 'Oi!' waiting for their full attention. 'Is there anyone among you who hasn't been inside the cordon at the barrel site?'

A hand went up, a female PC: young brunette, five ten, hazel eyes, square shoulders.

Jardine didn't seem to know her. 'Speak up then.'

Frankie bristled. If Jardine offloaded his anger on the PC, he'd wish he hadn't.

'I was deployed to prevent anyone approaching from the west,' the officer said. 'When I heard on the radio that a second body had been found. I made my way here on foot to see if I was needed.'

'You are.' Frankie beckoned her over. Sentry duty probably meant she was inexperienced, a probationer perhaps, not long out of training school. 'What's your name?'

'Fitzsimmons . . . Roz.'

Frankie glanced at Cooper. 'Don't go far, I may need another chat.' He was gone in a flash. 'Roz, grab a forensic suit, hat and mask. This is DS Dick Abbott, my MIT colleague and yours temporarily. You're the only two here who were not on site this morning.'

Roz smiled at Dick.

Every woman smiled at Dick. He might be married and twice her age, but he was a magnet for the opposite sex. Always had been. He could get more out of females, colleagues or witnesses, than any detective Frankie knew.

'Grab some gloves.' Frankie nodded towards the dead man. 'For obvious reasons, I can't handle what I'm about to ask you to do myself. Neither can Dick. I want you to search his pockets carefully. There could be a syringe in there. If you see one, leave it be. I'm only after his wallet, assuming he has one.'

Roz looked uncertain. 'I've never done that before, Sarge.'

Frankie remembered her first time. Gross. She was of similar age, around twenty years old. 'You have pockets, don't you?'

'Yes.' Roz looked down at her utility belt, then up again.

'You smoke?' Frankie asked.

'Yes—'

'Then pretend he's got your fags and there are no shops open. Go on, he won't bite. Dick'll hold your hand. We need ID.'

She hesitated.

'You're good for this.' Dick handed Roz a forensic suit. 'C'mon, if I have to look like a clown, then so do you.' He was good like that, offering encouragement to those young in service.

As she got the kit on, Frankie noticed one or two of the lads behind the tape having a laugh at her expense. 'Who's Mouth Almighty over there?'

Roz looked up. 'PC Harrison. Ignore him, guv. I'm used to it.'

'Like hell . . .' Frankie singled him out. 'Harrison! You think it's funny to belittle a fellow officer?'

The grin slid off his face. 'No.'

'I think you mean, no, Detective Sergeant.' Frankie had met many arrogant guys like him and was in no mood to let it slide. 'Well, you just volunteered for the grunt work. Maybe next time you're called out to a crime scene, you'll show proper respect for the dead, and a colleague who's taking her job seriously. Now piss off and wait at Hawkhope car park. You and I will meet again.'

Roz didn't smirk as he sloped off through the trees, though she probably wanted to.

'Off you go,' Frankie told her. 'Dick will keep you right.'

Dick led the way using the tread plates Jardine had put in place – one way in, one way out – then gave Roz the nod to proceed, reiterating the need to avoid sharp objects. She got straight to it, avoiding the eyes of the unidentified dead man. It was the same for every rookie cop. She found nothing in the left pocket and moved on to the right. When she was done, she stood up holding a soggy carton between thumb and forefinger. Dick leaned closer to examine the find, resisting the temptation to take it from her, then turned to face Frankie.

From where she was standing, she couldn't make out what they had found.

He felt her frustration. She was a hands-on cop, a good cop like her father. On so many levels, she deserved that promotion more than he did.

She spread her hands. 'What is it?'

'Roz found the fags,' he said.

'No wallet?'

'No, hold on.'

Dick turned away, complimenting Roz for a job well done, handing her an evidence bag from the forensic kit.

Placing the item inside, she sealed it tightly.

'Sign it too, please.'

Once she'd done the business, he took the bag from her, eyes widening as he stared through the polythene window at the warning label on the carton: Reykingar geta skaðað sæði og draga úr frjósemi. Pulling out his mobile, he tapped the words into Google Translate: *Smoking can harm semen and reduce fertility.*

'Oh shit!' The expletive put Frankie on alert.

'What?' she yelled.

He locked eyes with her. 'They're fucking Icelandic.'

13

Throughout his meeting with Bright, David had been ignoring the persistent vibration in his pocket. It happened again as he left the office. Pulling it out, he checked the screen. Several missed calls and two missed texts, all from Frankie. He scrolled through them. The tone of each was urgent. In police speak, a 'development' had serious connotations. The last text he received was touchy, her words circumspect, but her meaning clear: I need help – where the hell are you?

Tapping on her number, David was relieved when the call connected immediately. He got in first, apologised for bailing earlier. She didn't ask why he'd not picked up her calls and he didn't offer an explanation, just listened patiently as she told him what was going down at Kielder. She was well and truly rattled.

'Where are the Icelandic kids now?' he asked.

'On the fly—'

'Since when?'

'A couple of hours at least. Actually, nearer three.'

'Christ!'

'I'm sorry, David. We weren't to know. If the second body had been found an hour earlier, they'd all be in custody, or helping us voluntarily. I've put a stop on their vehicles. No update on that yet, unless you know something I don't.'

'This is the first I heard of it.' David palmed his brow, checking the corridor to ensure that he was alone, the polished sign on Bright's office door catching his eye. He made off, keen to get out of HQ before his guv'nor found him floundering. Frankie was tripping over herself to apologise. 'Not your fault,' he said. 'The search parameters weren't wide enough. If anyone is to blame, it's me.'

14

Pathologist Russell Stuart had already made a small sketch of the area. He was kneeling beside the second victim, in the middle of his preliminary examination, a large medical bag open on the ground beside him. From a distance, Frankie could only see the crown of his head. He was shit hot, older than Collingwood, the most senior Home Office Pathologist in the northern region for the past two decades. He'd worked a lot with her old man in the latter years of his service and she knew him well.

He sat back on his knees, thinking. He appeared to be talking to Dick, except he was too well mannered to do that without making eye contact. No, she decided, he was dictating his initial observations, giving a running commentary of what he'd found into the device in his hand.

Dick said something.

Stuart looked up and gave a nod.

Examination complete, he picked up his kit and made his way towards Frankie. He was a short man, early sixties, hair almost white at the temples, his face mask hanging loose around his neck by the time he reached the outer cordon and ducked beneath the tape a uniform was holding up for him.

She was champing at the bit to hear what he had to say.

He didn't stand on ceremony. 'Your man has substantial injuries to the back of his head and a small, very recent nick to his right forefinger.'

'Defence injury?'

'I'm inclined to think not. I'd have expected more of them if that had been the case. I rather think he didn't see what hit him.'

Hit him?

Frankie glanced briefly towards the reservoir. The water was decidedly choppy. When she was standing nearer to the shore an hour ago, trying to put a puzzle together and finding no clues to guide her, she'd heard the slap of liquid against large boulders that fringed the edge of the lake to the southern side of the wave chamber. She'd thought nothing of it at the time. Now though, it triggered a response. 'It's rocky close to the water's edge. Dangerous in places. Might he have fallen and struck his head on the way in?'

'Once perhaps, not twice.' Stuart arched an eyebrow. 'Unlike you not to pay attention, Frances.' He always used her given name. 'I said injuries, plural.'

Ten minutes later, having briefed her fully, he left the scene just as a PolSA team arrived. Frankie liaised with their team leader, then took out her mobile, calling David to confirm the pathologist's findings. 'So, there we have it, guv. An expert opinion: a murder case. Stuart is free to begin the post-mortem as soon as the body arrives at the morgue.'

'What do you think?'

'I don't know, is the honest answer. There's no break in the fence where the body was pulled from the water, no conveniently discarded weapon. When have we ever been that lucky? There are no signs of a fight, nor trail of blood, so the victim didn't crawl there and fall in. We're looking for a crime scene elsewhere. We need someone to calculate direction and drift, given the windy conditions.'

'I'll sort that.'

Frankie paused, putting her thoughts in order. 'For the life of me I can't read it any other way than a straight.' She meant a straightforward case, a violent death with a list of suspects they already knew about, not an investigation with no clue as to who was responsible. 'Whether we like it or not those kids are in the frame. Why else would they all tell us that there were ten in their number, when there were eleven? We need eyes on them.'

'I'll ask Mitch if he knows in which direction they were heading—'

'I did that already. He doesn't.'

Eleven kids, not ten.

A shiver ran down Frankie's spine as a thought pushed its way into her head. In the rush to get to Kielder for the second time that morning, she'd bypassed the Hawkhope car park, a decision she was now regretting. She'd been so busy issuing orders, keen to do things right, it hadn't occurred to her till now. David might not be the only one cocking things up.

Sensing trouble, Andrea whispered in her ear. 'You in trouble?'

Frankie rolled her eyes, an unspoken reply: maybe.

Another whisper. 'Who you talking to?'

'Is that Andy?' David asked.

'Yeah, I'm needed, I have to run. Call you later.'

A curt reply. 'Make sure you do.'

It was like a red rag to a bull. Frankie came apart: 'That's rich from someone ignoring my calls. When have I ever left you out of the loop? Can you honestly say the same thing?'

There, she'd said it.

She was angry, mostly with herself. She'd tipped her hand, shown David and Andrea how important those results were. Now they both knew what was bugging her. David didn't deserve an apology. He wouldn't get one either. She wanted to tell him that it wasn't affecting her ability to take control her end. He'd probably made up his mind that it was. Her conversation with Dick felt like light years away. Promotion to the next rank had preoccupied her all morning. This was her time, her moment, and she wanted it badly.

There was a beat of time before the line went dead.

Frankie checked her screen. 4G signal. Plenty of battery. She glared at her sister-in-law. 'The bastard hung up on me!'

Andrea made a face. 'You get what you give out, Frank. Why so arsy? I swear, you two argue more than me and Rae.'

Unlike Frankie, Andrea never lost her cool. Her job in Traffic required her to be calm in a crisis and she took it to the nth degree. Whatever situation she found herself in, overreacting was not in her nature. In a car chase, it could cost lives, her own as well as the person or persons she was pursuing. In her opinion, losing your rag was a waste of energy.

'C'mon,' she said. 'It can't be that bad. You're Superwoman. You could handle David wearing a blindfold and with your hands tied behind your back.'

'He's a pain in the neck.'

'And you're not? Isn't it one of your rules that if you've made an arse of yourself, you should front up? I think you may just have broken it.'

Frankie looked away, still simmering.

'Hey, what is it? You can tell me—'

'There's nothing to tell.'

'Yeah, right.' Andrea put a hand on Frankie's shoulder and gave it a squeeze, a piece of meaningful advice on its way. She spoke softly and sensitively, genuinely concerned. 'If you're going to get upset, best not do it in front of this lot, eh? Jardine and his team have clocked us. Keep it till you get home. Rae and I are in tonight if that would help—'

'I'm having dinner with Mum and Dad. Maybe . . .' Frankie cut off the question she knew Andrea was dying to ask: had she passed her board? Before she had a chance to voice it, Frankie said: 'Walk with me, I may need you. I have to speak to Jardine first.' By the time they reached him, her emotions were under control. 'Bex, which one of your crew checked the car park earlier?'

'Harrison. The guy you sent packing.'

'Don't wind her up,' Andrea said. 'She's not in the mood.'

Jardine looked at Frankie. 'Why do you want to know?'

'I need a copy of all vehicle registrations. Get him on the

radio. Tell him Tango 7003 will be with him shortly. He's to give her the list.' Frankie asked Andrea to follow it through, then left immediately. Ten minutes later, her sister-in-law confirmed her suspicions. The second victim had made his way to Kielder independently.

Frankie was asking herself: why?

15

Back at base, the incident room was set up for two new investigations Frankie didn't think were linked, though she had to concede that the finder of the first victim may have been responsible for the death of the second. The electronic murder wall was on a split screen, both cases on display, graphic crime-scene images already uploaded, sent through to the MIR by forensic photographers.

The door behind her swung open.

She turned.

David gave her a nod as he came closer, calling the team to order for an impromptu briefing, keen to bring them up to speed. Frankie felt no tension between the two of them. She'd said her piece and he'd responded by ending their call abruptly. So what? It wasn't the first time and wouldn't be the last. She detected nothing unusual in his demeanour as he began his delivery.

'As you've probably gathered, the barrel investigation is a non-starter until the post-mortem report comes through,' he said. 'Let's be clear. It is of equal importance but lower in priority. A fresh victim must take precedence over skeletal remains. For the time being we'll concentrate on Victim Two. Switch off your mobiles and pay attention. I wasn't involved, so DS Oliver and DS Abbott will take the lead on this one.'

He gave Frankie the nod to proceed.

'Before we begin,' she said. 'I want to clarify Home Office personnel so there's no dispute over who did what. The pathologist on Victim One, the barrel case, is Beth Collingwood. For Victim Two, it's Russell Stuart, who has confirmed an unlawful killing. The IP has deep wounds to the back of his head, cuts and bruising to his left cheek. There's grit in a facial wound that might help identify where he was attacked. Looks like he was hit with some force from behind, was perhaps incapacitated by the first blow and fell forward, injuring his cheek, then struck again with the same weapon. Unless he's called out again today, Stuart should have more detail for us by tomorrow.'

'Any idea on weapon type?' The question had come from PC Indira Sharma, the MIT's aide who everyone referred to as Indi.

'A blunt instrument. Sorry, I can't be more specific.' Frankie paused. 'There's a lot we still don't know. Until Professor Stuart gives us cause of death we can only speculate on whether the injuries were fatal or if the victim was knocked unconscious, pushed in and drowned as a result. The PolSA team found a hypodermic not too far away. Their search for both weapon and crime scene is ongoing.'

Frankie paused, Stuart's words arriving in her head.

The term 'blunt instrument' was a coverall. A generalisation. Any tool – hammer, wrench, tyre lever – any piece of wood or stone, like the one Kristjánsson had used to break open the barrel, held specific and measurable markings which would show themselves to an experienced medical examiner.

A memory stirred, one that was important to share it with the team.

'I found a tent peg at the barrel scene this morning. Given that Victim One died several decades ago, it had little relevance, but now we have a more recent victim with a caved-in skull, I've handed it to forensics. We could be looking for a camping mallet.'

'Is there any update on Kristjánsson and his group?' Mitch blushed as he asked the question.

'Not yet, though there is a flag on their vehicles to trace them using ANPR.'

Automatic Number Plate Recognition was a fast and efficient technology, a vital tool for tracking vehicles that passed between traffic surveillance cameras on motorways and main roads. There were ways round it, especially in rural areas where CCTV didn't exist.

'Let's hope our foreign visitors lack the geographical knowledge to avoid detection. One of Jardine's crew took the registration details of every car parked at Hawkhope at six a.m.. There were three, not two, vehicles with Glasgow plates there. Two Range Rovers and an Audi A3, which is on its way here on a low-loader as we speak.'

'How come?' Indi said. 'Couldn't it belong to anyone?'

'It could, but it doesn't. It's registered to a Glaswegian with form for violence and drug dealing spanning twenty years. His name is Gavin Campbell. On my way here, I spoke to Police Scotland. They say he's a lowlife with links to an Organised Crime Group and who sometimes uses the alias, Ross McDonald.'

'How is this relevant?' David asked.

'His girlfriend claims the car was stolen yesterday at some point in the afternoon. As far as she knows he didn't report it, which raises the question why. I have no proof, but the timing of the alleged theft coincides with Kristjánsson's plane arriving in the UK. If the second victim was also a passenger on that plane, he may be responsible for the theft, or Campbell-McDonald loaned him the vehicle. If I'm wrong, the worst I've done is upset an OCG. I think I can live with that.'

The MIT were laughing.

'The way I read it, we have three theories to consider. One: Victim Two saw the barrel go into the water and was silenced by whoever put it there. Two: the Icelandic kids rocked him off for reasons unknown to us. Three: our victim half-inched the wrong car, was followed and made an example of by the group Campbell-McDonald is associated with.'

'Good job,' David said.

'That's a bit premature, guv. We have no evidence to link the victim to Kristjánsson and his group. It's possible they came across him at Kielder, a chance encounter, but I don't believe it—'

'Me neither,' Dick said. 'They arrive in the same city at around the time Campbell's car was stolen? That's quite a stretch, guv. Unless it's Campbell in the morgue and he happens to have a penchant for Icelandic cigarettes.' He caught Frankie's dismissive expression. 'What? I'm just putting it out there—'

'It's not him,' she said.

'You don't know that.'

'I do. The first thing I did when I arrived was check the PNC. Unless he's lost twenty-five kilos, taken up a gym membership and managed to change the colour of his hair and eyes, it's not Campbell.'

She held up an A4 printout showing a fat, tattooed thug.

'My mistake.' Pointing two fingers at his head, Dick pulled an imaginary trigger. Everyone laughed and so did he. 'Sorry guys, it's been a long day. The good news is, we have a timeline of when the Icelandic kids landed in the UK and their alleged ETA at Kielder.'

'We need to evidence that,' Frankie said. 'ANPR should be able to track their journey south and establish if Campbell's Audi was in their convoy.'

Mitch raised a hand, a sheepish expression.

Frankie's stomach took a dive.

She'd seen that look before.

'The floor is yours,' she said.

'Sarge, the girls I spoke to said Kristjánsson spent months planning the trip.'

'Yes, he told me—'

'But did you know they were going to stay awhile? One of them told me they had a visit to the Observatory already bought and paid for. Apparently, Kristján and a couple of others are keen astronomers, the reason they chose Kielder as their holiday destination—'

'Why am I hearing this now?'

'It slipped my mind.'

'Fuck's sake, Mitch. This is a murder enquiry. Get onto them, and while you're at it, I want you ringing round any other tourist attractions you can think of: Kielder Castle, the Bird of Prey Centre and any I've missed. If they made any bookings I want to know about them immediately. Ditto boat and bike hire.'

'Yes, Sarge.'

David was shaking his head. 'Dick, I need a word.'

16

Frankie had been watching David's office door like a hawk. The blinds were down, a private, do-not-disturb conversation with Abbott already lasting ten minutes — too long to be a knock-back. The internal phone rang on Mitch's desk, startling her. The DC was nowhere to be seen and she got up to answer it, all the while keeping her eyes peeled for Dick coming out, keen to gauge his mood.

The witness, Maria Colman, was elderly. So quietly spoken, Frankie had to ask her to hold the line a moment. She covered her handset, telling the squad to keep the noise down. The room fell silent, a few shrugs, quizzical looks and whispers passing between MIT detectives, ranging from 'she's onto something important' to 'what's eating her?' Mather, the statement reader, could be awkward sometimes. Privately, David had told her that if he wasn't so good at his job, he'd be shown the door.

Abbott was still in his office.

Ignoring that thought, Frankie returned to her call, apologising for keeping Colman waiting. The old lady lived in Yarrow, in a house overlooking the reservoir. She'd called to say that she was out in her garden with her dog when she saw headlights, a vehicle screaming across the dam from Hawkhope shortly after midnight, maybe later. All morning, she'd witnessed police activity. While she didn't know what all the fuss was about, she thought it might be important.

It might.

Frankie wrote down her full name, excited by the prospect of a witness who possibly had more to give.

Colman gave the name of a house on the C200.

'I know it well,' Frankie said. In the space of a few hours, she'd passed the house four times on the way to and from Kielder. 'How long have you lived there?'

'Twenty years and counting, dear. It's extremely rare to see anything other than forestry vehicles crossing the dam at night, though for those looking for a quiet rendezvous there's nowhere better. They tend to crawl along quietly, so as not to draw attention, not like the madman I saw last night.' Colman seemed very sure of her facts.

'Any idea on the type of vehicle?'

'A noisy one.' Colman's cough was like a death rattle.

Frankie hoped it wasn't serious.

'Detective Oliver, perhaps I shouldn't have called. I could be wasting your time—'

'No, please continue.' Frankie could do with all the help she could get.

'I'm sorry, I don't drive and I'm not good with cars.' Colman immediately contradicted herself: 'If I had to guess, I'd have said it was diesel rather than petrol. Definitely not electric. If you're after the make or model, I haven't a clue. Oh, there is one other thing about the vehicle. It struck me . . .'

Another hacking cough prevented her from continuing.

'Take your time, Mrs Colman. Would you like me to wait while you fetch a glass of water?'

'No, thank you, dear. I'm all right – as all right as I'll ever be.'

She was making light of her condition. Frankie suspected that she was medically, possibly terminally ill, as manifest by her continued breathlessness. Colman's next words were barely audible. From what Frankie could make out, it was as if the woman had drifted off someplace else: a hospital ward, a funeral home, or heaven, if she believed in the afterlife. She'd completely lost the thread of a conversation the detective sergeant was keen to continue.

God, she hated her job sometimes.

Then again, Colman was trying to be a good citizen. Helping

the police might give her a reason to feel that she still had a contribution to make, a reason to get out of bed in the morning.

Frankie gave her a gentle nudge. 'The vehicle stood out in some way?'

'Oh, yes. It sounded to me like it was old . . . badly maintained, if you know what I mean. The air up here is unpolluted. I could smell exhaust fumes. The driver had his foot to the floor and it occurred to me that the damned thing might blow up if he didn't slow down.'

Frankie was aware that the MIT were earwigging, excited at the prospect of a potential lead.

She hoped they were right. 'Thank you, Mrs Colman. An officer will be out to take a statement. When would be a convenient time?'

'I'm not planning on going anywhere. I rarely get out these days. Hexham, on market day, once a month if I can get a lift. Otherwise, I'm pretty much housebound since my husband passed away. I'm ninety and not in the best of health. A neighbour keeps me stocked up. I still bake sometimes. Maybe I'll make some scones. You people must get hungry.'

'Please don't go to any bother on our account.'

'Except for my border terrier, cooking is my only pleasure. It'll give me something to do.'

What a nice lady. 'That would be very kind. Thanks for your time.'

'You're welcome. I hope it helps.'

'It does.'

Colman disconnected.

Getting up, Frankie walked across the room to the receiver's desk, handing her a note of the phone call. As intrigued as everyone else, Detective Sergeant Pam Bond digested the text. 'You want me to raise an action on this as a priority, Frank? There's not much else going on at the moment.'

'Please, ASAP. If Colman saw the vehicle, then others may have. Alert the house-to-house team. Get in touch with

Jardine. Tell him we need bodies to patrol all fishing locations, particularly late evening and early morning, so we can round up any potential witnesses. It's probably too dry to find tyre tracks on the access road. We need to retrieve anything that may have been discarded en route to the Belling peninsula.'

'Consider it done.'

'Thanks.'

Pam flicked her head towards Stone's office door. 'What's going on in there?'

Like she didn't know.

Frankie shrugged. 'No idea.'

'That sounded like "mind your own business".' Pam's smile faded, her eyes straying over Frankie's shoulder. She sat up straight. 'Guv'nor incoming. Your six . . .' She winked. 'Good luck, Frank.' Double O Seven knew exactly what was going on.

Frankie didn't know whether to laugh or cry.

When she plucked up the courage to turn around, a PC entered the room, diverting David's attention away from her. His expression was apologetic as he pointed at his watch, held up a hand, fingers spread out: Five minutes?

Frankie nodded. *Apologetic?*

This was not looking good.

17

David returned to his office and shut the door. Frankie scanned the MIR. No sign of Dick. No mystery: either he'd pissed off to lick his wounds or been told to make himself scarce. She searched for him in the MIR and beyond, opening and slamming doors, bursting into the male locker room, having to apologise to a couple of semi-naked coppers. The image of black socks, white underpants and skinny, hairy legs stuck with her as she returned the incident room.

Grim.

She called Abbott.

A mobile lit up on his desk, evidence that she was in a flap. It was lying there, along with a discarded pen, paperwork left incomplete, his well-worn leather jacket slung untidily over the upright of his chair, the first place she'd have looked had she been thinking straight. He was in the building, hiding somewhere.

She had to find him.

Too old to play hide and seek, she asked: 'Anyone seen Dick?'

Detectives were shaking their heads, their faces blank.

Frankie was good at reading them. There were no tell-tale signs that her colleagues knew something she didn't. *Damn it.* The mobile in her hand bleeped. An incoming text. She thought it might be the man she was looking for, asking her to meet him for a chinwag, somewhere away from the incident room, a chance to share positive news – a way of getting her out of the office while she took in the fact that he'd passed and she hadn't. The message was from David:

I'm done. Ready when you are.

Frankie was nowhere near ready, even though this was what she'd been waiting for her whole career, the chance to achieve the same rank as her grandfather, leaving only one rank to go to equal that of her father. He'd taken retirement at the earliest opportunity to go on a crusade of his own, an opportunity to look forensically at her sister's violent death that had lain undetected for a quarter of a century. Though broken by the loss, he'd been the best dad Frankie could ever wish for, holding onto his grief so that she and Rae would grow up without feeling that the dead were more important than the living. Her mother had also shown amazing courage for the same selfless reasons.

Frankie could weep just thinking about them.

With a sense of dread, she approached David's door.

Her moment had finally arrived.

She sat, crossing one leg over the other, trying to relax and breathe normally. She studied David closely, keeping her hands still and her gob shut. There were no signs as to how this meeting might pan out, none that she could see. She was losing her edge. His eyes were on the file in front of him – *her* file.

'Well . . .' He looked up. 'You aced your promotion board. Congratulations, Frank.'

She blew out a breath, then looked away, unable to rise to the occasion.

'Nothing to say?' A hint of amusement. 'You can't have been in doubt.'

'Hmm . . .' She waggled her hand from side to side. 'You had me going for a while.' An image of Abbott arrived in her head. 'Dick heard rumours hours ago. Given that we'd both seen you this morning, neither of us were holding out much hope.' It wasn't meant as a dig and she hoped it didn't sound that way. 'How did he do?'

'Didn't he tell you?'

'I've not seen him.'

'He didn't make it.'

Frankie felt a sharp stab to her chest. 'Why? He's a good detective—'

'Competency was never an issue, Frank. You know as well as I do that a good DS doesn't always equal a good DI. You're either ready or you're not. There can be no grey areas, you know that. It was their call to make, not mine.'

She pictured Dick alone, kicking an item of furniture or other inanimate object that couldn't kick back, wondering what more he could realistically do that he hadn't already done to impress those whose job it was to make and break careers. David was right. Solid police work often wasn't enough. Maybe Dick's face didn't fit or he'd upset someone who was blocking his promotion. Maybe he was considered too old. Bias, conscious and unconscious, was endemic in the police service.

'How did he take it?' she asked.

'His time will come.'

'Will it? He can retire in less than three years.'

'Maybe not then . . .' It was an honest answer. 'Whether or not he reapplies, I'll tell you something for nothing, he'll be the first in the queue to buy you a pint or turn into chief party planner when you're promoted. He thinks the world of you.'

'The feeling is mutual, but there'll be no party.'

'That's a shame.'

Her eyes misted up, her emotions threatening to spill out. David had clocked her momentary loss of control and may have misread it as the news sinking in. She wasn't about to correct him. Talks of a celebration had upset her. Joanna would've been proud of her today. Frankie was eleven years old when her sister went out and never came home. A party would be marred by the fact that she couldn't be part of it.

David was staring at her.

Now, she suspected, he knew where she was at.

On more than one occasion, he'd articulated his thoughts on her tragic background. As a third-generation cop, he felt she'd been exposed to too much death from an early age, hearing about it, talking about it, experiencing it first-hand. He understood that the scars of her past were driving her, that she'd joined the police in order to overcome her grief, to make sense of what happened to Joanna.

How screwed up was that?

'Thank you, David.'

'For what?'

'Everything you've done, for me and for Dick. If it wasn't for you, we'd still be in general CID with Windy.' She was referring to Superintendent Gale, a man none of them got on with. He was in charge when David had taken a demotion to return to Northumberland following Jane's murder.

'No thanks required,' he said. 'It's an honour to have you on my team, even though you can be . . .' He paused. 'Challenging on occasions.' He was trying to lift her. 'Don't worry about Dick. Do yourself a favour and think about number one today. This is just a stepping stone, but you're on your way. Soak it up and enjoy it.'

'Does he know?'

'He's probably worked it out.'

'Did he ask?'

'What do you think? I told him I wasn't at liberty to say until I'd spoken to you. I thought you might like to handle that yourself.'

Frankie appreciated that. It would be a difficult conversation. She was suddenly conflicted. When she was eventually promoted it would signal the end of her working relationship with David, the end of her deployment to the MIT for the foreseeable future, an association she valued above all else. Regulations required her to return to uniform while she waited for a posting, a factor she hadn't thought about . . . till now. Strange how ecstasy could turn to agony in the blink of an eye.

'Any idea on timescale?' she asked.

'You're in a rush to leave us?'

'No . . .' She was fighting her emotions. 'I was just wondering how long I've got.'

'You make it sound like a death sentence. Bright wants to promote you sooner rather than later.'

'Right.'

'For someone who's been working hard to get there, you don't sound happy about it. No need to panic just yet. I'd like to hang on to you until our current investigations are resolved. I don't suppose you're keen to pull on a blue suit any more than I am.'

She feigned a shiver.

David laughed. 'Your uniform stint won't be for long. When it's over, Bright intends to create a position for you within the Murder Investigation Team. The department would be struggling if retired detectives hadn't returned as civilian investigators. We can't have a situation where the monkeys are running the zoo. I can't afford to lose your expertise – that's if you're in agreement.'

She'd love that.

'When you return, I can keep you on as my bagman or cut you loose and pick someone else, someone who won't give me such a hard time—'

She was too tense to raise a smile. 'Have you made your decision?'

'That's a matter for you. Whichever way you jump, you have my backing. No rush. I'll hold the post open until you give me the nod. If you decide to continue as my 2ic, I'll ask Dick to fill in while you're gone, on the understanding that the arrangement is temporary. Give it some thought. We can talk about it when you're ready.'

'I accept.'

David smiled. 'I was hoping you'd say that. Drink later?'

'I can't, I'm having dinner with my folks.'

'Some other time then.' He was crestfallen.

'I'd love you to be there when I tell them.'

'I'd like that too,' he said.

18

Frankie took a round of applause as she opened the door. There were whoops and hollers, two-handed whistles and pats on the back from detectives and civilians who downed tools, leaving their desks to congratulate her. Their collective joy brought a lump to her throat. Dick was the last to approach, a big hug. No sign of envy on his face, though she was under no illusion as to how he might be feeling, having been passed over in favour of a relatively young upstart. Not wishing to piss on her chips, he hid it well. They had worked together for years and were about as close as it was possible to be.

'You been listening at keyholes again?' she whispered as they pulled apart.

'Didn't need to.'

Taking her upper arms, he swung her round to face David's office. The blinds were up. He was grinning like a loon, a show of pride and solidarity, actions that made sense of his overly long meeting with Abbott and his disappearance afterwards. David had probably hatched a plan to give Dick the nod as soon as the deed was done in order that he could either cheer or console her, depending on which way it went. Such generosity of spirit from both men was hard to come by. She was glad to count them as friends as well as colleagues.

A warm feeling washed over her as she returned to her desk, less exhausted now that the gatekeepers had spoken. Today's decision was epic, a game-changer. She could go further if she had a mind to. In the coming weeks, she'd be carried along on a high, thrilled by the prospect of what lay ahead, and yet sad that she'd be leaving the MIT, even for a short spell in uniform.

Whichever way you jump, you have my backing.

Her mind was made up before David had stopped speaking.

With so much still to learn, there was no way she'd forego the opportunity to continue as his 2ic. His willingness to share the experience he'd gained in the Met had been the making of her. She owed him and would deliver.

Sensing a presence, she raised her head.

Mitch was standing close by, hands in pockets, an odd expression, obviously nothing to do with her news. If she'd had to describe it, she'd have said it was a mixture of anguish and disappointment.

'Why the long face?' she asked.

'I just got a call from the ANPR control centre. They spotted the Range Rovers heading south yesterday, Campbell's Audi following close behind. Every time the four-by-fours stopped, so did the Audi. Whoever was driving it, they were definitely travelling together.'

'Any sign of them today?'

'Not so far.'

'OK, keep me posted.'

It was hot in the MIR, the air conditioning on the blink again. Desperate for air, Frankie got up to open a window, her mind back on the double-hander. It was unimaginable that two bodies had been discovered in such an idyllic spot as Kielder and on such a beautiful day. The question as to whether the deaths were in any way connected brought her focus back into the room.

Turning from the window, she realised that Mitch hadn't moved an inch. 'Sorry, I thought you were done. Did you have more to say?' She sat down, inviting him to do likewise, waiting for a response that never came. 'Well, there obviously is, so get it said before I drop off.'

'I've been thinking about Kristjánsson and his mates.'

'What about them?'

'We've been working on the assumption that they scarpered after I let them go. I'm not sure I buy it. They were such nice kids—'

'They're also witnesses who have nothing to do with our first victim and everything to do with the second,' she reminded him. 'The very least they can give us is an ID.'

Unconvinced, Mitch looked away.

'Should I give Dick the girls to interview in future? He's good with females.'

She'd made her protégé blush.

'Lighten up, man. That was a joke, not a criticism. Well, perhaps a friendly reminder never to be swayed by innocent faces or baby blue eyes. They might just turn to ice. Believe me, we've all been burned that way.'

'We have no proof they even know he's dead.'

'The point is, they know him. Give me one good reason why none of them mentioned him when questioned—'

'He was driving a vehicle belonging to an OCG. Maybe they wanted to distance themselves from an undesirable. I mean, he was a user, right?'

'User or not, we need to hear it from them.'

'Imagine yourself in their position, Sarge. They're young and abroad for the first time in their lives. It can't have been easy being pulled into this. They came expecting a fabulous holiday, a new experience. What they got was a run-in with police.'

'And your theory is?'

'Well . . . the ANPR can't find them—'

'No, because they're off-grid—'

'That doesn't mean they're guilty though, does it?' Mitch wasn't letting go. 'If they have nowt to do with the second body, there'd be no reason for them to run. Maybe they're not on the hoof. Maybe they decided to continue their trip and doubled back to the reservoir.'

Frankie studied him.

Mitch had a valid point. With twenty-seven miles of shore-line and plenty of forest trails to choose from, the Icelandic group would be spoilt for choice if they were looking for another place to set up camp. There were many off-road car parks and hardly any CCTV up there. If they had plans to see the best of what the area had to offer, they might stick around.

'Did you check on the Observatory booking like I asked?'

'I tried. Couldn't get an answer.'

'OK, keep on it. Failing that, get yourself up there. What you've told me could explain their disappearance. See if you can pinpoint where their phones are and get a message to Jardine. Have his crew check out the car parks again, but ask yourself this: what better place to hide than somewhere they think we might not look, somewhere we've already looked? They're not off the hook yet.'

19

The call from pathologist Beth Collingwood was totally unexpected, its content intriguing: could Stone possibly swing by the city morgue at around five o'clock? He'd offered to go straight there. She was busy finishing up and said she'd rather not go into detail over the phone. An update this early in the process, particularly on ancient remains, was a bonus to any Senior Investigating Officer with nothing to go on and little chance of finding vital evidence until identification was confirmed.

Telling her he'd be there at five, he rang off, his attention straying beyond his office door. During his call, Frankie had been deep in conversation with Mitch, a dialogue that seemed to have run its course. As the young DC moved away, David checked his watch: five to four. Grabbing his jacket and car keys, he approached Frankie's desk.

'Fancy getting out of here?' he asked.

Her eyes shifted to the office clock. 'It's a bit early to knock off, isn't it?'

'We're not knocking off.' He updated her on Beth's call. 'We have an hour to kill and I need to refuel.'

On the way to the city morgue, they stopped at one their favourite eateries, an out-of-town café on the edge of Jesmond Dene; a chance to gather their resolve after an early start, enough to sustain them before joining her parents for dinner at seven thirty. They had a nice surprise coming.

The café wasn't busy. Unsurprising at this time of the day. The nearby Coast Road was a notorious bottleneck, especially at rush-hour, a place to be avoided if you were heading out of town.

Fortunately, they were on their way in.

Ordering at the counter, they took a table near the window overlooking the dene, a deep wooded valley, surrounding by trees, donated to the city by industrialist and philanthropist Lord Armstrong in the late nineteenth century. A hidden gem and wildlife corridor, it drew locals and tourists like a magnet, offering a peaceful haven, a network of pretty paths and bridges spanning the River Ouseburn – all of it a stone's throw from the city centre.

Frankie tore her eyes away from the window. 'Did Beth say what she wanted?'

David shook his head. 'She seemed preoccupied, so I didn't push it.'

'Must be important. It's not often she asks to see us this late on a Saturday afternoon. She has friends and a social life. Remember them? I can't recall what time off feels like, can you?' She didn't wait for an answer. 'Seriously, when was the last time you went to the theatre or took in a live music event since you left the capital?'

A shrug from David. 'Three, four months?'

'Precisely. We're missing out.'

'You mean, meeting over a dead body doesn't count?'

Their afternoon snack arrived, presented by a waitress who, having overheard David's last remark, didn't engage in conversation. Frankie took a sip of tea and forked a large chunk of apple pie, the utensil poised mid-air ready to shove it in her mouth.

'I'll miss the team when I leave.'

'Shift work has its advantages.'

'Like what?'

'No on-call 24/7—'

'Sleep deprivation is what fires your jets. Don't pretend it doesn't.'

David could see the wheels turning in Frankie's head. She was a workaholic too. There had been little time for socialising since they had moved to the MIT. Occasionally, they went out with Rae, Andrea and, more recently, Ben – a game of darts or a movie. Neither of them were having much fun outside of work. They were both single and yet spent little time hanging out together. They had no excuse, there were many venues to choose from. They were seriously in danger of losing their identities.

She hadn't spoken for a whole three minutes – a personal record.

'We should arrange some downtime before you leave,' David said. 'Other people do. Mitch and Indi are always banging on about their nights out. They just booked for James Morrison's concert at the City Hall in November. If they can find the time, we can. Rank should have its advantages, right?'

She didn't answer.

'C'mon, if you're not having a leaving "do" we should do something to celebrate your news, just the two of us. What do you say?'

Frankie swallowed a mouthful of pastry. 'You're on.'

David couldn't keep the smile off his face. 'I'll see what's coming up. My shout.'

His vibe excited her. 'On one condition . . . you let me take you for curry afterwards. I like to pay my way.'

'If you insist.'

'I do.' Frankie pushed her plate away, a glance at her watch. 'It's almost twenty to. See off your latte. We should go.'

Stone's mobile rang as they arrived at the morgue. He asked Frankie to go in and said he'd join her in a moment. She walked on, entering the building through the main entrance, making a beeline for Beth's office. She was already there, stuffing her work gear into a well-worn rucksack, its straps frayed at the edges. Frankie had rarely seen her out of a forensic suit or surgical scrubs. Today, she was dressed in casual clothing: skinny jeans, a black T-shirt with the words Everybody Counts or Nobody Counts, Harry Bosch written across the front in red and white.

Frankie pointed at the logo. 'I like.'

Beth glanced down at the lettering. 'Not a bad philosophy to live by, is it? Help yourself to a coffee. There's juice in the fridge too.' She peered guiltily at a tea plate on her desk. It was full of crumbs, all that remained of an afternoon snack. 'As you can see, I'm all out of biscuits.'

'I'm fine. David and I stopped for a break on the way. We usually need a lining on our stomachs before meeting you.'

'Where is he?'

'Taking a call. He'll be along shortly.'

Right on cue, he appeared. 'Sorry for keeping you waiting.' He eyed the rucksack at Beth's feet. 'You heading home?'

'Or somewhere more exciting?' Frankie asked.

The detectives sat down, grinning at one another.

Beth's eyes drifted between the two. 'Did I miss something?'

'In joke,' Frankie said. 'We were just talking about the fact that some people actually have a life outside of work. You're the perfect example—'

'Not tonight . . .' In response to Frankie's narrowing eyes, Beth gave a resigned shrug. 'As of three days ago, I'm officially single, replaced by someone less selfish, apparently. Jed wants kids. I don't. Ever . . .' She spread her hands. 'God forbid that I should have any choice in the matter. "Tick-tock" was his parting shot, like I need a reminder of how old I am.'

'His loss,' David said.

Beth waved away the comment as if it were of no consequence. 'It's for the best. It was never going to end well. It was *always* going to end. I should've kicked him out years ago. I'm in the market for a new squeeze if you know of anyone looking for a date with someone who reeks of chemicals, spends more time with the dead than the living and would rather not procreate.'

Frankie wondered if that was a come-on to her boss.

Why should she care?

Except she did.

The emotion took her by surprise.

She covered it with a show of solidarity. 'Not all women are fulfilled by having children,' she said. 'Jed wouldn't know a good thing if it ran up and bit him. You might not have his undivided attention. You have ours.'

'You guys are great.'

Frankie had never thought Jed – a junior barrister who pranced around in a wig all day, acting like he was the greatest gift to womankind – was good enough for Beth. She was more street than strut. Not wishing to dwell on her personal life, or lack of it, Frankie hoped she wasn't about to be edged out of her boss's affections by someone smarter, cooler, more of a catch on every level.

So much for a show and a curry.

David was watching her.

It was as well he couldn't read her mind.

What the hell was she thinking?

Focus!

Frankie turned her attention to Beth. 'Please tell us that the skeleton in the barrel was a hoax, planted by an anatomy student with a sick sense of humour. We'll happily ship out.'

David laughed. 'It wouldn't be the first time we've been taken for a ride.'

'I didn't drag you down here to spare your blushes, David.'

'So why did you?' Frankie was beginning to feel like a gooseberry. 'Shall we start with gender?'

'The victim is definitely male.' Beth pulled a folder towards her. Opening it up, she presented them with a series of images, all timed, dated and numbered, hard evidence to present to a court of law when the time came. The photographs were ordered consecutively, showing the barrel being taken apart, the remains shifted to a stainless steel examination table, most of the bones now detached from one another. 'I suspect his hands and feet were bound with cable ties. I found three in soil removed from the bottom of the barrel and one hanging loose around a limb.'

'What the hell is that?' Frankie was pointing at a square perforation to the victim's skull.

'That's how he died,' Beth said. 'A catastrophic injury made by a pickaxe or similar instrument, the point of which would almost certainly have penetrated his brain. He was placed into the barrel in the same state as he came into the world, naked. All tissue was gone, which rules out the possibility of fingerprints.'

'Don't suppose you found any circumstantial evidence that spoke to his identity: ID, watch, credit card?'

'No, no and no—'

'You're depressing me,' David said.

'I did find one thing . . .' Beth showed them a blown-up image of a vintage micro mosaic cross. She'd placed rulers across and down the page to show the size of the piece: 40 mm in length; the crossbar 20 mm wide. 'Impressive, eh?'

'I'll say . . .' Frankie couldn't take her eyes off it. It was beautiful, intricate, the mosaic picked out in red, white and blue. The base of the cross was crafted in chrome. 'Wish it was mine. Do you still have it?'

'No, I sent it to the lab.'

'He was wearing it?'

'That would be difficult since his head was detached from his body.'

'If we can trace its provenance, we might be in business.'

'The cable ties are interesting . . .' Beth held up one of the images. 'As you can see, they're stamped with the brand name Ty-rap, invented by an American company Thomas and Betts in 1958 for the aeronautical industry. Not my job, I know, but I had a few moments to kill and did some research. They're still trading under that brand name, though in 2012 they merged with another company, ABB. There are millions sold around the world. The fact that these are nylon and not metal-toothed may be significant. Until the forensic anthropologist dates the bones, I thought you could look more closely at when nylon – if that's what it is – was first introduced. It might help identify in which decade the victim was killed.'

20

Any clue that might pinpoint time of death was a big plus. Stone and Oliver were buoyed by the items found inside the barrel, and there was more to come from Beth Collingwood. A broken arm that might lead to a positive ID if ante-mortem X-rays were made available. Then came the pièce de résistance. DNA might degrade, but it had a shelf life. Beth said it took years and years to completely break down. In addition, she was able to confirm that the soil on the bones proved, beyond any doubt, that the barrel victim had been buried for some time, exhumed and moved to the deposition site, a mystery that stumped murder detectives gathering for the evening briefing, including David himself. There would be a reason for it and he was relying on his team to find it.

'Who's available to stay late?' he asked.

There was no shortage of volunteers, Abbott among them. He was in no rush to get home and tell his wife that he'd failed his promotion board, a prospect he was probably dreading. Linn was Swedish, younger and more dynamic than him, a high-flying, smart and successful executive, a woman definitely on her way up.

David had a plan to bolster his flagging ego. 'Dick, the MIR is yours. Split the team, half on Victim One, half on Victim Two. Raise actions where necessary, prioritising the collection of soil samples from Kielder for use as a comparison. Pathologist Russell Stuart has promised to update us tomorrow on the second victim. As soon as we have a blood sample, we can run his DNA through the Icelandic database and Interpol. In the meantime, find out if anyone fitting the description of Victim Two travelled from Iceland to Glasgow yesterday. Airport staff should be able to tell you where, when and how Kristjánsson's flights were booked. If this is the first leg of a European tour, we need details of ongoing travel, a copy of an itinerary, assuming one is available. Frankie and I will be a couple of hours, tops.' He was unaware that events wouldn't quite turn out that way.

They left the building for the village of Woolsington where Frankie's parents lived, a twenty-minute drive west of their Wallsend base. They arrived on the dot of six thirty with every intention of returning to the MIR later. Her father came to the door to greet them. His arms were around her before she stepped inside. He loved his daughters equally, but these two shared a very special bond, unique in David's experience. At first he thought it was because she was the youngest of three, or because she'd followed her forebears into the police service. He'd since come to realise that the reason was a lot more personal. The likeness between Frankie and her late sister was astonishing, whereas Rae looked nothing like either of them.

David shook hands with Frank Snr, then with his father, also ex-job. Their association with the force stretching back to the mid-sixties. David had no doubt that Frankie had the potential to eclipse their formidable reputations within Northumbria's elite murder squad if she continued to apply herself. Ironically, the murder of a loved one had galvanised her into action, determined to find answers for other families affected by such tragedy. Her inner compass was intact, her insight unmatched by her peers.

Frankie was beginning to suspect that the family dinner, a frequent occurrence for the Olivers, was the second time she'd been set up that day. In close touch with his ex-colleagues, some of them still serving, she wondered if her father had heard through the grapevine that the promotion board had deliberated and made their recommendations known.

She glanced across the room.

If he already knew which way the pendulum had swung, her old man showed no signs of it. He was deep in conversation with David's nephew. As soon as her mother was told that David would be joining them, she'd invited Ben along. Frankie's father was asking how his internship at a local newspaper was going. He was working with Belinda Wells, an award-winning, kick-ass journalist with a fearsome reputation for hunting down the best news stories and running with them, but Ben was restless, his eye on a different future – a career in the police had been mentioned.

Andrea hauled herself off the couch, collecting Rae's wine glass, an unspoken message passing between them as she left the room to refill it. On her return, Andrea wandered over to speak to Frankie, a glass in each hand, dropping her voice to a whisper. 'I see you've made up with the Northern Rock.' It was David's nickname in police circles. Though Andrea didn't know it, they had one for her too: Eye Candy Andy. Frankie knew she wouldn't approve.

Stifling a grin, she feigned innocence. 'What are you on about?

'You two seem to be over your spat.'

'There was no spat.'

'This morning he hung up on you—'

'Did he? I don't recall. How come you're here anyhow?'

Andrea countered, a raised eyebrow. 'How come he is?'

'I invited him. What's your excuse? I thought you were staying home tonight.'

'You know Rae can't bear to miss out—'

'You mean *you* can't.' Frankie sipped at her Prosecco. 'Let me guess, it was your turn to cook and she didn't fancy spaghetti.'

'Ouch.' Andrea put a hand to her chest. 'You really know how to hurt people. Believe it or not, I do try.'

'Try harder. Who knows what you could achieve? You might even find you can make the Bolognese sauce to go with it.'

'Says the Queen of take-out.' Andrea chuckled. 'It's a good thing Mum's cooking tonight.'

David sat directly opposite Frankie in the dining room. He waited for everyone to be seated before sending her an unspoken message: *What are you waiting for? Tell them!* He'd chosen his seat on purpose, surreptitiously placing his mobile on the table, poised to capture the moment for posterity. She hesitated. The second nudge was less subtle than the first. David tapped the side of his wine glass with a fork, to gain everyone's attention.

Bastard! She wasn't ready.

Unceremoniously, she blurted out her news.

The only time she'd seen her family this excited was when Rae and Andrea decided to formalise their relationship and move in together. Then and now, her father was overcome with emotion, her grandfather too, so much so, Frankie couldn't look at them.

David got to his feet.

'Don't you dare!' she said.

Everyone laughed.

'I promise it'll be short,' he said.

A text alert killed the moment.

With five serving and retired police officers present, and their long-suffering other halves, there was no need to apologise for the intrusion. On autopilot, Frankie got up, wandering across the hallway into her father's den. It was her favourite room in the house – a place of safety where she often thought through difficult cases – but also his private incident room where he hoped one day to unravel the secrets of her sister's murder. As Frankie stood there, on such a momentous day for her personally, a quarter of a century rewound itself like the hands of a clock.

This was where Frankie had last seen Joanna . . .

She was here now.

Frankie shut her eyes, then opened them again, took a deep breath and checked her mobile, an urgent message from Mitch: We lucked out with Jardine. No sign of the four-by-fours at Kielder. Icelanders' phones are all off, but we may have caught a break. I got through to Kielder Observatory. Kristjánsson and three of his crew prepaid for a night sky safari.

She keyed a reply: Great work!

Yeah, except it's tonight.

Seriously?

Want me to deal?'

No, I'm closer.

21

David drove at breakneck speed to get them to Kielder Observatory, almost fifty miles away, much of it on narrow country roads. Fortunately, traffic was light. Short of Kielder village, not far from the Scottish border, they turned off the C200 and made a slow ascent through an open gate and uphill along a winding forest track for almost two miles, their wheels crunching on dry ground. There was no one about as they drove into the Observatory car park.

Exiting their vehicle, they took a moment for their eyes to adjust. Now their lights were off, darkness had taken on a new meaning. In order to make the most of the night sky, white light was discouraged here. David, who'd been several times before, searched the car park with the aid of a dimmed torch with a red filter.

Though she could hardly see him properly, Frankie could feel his excitement draining away.

'No Range Rovers doesn't bode well,' he said.

'Don't panic. Not all of Kristján's group are booked for the event. It's possible that the four that are were dropped off by the others or walked from wherever they set up camp – if that's what they've done.'

'Up THAT hill? I can't see it, can you? You'd need an oxygen tank to reach the top.'

She laughed. 'Maybe they took a wrong turn or are late then.'

He wasn't convinced and told her so. 'Come on, it's this way. Stay close, I don't want you breaking a leg.'

It felt awkward as he slipped his hand through hers. With no torch of her own, she needed him to guide her. She couldn't see shit. They reached a pathway lined by tiny red indicator lights. At the end of it, they entered a wooden structure on the right. It was warm and cosy inside, essentially a windowless classroom with dimmed lighting. A talk was in progress, four digital screens on the far wall. All eyes were on a giant screen at the front showing the solar system, the size of planets in relation to one another. The information on display was as mind-blowing as it was fascinating.

A female staff member walked in behind them, asking for their names. David showed ID and they moved silently outside. She was a young astrophysicist who, unlike them, was wrapped up warm against the evening chill. Even in summer, it was cold at Black Fell at night. Viewing the sky through telescopes mounted on various platforms was an icy job.

Stone introduced himself, receiving confirmation that the kids he was looking for were a no-show. Thanking her, the detectives left to maintain observations from their vehicle, a chance to polish off the food that Frankie's mum had hastily plated up for them, cold but edible. Having missed out on dinner, they were both famished.

As they ate, Frankie lost faith. Their unexpected change in plan was unlikely to take them anywhere. Observation duty, covert or otherwise, was always tedious. In such a remote spot, there was little to keep them occupied: the odd screech of a bird overhead, a movement in the undergrowth.

Time, it seemed, was standing still.

'I'm bored now.' Frankie was wishing she'd stopped inside, a chance to listen and learn. 'Is there any point in us hanging around? If Kristján is that keen on astronomy, he'd hardly miss an opportunity to play with a big boys' telescope, would he? You have to book these events months in advance and they don't come cheap.'

'I told you to stand down. You should have stayed to celebrate with your family. This was never a two-person operation—'

'You've been at it since five a.m.. It didn't seem right to bunk off while you were still working. We could call on Maria

Colman, the woman who saw the vehicle crossing the dam last night. She only lives down the road.'

'It's late. You said she was elderly and not in the best of health.'

'OK, we'll leave it then.'

David started the engine. 'Give Dick a call. See if he's any further forward.'

Frankie did as he asked.

Abbott picked up immediately. 'Hey! I was about to call you.'

'Oh?' Intrigued, she put the phone on speaker so that David could listen in.

'I owe you an apology,' Abbott said. 'While I was on to Glasgow Airport, I thought I'd check to see if Kristján and his group had somehow managed to circumvent the ANPR and arrange early flights home.'

'And had they?'

'No sign of them re-entering the Hertz drop zone to return their motors. Their registrations would have been picked up automatically. The woman I spoke to was kind enough to run their plates through her system. The keys were handed in at Newcastle Airport branch. The group flew out from there, London-bound, then on to Iceland.'

'Get on to their security,' David said. 'I want them detained when they land.'

'Too late, guv. They disembarked from Keflavík airport an hour ago.'

22

As they drove away from Kielder Observatory, Frankie swore loudly, angry that witnesses, any one of whom could be a suspect, had managed to slip out from under her. She hadn't seen it coming and neither had David. Nothing he said had made her feel any better. Unable to placate her, he took something from his pocket and handed it over.

'What's this?' She couldn't see in the dark.

'A good-luck gift. I'm going to miss having you around, Frank.'

Excited, she turned on the interior light.

It was a small gift wrapped in a crumpled charge sheet.

'Hilarious! What is it?'

He kept his eyes on the road. 'Take a look.'

Ripping off the paper, she almost choked when she saw what was inside: her grandfather's old police whistle, his most prized possession, a precious heirloom that he'd gifted to Stone for saving her life during a prior investigation.

'I can't accept this, David. Granddad gave it to you.'

'I want you to have it and he agreed. I've been waiting for the opportunity to return it and can't think of a better day to do it.'

'Thank you.' Frankie turned off the light before he saw how moved she was. 'I'm sorry about dinner.'

'There'll be others. Next time it's on me.'

'You think your unemployment benefit will cover it? I'm no cheap date and Bright will go nuts when he gets wind of our cock-up.'

'Not necessarily.'

David fell silent for a while, but by the time they made it to her Amble apartment, eighty miles away, they had hatched a plan. They arrived at half past midnight, nineteen hours after he'd called her out. She didn't ask him in or bother with her usual routine of a nightcap on her balcony overlooking the marina. Bypassing the shower, she fell into bed and was asleep before her head hit the pillow.

They were waiting at Newcastle International Airport when Detective Chief Superintendent Bright walked into the arrivals hall off an early flight from London Heathrow. Hitching his bag over his shoulder, he looked around for his driver, his eyes finding them instead. Frankie had waylaid his lift, keen to update him on developments and persuade him to sign off on their proposal. She'd also packed an overnight bag on the off chance he'd agree.

It was stowed in the boot of David's car.

Bright frowned as he approached. 'And there was me thinking I might get in a round of golf this afternoon. A delegation on a Sunday morning usually means trouble. From the look on your faces, I'd say it's serious.' He glanced at the adjacent coffee shop. 'Shall we?'

David took his bag and moved towards the café. 'What can I get you?'

'Double espresso for me.' Bright sat down. 'Frankie deserves champagne, though it's a little early.' He smiled at her. 'Congratulations on your recent news. Your father must be so proud.'

'He is, as am I. Thanks, guv.'

David took a seat. Coffee was on its way.

'I assume this is about the IP in the barrel?' Bright asked.

David shook his head. 'No, sir.'

'So why are you here?'

He explained that a second victim had been discovered at Kielder. 'I was with you when he was found, sir.'

'Any ID?'

'Not yet,' Frankie said. 'Though he had a packet of Icelandic tabs in his pocket.'

'You've linked the incidents?' Bright was looking at David.

'No, guv. It seemed sensible to split them, rather than link them.'

'Hold on, the finders for Victim One are Icelandic. Victim Two is the same nationality. Sounds like they're linked to me.'

'We have yet to confirm that he is Icelandic. The cigarettes might have been dropped and picked up by the dead guy.'

'Then I agree, it's not enough.'

'We have three scenarios,' David said. 'One or more of the Icelandic visitors are responsible for the second death; someone we don't yet know of is responsible; or the victim saw the barrel go into the water and was silenced by whoever put it there. We are leaning towards the first option. Unfortunately, we'd let the Icelandic group go before the second body was discovered. To safeguard the integrity of the scene, Abbott dealt with it, with Frankie guiding him at a distance.'

He gave her the nod to continue.

She didn't need asking twice. 'As of last night, we have unequivocal proof that Kristjánsson and his group skipped town. Cancelling their plans for a European tour, they flew home and not from their starting point in Glasgow. They departed from this very airport to London, taking a connecting flight to Keflavík, landing in Iceland before we heard they had done a runner.'

'There can only be one explanation for such a hurried exit from the UK, surely.'

'That's the premise we're working on, guv. David thinks that Abbott and I should fly to Iceland to question them. We have their details, so they shouldn't be too hard to find. There's a direct flight out of Glasgow at twenty to three this afternoon. If we leave now, we might just make it.'

Bright wasn't happy. 'Have you shared your plans with Abbott?'

'I took the liberty of putting him on standby, yes.'

'Then you'd better un-take it.'

'Excuse me?' Frankie was confused by his reaction. 'I agree I'm cutting it fine, but you know Abbott. He's ready to ship out at a moment's notice. I could meet him there, if necessary. Failing that, there's another flight first thing in the morning from Edinburgh.'

'Not what I was getting at. I'm unhappy with him going. Full stop.'

She kept the resentment from her voice, but only just. 'Might I ask on what grounds?'

'Nothing to do with timing, if that's what you're thinking, or budget.' Their coffee arrived and Bright slurped his off in one go, meeting her eyes over the top of his cup. 'Frank, I have every faith in you and Abbott. However, David's experience of international investigations will speed the process. At best, dealing with a foreign force can be tricky; at worst, a downright pain in the arse. Should you come up against a jobsworth, he or she might give you the runaround. These situations require diplomatic handling by someone of equal rank. As your SIO, I'd like David with you in case you encounter a problem.' He turned to David: 'What's the state of play with the barrel case?

'It's dead in the water, guv. No pun intended. Collingwood confirmed that the victim is male. His hands and feet were bound. He'd been struck with a tool, probably a pickaxe. We have a few enquiries to make regarding the cable ties used to secure him. Other than that, given the state of the remains, we're playing a waiting game until they can be aged and identified. We need an anthropologist to establish a timescale. That's a long way off and is as far as our leads go at the moment.'

'So nothing Abbott can't handle on his own?'

'No, sir.'

'Go!' Bright said.

23

As they left the airport, Frankie stood Abbott down, putting him charge of the MIR until further notice. Then, as he'd done the night before, David took the wheel, heading across country to the A69, west to Carlisle, then north on the M6, joining the M74 and on to Glasgow. Driving was his passion and Frankie was grateful for the opportunity to relax. Never having undertaken that journey on a weekend, she was surprised by how little traffic was on the roads. Given the only available flight to Iceland that day, what initially appeared a big ask to get them there on time turned out to be a pleasant, uneventful drive on a sunny Sunday afternoon.

In anticipation of Bright's agreement, she'd reserved two seats on the flight and checked out the shuttle bus that would take them into the centre of Reykjavík. Confirming the bookings en route, she saved their boarding cards to her mobile wallet and watched the world go by through the car windscreen, excited to be crossing international boundaries, keen to make the most of David before she left the Murder Investigation Team. He might still want her as his 2ic, but plans were frequently subject to change.

The thought that she might not end up in the MIT bothered her.

As they drove into Glasgow International airport, David was grateful for the overnight bag he kept in the car on a permanent basis, in case work took him out of town. He called his nephew on the hands-free, telling him that he'd be away for a day or two, depending on how things panned out in Iceland, and would let him know when to expect him home. Ben's voice sounded thick in his throat when he answered, his speech almost incomprehensible when spoken through a gaping yawn, several words seeming to merge into one long grunt . . .

'Yehwenever.'

'Must've been quite a party,' David said, looking around for a vacant spot in which to park. 'How's the head?'

'Fine. Slept in Frankie's room. Had no choice. Didn't get to bed till three.'

Frankie was grinning. 'Did Mum make you breakfast?'

'Yeah.' Another yawn and no hello for Frankie. 'Thinking of moving in, to be honest. Brekkie where I live is non-existent, unless I make it myself.'

'Go for it!' David said. 'How many times have I told you, you're cramping my style—'

Frankie nudged him with her elbow. 'Take no notice, Ben. He loves having you around.'

'Hmm.'

David swung his vehicle into a parking space. Grabbing his mobile, he got out of the car, lifting the device to his ear as he walked towards the terminal building. 'Gotta run, mate. We have minutes to spare before check-in closes. Don't be getting any party ideas while I'm away. Any breakages are coming out of your allowance.'

'Whatever.' The line was cut.

David's eyes met Frankie's, a wicked grin developing. His house was safe.

The two-hour flight landed just before four o'clock, local time, ten minutes earlier than scheduled. Frankie had slept for the second half of the journey, dreaming of ice-caves, angry volcanoes, vast glaciers and lava fields, landscapes she'd read about in the onboard magazine. Icelandair knew how to sell their country to its visitors. Keflavík airport terminal was no different. She wanted to browse the bookshop. Joking that she couldn't read Icelandic, David dragged her away. He was on a mission to speak to local police at the earliest opportunity.

'Do we have to get the bus?' she asked as they walked towards the exit.

'Not sure we need a hire car,' David said.

'Taxi?'

'You have an aversion to public transport?'

'No.'

'If we're lucky, local police might ferry us where we want to go.'

'You reckon? They have fewer officers nationally than we have in one of our area commands.'

'May as well give them something to do then.' David pointed to the bus stop as they emerged from the terminal. 'And remember, we're working, not sightseeing, much as I'd like to spend some time here. I've never been, have you?'

'Long time ago.'

Her depressed tone made him stop walking. 'You never said.'

'You never asked.' A big sigh. 'I wasn't in a good place at the time. Jo had died two years earlier. Still grieving, I didn't want to leave Mum and Dad. They thought it would be good for me to get away. The truth is, I cried the whole time I was here. Never ever tell them that. They think I had a great time.'

David put a hand on her shoulder. 'I'm sorry you had to cope with that.'

'It is what it is. This trip is hardly going to be a picnic, is it?'

24

The Flybus airport shuttle to the city centre ran every ten minutes. They hopped on the first one to arrive. David was well
prepared. Before boarding he'd done his research and had an
idea where they were going. He'd asked to be dropped off at
bus stop 14, close to the National Commissioner of Icelandic
Police, National Bureau of Investigation and the National Central Bureau of Interpol. A short walk away was the Miðlæg
Rannsóknardeild, a national resource that housed the Major
Crimes Unit – Iceland's equivalent of British CID – and other
police departments.

It was a comfortable ride, a fast route, the landscape changing
as they got closer to their destination, industrial buildings giving
way to pretty wooden houses, painted in a variety of colours.
Frankie had little to say about it. If David was reading her right,
she was thirteen years' old, caught up in a dark memory, unable
to appreciate her surroundings. He left her to her thoughts,
wishing they had time to take advantage of what the country
had to offer: a whale-watching cruise or helicopter ride across
an active volcano, anything to take her mind off Joanna. By the
time they reached the city and got off the bus, she'd come to.

'Where now?' she said.

David consulted his notes: 'Hverfisgata for police, Skulgata
for spies.'

They spotted the municipal police building without troubling
the locals for directions; a huge white office structure with
many floors. Inside, David asked her to call the MIR to check
on Dick, then went off to make enquiries. He hadn't tipped
anyone off that he was coming, fearing that they might ask
too many questions before he'd worked out how much he'd

like to share. Showing ID to a female officer at the front desk, he asked to speak with his Icelandic counterpart. She took a photograph of his warrant card, telling him that the SIO he needed to speak to was out.

'When might be a good time?'

'An hour, two?'

Frankie had warned him that no one was ever rushed in this country. Only Brits watched the clock. 'Could you be more specific? I've had a long journey.'

The officer behind the reception desk made a call, then hung up.

During the short exchange, David caught the words English and police. Nothing else.

The officer apologised for the delay. 'Detective Chief Inspector Jónsdóttir will be here at seven thirty. Would you like to wait? I can arrange some coffee and a sandwich.'

'No, thanks. I need to find a hotel.'

Earwigging their conversation, Frankie looked up from her mobile, urging him to get on with it. What was taking so long? *These situations require diplomatic handling by someone of equal rank.* Bright's decision to send David had been wise in theory, though it looked like he was being fobbed off. As soon as the thought arrived, Frankie changed her mind. He seemed relaxed, leaning on his right forearm, deep in conversation with a female officer whose expensive perfume she could smell from across the waiting area.

Their heads were almost touching.

Frankie moved closer . . .

As her guv'nor made to leave, the female copper spoke again. 'If you have no reservation, you should try the Hotel Reykjavík Centrum. It's modern and comfortable with a restaurant I like very much. The location is perfect, one of the oldest streets in Reykjavík. My shift ends in in five minutes. I could show you, if you like.'

Oh, for God's sake.

'That won't be necessary,' he said.

'Would you like me to call them for you?'

No!

Frankie willed David to turn around so she could stick her fingers down her throat. First Collingwood, now Blondie. Who next? She ruffled her hair, running a licked finger across each eyebrow, like it would make squat's difference to how she looked. Compared to the attractive officer behind reception, the British DS felt like a regurgitated dog's dinner. She did nothing to make herself presentable, especially on duty. Why should she? She was there to work, not play. If the rules of engagement were different here, she'd damn well make allowances.

'I'm a detective,' David said. 'I'll find it if you give me a clue.'

Frankie pressed her lips together, stifling a grin. The Icelandic officer had already given him one, only he was too dumb to spot it. Did she have to draw him a bloody map?

Omigod! She did.

'You're looking for Aðalstræti.' Like a tourist information clerk, the officer drew a pad towards her, tore off a street map and picked up a highlighter pen. You'd have to be going some to get this level of personal service at Middle Earth. David's new bestie wasn't about to let go just yet. 'You go here . . .' She drew a yellow line on the map. 'Turn here . . .' She marked another straight line, longer than the first, then looked up to check on her handsome British guest, a penetrating gaze. 'The hotel is right here.' She drew a cross.

'X marks the spot,' Frankie said, arriving at the counter. 'Guv, we need to make a move.'

If looks could kill.

25

Diplomacy was overrated, no matter what Bright said. Frankie walked away from the Major Crimes Unit at a fast pace, irritated that they were having to wait around to see Stone's Icelandic equal when they had a murder to investigate. The only break they caught was timing. Purely by accident, they had landed in the period of the midnight sun, the only few days of the year when it occurred after twelve o'clock. They were hoping to find Kristjánsson in Reykjavík. If they had to travel to his family home in Ísafjörður they'd never manage it before morning.

The mobile in her pocket vibrated.

She stopped walking to check the screen.

A message from her father: **Has the eagle landed? x**

She keyed a reply: **We're down. x**

We're up! So proud of you. x

His words brought a lump to her throat. **Love you, Dad. x**

David had caught up with her. 'Any news?'

'Not from my old man, though he'll be wanting chapter and verse on our investigation when we get home.' Frankie slipped her phone into her pocket. 'You know he can't help himself.'

'Did you ring Abbott like I asked?'

'Yeah, you were too busy schmoozing with Blondie to notice.'

David gave a pointed look. 'She was trying to be helpful.'

'She was trying it on.'

'She was out of luck. I don't date female officers. They're trouble.'

Frankie was tempted to add, you don't date female officers anymore, but thought better of it. It would start him thinking about Jane and she didn't want that. Not now. Not here, far from home, in a place outside of his jurisdiction. Her job was to make his life easier, not worse.

He was waiting for an answer.

She gave him one. 'Toxicology and post-mortem reports are in on our second victim. There was enough diamorphine in his bloodstream to put an elephant down. Grit and soil from his facial wound came from woodland. Trace evidence of coniferous needles, plant litter and organic humus confirms that he was killed in the vicinity of Kielder, not elsewhere.'

'The search for the scene is ongoing?'

Frankie nodded. 'Large parts of the Lakeside Way, north and south, are sealed off to the public. They're not happy about it. PolSA are concentrating on the shoreline and will move the parameters if necessary.' She paused. 'There was water in the victim's lungs. He was alive when he entered the reservoir.'

'Right.'

'Have you met Russell Stuart?'

'Not yet.'

'Didn't think so.' Frankie stepped aside to allow a mother and baby to pass. For a Sunday evening the street was busy. 'He's been on a year's sabbatical. He reckons the catastrophic injuries to the back of the IP's head may well have been fatal in any event. There was substantial brain damage. Disoriented, it's possible he fell into the water after the attack and drowned.'

'Any joy on his prints?'

'Negative.'

'What about DNA?'

'No match. He has no form in the UK. The labels on his clothing aren't on our system. Hardly surprising, if he's from here. Abbott uploaded prints and DNA results onto the international database. He'll let us know if they come up with anything. We need to speak with Kristjánsson urgently.'

'Has Maria Colman been seen yet?'

'Yeah, Abbott sent Mitch to Yarrow to take her statement. Most of it confirms what she told me on the phone. He had the sense to ask what happened next. Once the vehicle shot across the dam, she went inside. It didn't pass her cottage, which is odd because it's right on the roadside. Either the driver stopped when he or she reached the junction of the C200, or they headed west.'

'If that were the case, wouldn't Colman have heard it?'

'She's ninety, David.'

They walked on together, finding the hotel they were looking for, a light grey clapperboard house in a historic area close to Laugavegur, the beating heart of downtown Reykjavík. They booked adjoining rooms, dumped their bags and had a quick bite to eat in Uppsalir, the hotel's café bar-cum-restaurant, then walked to the Major Crimes Unit to meet with Icelandic investigators.

26

Detective Chief Inspector Jónsdóttir's office was large and airy, three times the size of David's at Middle Earth, and with a window overlooking the bay and the mountains beyond. Jónsdóttir was tall, mid-forties with sharp green eyes and fair hair. She was casually dressed in a dusky pink blouse, tight jeans and flat shoes. She had an air of authority about her. Her second-in-command, a male, was younger, approximately six three, thickset with a strong jawline.

Both were standing.

Jónsdóttir stepped forward, extending a warm welcome and a firm handshake to the Northumbria detectives, introducing herself only as Anna and her sidekick as Emil. The DCI was supremely confident, a woman who felt no need to define herself by rank. Icelandic women were at the forefront of the race for equality.

'I'm very pleased to meet you,' Frankie introduced herself and Stone.

'It's always a pleasure to collaborate with a foreign force,' Anna said. 'Though an unexpected delegation from British murder detectives has caused quite a stir among my colleagues. There must be a good reason why you didn't call to alert us that you were coming.'

There was a question in there somewhere.

'Our decision to come was taken at the last minute,' David replied.

'I'm intrigued . . .' Her expression spoke volumes. His comment had fallen woefully short of an explanation. She didn't challenge him, just pointed at two chairs. 'Please, make yourselves comfortable and tell us how we might help.'

They all sat down.

'Yesterday morning, two bodies were discovered within the space of a few hours at the same location, a reservoir in Northumberland in the north-east of England,' David said. 'The first was found by a young Icelandic graduate on holiday with nine of his friends. The remains are old, skeletal. Your countrymen and women are witnesses, not suspects. I'm dealing with that incident. Frankie is the lead investigator on the second.'

For continuity, David wanted her to handle it while he took care of the barrel case. She'd been to the scene. He hadn't. When he'd asked how she'd felt about stepping up, she didn't know what to say at first. She was proud to take it on. Hadn't expected to run a murder investigation on her own so soon. He had no doubt that she was good for it. His door was open if she got stuck.

He gave her the nod to proceed.

Anna and Emil listened as she outlined why they had come on the trail of Kristjánsson and co, explaining that the group had been questioned and released before the second body was discovered. 'I have the passport details of the ten we interviewed and an image of the second victim, a young man we have reason to believe is also Icelandic.'

Anna said. 'How so?'

'There was no identification on the body, no phone either, just a pack of Icelandic cigarettes. Hardly earth-shattering, I know. Of itself, the link is flimsy. The victim was found within a few hundred yards of the crime scene where the first victim was discovered, even less distance from the Icelandic encampment. You may be forgiven for thinking that the backpackers gave him the cigarettes. It would be an obvious assumption to make, except for one thing: every member of the party stated that they had not met or seen anyone since arriving at Kielder.'

'Show me the photograph.'

Frankie took a folder from her bag, removing a list of the Icelandic documentation Mitch had taken copies of at Hexham police station, a crime scene photograph attached to the back.

Passing them to Anna, she waited. The Icelandic DCI studied the list, then the image, before passing them to Emil.

Frankie knew instantly that her unidentified victim was familiar.

David did too by the look of him.

Anna didn't confirm it.

Frankie gave her a nudge. 'You know him, don't you?' It was a statement framed in a question.

Anna met her gaze. 'You're very perceptive—'

'That's what I'm paid for.'

'Let's not jump the gun.' David was warning Frankie to cool it.

'I'm not trying to wind anyone up, guv. Tempus fugit and all that.'

'Your colleague is right,' Anna said. 'I assume your trip to Iceland is time-limited—'

'We have a few days, maybe less.' Frankie was desperate to move things along. 'The victim's prints and DNA were uploaded to Interpol by a colleague of mine. We know that the car he used to get to Northumberland is owned by an organised crime syndicate based in Glasgow. If he was associating with people like that, he may well have convictions, in which case identification shouldn't take long.'

Anna examined the image again. 'This man has facial bruising. He looks like a person I've come across many times. If it's who I think it is, he has a tragic past and a long criminal record here in Iceland.'

'For?' Frankie asked.

'Drugs, dealing and possession.'

'No one will miss him,' Emil said.

Anna shot him down. 'That was both unnecessary and unkind.'

A casual shrug. 'Just telling it like it is—'

He'd angered Anna. 'If you'll excuse Emil for a moment, he'll make some enquiries.'

Without apologising, he got up to leave, her eyes like daggers in his back.

Frankie felt the vibration of her iPhone. 'Just a moment, Emil. I've been waiting for news from England. I think it just came in.'

Wrestling the device from her pocket, she accessed her inbox. The only unopened email was from Abbott. It contained a number of attachments: the post-mortem report; several close-ups of her victim, of particular interest the track marks on his arms and a tattoo on his neck she thought might nail his identity; images of the labels on his clothing, one of the cigarette pack Roz Fitzsimmons had found on his body.

She looked up, eyes on Emil. 'What's your email address? I'll forward it on.' He gave it and she sent it straight away.

'Thanks,' he said. 'I'll take a look.'

Finally, Frankie had reason to believe.

27

After Emil left the room, Anna eyed her British guests, a poker face that gave nothing away, then glanced at the list again. 'Unlike the man in the photograph, the names here mean nothing to me. I'll look into them. What makes you think that Kristjánsson and his backpacking friends are here in Iceland?'

'They flew in last night,' Frankie said. 'Airport security confirmed it.'

'Why is that odd if they weren't travelling with your second victim?'

'We have digital proof that they were, yet they kept quiet about it.' The two women locked eyes. 'Northumberland was the start of a European tour for some of the group,' Frankie added. 'Dumping their hire cars, in a place other than where they picked them up, within hours of speaking to police, suggests that they were running away, that one of them was somehow involved in the death of the second victim.'

'That's quite a jump.'

'You can see why we might make it.' David said. 'Whoever it was anticipated that we'd find the body quickly. Like Reykjavík, Kielder gets many visitors from around the world. At this time of year, it's teeming with holidaymakers.'

Anna said, 'You're suggesting a conspiracy?'

'We don't know,' Frankie said. 'We're here to find out.'

The Icelandic DCI didn't rubbish her theory without giving it further thought. She stood up to stretch her legs, opened the door of a wall cabinet that housed a small fridge. Taking three bottles of water from it, she handed Stone and Oliver one each, then sat down, unscrewing the top of her own. 'Might the group have cancelled their trip because they were upset?'

'We thought so too at first,' Frankie said.

'What made you change your mind?'

'Kristjánsson was nervous around me.'

'Hardly surprising. It's not every day you find a body. He's young. Maybe also shy.' Anna smiled. 'Did you frighten him, Frankie?'

David laughed. 'She frightens me.'

'Me too.' Smiling, Anna was about to respond when the internal phone rang. Excusing herself, she took the call, speaking in her native tongue, half an eye on her visitors. She scribbled a few notes on a pad before replacing the receiver. 'That was Emil. Your journey has not been wasted. The identity of your victim is confirmed.'

Frankie pulled a pad from her briefcase, clicked open a pen. 'Name?'

'Jón, J.O.N. No aitch. Last name Scheving, S.C.H.E.V.I.N.G.' Referring to her scribble, Anna gave a date of birth: 4.11.97. the only thing she'd written down. She crossed her arms, her face pained by a dark memory. 'It doesn't surprise me that he met a violent death. His parents, both drug addicts, were neglectful from the minute he drew breath. Their turbulent relationship dominated his life.' What Anna said next was totally unexpected. 'His father is serving time for his mother's murder. He flew into a rage while high and strangled her in front of the boy when he was eleven years old.'

Sadly, the narrative wasn't new.

Frankie dropped her head. She had been Scheving's age when Joanna was taken from her. She couldn't imagine what effect it might have had on her if she'd actually seen the murder taking place.

David covered for her. 'Which, I presume, is how you came across him?'

Anna confirmed it with a nod. 'He was traumatised by the experience. I couldn't get him to open up. Family liaison didn't come close. He was too far gone. Apart from the convictions I mentioned, Emil tells me he has one for sexual assault on an underage female I didn't know about.' She shook her head. 'What goes around . . .'

Snippets of her interview with Kristján replayed in Frankie's mind, raising her antennae. A suspicion forced its way to the surface. One she didn't want to acknowledge, let alone think about. 'Did you investigate the sexual assault?' she asked.

'Not personally, no. I was in the United States at the time, which is how I missed it.'

'Can you pull up the conviction, let me look at the file?' Frankie was pointing at the computer on her desk. The two DCIs looked at one another, curious as to why it mattered now that Scheving was dead. Frankie said, 'Trust me, it's important.'

Using her warrant card, Anna logged on, fingers flying across the keys as she typed in his name. She scrolled down, clicking on the sexual offence conviction, almost three years old. Her eyes widened as she took in the text on screen, her head turning slowly to view the list the Northumbria detectives had brought with them. Frankie didn't need telling that Jón Scheving's female victim was on that list.

She'd already made the jump.

28

In the past hour, DCI Anna Jónsdóttir had agreed to organise a joint operation with UK police. She'd transformed her office to accommodate her unexpected guests. It had become a mini-incident room, complete with a whiteboard containing a grid of names, gender, dates of birth, written up in order of priority; a pile of papers now on her desk. She was on her feet, ready for action, a list of addresses in her hand, verified by Emil as current. He'd been hanging on to her every word, excited to be working alongside an experienced murder investigation team.

'So,' Anna said to Frankie. 'How would you like to play this? There are four of us. Other personnel are on standby to help, assuming you want to bring the suspects in at the earliest opportunity.'

'Apart from Eva Jacobsdóttir . . .,' Frankie said. As Jón Sche-ving's victim and Kristjánsson's girlfriend, the word motive had entered the frame. 'Given the nature of the assault she suffered, I'd like to interview her at home, if it's all the same to you. For what it's worth, I hope she or one of her pals hasn't done something stupid. They're nice kids. I'll get no pleasure seeing one or more of them locked up.'

Anna shared the sentiment.

Frankie could see it in her eyes.

'Just to clarify,' David said. 'We're not asking for arrests at this stage.'

Frankie kept her focus on Anna. 'David's right, we have bugger all hard evidence. We ask for voluntary cooperation. If they refuse, then it's over to you, Anna. You're the one with the clout over here. For obvious reasons, I favour a coordinated strike. We don't want them alerting one another that we're in town.'

'If we can find them,' Anna said. 'They're young. Chances are, some of them may be out tonight.'

'I appreciate the problem of locating them at the weekend. I hope we're not tying up too many resources.'

The Icelandic DCI waved away her concerns. 'My officers will find them. You and I should stay with Eva until we round them up. That way we can be sure she doesn't tip them off.' She caught the eye of her 2ic. 'Emil, are you ready?'

'Yes, let's do this.'

'Consult with the troops and meet us outside in ten.'

David was happy to take a back seat, literally and figuratively, allowing Frankie and Anna to take the lead. Already, they were getting on as if they had known each other for years, part of the international police family bonding them instantly, temporary colleagues preparing to strike.

Anna led the way.

The waiting Volvo Cross Country had blue-and-yellow livery and Icelandic insignia, the word LÖGREGLAN on the side and POLICE on the bonnet. On the rear of the vehicle, presumably for the benefit of tourists, was a smaller POLICE sign, the image of a telephone and the number 112. David would remember that. Working in unfamiliar territory, you never knew when you might need an emergency response.

They all climbed in, Anna behind the wheel, Frankie her front-seat passenger, David and Emil in the back seats, several double-crewed police vehicles bringing up the rear. As they drove through the narrow streets of Reykjavík in convoy, there was all manner of street art to take in, along with the vibrant café culture as restaurants and bars filled up. Plenty of curious stares were directed their way by locals and tourists, an operation on a scale rarely seen in the Icelandic capital drawing their attention. Minutes later, Anna dropped David and Emil close to Kristjánsson's home, a flat rented and paid for by his father, according to his lease.

Eva lived in Mosfellsbær, a fifteen-minute drive from downtown Reykjavík. Alone in the car with Anna, Frankie felt tense. The minute David and Emil jumped out, the atmosphere had changed – and not for the better. The DCI seemed preoccupied. Never one to hold back, Frankie had to ask.

'Something wrong?'

'I was thinking about Scheving.'

'What about him?'

'There's no doubt that he was traumatised by the loss of his mother and the manner in which she died, but I made it my business to read the statement he gave when charged with sexual assault. It angered me. According to him, there was no crime. Eva was a willing participant—'

'You do surprise me.' Frankie couldn't help herself. It was the answer all sex offenders gave. 'Must've passed him by that she was fourteen and he was five years older.'

Anna shook her head in despair. 'I always felt so sorry for him.'

'And yet, just like his father, he thought every female was fair game? Save your sympathy for his victim. It can't have been easy for her either. I've seen so many young girls come out of court more damaged than they went in. Litigation hands men the opportunity to rubbish reputations and spread their poison in order to justify their crimes.'

'You're preaching to the converted.' Anna glanced into the passenger seat. 'Are you OK?'

'I'm fine.' In her rear-view mirror, Frankie noticed the remaining police vehicles peel off, heading to different addresses. 'Take no notice of me, I'm just sounding off . . .'

For girls like Eva, Joanna, and every other female victim she'd ever known.

'Did you interview Eva in the UK?' Anna asked.

'Yes.'

'What's she like?'

'Quietly spoken and polite. Maybe too polite, the type a guy like Scheving would target and take advantage of.'

Anna slowed, ducking her head, checking street signs.

'Did Eva report the assault?' Frankie asked.

'No, her mother did. The girl didn't want to talk about it. The file suggested she was a reluctant witness at first—'

'Can you blame her?'

'Eventually, she found the courage to give evidence.'

'Good for her.' Frankie meant it. 'I'd be interested to know if Scheving ever visited his father in prison—'

'Surprisingly, he did.' Anna turned left, accelerating uphill.

'Let me guess, his father claimed provocation.'

Anna's confirmation came as no surprise.

Frankie was growing more and more irate. She'd heard police officers use the same defence in order to keep their pensions. Men who should've known better. In some cases, it was common knowledge that they were violent at home, exercising coercive control over female colleagues at work. They were a disgrace to the office they held.

There was an edge to her voice when she spoke. 'Everyone can find an excuse for lashing out if they look hard enough. No matter how Scheving wanted to paint it, he was the adult, Eva a child.'

Anna took her foot off the accelerator, a concerned glance into the passenger seat, dipping a toe in choppy water. 'If you don't mind me saying so, you seem angrier than is healthy about a historic case . . .' She waited until the silence between them became unbearable. 'In my experience, it's sometimes easier to offload to a stranger than a close colleague. If there's anything bothering you, I'm a good listener—'

'Is this it, the red door?' Frankie wasn't going there.

29

The chatter on the radio increased as Anna parked the car, ending their conversation. The transmission was short, Emil's voice upbeat. Pulling on the handbrake, Anna spoke to him, then turned to face Frankie. 'Six of the ten on our list have been found, including Kristjánsson. They're on their way to the station. My team will continue to search for the rest. Your strategy appears to be working.'

Kristján's voice arrived in Frankie's head: *You get a lot more from everything if you plan.*

He wasn't the only one who'd done his homework. She was well prepared. Out of the car now, her Icelandic escort was already halfway up the garden path of a pretty, typically wooden dwelling with a wrap-around balcony and a well-stocked front garden, overlooking the North-Atlantic Ocean. Two vehicles were parked on the driveway, a black Ford Expedition and a red VW Up.

Making a note of their numbers, Anna pushed the doorbell.

A man of around forty pulled the door open, surprised to find two strangers standing there. He was deeply tanned, casually dressed in long shorts and a T-shirt with what Frankie realised was a city map of Reykjavík printed on the front.

Holding up ID, Anna asked if they might go inside to speak with him.

He stepped aside to allow them in, directing them to a cosy living room. There were voices coming from an adjacent room. Taking a step to the side, Frankie glanced into it. She could only see a large smart TV mounted on the wall.

Explaining the purpose of her visit, Anna introduced the British detective, asking to speak with Eva – an urgent matter that couldn't wait – repeating this in English for Frankie's benefit.

The man switched his focus to Frankie. 'If it would save time, conduct your interview in English. I teach it in high school. My name is Jacob. Welcome to my home. Is this about the body they found?'

'Yes, sir.'

If Jacob was referring to the barrel case, then Frankie's answer was technically incorrect. She had every reason to keep her powder dry until she had eyes on his daughter. Laughter and a conversation she couldn't understand drifted in through the open door. The voices, one male, two females; Eva and her mother presumably – a brother?

Shit!

Remembering the two vehicles they had passed on their way in, Frankie had to think on her feet. 'We understand that your son Aron no longer lives at home with you.'

'Your information is correct. He has a place in town.'

With any luck, Frankie hoped, Emil had already found him. Aware of Aron's quick temper, she was taking no chances. Leaving home didn't necessarily mean that he wasn't in the house. 'It being Sunday, I wondered if he might also be here with you this evening.'

'He's out with friends,' Jacob gave a shrug. 'I have no idea where. Would you like me to call him?'

'No, it's fine. We'll try his flat later.' Frankie glanced into the TV room, one less problem to deal with. 'I'd like to see your daughter now.'

He called out to Eva.

His offspring was smiling when she arrived in the doorway. She froze when she saw Frankie. 'What are you doing here?'

'I'd like to ask you a few more questions.' Unaware of Icelandic law relating to young persons of her age, Frankie played it safe. 'I'm happy that your father is present while we have that conversation.'

'I'm not.' Eva snapped her head around. 'Leave us, Papa?'

30

Eva's bluntness had drawn no negative attention from either her father or Anna. Icelandic women, even young women it seemed, were liberated; they knew their own minds and were unafraid to speak up. Still, this was not the girl Frankie had taken a statement from at Hexham nick; more like the one hiding in Kielder Forest, keeping a close eye on Kristjánsson. Her father left the room and they all sat down, Anna merely an observer who had agreed to chip in only if it became necessary. That was fine with Frankie. She had no authority here. With no time to mess around, she chose a direct approach.

'Why did you run, Eva?'

'Run?' A frown developed as the girl came closer. 'What do you mean?'

'Well, you're here and not in England. You told me that you and Kristján had plans to travel further afield and yet you all returned home the minute you were allowed to leave.'

'What of it? We changed our minds.'

'I realise you'd had a shock, but it seems over the top to cancel a holiday you'd taken months to plan and pay for—'

'Not really.'

'Yes, really.' Frankie's tone hardened a little. 'Eva, I've come a long way. You need to be honest with me. Last night, you were booked into the Kielder Observatory. Kristján was keen to go. You didn't cancel. You just failed to turn up. I've been asking myself why the rush to get home when it meant missing out.'

'There was no rush. We'd had enough and decided to leave.'

'That's all there was to it?'

'Yes, I swear.'

'And yet you didn't return to Glasgow, where you might arguably have been able to change your arrangements without having to take out a mortgage. Instead, you dumped your cars and flew out from Newcastle on the first available flight to London and on to Keflavík. That must have taken some organising at short notice, and great cost. It seems perfectly reasonable to assume that you were running away.'

Eva didn't answer.

'Whose idea was it to leave?'

'I don't remember.' She was lying.

Frankie gave her a not-so-gentle nudge. 'Tell me about Jón Scheving.'

The girl's expression was like stone. 'What of him?'

'Can you explain why you never mentioned him when we spoke?'

'You never asked about him—'

'No, but I specifically asked if you'd seen anyone during your stay in Kielder. That question was put to everyone in your group by myself and my colleagues. It received a negative response. You all made statements to that effect. You can see why I find it odd that none of you mentioned Scheving when questioned—'

'We didn't want to be associated with that piece of shit.'

Mitch had said as much to Frankie. 'I understand . . .' She held Eva's gaze, her tone more sympathetic now. 'You two have history, the worst kind. I don't wish to upset you, but you all lied to us. I want to know why.'

Eva's eyes were vacant. A faraway look, another time, another dark and dangerous place. The shutters went up. Frankie felt like a shit putting the seventeen-year-old under pressure, but her aim was to get at the truth. That required her full focus, no matter how painful for a suspect with a motive to kill.

'We found his body,' Frankie said.

'What?' The girl's eyes widened. 'When?'

'Soon after we let you go.' She was either a good actress or genuinely shocked. Frankie couldn't make up her mind which. 'When did you last see Jón Scheving?'

Eva looked away, her chest rising and falling beneath her T-shirt as she struggled to keep her breathing under control. Frankie allowed the silence to stretch out between them, hoping the girl would feel compelled to fill the void.

She didn't.

Frankie glanced at Anna, her cue to intervene.

'The detective asked you a question,' she said. 'When did you last see Scheving?'

Eva took a moment longer. No matter how much pressure she was under, she wouldn't be rushed. 'It was late, around midnight. I can't say for sure. He was drunk and abusive. We didn't invite him to join us, if that's what you think. We bumped into him at the airport. He was on our flight to the UK and tagged along. Kristján tried to talk him out of it but he wouldn't take no for an answer. He followed us. No one wanted him there. He knew it and walked off in a huff. I was relieved to see him go. We all were.'

'Who else saw him leave?'

'That's a stupid question—'

'Which requires an answer,' Frankie said firmly.

'Everyone. We didn't look for him. Why would we? And in the morning, we found the barrel, then you turned up. Afterwards, like I told you, we just wanted to come home.' Eva studied Frankie closely, ignoring Anna as if she wasn't in the room. 'Where did you find him?'

'I can't tell you that.'

'You mean you won't.' Eva dropped the attitude. 'Was it an overdose, a car crash?'

'You're smart. I'm sure you can work out why I can't go into detail.'

'You think I had something to do with his death?'

'Did you?' Frankie asked.

Eva laughed, a derisory glance at Anna, a word or two in Icelandic.

Frankie had no idea what she'd said. Her best guess would be: Is she for real?

'You think this is a joke, Eva?' Anna said in English, hard eyes on the girl. 'I can assure you it's not. A man has been murdered. You and your friends are under suspicion. For your own good, you should take the matter seriously. If you know what happened to him, you must tell us now.'

'You think I could care less about that pig?' In what Frankie could only describe as rage, the girl flipped, her eyes as cold as ice. 'In and out of court, he put me through hell, making me sound like a whore who was begging for it. I'm glad he's dead.'

'You had every reason to hate him,' Frankie said.

'I didn't kill him. I wish I had.'

'You don't mean that. What he did to you was unforgivable but not worth ruining the rest of your life for.' The blood drained from Eva's face. Frankie hoped she hadn't already done that. 'Who knew he'd assaulted you?'

'No one. Do you think my friends would have let him follow us to Kielder if they had?'

She had a point. 'Not even your brother?'

'No, my case was heard in camera. Only my parents knew.'

Frankie's tone softened. 'Eva, if you didn't kill him, someone else did, perhaps one of your party. I'm here to investigate that possibility and I'm going nowhere until I know for sure.' She allowed Eva a moment to process the reality of a situation that could put her, Aron, or one of their friends behind bars. 'Take your time, there's no rush. Did you see or hear anything? An argument perhaps?'

No response.

'Eva, talk to me. C'mon, Scheving is dead. He can't hurt you anymore. If you know something, no matter how small, I need to hear it. Help me to understand, because this is not going away until I get the truth. And I will find it, I can promise you that.'

No reaction.

Frankie backed off, remembering what Kristján had said about Aron: *he's very protective of her.* Had her brother taken revenge? Had she? Or was it Kristján? Was he trying to shift the blame? Frankie had seen the way he looked at the girl, the way she looked at him. If he knew of the assault, it gave him motive to kill. It also made sense of his nervousness around Frankie and his reluctance to admit to a relationship with Eva.

A text came in.

Anna went for her pocket. Her nod was almost imperceptible: she had news. A heavy weight settled in Frankie's chest as the text was forwarded. The other nine suspects were all at the station. Enough for now . . . time to go.

Frankie stood. 'One last question, did you see anyone else that night?'

'Not that I recall.' Eva took a moment to think. 'Yes, actually. One vehicle. We had to put out the fire in case the driver saw us. Kristján thought it might have been a forest ranger.'

'When was this?'

'Just before Scheving left the campsite.'

'Did you see the vehicle, can you describe it?'

'All I saw was the headlights through the trees. It flew past without stopping.'

'Travelling in which direction, towards or away from Hawkhope car park where you left your vehicle?'

'Away.'

'Did you see or hear the vehicle again?'

Eva shook her head.

There was no guilt present, no sign that she was on the verge of a breakdown, having been presented with questions that would cause most people to react. Quite the opposite. She displayed no emotion whatsoever, even when Anna asked her for a sample of saliva. Opening her mouth as it was taken, Eva met Frankie's gaze head-on, a look that would keep the detective sergeant awake tonight.

31

David and Emil were busy interviewing when the two female detectives arrived back at Anna's office. Time to regroup and get better acquainted, an opportunity to go over Frankie's relatively brief but illuminating interview with Eva. There would be others. The girl could count on it. Frankie wasn't finished with her yet. Eva hadn't denied that Scheving had joined the group in Kielder or made any attempt to conceal how she felt about him.

She had more to give and so did the others.

Victim or not, Frankie wondered if she'd been staring into the eyes of a cold-blooded murderer, an accomplice – or neither? There was only one certainty in play here. If one of her friends was responsible, Eva wasn't about to implicate whoever had caved in Scheving's skull. That unsettling thought was interrupted a few minutes later by a knock at the door.

Emil entered. 'All done.'

Frankie turned to face him. 'That's what you think.'

With David's approval, an interview strategy had been painstakingly worked out before the detectives all left the MCU to round up the group Anna had casually referred to as 'the ten'. Frankie asked Emil if any had mentioned seeing Scheving. The answer was no. They had all stuck to their story: that they saw no one at the campsite.

Frankie panicked. 'You haven't let them go?'

'Not yet, David asked me to hold them until you got back, though I'm not sure why. There's no evidence on any of them. No motive either.'

'Eva is popular, a friend. Doesn't that give them all motive?'

'I suppose, but you can't keep someone in because they know her.'

'With Anna's permission, they're stopping in until I say otherwise.'

Emil glanced at his boss.

Anna gave a nod. 'They've lied to us, Emil. Eva confirmed that Scheving was at the campsite and that everyone saw him leave, which puts them all in the frame. She also mentioned a vehicle that could be of interest to the investigation in the UK.'

'Sounds positive.' Emil met Frankie's gaze.

She confirmed it with a nod. 'Any idea how David's progressing?'

He pointed at the computer on Anna's desk. 'Let's find out.'

Logging on, Anna pressed a few keys, turning the screen around so that all three could see it, a new addition to her system that allowed her to view an interview in progress from the comfort of her office.

In the interview room, David had his back to the camera, his arm draped over his chair, right foot resting on the left knee. He looked relaxed and in control.

Unsure which of the group was facing him, Anna caught Emil's eye. 'Which one is he?'

'Kristjánsson,' Emil and Frankie said in unison.

'I had to look hard,' Frankie added. 'He wasn't wearing glasses when I interviewed him in the UK. He looks very different with them on.'

'Camouflage,' Anna said casually. 'It doesn't surprise me that David left him till last. He's making him sweat most probably. I'd have done the same in his shoes.' She looked at Frankie. 'He seems nice, your boss.'

'Don't be fooled by his laid-back approach. He's smart and can mix it with the best of them. I'm hoping he's had more luck with Kristján than I did.'

Anna smiled. 'You two seem close.'

'We have our moments.'

'Have you worked together long?'

'Couple of years. He's northern, like me, though you

wouldn't know that by his accent. He moved away from North-umberland, joining the Met when he wasn't much older than Kristján. Made quite an impact too. He impresses the hell out of me every day.' The thought that she might see a lot less of him going forward had been preying on Frankie's mind. She hoped she'd end up on his team, not in some hellhole in the back of beyond following her official promotion.

That was by no means guaranteed.

She pointed at the screen. 'Can you get the audio up too?'

Anna tapped more keys and they all listened in.

David was recapping, checking his notes, ticking off key questions they had agreed to put to all of the suspects before rounding them up.

Kristján was uncommunicative and yet anxious to get the interview over and go home.

A text message arrived on Frankie's phone at the exact same time as Stone went for his pocket. It was from Abbott to both of them: **Scheving DNA match: Post-mortem blood samples. Blood found at Kristjánsson's campsite.**

32

In the interview room, David had finished checking Abbott's message. When he spoke, his tone was harder than before. 'I'll ask you once more, who else was at the campsite?'

'No one.'

'You're not helping yourself, son.'

'Kristjánsson is losing his bottle,' Anna said.

'And Stone his temper,' Emil added.

Frankie stared at the screen.

David held up his mobile and gave the lad a shove. 'I now have unequivocal proof that you're lying. I'm not going to tell you what it is. You'd better come clean or I'm going to think you're guilty of something far more serious than withholding information.'

Kristján broke then. 'He was not invited.'

'Who? I need a name—'

'Jón . . . Scheving.'

David crossed his arms. 'Now we have that out of the way, perhaps you could explain how his blood was found at your campsite.'

The lad hesitated. 'He cut his finger on a beer can.'

'You sure about that?'

'I saw him do it.'

'Where's the can now?'

'I don't know, do I? If it's not at the campsite, he must've taken it with him when he left.'

Frankie made a mental note to chase that up and sent David a text: Take a break. Need to speak to you – now.

Pausing the recording, he immediately got up.

Kristján spoke again before David reached the door. 'Scheving's an asshole.'

Retracing his steps, David retook his seat. He pressed a button on the audio apparatus, asking Kristján to repeat what he'd said for the benefit of the recording. He did so, word for word.

'Did you fight?' David asked.

'Me? No. I was angry with him for sure. He was provoking Eva, arguing with Aron, waving a knife around.'

Frankie glanced at Anna and Emil. 'No mention of an argument or the knife from Eva. And there was no weapon found at either scene.'

All three turned their attention to the screen.

'What was the argument about?' David was asking.

'I don't know, I only saw the tail end of it. It never came to anything. Scheving just left.'

'To go where?'

'No idea.' He blew out a breath. 'Am I in trouble?'

'Depends what you've done.' David paused. 'When did you next see him?'

'I didn't, I swear.'

'Whose idea was it to abandon the trip?'

'Mine.'

'That's interesting,' Frankie said to the others, without taking her eyes off the screen.

'Why?' Emil asked.

'Eva couldn't remember whose idea it was to leave,' Anna said.

'Those I interviewed didn't deviate from that,' Emil replied.

Now Frankie looked at him. 'I don't buy it. One might forget, not all of them.'

On screen, David sat forward, elbows on the table, hands cradled in front of him, eyes fixed on Kristján. 'I want you to answer this very carefully. Is that all you have to tell me?'

'Yes, no . . .' Whatever he was about to say, he seemed terrified to come out with it. 'I put pressure on the others not to mention Scheving to DS Oliver and her colleagues. It was a stupid mistake. I regret it and take full responsibility. I'm sorry. Scheving isn't someone any of us want to be associated with, here or over there.'

'Why is that?'

'He's a junkie.'

'So why ask him along?'

'I didn't. He crashed our party.'

Frankie was tempted to do the same.

She wished she was in there, a chance to kick David under the table, a hint that she had an important question of her own. She would insist on an explanation. Had Kristján and Eva concocted an elaborate story to explain how Scheving came to be with them in the UK? Wouldn't bright, articulate kids have come up with a more plausible scenario? At such a pivotal moment it was unwise to send another text asking her SIO not to proceed. She did it anyway: **Need a word, guv.**

Seconds later, the door to Anna's office flew open. David frowned at her. 'This had better be good, Frank.'

'I have new information you need to be aware of, guv.'

'Then why so glum? You might have your first case nailed down by close of play.'

'I don't see that as a true reflection of how things stand,' she said.

Anna and Emil raised a smile to one another. Watching the Brits disagree was like looking in a mirror.

Frankie didn't join in. She had a sense of misdirection. There was a rabbit off somewhere.

'OK, what have you got?' David said.

'Eva confirmed that Scheving was at the campsite and yet Emil tells me those he interviewed are holding the party line.'

'They're off the hook,' David said. 'Kristján admitted that he coerced them into it—'

'Yeah, we heard.' Frankie gestured to the computer on Anna's desk. On screen, Kristján was sitting where David had left him, head bowed. 'Why would he suddenly volunteer that information?'

'There could be a number of reasons, to clear his conscience being top of that list. He's not stupid, Frank. He knows that we wouldn't travel internationally if the matter wasn't serious. If one of "the ten" were to break down, it wouldn't look good for him, would it?'

'Or, he could be protecting someone other than himself,' Anna suggested. 'We only caught the last part of your interview. Does he know that a second body has been found?'

'Not yet.'

'That's interesting,' Frank said. 'Did he mention seeing a vehicle?' David shook his head and she carried on. 'Eva claims there was one, travelling west on the access road from Hawkhope at around midnight. Shortly afterwards, Scheving left the campsite and the group called it a night. Eva didn't see the vehicle again, but it could be the same one our witness Maria Colman saw coming the other way. What killer would miss the chance of placing someone else at a crime scene?'

33

Leaving Kristjánsson to sweat, the four detectives held a mini-briefing in Anna's office. Undoubtedly, lies had been told. Anna felt compelled to point out that there was no hard evidence on which to base an arrest. She couldn't justify holding the witnesses for much longer. Having got wind of their plight, one or two of their loved ones had arrived at the Major Crimes Unit demanding to know what was going on. Pressure was building to charge or release them. The British detectives agreed with her assessment, David expressing his concern over Frankie's questioning of Eva, the only one of 'the ten' currently at home with her family.

'I wouldn't worry too much about that,' Anna said. 'Nordic women, even young ones, won't be pushed around. Not that Frankie was pushing very hard on this occasion. Eva is clever enough to avoid dropping herself and her friends in it. It's a question of who's covering for who.' She paused; thinking time. 'Maybe it was self-defence. Eva said Scheving was stoned. After he left the campsite, maybe she went looking for him, a chance to tell him what a piece of shit he really was. He tried it on with her. She flipped and shoved him into the water—'

'Our pathologist categorically ruled out accidental death,' David said. 'That's why they're all keeping schtum. By my reckoning, we have ten suspects and no clue. Detecting this one is like a game of *Take Your Pick*.' He explained to Anna and Emil that he was referring to a game show broadcast on TV in the fifties and sixties, his late grandmother's favourite of that decade.

'I'm not sure who killed Scheving,' Frankie said. 'But I don't believe Eva is responsible. He was struck twice from behind by someone tall enough to inflict catastrophic head injuries.

Given the size of him, and her diminutive figure, she's physically incapable—'

'Unless he was seated or lying down,' Anna said.

'Anna has a point,' David said. 'If he was off his face, he may not have been aware of someone approaching.'

'A sitting duck? Great, an unprovoked attack is all we need . . .' Frankie ran a hand through her hair, eyes on David. 'She's such a wee thing, just a few years older than Joanna when—' Realising she wasn't in her own MIR among close colleagues, she checked herself. Her fingernails were digging into the palms of sweaty hands. Anna was studying her. Now she knew that there was something else bothering her.

Something deeply personal.

Frankie moved on. 'Eva made no secret of the fact that she hated him. But I can't see her taking a hammer to his head, can you, Anna?'

'No.'

'The thought of her spending more than a few minutes in a cell makes me sick to my stomach. She's a victim too, don't forget. If it turns out that she's responsible, she needs help, not punishment.'

'Not if she went equipped,' David reminded her.

Frankie didn't argue. How could she? Taking a weapon along was a premeditated act, proof of intent to do harm. No barrister could put forward diminished responsibility as a defence if that were the case.

David had read her mind. 'Look, we don't have enough to point a finger at anyone yet. The way I see it, they're all under suspicion, three with a definite motive: Eva, Aron and Kristján.'

'Except Eva swears the two lads didn't know of the assault by Scheving,' Anna said.

'She can't know that any more than we do,' David warned. 'Maybe Aron was taken into her parents' confidence and told not to say anything, or he overheard them talking when his sister wasn't around. If he told one of the others, they could all know by now.'

'Eva seemed genuinely shocked to hear of Scheving's death,' Frankie said. 'If she didn't kill him, she may have come to the same conclusion as us, protecting any one of them without knowing what happened. We should examine all ten statements for discrepancies and see where it takes us. Even the most accomplished liar makes mistakes. It will give us leverage to challenge their accounts. We jump on anything that doesn't add up.'

'Works for me.' Anna looked at her 2ic. 'Have any of them ever been in trouble, Emil?'

He shook his head. 'There's nothing on our system. I'll keep digging. They seem to have been model citizens up to now.'

'Offenders rarely go from zero to murder,' Frankie pointed out. 'We need to tread gently. We don't want to get this wrong.' *I don't want to get this wrong.* 'These kids have their whole lives in front of them. Eva has dreams of being a doctor, for Christ's sake.'

Anna looked at her. 'You must follow the evidence—'

'Yeah? Tell me something I don't know.'

David shot her a look. An apology was in order.

Frankie gave one. 'I'm sorry, Anna. That was uncalled for.'

'I'm not that fragile.' The Icelandic DCI smiled. 'Look, as far as I can see, there's only one option on the table. We ask them to surrender their passports voluntarily and let them all go home.'

'That sounds sensible,' Frankie said.

David and Emil were nodding.

Privately, Frankie agreed with Mitch's assessment: Kristjánsson and his friends were nice kids. It would give her no satisfaction if it turned out that Scheving had been murdered by one of them. There would be no celebration at the end of the investigation. No winners – only losers.

34

Keen to get out of the Major Crimes Unit, Anna suggested they call it a night and resume their debriefing in the morning, inviting the British MIT officers to a bar down the road for a quick drink before she headed home. It was a short walk away, a cosy place, fairly empty when they arrived, a watering hole for local officers Anna told them, a place to shake off events of the day or sink a few beers to help them sleep.

Emil brought the drinks to the table, swung his leg over a chair, sat down and lifted his glass. 'Welcome to Iceland.' They clinked glasses. 'Where are you staying?'

'Reykjavík Centrum on Aðalstræti,' Frankie said.

'Oh,' Anna seemed pleased with their choice of hotel. 'Romantic—'

'Funny you should say that . . .' Frankie put down her glass. 'One of your officers recommended it. Even offered to show David where it was. If you ask me, she had an ulterior motive.'

Emil grinned at Anna. 'He's been talking to Freyja—'

Frankie nudged David's arm. 'He means Blondie, in case you're in any doubt.' She eyeballed their Icelandic hosts. 'He's a bit slow on the uptake.'

'I told you, I'm not here to play, I'm working.'

'And available,' Frankie joked. 'You could've been in there. From what I could see, Freyja was quite taken with you.'

'She's harmless, and spoken for,' Anna said. 'Besides, I meant romantic in the historical sense. Part of your hotel dates from the eighteenth century. It was built above the ruins of a longhouse from the Viking era. Did Freyja mention that it displays Iceland's oldest human remains?'

'No,' David said. 'And I've had my fill of remains for one week.'

'They date back to AD 870.'

He put down his pint. 'I hope the pathologist dealing with my skeleton can be as specific when I return to the UK.' The small talk hadn't helped take his mind off work any more than the change of venue had. 'The barrel find was the reason Kristján gave for returning home. He came up with the same story as Eva, pretty much. Whether it was rehearsed or not is open to question. As you all saw, the lad is a bag of nerves—'

'You can't read anything into that,' Anna interrupted. 'Being pursued by the SIO of a foreign force is bound to have shaken him up.'

'Only if he has something to hide—'

'Not necessarily,' Frankie said. 'Imagine Ben in his position. Wouldn't he be anxious?'

Anna looked at David, a surprised expression. 'You have a son?'

'A nephew. He lives with me since his father passed away. Frankie's idea.'

'And he's doing a great job of looking after him,' she said proudly.

'How on earth do you have the time?' Anna said.

David laughed. 'I don't.'

'Me either. My mother is desperate for a grandchild.'

'Mine too,' Frankie said. 'I can't help her.'

She wondered if Anna considered herself too old or if she'd made the decision not to have children in favour of occupational advancement as Beth Collingwood had? Frankie was sure that the greasy pole would be a lot less slippy in this forward-thinking country, an Icelandic law in place to protect working mothers from professional oblivion. Many women in the UK were sacked while on maternity leave, an illegal practice that still went on, those doing the firing couching their dismissal in terms that allowed them to end their contracts regardless of employment law.

Pushing that grim thought away, she asked David and Emil

a question: 'Did the nine you interviewed all give saliva samples willingly?'

They confirmed it.

'That would suggest they have nothing to hide – or they think that a DNA match isn't possible now that the body has been immersed in water. Maybe we'll get lucky, or unlucky, depending on your point of view.' Frankie was about to elaborate when her mobile lit up on the table. She lifted the device, expecting her father. It was Abbott. She glanced at her watch, wondering why he was calling at this late hour. 'Excuse me, I should take this.' She got up and walked outside into the cool evening air.

35

She tapped to answer the call. 'Hey, Dick. What's up?'

'I have news.'

'Good or bad?'

'Both. Beth Collingwood has some clout. Can you let the boss know that his skeletal remains are being examined by a forensic anthropologist as we speak?'

'Will do. Do we know who?'

'Professor Michael Leonard.'

'Not someone I'm familiar with. Anything else?'

'The PolSA team expanded their search area. They found a one-man tent at Gordon's Wall. No ID but we have reason to believe it may belong to our second victim.'

'Gordon's Wall? I've never heard of it.'

'It's the remains of an old bastle house enclosure, about halfway between Hawkhope car park and the Belling penin-sula. The camping gear was well hidden under some rotting branches. They found nothing of interest in the storage pock-ets, but whoever put it there didn't search it properly. There was a stash of drugs in the gear loft. The metal tent pegs match the one you found at the campsite.'

'Interesting. Any prints?'

'None. No sign of a weapon either. We need the divers down for that.'

'And where do you propose they start looking? There's two hundred billion litres of liquid in the reservoir and it's bloody deep. They'll never find it and won't even try.'

'No, I don't suppose they will,' Abbott said.

'And the bad news?'

'You're not going to like it, Frank.' He let out a heavy sigh. 'Someone, presumably one of your suspects, posted a close-up, high-definition image of our first victim on Instagram—'

'Tell me you're joking! We just let the little bastards go.' It came out like an explosion. 'Didn't Mitch check their mobiles? I specifically asked him to.'

'Yes, and he swears there were no images of the barrel on any of them. We can only assume that it was shot on a camera and uploaded later. The named user was not one of the ten kids we interviewed. The account is brand new. He or she probably used a false name.' A long pause. 'It gets worse. Whoever was responsible also made a short animation which has gone viral. I mean worldwide viral, attracting an unprecedented level of interest. Our internal phones are so hot I've had to draft in extra personnel to cope. In the past couple of hours, I've been fielding calls from all over the globe.'

'Whoa, back up. I don't understand.'

'Social media bods are having a field day and not just on Instagram. You need to view the clip. It depicts a lost under-water world—'

'You mean Plashetts?'

'Yeah, a place no one ever heard of till now.'

The village once housed a thriving mining community whose homes were flattened to make way for Kielder Water and a giant dam that changed the history of a peaceful valley. Many chose to believe that the place still existed beneath the water, dark and derelict, Northumberland's very own Atlantis. It was the stuff of folklore, some insisting that when the water level fell, the spire of a lost church could be seen and children's voices could be heard floating up from their sunken school. These myths had drawn many a curious visitor to the area.

'Of course it's bullshit,' Abbott continued. 'But many tour-ists due to leave are sticking around. Jardine says more are arriving with nowhere to stay. The public all want a piece of this. Put it this way, it's done more for the Northumberland tourism industry than Roman heritage, the Angel of the North and Border Reivers ever could. I'm praying for rain. If this good weather keeps up, by morning it'll be like a circus up there. The story has taken on a life of its own, Frank. Google #thedeep. Everyone else is.'

Slowly, Frankie turned to look through the window of the bar. Emil was at the counter getting another round in, Anna and David still at the table. He was laughing at something she'd said and seemed much more relaxed than when Frankie had come outside. There wasn't a hope in hell of his good mood continuing. When she repeated what Abbott had just told her, he'd go apeshit.

'Frank, you still there?'

'Wish I wasn't. Listen, you have too much on to waste your time on this rubbish. Hand it off to the press office—'

'I tried. It's too big, they can't contain it. Bright doesn't trust me to handle it either. A damage limitation exercise is the way he put it. Sorry to spoil your fun, but he wants you here ASAP.'

His comment threw her.

The idea of returning home alone was unappealing. Flying to Iceland with David's support was one thing. If things went wrong, he'd take the flak. Separated, it would be a very different ballgame. The thought stressed her out for reasons she couldn't get her head around.

'Did he ask for me specifically?'

'If your name is Frank, he did.'

'Well tough. It's not possible for me to leave now.'

'You tell him then. I'm out—'

'Don't be such a wuss. Things are moving this end. All ten of Kristjánsson's group have been re-interviewed and swabbed and victim ID is now confirmed.' She spelled out Jón Scheving's name. 'He has form, including a conviction of sexual assault on Eva Jacobsdóttir when she was fourteen years old.'

'Jesus! Well there's your motive.'

'Maybe . . .' Frankie ran a hand through her hair, another glance into the bar. 'Look, Bright knows I'm handling the second victim, David the first. Tell him that two of my suspects have coughed to Scheving's presence at the campsite and more. Also, that the Icelandic police are fully on board. The SIO here is DCI Anna Jónsdóttir, if he wishes to confirm her willingness to cooperate. It would be nonsense for me to fly home now. Don't worry, David will support me.'

'What makes you so sure?'

'I'm telling you, he'll be home on the first available flight.'

36

Frankie accessed Google. As Abbott had described, the animation had been copied and shared across all social media platforms, stirring up a frenzy. It was trending in the UK, its hashtag #thedeep capturing the imagination of millions. The short clip depicted a ghostly cartoon village, buried beneath the water. Multicoloured fish swam in and out of smashed windows. Reed beds were present where gardens used to be. As she continued to watch, the barrel began to move upwards, floating through a raft of air bubbles, gyrating from side to side until it bobbed to the surface, revealing a screaming skull through a gaping hole. Its creator possessed a sick sense of humour, the type that played to an audience who liked nothing better than to jump on someone else's grief. The ghastly skit lasting two minutes was accompanied by the catchy tune of 'Dumb Ways to Die'.

Staring blankly across the street, Frankie's anger rose.

Dumb it may be to end your days in an old container, but this was no laughing matter. The skeleton was once a human being whose relatives had probably been searching for him for years. Depending on his age at time of death – assuming Beth Collingwood's opinion was correct that the remains were decades old – his parents may already have gone to their graves never knowing what had happened to him.

She was appalled by such a public display of insensitivity.

The dead man may have a living wife and offspring who might have seen the animation and would be upset by it when notified of his death. Though the circumstances were not the same, that sad thought resonated. Witnessing the heartbreak of her parents and extended family in the aftermath of her sister's murder, Frankie could relate on a personal level. They had a body, but no closure. The event had overshadowed her life from that moment on and made another path impossible. It was preordained that she would choose to help victims of serious crime. She'd work the case as if her sister's remains were in that barrel.

Frankie pushed open the door to the bar, standing aside to allow someone out before entering.

As she stepped over the threshold, a text arrived: DAD.

Ignoring it, she pocketed her mobile.

Three pairs of curious eyes stared at her as she approached the table and sat down, updating David, Anna and Emil on developments in the UK. If what the PolSA team had found turned out to be Scheving's tent, it was a major breakthrough, one that might move her investigation a step closer to a resolution.

'Skál to more good news.' Anna raised her glass.

David and Emil did likewise.

She eyed her glass on the table but left it there.

The butterflies in her chest were flapping wildly. These kids were making a fool out of her. 'It's too early to celebrate,' she snapped. 'It may look like we're in business. We still have a long way to go.'

David looked at her, a frown developing. 'Small steps, Frank. It's one less problem—'

She cut him off. 'We have another, guv. Or should I say you do.'

'Which is?'

Frankie briefed him on the state of play at Kielder. Anna and Emil exchanged a worried glance when she mentioned the fallout from the animation and the fact that it was proving difficult to access the social media account used to post it. This was not good. More questioning was on the cards. They all knew it. There was no way both British detectives could leave just yet.

37

When David and Frankie returned to their hotel, she asked him to join her in her room to watch the animation, something best done in private. Despite what she'd said to Abbott, she wasn't entirely sure who'd stay in Iceland and who'd return to the UK. If David was the one leaving in the morning – a big *if*, given Bright's opinion that rank should overrule reason – she had stuff to say that couldn't wait, a thought she shared with him on the way up in the lift.

While he accessed the video clip on his mobile phone, Frankie raided the minibar for drinks – Dutch courage before she dived in – then joined him at a table beneath the window, overlooking the street. It was quiet outside, very little going on, a young couple strolling hand in hand towards the town centre, an older couple heading the other way, deep in conversation.

Frankie wished she could trade places.

Troubled by her case, she wondered how she'd do her job with her hands tied, having to rely on Anna in order to proceed; how much she'd have to rely on herself with David gone, a prospect that ordinarily would thrill, not frighten her.

He spoke softly. 'Everything OK?'

'Hmm.' She didn't look at him.

'For someone who ID'd a victim and can place him near the crime scene with ten suspects in the frame, you seem a bit tense.'

Her eyes were firmly fixed on his now. 'I'm not partying yet.'

'You soon will be. This case is practically cut and dry.'

She didn't share that view. 'I keep going over the evidence. It all seems to be pointing in that direction, but something's off about this case. I'm damned if I can work out what it is.'

'Go on.'

'I probably shouldn't share this, with you of all people. I'm not certain we're on the right track.'

'Why?' David relaxed into his chair, waiting patiently for her to continue.

It felt odd that her bed was a few feet away. The location was too intimate. She was wishing they were having this conversation in the MIR at Middle Earth, surrounded by their crew, or in the bar downstairs; anywhere but here.

'Look, forget I said anything.'

'Make your mind up. First it can't wait, now it can. Which is it?' David glanced at his watch. 'It's time we hit the sack, so stop buggering about and get it said.'

This was hard for her. 'I feel like I'm heading toward a dead end.'

'Why? What we now know about Scheving's link to Eva changes everything—'

'I know it looks like an Icelandic national was responsible for his death—'

He cut her off. 'Frankie, the evidence is staring you in the face. They all had contact with him the night he died, even though some of them still deny it. We . . .' He back-pedalled. 'I mean, you now have motive.'

'I still think we're missing something.'

'Like what? If the assault on Eva was common knowledge, she and the rest of them also had means and opportunity. If this were my case, the question I'd be asking myself is which of the ten I should put the thumbscrews on. Then there's all the other stuff—'

'What other stuff?'

'The degree of planning for one.'

'How d'you mean?'

'Given the history between Eva and Scheving, how believable is it that the group bumped into him by accident and he just tagged along? I accept that he's not on any of their travel documentation. It was a group booking, ten names, not eleven.

What if the group knew he took a regular flight to Glasgow?'

'You're suggesting they engineered the meeting?'

'They could hardly risk a link between Scheving and their trip.'

'Or maybe you've been watching too many conspiracy thrillers.'

'Coming from you, that's hilarious.'

'Sod off. I'm being serious.'

'Hey! You brought it up.'

Hurt by his casual attitude, Frankie looked away. Ordinarily, she'd have laughed off his comment. Her appetite for such films and TV dramas was legendary within in the MIT, and he often teased her about it, finding it bizarre that she indulged a pastime so close to her day job. He wasn't the only one. What she was now dealing with wasn't a work of fiction, it was fact. And the evidence was leading her to a place she didn't want to go.

'Frank, don't sulk. I was joking, not getting at you—'

She snapped her head around, eyes blazing. 'Weren't you?'

'No, calm down.'

She threw back her drink, meeting his gaze over the rim of her glass. 'If you want the God's honest, it'll kill me to lock any of these kids up for wasting scum like Scheving—'

'Careful, you don't get to decide on who's deserving and who's not.'

'Yeah, yeah. Doesn't mean I have to like it. And, for the record, I'm not discounting the credibility of your suggestion. It occurred to me too. I just can't believe that, singularly or collectively, the group cooked up an elaborate plan to lure him into their company with a view to doing away with him.'

'Even as payback for what he did to Eva? From where I'm standing, that's how it's looking. You said yourself, you distrust Kristján, and rightly so. Did you conveniently forget that he lied to you, hiding the fact that he and Eva were an item? Explain to me why he'd sidestep such an innocent question.'

'People lie for all sorts of reasons.'

'Do they?'

'Yes. He probably thinks that his relationships are none of our business. Not all of us like to share. Some of us are degree standard when it comes to hiding our feelings.'

David's eyes grew cold. He thought she was having a dig. She wasn't. Since they began working together, he'd hidden stuff that was deeply personal. Then again, so had she. 'Are we still talking about Kristján and Eva?' he asked. 'Or did you bring me up here just to have a go?'

'No, of course not. Why would I?'

'You tell me.'

She didn't answer.

David kept his focus on the investigation. 'OK, so let's go through the evidence. The group had no accommodation booked. Fair enough. They were rough camping. I get that. But, by his own admission, Kristján had been planning this trip for months. He knew the Kielder landscape. It wouldn't take a genius to work out that there's sod all CCTV up there. It's a remote spot where he, or they – if anyone else was in on it – might conceivably have got away with murder. Let's face it, had it not been for the appearance of the barrel, they could've been in and out and we'd have been none the wiser, possibly for months or even years—'

'Only if they'd buried Scheving's body. They didn't.'

'Doesn't mean that it wasn't their intention,' he warned. 'Maybe he made a superhuman effort to run for his life, fell into the water and drowned before they had the opportunity.'

'The pathologist ruled that out.'

'I've known it happen, Frankie. Or maybe they were disturbed.'

'By whom?'

'I don't know, some night owl taking a late walk, a run, a bike ride. We're not the only weirdos who stay up late.' He paused. 'Then there's the other explanation. They might have been seen by whoever dumped the barrel.'

'Or the other way around.'

Frankie was testing his hypothesis, challenging him. As his 2ic, that was her role. As his equal on a double-hander, even though she was talking perfect sense, she lacked the conviction of her words. Had he sensed it? Was he wondering why her confidence was slipping away? Getting up, she grabbed another couple of drinks from the minibar, handing him one as she returned to her seat.

Sitting cross-legged, she unscrewed the top of her miniature and refilled her glass. 'So, as far as you're concerned, I should be on starter's orders, ready to put this case to bed. There are holes in your argument, David. Why on earth would Kristján call us when he found the barrel when he could just as easily have left it alone? Your theory only works if Eva wasn't part of the equation. Remember, they were together when the barrel was found. It was her phone he used to call the control room. If he hadn't called it in, it would have raised her suspicions. What other choice did he have? If so, it puts her in the clear.'

'OK, I can't answer that. You said yourself you didn't push too hard with Eva. Try leaning on him instead. The others see him as their leader. If he folds, so will they.'

Frankie didn't respond.

Kristján wasn't the only one she needed to lean on. Privately, she wanted nothing to do with the investigation. She wanted David to order her home, an event that would put her out of her misery, even though the barrel incident attracting so much press attention in Northumberland was his, not hers. In that respect, she was surplus to requirements in the UK. Her head was throbbing. There was a fine line between innocence and guilt.

David's expression changed suddenly.

She had an idea that he was about to force her hand.

It didn't take him long to put it into words. 'This is your

baby. If you think can manage on your own, stick with it here and I'll book a flight.'

'If?' Her hackles were up and it showed. A moment ago, she wanted to leave. Now she wanted to stay. Her thoughts swung wildly between the two. 'Are you suggesting I'm out of my depth? Because I'm not.'

He crossed his arms, his brow creasing. 'Is that what you heard come out of my mouth?'

Frankie's cheeks were burning, nothing to do with the whisky she was drinking. 'No, maybe, I don't know. I'm tired, not thinking straight. I'm sorry, I shouldn't have said that.'

'No, you shouldn't. Have you any idea how proud I am of you?'

She bit. 'Bright implied I wasn't ready.'

'That's your interpretation, not mine.'

'That's what it sounded like to me—'

'Frank, that is not what happened. He was sheltering you, if only you had the sense to realise it. He knows how hard it is to lead an investigation away from your own stomping ground, more so across international boundaries where you have zero authority to act and without your team behind you.' He made a show of looking over his shoulder. 'Besides, unless I'm mistaken, he's not here to make that call. In case you'd forgotten, foreign soil or not, I'm still the SIO. I'm not telling you how to run your investigation. I'm merely offering a point of view, as I would if we were conducting a briefing. This is one you'll have to work out for yourself. Now we've met Anna and Emil, I can see no earthly reason why you can't handle it alone.'

'What if Bright insists that you stay and I go?'

'He won't know until after the event. Let me worry about that and concentrate on the case. Kristján is smart, but not smart enough to hide the fact that he's still withholding information. He's thrown a nugget of truth our way to keep us happy. If you want my opinion, he's scared of something altogether darker than the pissed off inspector-in-waiting.'

'I'm not pissed off—'

'Could've fooled me. If I leave and you take the reins, I'm willing to bet that it'll run in your favour. Kristján will be lulled into a false sense of security. When that happens, he'll trip himself up. He'd be a fool to underestimate you. Others have made that mistake and lived to regret it, me included. That's not what I'm doing now. I'm merely trying to help.'

Frankie smiled for the first time since they had come upstairs.

It was a front – she was still wavering.

David gave her a shove. 'I'm not saying it'll be easy. You'll be walking a tightrope here with Anna firmly in charge. If the two of you disagree, you'll have to fight your corner. As you've just demonstrated, you're good at that. Remember, over here you're the face of Northumbria Police, so try and be less sweary about it. I'm a phone call away if you need support, day or night. Are we on?'

Frankie climbed down. 'It's me I'm worried about, not Anna.'

'Why? She's agreed to give you a free hand. For obvious reasons, you'll have to go through her if you feel an arrest is justified. Make no mistake, if it turns out that one or more of the ten are involved in Scheving's death, she'll pursue it with every weapon in her armoury. She said so.'

'Assuming I can get them to open up—'

'They're toast. If anyone can, it's you. Once they realise that one of them is facing a life sentence, they'll drop the facade and start blaming one another. That's your in. Make sure you take it.' He paused, his voice quieter when he spoke again. 'This is your shot, Frank. Your chance to prove to Bright how ready you are to step up. Solve this one and you can write your own ticket.'

'Yeah, no pressure.'

Frankie was about to go into meltdown . . .

38

David had no idea how long she'd been staring blankly out of the window, looking down on the street below. At some point, she'd jumped up, began pacing up and down, her hands balled into fists. It was so unlike her. Only when he shifted in his seat did she remember he was still there.

She swung round. 'Can I ask you something?'

'Fire away.'

A beat of time. 'Did nothing faze you on the way up?'

'That's an odd question.'

'Is it?' She glared at him.

'Frankie, sit down. What's wrong?'

'I'll tell you what's wrong . . .' She perched on the edge of her bed, elbows on her knees, hands linked together, supporting her chin. 'I feel like a fraud. When I made DS, I never felt like this. Not once. You seem so certain of which way the wind is blowing. I can usually call it too. Not this time. I'm terrified that I'll mess up before I'm officially promoted. It's draining my concentration.'

'Did you think all you had to do was to rock up here and it would all fall into place?'

'Of course not—'

'Good, cos that's not how it works.'

'I know that.'

'This is about Eva, right?'

Her eyes flashed. 'If you mean Joanna, don't you dare go there.'

David didn't react. His voice was calm when he spoke. 'Please don't put words into my mouth. When have I ever insinuated that you can't do your job because of what happened in the past?'

'Fair enough. I apologise. You were right, it is Eva. She's damaged, David. Possibly beyond repair. If I push too hard, she might break. I can't have that on my conscience. She acts tough. Underneath that shell, she's fragile—'

'Then you have something in common.'

'Not funny.' She glowered at him. 'What if we're wrong about her, about all of them? It would kill me if I make a move and find out that these kids are entirely innocent, criminally speaking—'

'If you don't want to take the lead, say the word—'

She snapped. 'Now who's misinterpreting? You know I've wanted this my whole life—'

'Then what is your problem?'

She threw her arms out, a gesture of frustration, self-doubt and a lot more. David had never seen her so wound up. He was beginning to worry. Had he overstepped the mark, handing her the opportunity to show what she was made of too early? The idea vanished almost as quickly as it appeared. What she was describing was first-case nerves. Imposter syndrome. He had to find a way to boost her flagging morale without making her feel ten times worse.

'Relax,' he said. 'We've all been there.'

'I haven't!'

'Then count yourself lucky.'

She glowered at him.

He softened his tone. 'Listen to me, what you're feeling now is perfectly natural. Anyone who tells you different is a liar. You have to push through it. The shit won't hit the fan if you follow the evidence. Everything you see and hear is a signpost. Isn't that your father's mantra? It's good advice. Stick to it.'

Her head went down.

She sat motionless for a while.

This was not the reaction David was hoping for. As soon as the words were out of his mouth, he realised that bringing her father into it was the wrong call, an added pressure she could do without. Even at school, her friends thought it was cool that her father was a detective. They were fascinated by the fact that he caught the bad guys and had been hailed a hero in the local press on many occasions. David could think of no better way to get through to her.

She adored her dad and talked about him constantly.

'Frankie, you have generations of experience behind you and nothing whatsoever to prove to your dad or me. The only one you need to satisfy is yourself. In all the time we've worked together, when has your instinct ever let you down? If you don't think Eva's involved, bring me the proof. This is no time to lose your bottle. These investigations are as serious as they come. They have huge implications, for the family of the victim and potential suspects. There's no room for error. The higher you go up the ladder, the more measured you have to be. Having doubts is a strength, not a weakness. Honestly, if you didn't have them, I'd be concerned.'

They stared at each other for a long while.

It was painful watching her question her worth. The day had brought about a seismic shift in how she viewed her job and her ability to carry it out. She'd morphed from gung-ho to ultra-cautious in the space of a few hours. David suspected her anxiety had been triggered by news that one of them would have to hotfoot it to Middle Earth.

'You're right to exercise caution. If "the ten" are innocent, the fact that they're suspects in a murder investigation will have a profound effect on them. If guilty, their lives and those of their loved ones will implode. That's a heavy load for anyone to carry.' Finishing his drink, he hauled himself off the chair, ready to deliver an ultimatum. 'I have a flight to organise. Your call: is it mine or yours?'

'I'm staying.'

39

Frankie woke feeling the benefit of sleep, albeit for only a few hours. She was looking forward to seeing David, though still embarrassed by her wobble the night before. She couldn't argue with his wisdom. Nevertheless, she wouldn't jump until she'd double-checked every speck of evidence, then cross-checked it again using Anna and Emil as a sounding board, briefing them on David's thoughts and hers. Calmer now, she was ready to face the challenge of flying solo, not dreading it.

Making a written note of her priorities, she left her room and knocked on David's door. When he didn't answer, she took the lift to the ground floor in the hope she'd find him having breakfast. He wasn't there. Odd. Maybe he'd gone for a run to clear his head. She took a seat alone, facing the entrance, expecting him to wander in any minute.

Maybe he wanted to eat alone.

A young man approached, casually dressed, nice looking and with a cheery smile. She stifled a grin as he greeted her in English. British guests were easily identifiable in Iceland, she concluded. They hadn't met last night.

She was sure of it.

He handed her what she thought was a menu. It was in fact an envelope with her name on, handwritten by David. Her pulse began to quicken, a million questions racing through her head. Had he reconsidered overnight? Was he grounding her, sending her packing? Did the envelope contain proof of booking, a boarding card, an explanation as to why he'd changed his mind?

'Something to drink?'

She looked up. 'Sorry?'

'Coffee, hot chocolate? Ours is the best in town.'

'Go on then, you talked me into it.'

'Anything to eat?' He held out a menu.

'No, thanks.' Her appetite had deserted her. 'The hot chocolate better be good.'

'You don't like, you don't pay.'

She smiled. 'I'll hold you to that.'

Tucking the menu under his arm, he cleared the next table, then moved away. Frankie ripped open the note, curiosity getting the better of her . . .

My flight is at 07.50. Anna offered me a lift. ETA in Glasgow, 10.10. Can you let Dick know I'll reach Middle Earth around one? Forgot to charge my phone last night. Unable to text him or you. Didn't want to wake you. Call you later for an update. Good luck! D x

The note had been scribbled quickly. Gutted that he'd left without seeing her, Frankie checked her watch: five past seven. Even if she could get to Keflavík airport – without wheels, she couldn't – David would be through security by now, on his way to the departure gate long before she arrived. There was no point following. She was on her own, in charge of her own destiny. It was make-or-break time.

By the time she made it to the Major Crimes Unit, Anna was in her office alone. Almost horizontal, with her feet up on her desk, her attention was focused on the report open on her knee. She was concentrating, oblivious of anyone standing in the doorway.

Frankie knocked gently, then entered.

'Hi!' Anna smiled broadly. 'Sleep well? David said you were up late.'

Frankie wondered if he'd also shared her investigative indecision. No, she decided, he had more integrity than that. He'd never rubbish his crew to anyone, for any reason, especially an SIO from a foreign force. It would be counter-productive, making an already difficult job impossible for both women. More likely he'd have done the opposite and bigged Frankie up, raising Anna's expectations. He'd also have taken the opportunity to make the DCI – who, by her own admission hadn't dealt with many murder investigations – feel that she was a valued ally whose local knowledge and authority they couldn't do without. For the foreseeable future she'd be assisting Northumbria's elite murder squad.

Taking her feet off the desk, Anna sat up. 'You want coffee before we go?'

'Go?' Frankie grimaced. 'I just arrived.'

'We have a death message to deliver.'

40

The prison in Hólmsheiði currently housed forty. No one bar the governor had been warned that police were coming, the purpose of their visit, or the fact that one of them was a British murder detective. Giving advanced notice was never a good idea, especially in a prison this small. Rumours of such an unprecedented event would spread like wildfire. That meant Anna and Frankie had to be cautious; they couldn't risk news of Jón Scheving's death reaching his father before they were inside an establishment that seemed altogether more relaxed than its British equivalent.

Showing ID at the gate, they were met by the governor, a friendly face. He introduced himself, then summoned his Head of Security, a mountain of a man in his mid-forties only a fool would pick a fight with. The officer was dressed all in black. His first name was Óli. His surname sounded so foreign to Frankie's ears, she didn't take it in.

'The detectives are here to see Scheving,' the governor said casually.

'At this early hour?' Óli was told the nature of their business.

'You are to act as their escort,' the governor said. 'Look after them.'

'Yes, sir.' Óli watched his boss exit the gatehouse, a frown developing as he turned to face Frankie. 'You came from the UK to give Scheving bad news?'

'Under the circumstances, it's the least I could do.'

'You don't have a telephone?'

Frankie smiled. 'In my experience, distressing information is best conveyed face to face.'

'You don't trust us to do it right?'

Were all Icelanders so blunt?

Frankie lied. 'My guv'nor prefers it this way.' She had no intention of disclosing the fact that the person who ended Jón Scheving's life might be a local.

Recognising her dilemma, Anna quickly changed the subject, asking Óli a question. 'Scheving is a former oil worker, right?'

A nod from the security officer.

'Does he speak English?'

A shrug. 'Maybe. We don't have a lot of use for it here.'

Anna suggested that she take the lead, concerned that Scheving might not be fluent enough to receive news of his son's death, other than in his mother tongue. Frankie agreed. Giving the death message was the most draining task for any officer working in the MIT. David had advised her to keep a low profile and be led by Anna.

'Please don't mention this to anyone until we leave,' Anna said to Óli.

'I understand.'

He led them to the professional visitors' room, which was small, windowless and bare: a table, four chairs and little else. Asking them to wait, the security officer went off to locate the inmate. Anna set her briefcase on the table. Opening it up, she pulled out a notebook, checking the estimated time of death with Frankie, confirming how much she was at liberty to tell his father, should he ask.

A few minutes later, through a narrow window in the door, Frankie noticed Óli returning with the man the detectives had come to see. Scheving Snr was of average height and build, with piercing blue eyes. He wore loose casual gear, his own. No prison-issue clothing here. He walked through the door with an arrogant swagger. His sullen expression changed when he saw that his visitors were both female. He didn't acknowledge Frankie. He was more interested in Anna's shapely legs.

She had her back to him.

Frankie noticed a deep scar down the left side of Scheving's cheek; a recent blade injury, she suspected, though he probably just 'slipped in the shower' – the coverall excuse following a fight. Snouts didn't go down well behind bars. Victims who knew what was good for them remained silent. Though the regime here seemed casual it was still a prison; there were consequences for anyone stupid enough to ignore the pecking order inside.

Scheving was probably one of those.

As Óli left the room, Anna turned slowly, making eye contact with the lifer.

Like a madman, he shot across the room, hurling himself at the DCI, sending her flying. Forming his hand into a fist, he pulled his arm back, ready to strike while she was still on the floor. Instinctively, Frankie launched herself at him, knocking his arm away before it made contact, hauling him off as best she could. There were no international boundaries where the police family was concerned. If an officer was down, you went to their aid.

Jurisdiction could go fuck itself.

All hell broke loose. The alarm went off – a deafening pitch. Either someone had caught the incident on CCTV or the commotion had penetrated the door. Frankie heard people yelling, boots in the corridor getting closer, a sound she was all too familiar with. Help, it seemed, was on its way.

Not quick enough . . .

Pulling himself clear, Scheving took a swing at Frankie, his fist connecting with her upper lip, splitting it wide open, sending a fine spray of blood across the room. Stunned by the ferocity of the blow, she stepped away, temporarily off balance. As he came back for more, Anna was on her feet. Turning herself sideways – making her body smaller and therefore less of a target – she raised her right leg, driving the heel of her shoe into the side of Scheving's knee, felling him in one fluid movement.

Bruce Lee had nothing on her.

The door flew open.

Two prison officers arrived – batons drawn.

'What kept you?' Anna's tone was sarcastic.

Neither officer answered. They were trying to restrain the inmate.

Óli barged his way past them. 'Scheving, knock it off!'

'Why is everyone speaking English?' he yelled. 'Get the fuck off me!'

'Shut it!' Óli's eyes widened as he caught sight of Frankie wiping her face with a shaky hand. 'You OK?'

'Still breathing, aren't I?'

Óli apologised. 'I'll remove him.'

'No, you don't!' Anna covered her left ear with her hand to deaden the sound of the alarm. 'We have important business here. I can't hear myself think. Turn the damn thing off.'

Óli gave a nod to one of the officers.

He let go of Scheving and immediately left the room.

'We're good,' Anna said to Óli. 'You can go too.'

'Not possible. Your security is my responsibility.'

'It's a bit late for that, wouldn't you say?'

'What about me?' Scheving was still struggling. 'You fuckers are supposed to protect me.'

'Cut it out!' the officer holding him said.

Óli rounded on the inmate. 'Shame we can't protect you from yourself. Assaulting the police probably set your chances of release back another five years—'

'Shame you weren't here to see it. They provoked me.'

Óli gave a quick retort. 'Isn't that the excuse you made when you killed your wife? If anyone believed that, they won't any-more. Did no one ever tell you that violence against women is unacceptable, in or out of prison? Just as well you like football.'

'What?'

'You just scored an own goal.'

Frankie stifled a grin. Óli was beginning to grow on her.

41

Anna explained that they needed a word with Scheving and they needed it now, in private. Óli shook his head. He was going nowhere. The right call if he wanted to keep his job. He head-pointed toward the door. Reluctantly, his remaining colleague let go of Scheving, left the room and parked himself outside with a clear view into the room. Having established that Scheving had a good grasp of English, Anna gave Frankie the heads-up to proceed.

Frankie waited for someone to cut the alarm, her eyes never leaving the lifer. Men with nothing to lose were unpredictable in the extreme. She wouldn't give him an inch. He took a step forward, his hand closing around the upright of a wooden chair, a lethal weapon should he choose to use it.

Óli shot him a warning. 'Lift that chair and I'll break your arms.'

Frankie couldn't have said it better herself.

A beat of time.

Relaxing his grip, Scheving scraped the chair away from the table. It made a screeching sound, like chalk across a blackboard. He threw himself down in the seat, eyes on Anna. If manspreading was an Olympic sport, he'd win gold. Seeing her revulsion, he grinned, exposing bad teeth, one of which was missing.

Maybe also lost in the shower.

Satisfied that he'd got the message, Frankie took the seat opposite, her back to the door. Anna sat next to her, the table acting as a barrier should the inmate kick off again.

For exactly the same reason, Óli remained on his feet, towering over him.

Scheving glared up at him. 'You know this bitch has it in for me. She helped put me away?'

'Someone had to,' Anna said. 'You want to leave? Be my guest. My colleague has come a long way to talk to you. It's all the same to us if you don't want to listen. Go back to your cell. We'll pass on what we know to the governor—'

'You're here now.'

Frankie wasted no time. 'I don't think we were properly introduced. My name is Detective Sergeant Oliver.' Her first name was none of his business. 'This is not a welfare visit. I have some very bad news concerning your son—'

'What the fuck do I care?'

Despite the free-for-all that had been going on for a good few minutes – it felt more like an hour – this was not the reaction Frankie had anticipated. She'd travelled a thousand miles to solve his son's murder. She could've asked Anna to deliver the bad news to his next of kin but had decided to extend his father the courtesy of a personal visit while she was there.

He must know that the news wasn't good.

If she was anticipating shock, raw grief or unimaginable pain, Scheving Snr wasn't about to oblige. He began to laugh loudly, a crazy Jack Nicholson type laugh that made her wonder if he was all there, or even if he was high.

He had the coldest eyes she'd ever seen.

'What's the fucker done now?' he said.

'Nothing . . .' If this psychopath expected sensitivity as Frankie broke the news, all bets were off. 'Your son is dead.'

'What of it?' He raised an eyebrow, the only physical movement he made, though there was something going on behind those eyes. It wasn't sorrow or disappointment. 'You wasted your time coming here. He's been rocking himself off for years. Couldn't even do that right.' He smirked. 'I'd have done a much better job on him.'

Frankie wanted to leap across the table and beat the living shit out of him, but she figured he might enjoy it. She wouldn't give him the satisfaction of knowing he was getting to her.

He was.

She'd visited his son's flat en route to the prison. It was shit-pit, the home of a young man who'd given up on life, a young man who'd passed the point of no return. The only nod to his past was a framed photograph of a woman Anna confirmed was his mother.

'What?' His father glared at Frankie. 'Did you imagine tears, an outburst of emotion, repentance for not having been around for him? Well, fuck you, fuck all of you.'

There it was again. That look.

Now she thought she understood.

His reaction was that of a worried man. This triggered a theory in her head. For a few moments, she remained silent, piecing together all she knew about his son. If her hunch was correct, she now knew how he'd come to be in possession of Campbell's car, the one he'd borrowed or stolen in order to follow Kristján and his friends to Kielder. If she was right, Jón Scheving had been acting on behalf of a manipulative father who didn't and never had given a toss about him.

In her head, Frankie was in the grim bedsit she'd visited that morning. Jón's violent death hadn't happened in Iceland but she was after evidence that might shed light on his life. She and Anna had carried out a very basic search and stumbled upon a lot of personal stuff: self-portraits symbolising death on every wall; missed appointments with a psychotherapist unopened in the hallway; hospital discharge letters indicating self-harm and offering counselling; all of it providing a bleak insight into the state of mind of her victim. Anna agreed to look into it further. Frankie had asked her if she could get a team of CSIs in to process the place fully.

Now she was back in the prison interview room.

While Anna watched Óli, Scheving watched her.

No longer enjoying the view.

He was simmering with rage.

Frankie leaned in to regain his attention. 'Mr Scheving, you seem more angry than upset. As if Jón's death were nothing more than a minor inconvenience.' She paused, faking an epiphany. 'Oh, I get it. Your only visitor is gone, along with your supplier. Now it makes perfect sense. Oh dear, how are you going to get your fix now?'

He didn't admit or deny it.

He glared at her: pure hatred.

Ignoring him, Frankie turned to face Anna, asking her what kind of man would put his only son at risk by asking him to source gear and smuggle it past customs and security, knowing the risks involved.

She played along: 'I did warn you.'

The inmate played right into their hands. 'He did as he was told!'

'Unlike his mother,' Anna said.

'What can I say? She had more balls. He was weak, shaking like a leaf every time I went near him. A mummy's boy who needed to be taught a lesson. You people should understand the concept of discipline—'

'And there you have it,' Óli said. 'The real Scheving has crawled out from under his stone.'

It sounded like an admission of guilt to Frankie. To have made sense of his son's frequent trips to the UK and his involvement with a Scottish OCG was no mean feat. This surely was progress, intelligence that would now be investigated by Óli internally and passed on to Police Scotland's Serious and Organised Crime Unit so they could block any future attempts to smuggle drugs into Iceland.

And, finally, she delivered the rest of the message. 'Your son was murdered in the UK, Mr Scheving—'

'Can I sue?' He slapped his right thigh and let out another crazy laugh. 'You should've looked after him better.'

'No,' Frankie said. 'You should.'

42

David had only been at Middle Earth a few minutes. Already he felt lost without Frankie by his side. Ordinarily, he never ever worried about her. He was now, more than he cared to admit, even to himself. He pushed the thought away. Her anxiety last night was a minor blip, no more. Still, she knew what time he was touching down in Glasgow and hadn't bothered to pick up the phone. Unusual. Maybe she was pissed at him for not waking her before he left the hotel. Maybe she'd slept in when he didn't text to say he was up and about. Maybe just busy. He thought about calling her now. He decided not to. She might misconstrue it as interference. The last thing she needed was him on her shoulder.

With her stabilisers off she'd learn to ride.

David glanced around the room. Not a detective in sight, only civilian personnel, most of them manning the internal phones that rang constantly. Odd. He studied the updates on the electronic murder wall, noting that the anthropologist, Professor Leonard, had left his private number. A note – SIO TO CALL ASAP – was written next to it. Positive news? Perhaps. Maybe progress on the barrel remains. If so, David could finally begin the process of identification.

Pulling out his mobile, his forefinger hovered over the call button, in two minds whether to call Leonard or Frankie. Before he had time to decide, advancing footsteps came from behind.

'Guv?' Abbott's voice.

Pocketing the phone, David turned to face him.

'Sorry, no one told me you were here.'

'Just in. Frankie didn't pass on the message?'

'Message?'

'Never mind.' Another glance around the room. 'Where is everyone?'

'I gave 'em the day off.' Abbott grinned. 'Briefing room. Bright's on the warpath—'

'Shit! Any particular reason?'

'Does he need one?'

'That wasn't a trick question.' He checked his watch. 'It's only half one. A bit early for a briefing, isn't it?'

'You obviously haven't seen your in-tray.' Shaking his head, David glanced at his office door. Abbott added, 'I put the day's news on your desk and was about to add this one. It's hot off the press.'

Until now, David hadn't noticed the *Evening Chronicle* in his hand.

Dick held it up with two hands.

The front-page headline was guaranteed to shift copies. The font was larger than usual. White block capitals on a black background was usually reserved for stories affecting the public purse, politicians falling from grace, or a major sports item. The favourite today was a particularly grizzly murder of a man who was not ready to stop living.

HELL AND HIGH WATER
Gruesome find emerges from #thedeep

David's eyes widened as he read the article. Locals were being hounded by journalists who wanted in on the action. They wanted to know who the dead man might be, who was missing and who among the community had previous for violence. Those who professed to believe the hype attached to Plashetts were making unfounded predictions that the body in the barrel was the first of many. That a serial killer had hidden his victims before the valley was flooded and that more bodies would follow, a ghostly reminder of the carnage villagers were forced to endure when their homes were taken away. **#thedeep** wasn't the only hashtag associated with the story, the most popular being **#thecurseofkielderwater**, which had also gone viral.

'Jesus Christ!'

'The nationals are worse,' Abbott warned.

'Shit! I need to call Bright before he gets wind of my arrival and comes looking for me.'

David speed-dialled the number. The call went straight to voicemail. He didn't leave a message. No sooner had he hung up than he heard footsteps approaching from behind. He could tell who it was by reading the wary expression on Dick's face.

David swung round to face the head of CID.

'You rang?' Bright said.

'Yes, I—'

'Let's take it in your office, shall we?' He was already on the move, David following him in. 'Shut the door . . .' Bright sat down at David's desk, leaving him standing on the other side of it. 'I specifically asked for Oliver and got you. What's going on?'

'It was my decision, guv.'

'I should bloody hope so. You're her SIO.'

David gave him the rationale. 'She's in too deep, guv. Whichever way the pendulum swings over there, there's history that needs further investigation, complicated by the fact that one of the Icelandic tourists, Eva Jacobsdóttir, was assaulted by Jón Scheving, our second victim, when she was fourteen years old—'

'So I gather, but that doesn't answer my question.'

'Guv, the last thing Eva needs is another male pushing her around. She requires careful handling and consistency. Oliver is well placed to give her that.'

'She's a detective, not a fucking social worker.'

'With respect, sir, you signed off on our strategy to split the team. Scheving's murder is Oliver's baby, the barrel case is mine.'

'That was before we crossed into international territory. You'd better hope that she's up to it.'

'She is, guv.' *I hope she is.*

They left David's office together, Bright returning to HQ, David heading for Abbott's desk.

Dick looked up. 'Everything OK, guv?'

'Yeah, living the dream.'

Dick lifted his hands in surrender. 'Just asking.'

'Just telling. Get Mitchell in here. I need him to do something for me.'

'On it, boss.'

When the DC arrived, David handed over a parcel, giving clear instructions to hand-deliver it to the laboratory for analysis. 'It contains DNA samples from all ten Icelandic suspects. Anna was going to send them to Sweden—'

'How come?'

'She has no sophisticated forensic crime lab there. Tell our lot that Bright wants it fast-tracked. If they argue, refer them to me. Frankie needs all the help she can get.'

43

Frankie stared at her fat lip in the mirror. If Anna had warned her how volatile Scheving's father was, even after his arrest, she might have anticipated a negative reaction and been ready for a fight. If not telling her was a test of her resilience, Frankie had passed with flying colours. She'd come across some hard bastards in her time. Scheving Snr was a piece of work. What his son had done to Eva was horrible but, in light of his background, Frankie felt a modicum of sympathy for him. With a father like that, what chance did he have of making something of himself? Driven by fear, Jón's options were probably limited: give in to his demands or end up on a slab like his mother when his father was released from prison.

Frankie checked herself.

If Joanna's killer was ever identified, would she feel compassion if he came from an abusive home? Would she forgive him? *Would she fuck!* If capital punishment were available, she'd volunteer to flick the switch. Anna had mentioned only yesterday 'what goes around' comes around. That was too easy a let-off for guys like Jón. A traumatic childhood might explain his behaviour. In no way did it excuse it. He'd rejected help and made the wrong choices. The responsibility for what happened thereafter was his and his alone.

Now he was dead.

Did anyone give a damn?

Did she, *really*?

The internal argument continued with David on her shoulder. . .

Careful, you don't get to decide on who's deserving and who's not.

He was right, of course, except life wasn't always black and white; more often than not it was shaded grey. Frankie didn't need reminding that she had a duty to all victims. A life, any life, taken by force deserved justice, but therein lay the rub. Privately, she felt that Jón got what was coming. Professionally, she was employed to uphold the law. No vigilante should get away with murder.

As she wrestled with her conscience, the disturbing artwork she'd seen in Scheving's flat entered her head. Though the sketches were full of violence and self-hatred, Jón Scheving had a rare gift for drawing, one that might have taken him to a better place had he chosen a different path. Frankie would never forget those haunted eyes. Clearly he had a death wish.

The sympathy was back.

Her mobile rang.

The fact that it was David made her feel guilty.

'Hey! How's it going?' she said.

His voice was intermittent. A poor signal or none was not unusual in and around Kielder Water. '. . . it's like . . . Clogged roads, illegal camping, national and inter . . . broadcasters . . .' Long pause. '. . . a piece of the story. I've not seen anything like it since . . .' More static. 'Dick . . . right . . . animation . . . Frank, are . . . there?'

'Only just. Guv, I'm losing you.'

'Bollocks. Can't . . . I'll . . . you later.' The line went dead.

Frankie hung up, imagining the media circus in full swing. Dick was right: the animation had taken social media by storm. David needed that like a hole in the head. She wondered how Bright had reacted to his being back in the UK. She bet it stung like hell, like the antiseptic lotion she'd applied to the cut on her lip. She left the ladies' room and went off to have it out with Anna. If she pulled another fast one, test of resilience or not, they would seriously fall out.

Without knocking, Frankie burst through Anna's office door. Anticipating what was coming, the Icelandic DCI apologised immediately, asking if Frankie required medical attention. She declined. She'd had worse and didn't push for a reason why Anna hadn't warned her that he might go on the attack. She was obviously feeling guilty, her expression indicative of someone who had a more immediate issue to discuss, and who was desperate to share.

'Come closer,' she said, logging on. 'I have something to show you.'

Intrigued, Frankie pulled up a seat. 'Are you going to give me a clue?'

'It's to do with Kristjánsson—'

'I thought he had no form.'

'He doesn't. Emil has been concentrating on cases that have been shelved. He found a historic case that may or may not be relevant to your current investigation.'

44

Professor Leonard was around six four, early fifties, sharp-featured, a leading anthropologist who'd been involved in many high-profile criminal cases. Before setting off to meet him for the first time, David had looked him up. It paid to know who you were dealing with. The scientist had an impressive track record. He was a revered expert witness not only in the UK but worldwide. If anyone could help determine the age of the remains the MIT referred to as the 'barrel' victim, it was him.

David proffered a hand. 'Pleased to meet you, sir.'

'Likewise.' Leonard's was a firm handshake. 'I gather you just flew in from Keflavík?'

'This morning.' David helped himself to a coverall, cap and mask and began to put them on.

'Wonderful country,' Leonard said. 'My wife, Katrín, is Icelandic. Ex-police, as it happens. We met in 1999 on an investigation much like your own. The Icelandic authorities wanted a second opinion on skeletal remains that had lain undiscovered for years. Young walker. The poor girl had wandered off course and fallen into a ravine. Despite an extensive air search, rescuers failed to spot her.'

Adjusting his cap, David moved toward the mortuary slab, the ribcage of the skeleton still intact, the rest of the bones arranged in what he presumed was the correct anatomical order. He caught Leonard's eye. 'I take it you've seen Collingwood's report?'

'Indeed. There's nothing in it that I disagree with.'

'Beth is very thorough,' David said.

'Always. It must be so frustrating having to wait around for us to do our jobs, Stone.'

'I'm used to it.'

'Don't be too downhearted. Hopefully, what I have for you will be worth the wait.'

'I hope so.'

'As you know, Beth found evidence of a healed comminuted fracture to the left ulna. In layman's terms that means the surrounding bone had shattered. It would have required surgical intervention, so hospital records might confirm an ID if you come up with a list of potential missing persons.'

'Did you manage to extract DNA from the bones?'

'I did. There's no match on the UK database.'

'Makes sense. We have reason to believe he might be Italian.'

Leonard peered over the top of his titanium specs. 'On what grounds?'

'Beth found a crucifix with the body.'

'Ah, yes. She sent images.'

'It's not any old crucifix. Its hallmark is Roma, dating back to the 1920s. It's a fabulous piece, in good condition, with a small amount of age-related surface wear on the underside, one of the nicest exhibits I've come across in relation to a criminal case. It must have been very precious to someone, possibly a family heirloom.'

'Doesn't make him Italian.'

'Hope is all I have right now,' David said. 'I don't have the benefit of a crime scene. I suspect the crucifix may have been pulled loose during a fight. If it was round the victim's neck when he was buried – and this is pure guesswork on my part – it may have remained attached when the skeleton was moved, possibly hidden in the earth surrounding it. I'm awaiting results on the soil sample.'

'Who did you ask?'

'Professor Dawson, James Hutton Institute.'

'There's no greater authority.'

'That's what I thought. You two know each other?'

'We move in the same circles. What are your thoughts on the crucifix?'

'I'm as convinced as I can be that it wasn't dropped by the perpetrator by accident. If not worn by the victim, I think it more likely that it was placed deliberately in the barrel by whoever put him there.'

'For what reason?'

'That, I can't imagine. Forensics found a minute section of hair caught in the chain, hardly visible to the naked eye. It'll be interesting to know if the DNA matches the sample you extracted from the bones.'

'Well, best of luck. Doesn't sound like you need me.'

'I wish that were the case.' David smiled. 'Give me a fresh body any day.'

'I'm not able to give a biological profile of the victim. And even if I could, would it help? Kielder attracts many visitors from around the world. There is a lot I can tell you though,' Leonard continued. 'The IP is a white adult male, in the region of thirty at the time of his death, give or take five years. You're in luck. Any older and I'd have been less specific. He's left-handed. Height, five seven, five eight – or 170 to 172 centimetres, if you prefer metric. Death occurred around forty to fifty years ago. That's as far as I can narrow it down. You'll have my preliminary report on your desk by morning.' Almost as an afterthought, Leonard added, 'As a rough guide, you're looking at the mid-seventies.'

'That's interesting.'

'How so?'

'My team did some research on the cable ties that bound him. Plastic and nylon ones were only introduced then.'

'Impressive.'

'Thank you, sir.'

David left him to it. He had a lot of respect for scientists whose skill went beyond that of a criminal investigator. Added to Beth's observations, the information provided by Leonard would form an integral part of the identification process. There was still a long way to go, for him and the Murder Investigation Team, but he had much to work with.

45

Anna's computer had inexplicably gone down. She'd had to wait ten minutes before logging on again, with Frankie breathing down her neck, fingers tapping impatiently on her desk as she waited.

'It's not the first time Kristjánsson has come across a dead body,' Anna said.

'What?' The word left Frankie's mouth like an Exocet missile. 'What are you talking about?'

'Five years ago, he found his grandfather's body outside his home in Ísafjörður. His house stands alone in a remote area by your standards. It was winter. He was found at the rear of the property, lying face up beside the log store.'

'Jesus!'

The file loaded.

Frankie noticed that it was marked as NFA: No Further Action.

Anna clicked to open it, a series of images appearing on screen.

Frankie studied them. It was difficult to determine the age of the dead man. He was younger and less frail than she'd expected. The casualty – or victim – was prostrate, as stiff as a post, eyes wide open, lashes and eyebrows white with frost, lips almost blue. A frozen hand was reaching up from the ground as if begging to be saved.

How sad.

Frankie couldn't help thinking of her own grandfather, to whom she was very close. She hoped he'd pass away in his sleep, warm and cosy in bed; his two Persian cats, Shiraz and Merlot, at his feet.

Anna's voice jolted her from her daydream. 'There was a

question mark over the incident, a time-lapse between time of death and notification to our control room.'

'By Kristján?'

'Yes.'

'Allegedly, they were close. He was inconsolable on the phone.' Anna let out a worried sigh, as if she'd rather not continue. 'He claims he got there too late to help him.'

'You have doubts?'

'Others did. I was not involved. If I had been, I'd have remembered.' Anna paused. 'By all accounts, Kristján's behaviour that day was out of character. He skipped school in a foul mood after an argument with one of his teachers. He failed to mention it when spoken to.'

'He was questioned by police?'

A nod from Anna. 'Naturally, there was a post-mortem. The preliminary result confirmed a heart attack, though the old man had an injury to the back of his head and the coroner wouldn't release the body for cremation. An inquest was opened and adjourned. When it took place, Kristján attended as star witness. Given his age, reporting restrictions were imposed, preventing his identification. The only other witness was the family doctor who pronounced the old man dead at the scene.'

'How old was he?'

'Sixty-six and in good health. Hadn't sought medical attention for years. His death was therefore unexpected and unexplained. It was unclear if the old man had suffered a coronary and fell or was struck and suffered a cardiac arrest brought on by shock. The evidence was inconclusive. In the end, the coroner returned a verdict of accidental death. Case closed. Anyway, I thought you should know about it. I promised David complete transparency.'

'I appreciate it, Anna.'

Frankie remembered snippets of her last conversation with David before he left the country: *This case is practically cut and dry . . . The evidence is staring you in the face . . . You now have a potential motive.* Was he right? What possible motive could Kristján have had to kill his beloved grandfather, unless he stood to benefit from his death?

46

'OK, everyone, mobiles off. We're finally up and running on the barrel case . . .' It was six o'clock on the dot. David was facing a full team in the briefing room, about to give feedback on Leonard's observations. He waited as phones were turned to silent and conversations ended. 'We now have an approximate age and height for our victim, as per your briefing sheet, an approximate timescale to go on. It's not great, but we're getting there.' He scanned the room, taking in every face, making sure there were no slackers. He had everyone's attention, especially DC Mitchell's.

'Mitch, I want you to concentrate on mispers. That's your one and only priority. We're looking for males between twenty-five and thirty-five who disappeared in the mid-seventies.' He turned to Abbott. 'Is there any news on the barrel yet?'

'We had some input from Woodhope Cooperage,' Dick said. 'The cask is made of American Oak. Apparently, they last up to eighty or so years. The one Kristján found was well-worn but airtight. Every barrel is marked with the initials of the cooper. Unfortunately, the craftsmen and the cooperage ours came from are long gone.'

'Is there any news on the unidentified vehicles Maria Colman and Eva mentioned?'

'Aren't we assuming they're one and the same?' Mitch asked.

'Either way,' Dick said. 'There were *no* forestry vehicles operating that night.'

'OK, keep on it,' David said. 'Until further notice, Dick will act as my 2ic. Frankie remains in Iceland on the Scheving murder for the time being. Those of you on her team will continue to pursue any lines of enquiry on her behalf this end.'

'Guv?' Indira Sharma's hand shot up. She was part of Frankie's team. 'I have news she needs to hear right away. Forensics fast-tracked the samples you brought from Iceland. They have a DNA match.'

'For what?'

'They amplified and typed a set of prints from the tent pegs the PolSA team found at Gordon's Wall, obtaining low copy number DNA. It belongs to Kristjánsson. He must've been in a sweat when he handled them. Not surprising, I suppose. He probably had limited time to hide the tent and its contents.'

'Now we're getting somewhere.' David said.

'There's more, . . .' Indi was on a roll. 'Forensics also found a small amount of Scheving's blood on the corner of an exhibit retrieved from the barrel site, the towel belonging to Kristjánsson, to be exact. Explains why he swam that morning. I can't think of another reason to take a dip at Kielder, at any time of the year, can you?'

Frankie failed to mention the poisonous thoughts whizzing round her brain to Anna. 'This could go either way,' was all she said at first. Then, feeling the need to qualify her comment, she added, 'On the one hand, Kristjánsson's negative experience with police here in Iceland explains why he was so nervous around me, around David. On the other, he may be conning us.'

Anna said: 'Can you call it?'

'Not yet, I can't.'

'Me either. I asked Emil to look into his grandfather's estate to see if there was any financial benefit to Kristján.'

'There was. It paid for his trip to the UK.'

Anna raised an eyebrow. 'He told you that?'

'Without hesitation. I'm pretty sure he said his grandpa "left" rather than "gave" him the money. Until now, I had no reason to query it. Why would I? More to the point, why would he mention it? He must've known that we'd find out that he was questioned over the sudden and unexplained death. Wouldn't he be more likely to conceal it?'

'For all this, you're still not sure of his guilt, are you?'

'The evidence is pointing his way. Problem is, it's circumstantial. I could be a mile wrong. Deep down, I just don't feel it's him . . . or Eva, for that matter.'

'Maybe we need to look closer at her brother then.' Anna paused. 'Emil didn't seem that keen on Aron. He said he was a bit too sure of himself. I trust Emil's judgement. He's a good judge of character. Might it be worth us tackling Aron together?' Anna stopped talking as a ringing mobile cut her off. Hers was on the desk, lifeless.

Frankie checked hers. 'It's David. Mind if I take it? We've not spoken since he left.'

'Have you fallen out?'

'Why would you think that?'

'No reason.'

'Then why ask?' Frankie glared at her.

'Are all Brits so touchy?' Anna was joking.

Frankie wasn't laughing.

'Relax,' Anna said. 'He never mentioned you when I gave him a lift to the airport. He seemed preoccupied, very different from the night before. I found it odd. And when I asked him if he had a message for you, he said no. I sensed an undercurrent, that's all.'

'He left a note.' Frankie swore as the phone died in her hand.

'I'm sorry, I didn't mean to pry.' Anna stood. 'I'll give you some privacy.'

Frankie had embarrassed herself reacting like a fifteen-year-old to what was no more than an innocent question from her host who, it had to be said, had bent over backwards to accommodate her. An apology was in order. The DCI was already gone, the door closing behind her. For a split second, Frankie thought she should go after her, then a text arrived.

Drop what you're doing and call me.

She hit speed dial.

There were no pleasantries when David came on the line. He got straight to the point, updating her on what had transpired at the evening briefing, progress on both murder enquiries.

Frankie concentrated on her own. Coming on the back of Anna's revelations, she found it hard to take it all in. The DNA match on the towel was a huge breakthrough. As David talked, her mind drifted to her base at Middle Earth, imagining the positive response such news would have brought about: detectives on their feet, high-fives, pats on the back, a hastily arranged drink after work.

'Frank? You there?'

'I'm here. It's a lot to process.'

'Yeah, all of it good. You have your smoking gun, enough hard evidence for an arrest. Kristjánsson has been deceiving us all along. He's now your target.'

'Really? I thought I was the lead on this one.'

'You are.'

'And if I'm not ready to lock him up?'

'Are you for real? You're on your way home. I need you here. Quit pissing about and find him.'

'Will you back the hell off and listen? I need more time—'

'You've had time.'

47

David was concerned with Frankie's unwillingness to play ball but had no time to indulge that thought. She'd work through the new evidence a damned sight quicker without a babysitter. Besides, he had other stuff to be getting on with. Tracing a man within a ten-year age range who'd gone missing in the seventies was at the top of that list. To speed things along, he'd asked Indi to help Mitch with the action he'd raised at the briefing, then returned to his office to catch up on emails and admin work. Running one incident was tough, running two was nigh on impossible without Frankie to take up the slack.

An hour later, he summoned Mitch and Indi to his office. It was a bit early to ask for an update on the state of play, but it would keep his mind off Frankie and give him ammunition to fire at Bright when he called later. That plan backfired. Nationally, there were many open misper cases from the period. In reality, little progress had been made.

Depressing.

'The scenarios are endless,' Mitch said. 'A percentage of those listed are people with a history of mental health problems ranging from mild depression to serious psychosis and all points in between. For others there are no clear indicators.'

'He's right,' Indi said. 'They just vanished, went out and never came home. The protocol hasn't changed that much since the seventies. The young and the elderly were prioritised. If our guy was in his twenties, assuming someone reported him missing, even if his actions were viewed as uncharacteristic by close family, he'd have been at the bottom of the pile—'

'Not in this office,' David said abruptly.

'No, sir.'

Mitch came to her aid. 'Cases were reviewed on a regular

basis, following reported sightings or tip-offs that led to new lines of enquiry. Some were eventually resolved. Sadly, the majority were not. The action you raised is likely to be time-consuming, guv. This was pre-computerisation—'

'The files were never digitised?'

'No such luck.' Indi thumbed towards the door. 'As you can see, Mitch and I are up to our necks in paper.'

David glanced through his open office door where he could see the evidence for himself. Their desks had been shoved together, towers of hard copy files on each of them and more on the floor. There were rarely shortcuts in police work. From time to time the job was exciting. Most of it was a painstaking slog through mountains of paperwork.

'Any hits?' David asked.

'Give us a break, guv.' Mitchell's mouth almost fell open. 'Indi and I hardly got started when you called us in. The files on our desk are men in the age parameters we were given, all reported in our own force area. We'll give it our best shot. You never know. Stuff gets missed. We might get lucky.'

'OK, you can go.'

Mitch hesitated. 'Guv, it's pretty isolated at Kielder. I was thinking that our victim may have gone off-grid, in the geographical sense, become disoriented and lost his way—'

'He didn't jump into that barrel by himself—'

Mitch blushed, taken aback by his guv'nor's harsh tone. 'The point I was going to make is that he may not belong here. If he vanished on purpose, he probably scarpered from elsewhere. He'd hardly stick around if he didn't want to be found. If he came north, he may have been here under an assumed name, which makes our task more difficult—'

'Did I say it would be easy?'

'No, guv.'

'Assuming he was reported missing, the minute his body was found his status changed. This is now a murder investigation,' David reminded them. 'That should focus your minds. I don't give a toss if it occurred fifty or five hundred years ago. It will be investigated fully. If we have to review every missing person file from here to Italy, that's what we'll do. Understood?'

'Yes, guv.'

Indi took a step away. 'Was there anything else, sir?'

'No. Keep searching. If you need more personnel, let me know and I'll see what I can do.'

As the detectives turned to leave, Indira caught Mitchell's eye, a message passing between them: *Who rattled his cage?*

48

Before Frankie could hide her troubled expression, Anna entered the room. Instinctively, the DCI knew that there had been a development, but not which way the evidence had fallen, whether it was it bad for the case and good for Frankie or the other way around. In all their conversations, Frankie had been wavering on the subject of an Icelandic national being responsible for Scheving's death. Anna told her that if she needed help to work things out, she'd make herself available as a sounding board. If not, she'd step away and let her get on with it.

Then the floodgates opened.

Frankie had been pouring her heart out for a good half hour. She couldn't believe she was having this conversation again, only this time with an SIO from a foreign force. It was the kind of exchange that was easier to have with a complete stranger than a friend, particularly one the British DS was unlikely to set eyes on once she left the country.

It felt good to talk freely.

'There's a lot riding on the investigation that brought me here,' she said. 'Not just because it involves foreign nationals, there are other reasons too—'

'What other reasons?' It was the first time Anna had interrupted since Frankie began offloading. 'I don't understand.'

'That makes two of us.' Frankie said. 'Not wishing to sound like a drama queen, I seem to have lost my bearings, which is embarrassing for a DS allegedly on her way up. I made a complete arse of myself before David left. I'm surprised he didn't take me off the case and send me packing on the first plane out of here.'

'Well, you're still in Iceland—'

'Hanging on by my fingernails.'

'David obviously doesn't think so.'

'Yeah, well I feel . . . I feel unworthy of the opportunity he gave me.'

'Why?' Anna sat back in her chair, an open, non-judgemental posture. When Frankie didn't answer, she carried on. 'I'm sure what you're experiencing is temporary. You've been travelling, working long hours. You're in need of a good night's sleep.'

'I wish that's all it was, Anna. My confidence has gone AWOL.'

'Oh, that.' Anna understood. 'Not unusual in our line of work. You're hunting a murderer. Whoever killed Jón Scheving is facing life imprisonment. That's a hefty load for anyone to carry. We all feel under pressure once in a while.'

'That's what David said.'

'Then what's your problem?'

'I don't know.'

'Yes, you do. C'mon, out with it.'

Frankie did know. 'It's silly.'

'Let me be the judge of that.'

'I shouldn't be feeling like this. I've been part of the MIT for ages. Dealing with murders is what I do. I'm on the brink of a promotion I've worked so hard for and . . .' She spread her hands, a gesture of frustration and helplessness. 'For the first time in my life, I feel like a complete and utter fraud. It's ridiculous. I'm looking over my shoulder at every turn, expecting someone will find me out.'

'Then I must be dim. I didn't spot an imposter.' Anna smiled. 'Fake it till you make it. That's what my boss told me when I stepped up.'

'You're just saying that to make me feel better.'

'You want me to drag her in here?' Anna waited, then picked up the internal phone.

'No, don't!' Frankie said. 'I believe you.'

Holding her gaze, Anna replaced the receiver on its cradle. She morphed from 'good listener' to straight-talking detective chief inspector in a flash. 'You have a lot to learn about me, Frankie. I do not humour my officers . . . Ever. Ask Emil. Let's get one thing straight. Right now, you're operating on my patch, which means you're *my* responsibility. I accept that you're at a professional crossroads. That said, I expect you to do your job. You need to get a grip. I suggest you start by remembering why you chose a police career—'

Frankie's eyes flashed in anger. 'And if I'd rather not?'

'The choice is yours. You can act on my advice or ignore it. Makes no difference to me. Go away and think about it. Close the door on your way out.'

'Is that a dismissal?'

Eyeing the paperwork on her desk, Anna spoke without looking up. 'I think I made myself clear.'

The lump in Frankie's throat expanded.

She was frozen to the spot, fighting hard to keep her composure. She didn't blame Anna. In her position, Frankie might have taken the same stance. There was no room for slackers on her team either. It might sound harsh to some, but a large dollop of realism sometimes drove the message home to an officer whose morale was flagging.

'Is that all or is there more to this than you're willing to share?' Anna had lost patience. 'Look, Frankie, if I stepped in something you feel is private, I make no apology. You're now under my command, so I'm making it my business. You have one minute to tell me what it is or you may leave.'

Frankie lied. 'I'm fatigued, that's all.'

'Rubbish. You're shaking. Look at you.'

For a moment, the detectives stared at one another, a game of blink first, a game that Anna excelled at and Frankie lost. Confirmation, if it were needed, that she was under par. She dropped her head, clasping her hands together in order to keep them still. It had been so hard to let go. Now Anna had issued an ultimatum, demanding that she push the door open further or ship out.

It was now or never.

No one had ever questioned Frankie's motivation to join the police service. Coming from a long line of coppers, it made sense to most people. However, Anna had scratched beneath the surface and found a wound that hadn't properly healed. Backed into a corner, Frankie had always found courage.

This time was no different, though it was killing her. 'My sister was murdered when I was eleven years old. Joanna was fifteen at the time.' Choking on her words, she cleared her throat. 'I'm sorry, Anna—'

'Don't you dare apologise.' The DCI handed her a tissue and stood up. 'Wait there. I'll get you some tea—'

'No, please, I'm fine. I'll turn into a basket case if you give me sympathy.'

Anna sat down. 'Does your team know about Joanna?'

'The head of CID knows. David does, of course, he's my boss. I prefer to avoid the subject where others are concerned. As far as I know, only one other colleague is aware of it. He respects my privacy and never speaks of it. Outside of that small group, you're the only one I've told.'

'You have my word that it'll go no further,' Anna said. 'I'm family too.'

That almost made Frankie tear up. The world over, coppers stuck together. Anna's comment had paved the way for complete openness and honesty. Facing a red card, there was more to gain than lose by telling the truth.

'When I found out that Eva was around the same age as Joanna when she was assaulted, I saw red. It triggered a lot of memories I've had a lid on for a very long time. I couldn't get Joanna out of my head. I kept imagining what she'd gone through. How terrified, alone and helpless she must've been.' Again, she cleared her throat. 'The case was never solved.'

There was a sharp intake of breath from Anna. 'Frankie, I'm so sorry.'

There was so much more Frankie could say. What was the point? She'd gone far enough. Telling Anna that her father was a policeman at the time, that he'd been called to a suspicious death unaware that his daughter was the fatality he'd heard about over the radio, served no purpose.

Unable to go the final mile, Frankie turned her head away, looking out through the window and yet not seeing what was on the other side of the glass. 'He's still out there somewhere, Anna. Having a great life . . . or maybe taking another. That's what I find so hard to handle. Not a day goes by when I don't think about it. Well . . .' She turned her head. 'Now you know. If you feel the need to contact David, I completely—'

Anna cut her off. 'That won't be necessary. From now on we focus on the investigation, assuming you feel up to it. If you're struggling, I want to know about it in real time, not after the event. Do we have a deal?'

'Deal. Anna, thanks for listening. I appreciate the support.'

'You can thank me by giving me the lowdown on what's happening in the UK. All of it, not the watered-down version. David left here convinced that Kristján was guilty of murder. Is that also your take on the matter?'

'No, well . . . at the time, the evidence was all circumstantial.'

'There's been a development?'

'A DNA match. Scheving's blood was found at the campsite and on Kristján's towel. Kristján's DNA was found on the tent pegs I mentioned. Unless he helped erect Scheving's tent, which I very much doubt, he's probably responsible for hiding the camping equipment. It's a definite link. I need to bring Kristján in, Eva too. We'd better get moving, I suppose.' She paused. 'Actually, I spoke to Emil earlier. He was heading out double-crewed. Do you think he could locate them for me? I'd like my shit together before I face them.'

49

It was unlike Stone to lash out. Mitch and Indira were right to wonder why he was in such a foul mood. He'd be wondering that himself, except he knew the answer: he was missing Frankie's company and wishing she'd call. That was not an acceptable excuse for taking a chunk out of his young colleagues. They were doing their best. Tracing a missing person was never going to be straightforward; finding one who'd been missing fifty years even harder.

David sighed.

He'd find a way to make it up to Mitch and Indi. Neither was alive in the mid-seventies, nor was he for that matter. No detective currently working in his Murder Investigation Team was. Apart from what they had picked up on the news over the years, they knew little of the time period described by some commentators as a grim decade: a miserable hangover from the swinging sixties; power cuts; industrial action; long picket lines and the three-day working week.

Dark times.

The MIR beyond David's office door was empty now. He'd sent everyone home. Lights were dimmed. The internal phones silent. He loved this time of night. With the office to himself, it gave him time to breathe, more importantly to consider his strategy going forward. What he needed was an understanding of the politics of the seventies and how it affected families, particularly in rural areas like Plashetts, the village demolished to make way for Kielder. It can't have been easy for them to give up the homes they had grown up in.

Using his warrant card, he logged on, accessing Safari. It wasn't hard to find what he was looking for. Historically, the creation of the reservoir had been well documented, from inception to completion, including the fact that it took two years to fill. The dates, he noted, coincided with those put forward by Leonard as the estimated time of death of the barrel victim.

Interesting.

Staring at the images on screen, he relaxed, hands linked loosely behind his head as he put the pieces together without the benefit of Frankie's input. She was a good bagman, someone he could bounce ideas off, guaranteed to let him know if she thought a theory was rubbish.

David read on . . .

According to online posts he found, thousands worked on the Kielder project in the mid to late seventies. At the time, there were strong objections to the scheme. The North Tyne valley community was angry. What David had learned presented him with a frame of reference and possible motive. He began to wonder if the skeletal remains Kristján and Eva had found might be those of an engineer or construction worker. Had there been a fight between crew? Had one of them clashed with a local activist? David had worked many an investigation where people had been killed for less.

A vibration in his breast pocket.

Sliding his mobile out, he checked the screen: Ben.

Without answering, David placed the mobile on his desk, irritated by the interruption. He didn't like the idea that the nephew he now shared a home with was canvassing the Kielder community at the same time as uniformed police officers were carrying out house-to-house enquiries, although of course he understood that the lad was only doing his job. Frankie had reminded him that unless Ben moved away – and neither of them wanted that – they were bound to be investigating the same stories simultaneously. It was something they would have to learn to live with – it was also fraught with danger . . .

As the SIO of a unit dealing with major crime, David couldn't afford a conflict of interest. His professional and personal lives could never, must never, collide. On the other hand, information was a bargaining chip he couldn't operate without. During his career he'd come to realise that the press were not always the enemy. When he was stationed in the Met, he'd developed a relationship that was mutually beneficial with the very woman who was now Ben's mentor.

His mobile stopped vibrating.

Seconds later, the device lit up again. David watched it shimmy across his desk sideways. One call, he could ignore. Two, in as many seconds, could be urgent. This parenting lark required a response, even though he was in no position to supply one half the time. His mind raced through possibilities: Ben had been sacked; he'd lost his door key; his new wheels had blown up or broken down; an RTA?

God forbid.

A fatal car accident had taken his father. What were the chances? David panicked. Experience had taught him that lightening occasionally did strike twice in the same place. He dismissed the thought. Wherever Ben went, Wells was his shadow. If anything had happened to him, somehow she'd have got word to David.

The call could wait.

Now she was in his head, Wells refused to go away, her over-pouty red lips, her unquenching thirst for alcohol. She was an outrageous flirt, but underneath all that playfulness lurked a no-nonsense pro. The real deal. The doyenne of journalism had many attributes: drive, ambition, intellect. Her sense of fair play was the most attractive part of her by far, the only bit he was remotely interested in, even though he owed her for favours he'd rather not think about now.

The journalist had one advantage over him. She could ask questions with impunity with no manual on investigative practice to adhere to, which made her a valuable asset. Ben too, because she'd taught him everything she knew. Maybe he'd picked up a snippet of gossip that could prove useful to David's case. As the idea arrived, so did the third call.

OK, this was getting silly.

Ben had won. His persistence would be rewarded, even though David was busy. As his mobile wobbled over the edge of his desk, he caught it with the skill of a cricket slip fielder with inches to spare before it made landfall.

'This had better be good, mate.'

'Nice of you to pick up,' Wells said. 'I was beginning to think you'd gone into hiding. How's it going?'

'Oh, you know, still feeding the piranhas.'

'We're a hungry bunch.' She laughed. 'Haven't you heard? There's a maniac on the loose at Kielder. Some of my lot are wetting themselves over it. Sadly, they outnumber those of us with any sense by about ten to one.'

David glanced at the screen to check on the incoming call. Definitely Ben's number. 'No offence, but I was expecting my surrogate son—'

'Don't sound so gutted. You got me instead. My phone died.'

'Is he there?'

'He's busy.'

'Doing what?'

'Schmoozing, by the looks. Was that still a word when you were born?'

'I get the drift. A mature point of view is what I need right now.'

'Ouch! My ego is well and truly crushed. I might be pushing sixty. I could still give a woman half my age a run for their money—'

David smiled. 'I'm sure you could. Not sure how you can help yet. I'll give it some thought. Now, is there a point to this call? Otherwise I'll have to run.'

'Well, as of this evening, Kielder is like Glastonbury on steroids. I kid you not. Some guys I've not seen for years just arrived in a Winnebago bigger than my flat. They've claimed their spot and are sitting around a campfire like a group of international boy scouts, shorts 'n all. You're missing quite a party. Fortunately for the Boy Wonder' – her nickname for Ben – 'there are young women here too. I suspect he's stopping over. I'm heading your way.'

'Why?'

'Why not?'

'I'm hoping to knock off shortly.' David spoke through a genuine yawn. 'I'm wrecked, Belinda. Can we do this another time?'

'No, I'm afraid this is a once in a lifetime offer.' She meant serious.

'It always is with you. Get to the point, I'm desperate to get out of here.'

'David, you can have anything you want from me so long as you beg nicely.'

Her attempt at humour had fallen woefully short of its mark. A weighty silence followed. The longer it lasted, the more uncomfortable David became. It was the first hint of trouble. The second, less subtle than the first, didn't take long to arrive. 'Actually, I'll be home in ten,' she said. 'Can we meet there? Your office isn't the best place to have a conversation we can't have on the phone.'

'I'm alone here.'

'You think you're alone there.'

50

After she got cleaned up, Frankie returned to Anna's office, feeling refreshed and a lot less stressed than she had earlier. As the DCI took care of her admin, Frankie spent the next hour watching the minute hand wind its way around the face of the clock, inch by painful inch, wishing she'd gone after Kristján and Eva herself.

She was startled when the internal phone rang.

Anna snatched it up. 'OK, Emil. The phone is on speaker. Frankie is here. Go ahead.'

'We're too late.' Those three damning words seemed to echo around the SIO's cavernous office. The DS sounded out of breath as if he was or had been running. 'Target 1 seen leaving his digs at 1300 hours carrying a large rucksack.' Target 1 was Kristján. 'He's not been seen or heard of since. I managed to talk his flatmate into letting me in to take a look around.'

'And?' Anna said.

'Looks like he skipped town. There's next to nothing in his room. None of his mates know where he is.'

'Any news on Eva?' Frankie asked.

'Negative. She's staying over with a friend, allegedly.'

'What friend?' she wanted to know.

'Her name is Helga Grímsdottir. She's a fellow medical student and I can't get hold of her either. On my way to her flat now, if I can find my car. Hold on . . .' A high-pitched beep – presumably his driver attracting his attention – followed by the sound of a car door slamming, a bit of rustling at the other end, then a diesel engine starting up. Emil rattled off an address. 'OK, go!'

'What?'

'Not you, Frankie. I'm talking to my ride. I got Helga's address from Eva's father. Jacob is showing no concern for her. These days, she comes and goes as she pleases. After the assault, he used to worry every time she stepped outside. It was stressing her out. He realised that if he didn't let her do her own thing she'd have no life.'

'He's right,' Anna said.

'Boss, I didn't ask to search Eva's room. I thought it best not to panic him. I just made out that I wanted to put some questions you'd forgotten to ask. Sorry, I couldn't think of anything else to say.'

'You did the right thing.'

'OK, I'll keep you posted.'

'Roger that.' The line went dead.

Frankie's head went down, mentally and physically. 'What happens now?'

Anna gave a shrug. 'You heard Emil. He'll keep looking.'

'We don't have time for that. I must talk to Kristján.'

'Don't panic. It won't get dark tonight. We'll find him—'

'When? I'm terrified he'll do something stupid. There was a note on that file you showed me suggesting he had psychiatric treatment following his grandpa's death. Guilty or innocent, he may attempt self-harm.'

'Yes, I saw that too.'

'Is there any chance we can put a tap on his phone and Eva's?'

Anna shook her head. 'Not on your life.'

'Even if it might save his? C'mon, Anna, chances are they're together. They must be.'

'That's a bit of a jump. Let's wait till we hear from Emil.'

'Even if they're not together they'll be in touch. We need to hear those conversations.'

'Is that how you operate in the UK?'

'Not illegally, if that's what you mean. Anna, please, I'm not asking you to pull any strokes on my behalf. I'm asking if you have the ear of a judge who can give you the authority we require—'

'As a last resort perhaps. Any judge will expect that all other avenues have been explored first. Besides, wiretaps aren't done in real time here. All recordings are archived automatically and made available after the fact. It won't take us anywhere soon. Old fashioned legwork will get us there quicker.'

'You heard Emil. Kristján's taken off with his possessions. He's unlikely to return to his flat anytime soon, is he?'

'Then we'll try his parents' house—'

'What?' Anticipating that she might need to visit the family following Kristján's imminent arrest, Frankie had checked out Ísafjörður on the net. The town was in the Westfjords region, a forty-minute flight or five and a half hours by road, if she was lucky. She was beginning to hate this bloody country.

51

Kristján felt anxious as he stared blankly at the horizon through the cabin window. Sight of a big sky would ordinarily lift his spirits. Not today. It was bad enough being questioned by DS Oliver in the UK. Now she'd followed him to Iceland, and brought her boss with her, the shit had really hit the fan. She was no fool but DCI Stone was a cut above, a more experienced detective who took the gravitas of his office seriously. He had eyes Kristján suspected could see right through him, an intelligence so sharp it frightened him.

Preoccupied with his thoughts, he jumped as a pair of arms slid around his shoulders, hugging him from behind. He hadn't heard or sensed Eva approaching across the wooden floor in her bare feet.

He turned to look at her.

Her hair was down today, the way he preferred it. Like liquid gold, it cascaded over her shoulders and arms, almost reaching her tiny waist. She looked so happy when they took off on holiday. Now her expression was grim, her face pinched and pale. He forced a smile he didn't feel. Although he received a kiss in return, it was fleeting and lukewarm, no passion behind it.

His heart ached to see how deeply troubled she was.

She walked around the chair, climbed up and straddled him, a knee on either side of his thighs. 'We can talk now. We're safe here. The police won't find us—'

'Is that why you wanted to leave the city?'

'Why else?'

'I don't know, Eva. I'm having second thoughts. We can't stay here. Running away didn't work last time. They came after us.'

*

Kristján appeared conflicted as he turned his head away, eyes full of resentment. Eva wondered how long his depressed mood would last. His father had told her that it had taken a long time for him to get over a previous episode, warning her against getting involved with him.

The man was a complete bastard.

Keeping Kristján well was the only thing that mattered to Eva, the reason she'd begged him to get out of Reykjavík for a few days to chill. Without passports, they were trapped, like the plot of the Icelandic TV drama that starred her favourite actor, Ólafur Darri Ólafsson. Bizarrely, he was also in the movie *The Deep*, which happened to be the title of the hashtag currently taking the world by storm.

As if they weren't in enough trouble.

Their friends knew who was responsible for the animation. Aron was the only person in their group who had the skill to create and post such a thing online. He said it was a laugh, except Kristján wasn't in on the joke. He'd told police that the barrel hadn't been photographed and was livid when he came across the clip. No point crying about it now. Once you hit send it was out there. Gone forever.

Kristján was more tense than Eva had ever seen him.

Putting her arms around his neck, she pulled him close, stroking the back of his head gently with her thumb, trying to soothe him. He didn't shrug her off exactly, just made it clear that he wasn't in the mood. He'd been distant for days. Eva was struggling to bridge the gap that had opened up between them.

'Kris, talk to me.' She was the only one who called him that and merely to piss off his father. 'We've hardly spoken since we got home. I can't help if I don't know the problem. If you have something on your mind, you know you can share it, right?'

He remained silent, his body rigid.

Exasperated, she climbed off him. 'I have no sympathy for losers who indulge in self-pity. I made an exception for you.

Everyone has a limit and I've reached mine. Have it your own way. You can't say I didn't try.'

'Eva, don't be like that.'

'Like what?'

To prevent her walking away, he grabbed her wrist, holding onto her.

She looked down at his fingers wrapped tightly round her wrist. 'Take your hands off me.'

He released his grip, a profuse apology on his lips. 'I just can't talk to you right now.'

She glared at him. 'You know, a long time ago, my mother told me that the only way to keep a secret is not to tell another living soul. I've lived by that ever since.' She gave him a filthy look, one she should perhaps have reserved for her mother. Unable to accept that her daughter was the victim of a sexual assault, the idea never to discuss it was hers. 'Just so you know, keeping things to yourself isn't all it's cracked up to be.'

Kristján's brow creased. 'What do you mean?'

'Doesn't matter.'

'Does to me.'

'I think you know already, not that it's any of your business.' She turned away, angry now. With her back to him, tears filled her eyes like small pools of salty water. She blinked them away. How the fuck had he found out? Why had she agreed to keep quiet about it in the first place? She'd done nothing to be ashamed of. Nothing. Her mother was plain wrong. Silence couldn't blot out the past. Every time Kristján laid a hand on her, that pig Scheving was in her head.

Kristján let the matter drop. They had been drinking heavily since they arrived at the summer house she called her bolthole. In reality, the small log cabin wasn't hers. It belonged to a great aunt, an old woman who hardly ever used it. It wasn't exactly breaking and entering – the key was hidden under a stone in the garden – still, he felt guilty being there without permission.

He didn't want a scene with Eva that might end in a fight. Everything he'd done in the past few days had been for her. The dilemma he faced was simple: should he confide in her now, or was it better she didn't know? He wasn't sure she had the strength and wherewithal to cope with a lengthy interrogation. There was no doubt in his mind that it was coming. Scheving's death wouldn't go away on its own.

Secretly, Kristján was pleased to have got away, affording him the opportunity to think. It was only a matter of time before the cops turned on them, trying to trip them up, his word against Eva's. Already, they had poisoned his old man's mind against him. Once you planted the seed of doubt in someone's head you couldn't take it away. It was in there for keeps.

His father didn't yet know he was being questioned over a second, unrelated death. He soon would. And when the police came knocking, the seed would grow and their estranged relationship would be as good as over.

Without family support, Kristján would struggle.

What he'd done this time round was bad.

What he suspected Eva had done was worse.

She was staring at him, on the verge of speaking. Slugging back her drink was a hint that he might not like what she had to say. She cleared her throat. 'When your grandpa passed away, your father said you were a mess for months.'

'It's called grief. What's your point?'

'He said you'd gone weird, wouldn't talk to the police or him, just like now. Did you do something bad back then?'

'No!' It was an odious accusation he never saw coming. 'How could you even think it? It was an accident. You know it was. Eva, if you don't believe that, we're done—'

'What about now? Did you hurt Scheving?'

He threw it right back at her. 'Did you?'

Her brows almost met in the middle. 'What?'

'You heard me.' Kristján stared at her with hard eyes, while images of Scheving forced their way into his head: his sinister smirk, his drug-fuelled eyes, his tent, his knife. 'Eva, I heard you scream.'

'What are you on about?'

'That night at Kielder, I heard you.'

Eva lit a joint, drew on it, blew a plume of smoke high in the air. 'You're off your head, you know that? What you heard was the wind, a creature in the woods, an owl perhaps—'

'I heard what I heard.' Kristján waited a beat. When she didn't answer, he carried on. 'I went out looking for you.'

'Oh really? Did you find me?' Her tone was laced with sarcasm. 'I think you'd had too much to drink. You saw me to my tent, remember—'

He cut her off. 'I meant later, after we all went to bed.'

'Not me. You must've been dreaming.'

'And I suppose you didn't ask me to get rid of Scheving either, or crawl into my tent crying that night. Why was that? I have to know.'

Another long drag on her joint. 'I, I don't know . . .'

'A few days and you can't remember?'

'So much has happened since.' Eva felt hot. Finding an elastic band, she tied her hair up. 'No, wait! I had a nightmare—'

'How convenient.'

'Believe what you like.'

Kristján stood up. A plea for honesty. 'When I returned to camp, you weren't in your tent. I checked. Later, when you came to mine, you were upset. I asked if you'd seen anything. You wouldn't answer. Unless you tell me different, I think I understand what might have happened.'

'You're crazy. I told you, I had a bad dream. I got up and went for a walk.'

He wanted to believe her. He wanted her to believe him. Distrust was a hateful emotion. It destroyed relationships and drove a wedge between people. The stress triggered a flashback, a body lying face up, an image he'd rather not think about. 'Do you really think me capable of harming anyone?'

'What? No, of course not, I shouldn't have said that.' She touched his hair.

He batted her hand away.

'Kris, I'm sorry. I don't want to fight. Please sit down—'

'I don't want to sit down!' He was yelling now. 'You started this—'

'I hurt you. Now you want to hurt me. I get it.'

He glared at her.

'Fine! I'm too wired to play games. You want answers? Well, so do I.' Eva's patience had run out. She wasn't about to let the matter drop. She replayed his dialogue. It was the first she'd heard of him leaving the campsite that night. 'Precisely what is it you think I've done?' she said. 'And what in God's name might I have seen that night? Yes, I asked you to ditch Scheving. I didn't mean kill the pig. If I wanted that I'd have done it myself. You wouldn't have the nerve.'

52

Belinda Wells was a class act. She lived a fifteen-minute drive from Middle Earth in an art deco apartment overlooking Newcastle's Town Moor. From there she could walk to the city centre if she had a mind to. She didn't. The only part of her body she exercised regularly was not something David wanted to think about while sober, unless you counted her overly large mouth. That was different. Eating, drinking and gossiping about other people's business floated her boat. It was what she lived for, how she found things out. The woman could talk to anyone and they would talk back. She may no longer be employed by a fancy broadsheet but, during her distinguished career she'd been involved with some of the most high-profile, public-interest stories to have made headlines. He knew no journalist more qualified to get beneath the skin of a scandal. Winning prestigious awards, being shortlisted for many more, meant nothing to her. What got her up in the morning was whistle-blowing in print.

She was born to break the news.

They had grown very fond of one another when they lived in London. Though they'd seen less of each other since they moved north, complex investigations had brought them together from time to time. They had an arrangement that worked. After a shaky start, Wells had even formed a close relationship with Frankie Oliver. And since David's nephew was now her pupil, the four of them socialised from time to time, a drink after work, but not often.

A meeting at Wells' place wasn't unprecedented. It was unusual. David's home was in the opposite direction. He figured that whatever she had to say would be worth the detour. Leaving the Central Motorway onto the Great North Road, he was forced to brake hard. Vehicles were queueing to the slip road, blue lights flashing up ahead. With time on his hands, unable to move forward or back, he called Frankie for an update on the situation in Iceland, hoping that by now she'd have calmed down, come to her senses and made an arrest. He suspected she hadn't, else he'd have heard about it.

Receiving no answer, he threw his mobile on the dash.

A few minutes later, she called him, tripping over herself to apologise, asking if he'd mind waiting. She was on her way out of the Major Crimes Unit with Anna and wanted to talk to him privately.

He heard them say goodnight.

Seconds later, Anna called out to Frankie. 'If you need to talk.'

Silence.

In his head, David pictured the DCI forming her hand into an imaginary phone, holding it to her ear. Frankie hadn't answered – perhaps because she knew he was listening in – or maybe she'd done so with a nod.

His eyes found the digital clock in his vehicle: 21:20. It was an odd offer for Anna to make so late at night. Why would Frankie need to call? Was she in trouble? Was he overthinking this? Probably. Anna Jónsdóttir seemed the type to go the extra mile for a British guest alone in a foreign land.

'Guv, are you there?'

Frankie only ever called him that when in the hearing of others, when things were not going to plan or they were having a row. Once she'd said her piece, or things calmed down, she'd revert to first-name terms, his preference. Unlike some senior detectives, it wasn't David's style to insist on guv, boss or sir. In that respect, he was no different from his Icelandic counterpart. He knew one thing. He wouldn't want to play piggy in the middle if those two ever kicked off.

'Guv?'

'Sorry, I was miles away.' He couldn't tell her where.

'Anything I can help you with?'

'Not sure, I'm still joining dots.' He kept it casual so as not to raise her hopes. Although the barrel case was his, they would both be working on it just as soon as she tied up things her end. It made sense to keep her abreast of developments. Then again, she had a lot on. He didn't want to overload her.

'What dots?'

David smiled. Her professional curiosity had no OFF switch. 'Well, our misper had a nasty break to his arm. Leonard said it was the type of fracture where the bone is broken in more than one place. They're difficult to heal, often requiring surgery, usually the result of a high-impact injury, a fall or some such. Then, while researching the building of Kielder Water, I came across an anniversary piece written thirty-five years after the reservoir was officially opened by the Queen in May 1982. It contained some interesting stats. The manpower was staggering, fifteen hundred at its peak. That's a lot of hard men, diggers and bulldozers.'

'Imagine the testosterone—'

'Exactly. Plenty of scope for fights and accidents, or even fights made to look like accidents. The timeline fits too, mid to late seventies. Just saying.'

'Sorry to piss on your chips, but I'll take your bulldozer and raise you a tractor.'

David laughed. He understood where she was going. The area surrounding Kielder was forestry and farmland. They also used heavy-duty plant, all manner of dangerous machinery and employed their own muscle. 'OK, you win,' he said. 'I'll add lumberjacks and farmers to the mix and do some more digging.'

Frankie's turn to laugh. 'If you're right and the victim was a civil engineer or construction worker, there must be a workforce record of accidents somewhere.'

'Yeah, I'll try and track it down.'

'I have an idea. Leave it with me.'

Not once had she mentioned her own investigation. It didn't bode well. He gave her a nudge. 'What's the state of play your end?'

Her good mood vanished. 'Promise not to yell at me? I'm sorry, guv. I wasn't quick enough. Kristjánsson got the jump on us again. He's in the wind. A search is underway.'

David was disappointed to have his suspicions confirmed. 'Is that why Anna thought you might want to talk later?'

'What? No. I don't need my hand holding.'

'So why did she ask?'

'It was girl stuff.'

'You're a rubbish liar.' He switched his engine off. 'What about Eva?'

'Most likely with him. Their phones are off. He's not been seen since one o'clock, she left shortly afterwards. They could be anywhere by now, except out of the country. Good thing Anna confiscated their passports. I'm going to the hotel for a few hours kip. Emil volunteered to stay on – he's been deployed to find them. If that doesn't happen by the time we regroup in the morning, Anna and I will either fly to Kristján's family home or give his father a call.'

'You're better off seeing the whites of his eyes.'

'We have Skype here too.' Given the seriousness of the situation, her joke was ill-timed. She knew it and moved quickly on. 'I appreciate it's harder to sniff out a lie that way. Anna thinks we'll be wasting precious time if we fly or drive up there only to receive a negative response. Besides, Kristján's father is unlikely to protect him—'

'Why not?'

She didn't answer.

'Don't play games, Frank. I asked you a question.'

'Kristján has more than one question mark hanging over his head.' She cleared her throat. 'I should've told you this earlier—'

'So why didn't you?'

'You were chewing my head off, ordering me to make an arrest. I couldn't get a word in edgeways—'

'Yeah, it'll be my fault. Isn't it always?'

'On this occasion it was.' She paused. 'Kristján was spoken to by Icelandic police a while ago. He was never charged with anything. The matter was marked NFA. However, it caused a rift between father and son.'

'What matter?'

Internally, David almost blew a gasket when she finally came out with it. That was probably what she was expecting and bloody well deserved. She frustrated the hell out of him sometimes.

'What part of "keep me posted" did you not understand?' he asked.

She apologised again, even though she thought the blame lay at his door.

He managed to keep his voice level and his tone soft. No point antagonising her when she was so far away. 'Well, you're there and I'm not, so you'll have to deal with him as you see fit. It sounds like you have a fair few questions to ask. If the investigation into his grandfather's death is closed, you do not go there, do you hear me?'

'I have no intention of looking into it.'

'That's the right answer. Hold on . . .' Turning on his ignition, David followed the lead if the car in front, pulling his vehicle over as another blue light sped by, this one an ambulance. He turned the wheel, retaking his place in the tailback. He heard Frankie yawn. He was shattered too. He intended to make it quick with Wells and head north, assuming he wasn't stuck here all night. The traffic still hadn't moved.

'What's going on?' Frankie asked.

'RTA ahead. India 99 in the air.'

'Where the hell are you?'

'A1. I'd like to say heading north to the Blue House round-about but I'm stationary.'

'Shouldn't you be heading home?'

'I have a meeting with Wells.'

'About what?'

'Buggered if I know. She was about to leave Kielder when she called. Whatever it is, she wouldn't come to the office.'

'Maybe she has something for us.'

'That she couldn't discuss on the phone? Unlikely. You know what she's like. I'd be better off trying to decipher her shorthand. Half the time, she talks in code.'

'She also talks a lot of sense. David, be careful. If she wants to meet at this hour, wouldn't give you the heads-up on the phone or meet at Middle Earth, she's giving you the gypsy's warning. You wearing Kevlar? Sounds like you're in for a bumpy ride.'

David?

He smiled. The real Frankie Oliver was back.

53

Wells buzzed him in. He didn't need to explain why he was late. From her top-floor apartment window, she'd seen blue lights in the distance and watched a Great North Air Ambulance Service helicopter land on the Town Moor to airlift a critically injured man to Northumbria Specialist Emergency Care Hospital at Cramlington in order to save his life. David had listened in to the drama on his police radio, including transmission from the GNAAS asking for an exact location to land. For the casualty, it was touch and go.

Wells didn't offer him alcohol. She knew he wouldn't accept with a long drive to his home in Pauperhaugh ahead of him. Instead, she made tea.

Handing it to him, she collected her gin, including the bottle from the kitchen counter, invited him to join her in the living room. She moved along the passage like a cheetah. Kicking off her shoes, she threw herself on the sofa, tucking her shapely legs under her bottom, cradling her drink. He took the seat opposite. For a moment, she studied him without saying anything, until the proverbial elephant edged its way into the room and made itself comfortable.

As always, she ignored it.

'Love the designer stubble,' she said. 'The shagged-out look really suits you.'

'I doubt that.' David stroked his chin. It was way past five. His shadow had become a beard hours ago. It was beginning to itch, as was his curiosity. 'It's been a long day, Belinda. Much as I'd love to stay and chat, I'd rather get this over and done with before I drop, if it's all the same to you.'

'You won't like what I have to say.'

'I didn't expect to.'

She rarely hesitated. Rarely allowed her poker face time off, and yet she seemed uncharacteristically tense. He detected a flicker of concern before she had the chance to hide it. Wells was someone who always had a pithy reply at her disposal. When it didn't materialise, it confirmed that dragging him across town was necessary and couldn't wait till morning.

'So?' He waited a beat more.

'Adam English is here,' she said.

The news took his breath away.

Of all the things she might have said, this was the very worst, the most unexpected. Adam English called himself a journalist. The man was a snake, out to make a name for himself at any cost, the type to concoct his own version of events and publish regardless. He'd made a career out of screwing people, blurring the lines between fact and fiction. Following the murder of his Met colleague, David had been on the wrong end of his lies and innuendoes.

David and DS Jane Vincent worked together in a Major Incident Team. They were professional partners, not romantically linked. He was in her house when her ex burst through the door and shot her dead in front of him. David couldn't deny his feelings for Jane, but they had never been acted upon. Not so, according to English. He saw an opportunity and went for it.

Wells lowered her drink. 'Are you OK?'

'Depends what mind games he has lined up for me this time.'

'I just thought I should warn you.'

'Will it do any good?'

'Probably not.'

Their eyes met across the room.

They sat in silence for a while, remembering the rubbish English had written at the time, inventing a story where there wasn't one, dishing the dirt, alleging that David's conduct as Jane's boss was out of order, given that she was in a relationship, albeit an abusive one. The events preceding the witch hunt would never leave him.

Recently, the flashbacks had begun to subside. Now they were working overtime. The images in his head were bad, the soundtrack unbearable: the shot that killed Jane; the animal-like wail that came from his mouth as she slumped to the floor; her futile plea not to let her die; the sirens of Met police rushing to the scene; the ambulance crew asking him to let go of the casualty; his voice yelling at them to back the fuck away.

Her flame had already gone out.

'David, breathe,' Wells said.

He re-entered her untidy living room disoriented, his eyes finding the empty sofa, newspapers scattered across the floor, shoes, an empty glass. Belinda was on her feet, standing right beside him, her icy cold fingers pressing his sweaty ones against the glass she'd placed in his hand, her voice gentle in his ear.

'David, take it please.'

He tried to give it back.

'Drink it, man. I'll make up the spare room.'

He glanced up at her. 'And how would that look if English has me under surveillance?'

'I don't know and I care even less.'

'He has previous for it,' David warned.

'And it was totally out of order.' Wells was aware that for months after Jane's death English had followed David around like a dark shadow. 'Anyway,' she sighed. 'It's not me I'm worried about, nor is it only you this time—'

He frowned. 'What do you mean?'

'I hope I'm not overreacting.' Lifting her glass from the floor, Wells poured herself another drink from a half-empty bottle of gin, took a slug, then perched on the edge of the sofa. 'I overheard him spreading his poison at the campsite.'

'About me and Jane?'

'Not this time, though one other name was mentioned—'

'Whoa, back up. You've lost me.' Confusion reigned but then David caught on. He was close to only one person. 'Are we talking about Ben?' He didn't wait for an answer. 'Is that why he's not here? You keep him the fuck away from English or there'll be another murder up there. I'll swing for him if he messes with me again.'

'It's not Ben,' Wells said. 'Northumbria's Media Team issued a formal statement on the deaths at Kielder. Bright signed off on it. All journalists were given a copy. You were named as SIO.'

'That's standard practice.'

'Well, some indiscreet press bimbo mentioned that you'd gone to Iceland with Frankie, at which point English started making his mouth go. He painted you as a Lothario who can't keep his hands off the female members of his team. As you can imagine, others listened. He shafted you once, David. He's not going to get the chance to do it twice and drag Frankie down too, not if I have anything to do with it.'

54

Eva had lied to her father. She'd made no arrangements to stay with a friend overnight. Her fellow medical student Helga Grímsdottir told Emil that she knew nothing about it and hadn't seen Eva since she took off for the UK. Concluding that Kristján and Eva had gone into hiding together, as Frankie had suggested, Anna decide to send Emil to Ísafjörður while she Skyped Kristján's father to ask if his son had returned to the family home.

The man spoke little English, so the telephone interview was conducted in Icelandic. Frankie didn't need to master the language to know that it was a useless exercise. From the man's tone and body language she could interpret that he hadn't a clue where the lad was.

'Takk,' Anna said, ending the call.

She slipped her phone in her trouser pocket. No jeans today. She was dressed in a navy suit, a crisp white shirt, her hair tied up in a soft feminine bun with braiding intertwined. It was a good look that suited her, very attractive, a style Frankie wouldn't dream of trying to replicate.

'Well?' Although she knew the answer, she had to ask.

'No joy.' Anna glanced at her watch, then up at Frankie. 'He'll be in touch if Kristján shows up, with or without Eva. I have to go out for a while. If I hear anything, I'll let you know. Emil will do likewise. He should be landing about now. If Kristján is in the area, he will be found.'

'I wish I had your confidence.'

'Believe me, Emil is good at this. Ours is a very small world, Frankie. Ísafjörður even smaller, only two and half thousand people live there. It would be harder for Emil to miss than find them.'

'I may as well have gone with him. I'm in the way here.' Since early, Anna's phone had been ringing off the hook, a long line of detectives Frankie had never seen before in and out of her office, all talking excitedly. Anna had been in her element issuing orders Frankie couldn't understand. 'You have multiple investigations to be getting on with, interviews, briefings, lock-ups on the horizon.'

Anna didn't admit or deny it.

Frankie never had been any good at fishing. 'I'll die of bore-dom if we don't find those kids soon. Is there anything I can help you with? I'd offer to man the phones if your lot spoke Geordie.'

'You can help by keeping the faith.' Anna glanced at the wall clock above the murder wall. 'Are you going out or waiting here for news? It's up to you.'

'No, I need some air.'

Frankie walked her from the building. There was obviously something going down. Anna didn't mention what it was and she didn't ask. Ignoring her wave, Anna took off at speed, leaving her British guest affronted on the pavement. 'Have a nice day,' Frankie whispered sarcastically.

For a couple of hours, Frankie had been wandering around Reykjavík city centre in the vain hope of spotting her targets. She was cold and miserable. While the UK was enjoying amazing weather, it was raining in Iceland. She bought a waterproof jacket in one of the outdoor clothing shops, then made her way down to the old harbour, a much bigger display of boats moored there than those whose owners had chosen Amble marina as their home, as Frankie had done. At midday, she found herself at the Harpa Concert Hall. It was a beautiful building with geometrically shaped glass panels, as attractive inside as it was without – only warmer, away from the wind whipping inland from the sea.

She bought lunch – an open sandwich and coffee – then

sat down, wishing she had a book to keep her company. She checked her mobile: no messages from Anna, Emil or David. Curious to know why Wells wanted to meet him, Frankie opened her contacts and tapped on her number. The call cut to voicemail. Leaving no message, she tried David instead. Same response. Frustrated at having nothing to do, she made a mental note to call them later, Ben too if she got the chance. First, her old man . . .

The call was answered immediately.

'Hey, Frank. How's it going? You getting anywhere?'

'Some.'

'Why so down in the mouth then?'

It had come out wrong. She was tempted to admit that she'd lied, that she was making a right hash of things and wanted to go home and curl up on the sofa in his den. She held her tongue. Her father had already gathered that things were not great in Iceland. Nothing got past him . . . ever.

'If you two need a hand, I'm available,' he said.

His leg-pulling failed to lift her. 'One, Dad. David flew home yesterday.'

'Ah, that explains your mood.'

'What mood? I'm not a teenager—'

'So don't act like one.' He chuckled. 'Be proud, Frank. It's not often a DS gets to run the show abroad. How come David left anyhow? You didn't piss him off again, did you?'

'Bright wanted one of us to handle the circus up at Kielder.'

'Oh, that. It's a bit late for containment, Frank. The press are camping out on the banks of the reservoir, waiting for the next body to pop to the surface like the Loch Ness bloody monster. They're literally coming to blows over the best pitch. There's no longer peace up there. I saw umpteen public order offences on this morning's news. You'd think war had broken out. As for preserving the crime scene, forget it. The damage is done. What Bright needs isn't David, it's the TSG.'

Frankie tuned him out.

A Tactical Support Group descending on Kielder Water wasn't funny. What her father was describing was the exact opposite of what was going on through the window. The rain had stopped and the sun had come out. People were wandering around at a leisurely pace. A small group of tourists were posing for a photograph. Happy faces. Arms round each other. Selfie sticks. No pushing and shoving here.

Her father was still talking . . .

It sounded like the illegal encampment and additional footfall, if she could call it that, was causing problems of epic proportions for the MIT, mirroring the mayhem of the construction village that sprung up years ago. Thinking about it gave her an idea.

'Granddad's not with you by any chance, is he?'

'He is, but he'll have to wait in line. You're not getting away from me that easily. Now give. I want chapter and verse on what you've been up to.'

'Didn't you retire?'

'Did I?' He laughed.

'My work is confidential.'

'I'm your dad. Ex-job, remember?'

'As if I could forget. Even if I wanted, which I don't, I can't talk right now—'

'Oh, I get it. You're moving up. I'm moving out—'

'That's not the case and you know it.' She dropped her voice to a whisper. 'I'm in a public building.'

'That's the oldest excuse in the book. Try again.'

'I am!' She took a photograph and sent it to him. 'Now do you believe me?'

'You could've taken that earlier.'

'I didn't.' To prove a point, Frankie accessed the image, took a timed screenshot and sent that too. 'Happy now? And if you're wondering why I have time to play truth or dare, use your imagination. Now put Granddad on, I need to talk to him.'

55

A hefty report landed on Stone's desk with a solid thump. He eyed the first page:

Witness Statement

(Criminal Procedure Rules, r. 16.2; Criminal Justice Act 1967, s. 9. Magistrates' Courts Act 1980, s.5B)

The James
Hutton
Institute

Police Reference	18010071544:	Operation Deep
		Instructing Officer: DCI David STONE
Lab Reference	CFC/9595392/19	Page 1 of 36
Hutton Lab Reference	2019-LAD/022	

Statement of	Lorna Dawson	James Hutton Institute
Age	Over 18	Cragiebuckler
Occupation	Forensic Soil Scientist	Aberdeen
		AB15 8QH

This witness statement, consisting of thirty-six (36) pages each signed by me, is true to the best of my knowledge and belief and I make it knowing that, if it is tendered in evidence, I shall be liable to prosecution if I have wilfully stated anything which I know to be false or do not believe to be true.

Signature   *Lorna Dawson*

Dated 25 June 2019

---

1. Qualifications and Experience

I am an expert in the scientific matters addressed in the statement and I have been requested to provide a statement in relation to the matters outlined. I confirm that I have read guidance contained in a booklet known as Guidance Booklet for Experts – disclosure: Experts' Evidence, Case Management and Unused Material, which details my role and documents my responsibilities in relation to revelation as an expert witness.

I have followed the guidance and recognise the continuing nature of my responsibilities, and in accordance with my duties of revelation, as documented in the guidance booklet.

1. I confirm that I have complied with my duties to record, retain and reveal material in accordance with the Criminal Procedure and Investigations Act 1996, as amended;
2. I have compiled an index of all material, and will ensure that the index is updated in the event I am provided with or generate additional material;
3. In the event that my opinion changes on any material issue, I will inform the investigating officer, as soon as reasonably practicable and give reasons.

I understand that my overriding duty is to the court and I have and continue to comply with that duty. The statement and the declaration required by Criminal Procedure Rule 19.4 (j) is appended to this statement.

Signature   *Lorna Dawson*   25 June 2019   Page 1 of 36

David turned the page. It took half an hour to read and digest all thirty-six pages of the document relating to the soil found caked around the skeletal remains of his unidentified victim, much less time to precis the crucial information it contained into a couple of sentences the MIT would understand. Leaving his office, he entered the MIR and called his team to order for an impromptu briefing. He was in full flow when the door burst open, Abbott apologising to everyone for crashing in. He remained standing, his attention firmly on his guv'nor.

Irritated by the interruption, David handed him the report, a clue as to what he was about to share with the team. Soil sample analysis fascinated David. To the untrained eye, mud was mud. It never ceased to amaze him how, through physical, chemical and biological analysis, scientists could unlock the unique properties of soil samples and narrow down the most likely origin.

'In layman's terms, the soil isn't from fell sandstone found in and around Kielder. It's a different geology altogether.' David consulted his notes. 'Professor Dawson said the samples recovered from the victim contain nutrient additives used in agriculture. They're low in organic matter, sandy in texture and had been limed. So we're looking for an area of arable farming that's been fertilised. The alkane and alcohol profile shows oil seed rape biomarkers in the soil. Apparently, the little black seeds are very resistant—'

'That's all we need,' Charlie, the office manager, moaned. 'Dozens of farms grow it.'

Abbott caught his eye. 'We have a starting point—'

'Not much of one,' Charlie bit back.

'Cup half full,' Dick countered. 'They're scientists, not magicians.'

'Cut it out, you two! I'm not finished.' David nodded at Mitch, who passed copies of the report to everyone. 'The most likely area of origin is the border region. The soil is granite patent material, an arable field that grew cereals and had a Sitka spruce forest nearby—'

'Bored now.' Charlie faked a yawn. 'Sounds like a job for the local boy scouts.'

Abbott glared at him.

Seeing his grim mood, asked: 'Any news from you, Dick?'

'As expected, Scheving's prints are all over the OCG's Audi,' he said. 'Along with Gavin Campbell's and several other well-known dealers. I've passed the info to Police Scotland. Also, I took a call from a motorcyclist who may have information that will help us. The guy's name is Neil Richmond. He was on his way home from the borders on the night before the barrel was found. Short on fuel, he headed to Kielder village where there's a garage open twenty-four hours. He got there at around eleven fifteen and found that it only takes cash. He only had a credit card, so he had to call his wife.'

'Does this story have a point?' David asked.

'It did when I started,' Abbott said. 'Something eating you, guv? First Mitch and Indi, now me. If you tell us what's up, maybe we can help fix it.'

David found Mitch and Indi in the room – they eyed the floor, looking for a hole they could climb into – then refocused on Abbott. It wasn't like Dick to backchat. As for what was eating *him*, the SIO had no clue. David wasn't so much bored with his input as distracted, his mind on other things. Adam English hadn't done anything yet. He would, though. That was the kind of journalist he was. It was only a question of time.

All around the room, officers and civilians were uncomfortable, avoiding eye contact with Dick, all waiting for David to put him in his place.

He hesitated.

Though Abbott had taken the news well initially, he was still raw, pissed off at being knocked back for promotion, finding it hard to accept that Oliver was swanning around abroad while he was stuck in a rut with very little, if any, chance of ever making the next rank. Aware that Bright didn't rate him as highly as her, having recognised the signs in other colleagues feeling undervalued and under pressure, David felt sorry for him.

Abbott was in a bad place.

Then he went too far. 'Do you want to hear what I have to say, or not . . . guv?'

He'd deliberately thrown down the gauntlet, disrespecting Stone in front of the squad. The two men had become close colleagues. Abbott was now out of order. Well over the line. It couldn't go unchallenged. Most SIOs would have jumped on him, some physically. Others would have ordered him out of the MIR. All would have given him a dressing down in front of his peers to let everyone know who was boss.

Detectives held their collective breath, urging Abbott to back off and apologise. He was well-liked in the squad, one of Frankie's besties, a man David had handpicked for the squad when he moved from general CID. Grateful for the posting, Dick hadn't put a foot wrong. Not once. These were mitigating circumstances the SIO took into consideration.

He let it go . . . for now.

'Get on with it then,' was all he said.

No apology was forthcoming.

Abbott carried on as if nothing untoward had happened. 'So, Richmond's wife arrives at Kielder village an hour later, in her pyjamas, none too happy at being dragged out of bed. It's not the first time she's had to come to his rescue. She dumps the gas and takes off. Her bloke fills up, leaves the empty can at the garage, and rides off after her. As he pulls out, he comes very close to a collision with a vehicle he claims had no lights on—'

'Not even dipped?' David queried.

Abbott shook his head. 'The vehicle damn near wiped him out, Richmond said.'

'Time was this?'

'Twelve fifteen.'

'Will Richmond make a good witness?'

'Should do. He's a headteacher, as it happens. Articulate. Nice with it.'

David was intrigued. 'So why are we hearing about this now?'

'Richmond thought no more about it until he saw our appeal for information on the news. Realising that it was the same night he almost came a cropper, he checked his headcam and found blurry footage which may or may not be of use to us. I was intending to follow it up later. Rather than incur the wrath of his missus, I arranged to meet him at a pub not far from his home.'

'You look like you could use a drink,' Charlie said. 'I know I could.'

'Me too,' Pam said.

'Make it a single,' David said. 'And don't hang around. With Frankie away I need you on your game. It's a school night for you too.' Everyone laughed, the tension draining away, Dick's smart mouth forgotten already . . . except by the SIO. 'When this briefing is over, before you disappear, I'd like to see you in my office.'

56

Frankie had moved out of the Harpa Concert Hall. She crossed the main road heading for Reykjavík centre and her hotel, street cover protecting her from the biting wind. It took ages before her paternal grandfather came on the line. As she waited, two images flashed through her mind. One of him sitting warm and cosy in her father's den, a mug of tea in his arthritic hand; the other of a younger man she didn't know, lying on the ground, frosted lashes, blue lips, a schoolboy standing over him: Kristján.

'Where the hell are you?' she whispered.

'Hello?'

It felt good to hear her grandfather's voice. 'Hi, Granddad. How are you?'

'Missing my best girl.'

'Ha! You'd be saying that if Rae were on the phone, I bet.'

'Of course. Your dad said you wanted my help.'

'Do you have time? He told me you were heading home soon. I don't want you to miss your bus.'

'Don't worry about that,' her father butted in. 'I'll take him.'

Frankie didn't have a lot to smile about, though her father's perpetual curiosity made her giggle. She might have known he'd have put the phone on speaker so he could earwig the conversation she was about to have. He hadn't left his enquiring mind or thirst for knowledge at the door of HQ when he retired after thirty years in the force. He took it home with him, along with his most prized possession, his warrant card.

Her grandfather was even worse.

On this occasion that suited her. With almost ten years under his belt with Northumbria Police by the time construction work began at Kielder in 1975, he might have insight to share. 'Granddad, if you're with Snoopy' – Frankie's nickname for her old man – 'then you'll be aware of the incidents my squad are dealing with. I'm sure he's relaying all the gossip.'

'Don't blame your dad, pet. You can't turn on the telly, listen to the radio or open a newspaper without hearing about it.'

'So I heard.'

'Is that why you wanted to talk?'

'Yes, and what I have to say goes no further. Dad, that goes for you too.'

'That's a given,' her father said.

Frankie would trust either of them with her life. 'We have reason to believe that one of the victims was murdered in the mid-seventies, give or take a few years. It only just occurred to me that Granddad was stationed at Bellingham at the time.' She raised her voice slightly. 'Have I got that right, Granddad?'

'Correct. I was a probationer from 1966 to '68, spent four years in Newcastle, then transferred to Bellingham nick in '72, which is when your nan and I moved there.'

'When did you leave?'

'End of 1980.'

'Your shift covered Kielder, right?'

'It did . . . everyone was moved out in 2014, long after I retired. Like a lot of others, the building was sold off.'

'You were there during the construction of Kielder Water?'

'I was.'

'Can you remember what it was like when the diggers moved in?'

'Pandemonium . . .'

His croaky voice was lost on the wind which had suddenly changed direction. It was affecting the quality of the sound on Frankie's mobile. Asking him to hold, she walked around the corner to shelter in a closed shop doorway.

'Sorry, I didn't catch that. Can you repeat?'

There was a moment of confusion at the other end, then a frantic whisper from her father to son. 'What did I just say?'

Her grandfather was obviously racking his brains and getting nowhere.

'It's fine,' Frankie said. 'Don't worry, it'll come back to you.'

Another pause, another whisper. 'Tell her. She'll think I'm past it.'

'He wants you to know he's not gaga.' Her father could never be serious.

'I know you're not, Granddad . . . Dad, I'm not so sure about. He forgets things all the time.'

'She's right.' Her father chuckled.

'What did Granddad say then, know-all?'

'He said he'd never seen anything like it when the diggers moved in.'

Frankie felt sad that her grandfather couldn't recall what he'd said a moment ago and yet fifty years presented no difficulty. There was nothing to recommend getting old. You could get specs for failing sight, aids for hearing loss, false teeth to replace those you'd lost, a toupee if you went bald. There was sod all you could do about memory loss.

She didn't dwell on or draw attention to it. Instead, she asked him a direct question, one that would make him feel valued and listened to, without sounding patronising. 'Dad can't help me with this one, Granddad. I really need your expertise. Think of it as unofficial consultancy. No pay. Just the gratitude of your old force. Can you elaborate any on what it was like then?'

He seemed to perk up immediately. 'Feelings ran deep, Frances. Environmental outrage isn't a new concept. There were some memorable clashes between planners and locals, physical and verbal. Families were split apart when loved ones threw in their lot with incomers, finding well-paid employment on the construction site, along with an army of workers recruited from all over the country.'

Frankie hadn't considered council planners. As far as she knew, neither had David. 'That's really useful.'

'Is it?'

'Yes. You said physical and verbal. Were the police involved?'

'Low level. No charges were ever brought. Neither side wanted any trouble. The council needed people onside. They were keen not to antagonise the community.'

'What about after construction got underway?'

'What about it?'

'Were the crews well behaved?'

'In the main. Why?'

'We're keeping our options open. David has a theory that our victim may have been an engineer or manual worker.'

'Wouldn't surprise me.' Her grandfather paused. 'What was that?'

'What?'

'That noise.'

'A text coming through,' Frankie said. 'Hold a sec, I might have to run.'

She examined the screen. Emil was a man of few words. **Can't get thro. Call me.**

'Listen, I've got to go. Thanks, Granddad. Speak soon. You've been really helpful. You too, Dad. When I pass this on, I'm certain David will be in touch.' The line went dead and she keyed in Emil's number. Before he answered, she was on the move. 'Emil, speak to me.'

'I called in on Kristján's father. Given your Skype call, he wasn't expecting me. He was resolute. Hadn't seen his son. Didn't particularly want to. I have no reason to disbelieve him. My search of the area was fruitless. No sign of Kristján here in Ísafjörður. I have good news though.'

'Tell me.'

'Remember the medical student, Helga?'

'What about her?'

'Concerned that we were looking for Eva, she called Jacob. When he realised that Eva hadn't been staying at her place as planned, he got worried and started quizzing her. The two girls are the best of friends. He figured that if anyone knew where Eva was hiding, Helga would. It turns out he was right. Eva's aunt owns a summer house. The girls stayed there once without asking. Their little secret.'

'Great job, Emil!' Frankie picked up the pace, keen to find Anna.

'It explains why the two girls haven't spoken since she returned home,' Emil said. 'I'll text you the address. Oh, and you should know there's no phone at the cabin. I checked. No activity on either Kristján or Eva's mobiles since they were last seen in Reykjavík. Unless they switch them on again, Helga can't warn them you're coming.'

57

Clicking the end of his ballpoint with his thumb continually, David reflected on what had gone on in the MIR. He was disappointed. No, angry. Expecting more from the man he'd appointed as temporary 2ic in Oliver's absence. Abbott's antics were unacceptable. The promotion board had made the right choice. He wasn't a patch on Frankie Oliver. She may be arsy on occasions – for good reason – but she was fiercely loyal. Had never, would never give him grief outside of the privacy of his office. Even then, it was never personal.

The tap on the door was hardly audible.

Abbott stuck his head in. 'You wanted to see me?'

'I do.'

The detective sergeant looked sheepish as he entered the room and closed the door behind him. He approached David's desk and stood to attention – hands behind his back, feet slightly apart, shoulders straight, chin up – like a rookie in uniform who knew he was about to get a tongue-lashing from a senior officer. If he was expecting to be offered a seat he had another thought coming.

Throwing his pen down, David held his gaze. 'Mind telling me what all that was about?'

'Guv?'

'Don't play games. You know damn well what I'm talking about. When I asked if there was a point to Richmond's call, it was said in jest. You took it the wrong way. Explain yourself.' When Abbott failed to respond, David carried on. 'You think you can take a swipe at me and get away with it?'

'I wasn't—'

'Yes, you were.' David crossed his arms, eyes firmly on the DS. 'If I choose to have a go at any member of this team, it's no business of yours. *If* I ask you a question, you don't ask one back. *If* you have something to say, you bring it to this office and we talk man-to-man, otherwise you and I are going to fall out. You never, *ever* bad-mouth me in front of the squad. Is that clear?'

Swallowing hard, Abbott offered a grudging apology.

'That's better. Now sit your arse down. You and I need to resolve this.'

'That won't be necessary, guv. I was out of order—'

'Sit. Down. And don't tell me you're fine, because clearly you're not. You can drop the pretence. I've been watching you. You're struggling. Ask around. Anyone who cares about you knows it. And before you ask, none of the squad has said a word to me. They have your back, as you have theirs. Now, apart from the obvious, do you have a problem I'm not aware of?'

'No, guv. I'm gutted, that's all.'

'Dick, I'm not stupid. I know what the next rank meant to you—'

'Do you . . . really?'

David wanted to tell him that he'd been there too. He hadn't. From DC to DS, from DS to DI, DI to DCI, he'd been promoted at the first time of asking. 'Look, it's not as if you've come in for scathing criticism. I can assure you, there were no such comments made. It just wasn't your time. That's all there is to it.'

'They said that two years ago—'

'Christ sake! It's old news. If moaning about it would alter the decision, I'd say fill your boots. It won't. And I have neither the time, nor the inclination, to play nursemaid. You need get over this fast and move on.'

'I have.'

'If you had, we wouldn't be wasting precious time having this conversation. You cannot allow this setback to affect your work. We're dealing with a two-hander. I need you. The team needs you. Off your game, you're fuck all use to us.' David could see that his words had hit home.

Abbott sat there, a ball of pent-up emotion. Closed off. His mouth a thin white line, his jaw sharp enough to slice bacon. Giving a resigned nod, he was about to open up when a knock at the door stopped him, the interruption coming at the worst possible moment.

'Not now!' David yelled.

Over Abbott's shoulder, Mitch could be seen through the glass. He shifted his weight from one foot to another like a kid who desperately needed to use the bathroom. He wasn't going anywhere. He wanted in. And yet seemed terrified at the prospect of entering the room in the middle of what he'd worked out was a reprimand. He'd rather run naked through HQ.

And still he persisted.

David glared at Abbott. 'Is this your doing? If so, ten out of ten for effort. Distracting me isn't going to work, Dick.'

Abbott looked over his shoulder, then at the SIO. 'Nowt to do with me, guv.'

'If I find out that you put him up to it, yours will be the shortest period of acting up in the history of the force.'

'Like I said.'

'Fair enough . . .' David had never known Abbott to lie. 'But I'm warning you, quit sulking or we *will* have that conversation. You have options: suck it up or ship out. To be honest, the way I feel right now, I couldn't give a shit either way. This is your call, so I suggest you go away and think about it.'

'I'm sorry. It won't happen again.'

David flicked his eyes towards Mitch. 'Let him in on your way out.'

Abbott hightailed it.

As the door swung open, David was conscious that the MIT had downed tools, all eyes on Abbott. Exchanging a worried look as they passed each other, Mitch crept into the office, red-faced and sweaty. There was something going down his angry SIO wasn't going to like.

'Sir, I'm sorry to interrupt—'

'What is it?'

He cleared his throat. 'The Detective Chief Super is on his way in. Before he gets here, you really need to see this.' He handed over a newspaper. The frontpage headline was a public relations disaster:

DUMB WAYS TO LIE: meet the Northumbria cop with more secrets than #thedeep

58

As soon as Emil had put the phone down, Frankie stepped up her pace, keen to reach the Major Crimes Unit as quickly as possible. By the time she reached it she'd devised a plan which involved going out on a limb, doing something that would never appear in a murder investigation manual or any other rule book – in Iceland, the UK or anywhere else for that matter.

Stopping short of the entrance, Frankie sheltered in a doorway and took the opportunity to call her old man. She wanted his take on what she had in mind and said as much when he picked up, only he was acting like he hadn't heard a word of it.

She'd heard a soft humming sound. 'You in transit?'

'Yeah, driving your granddad home.'

'Can you call me when you drop him off.'

'He's already dropped off – can't you hear him sending the zeds up? I can hardly hear myself think.'

Frankie smiled, pictured her grandfather hanging like a bat from his seat belt, probably tired after her questions earlier. Finally, she conjured up the courage to make her father listen. It came as no surprise to him that the call was work-related. In the middle of a big case, it usually was. He'd taught her everything she knew and he loved that she valued his opinion above all others.

She had never needed his wisdom more than she did now.

It took a while to offload, but once she'd got going it came pouring out of her, a stream of doubt she couldn't stop. 'All the evidence is pointing in one direction. It's screaming at the top of its voice that Kristján is responsible. David's convinced of it. But I'm not – not yet, anyway. I believe the kid lied to us. I believe he hid the tent. I can't explain the blood on his towel. I think he may be covering for someone else and that someone might be Eva. Until I know for sure, there'll be no arrest.'

'Sounds like you're on top of this.'

'Really, Dad?' Frankie wasn't sure.

'Lead investigators have latitude,' he said. 'What exactly are you up to?'

'You won't like it . . .' She took a deep breath. 'I'm planning an informal interview . . . with both of them . . . together.'

'Bold move—'

'Is that a euphemism for suicidal?'

'I didn't say that.'

'You didn't have to. I can hear it in your voice.' Frankie glanced up at Anna's window, wondering if she'd be cool with her plan. Whether she was or not, that was the way it had to be, the only course of action that Frankie thought might work.

'So long as you're sure it's the right thing to do, Frank—'

'Dad, I've never been surer of anything in my life. The only way I'll get them to talk is to put them in the same room to answer questions.'

'You've run it past the Northern Rock?' Her father often referred to David by his nickname.

'You're 'avin a laugh,' she said. 'He'll hit the roof when he finds out—'

'Not if you're right.' Nothing fazed her father. 'Look, ordinarily suspects should be questioned separately—'

'Yeah, state the obvious, why don't you?'

'Will you shut up and listen?' He didn't wait for an answer. He knew he wouldn't get one. An apology? Forget it. She was seeking reassurance. 'The word "ordinarily" was a hint, Frank. There are exceptions to every rule, times when you have to step outside of protocol to get a result. Some suspects would rather die than tell us what they know, especially when a loved one is also in the frame. Eva's motive is a strong one. Let's face it, she went AWOL with Kristján for a reason.'

'Yeah, most probably to buy them enough time to get their story straight.'

'Exactly. If you question them separately, they'll say what they've agreed on and never deviate. I've known offenders I could keep apart for ten years and they'd never rat on each other under interrogation. Their truth is whatever they've decided it'll be.'

'Thanks, I needed that. Being at odds with David has knocked me for six.'

'It happens,' her father said. 'My lot had a guy locked up for murder once. He'd been detained and interviewed. The victim was tied up. Everything pointed at the boyfriend. The couple were into bondage. We had videos of them having sex together. We found her tights in his house and a whole lot more besides. My guv'nor was so convinced of his guilt he'd booked the police club to celebrate. I was the only dissenting voice. My head told me he'd done it. My heart said otherwise.'

'And had he?'

'No. We caught the right guy eventually.'

'Well, I don't think Eva is a killer either. I just think they're holding back.'

'Maybe they're both protecting someone.'

'Maybe.

'Hold your bottle, Frank. Believing in yourself isn't easy. If you think your colleagues are wrong, stick with it. Find the proof and present it to them. Have your joint interview. Sit these kids down and be honest with them. Who knows, if you bash their heads together, they might cough to what they know, assuming they know anything.' Her father chuckled. 'It always worked with you and Rae.'

Frankie's laughter didn't last. 'If you're wrong, those wise words could have me dismissed.'

'Sometimes you have to fly solo. I trust my gut, Frank. Do you?'

She sidestepped the question. 'If David asks, we never had this conversation.'

'What conversation?'

She bloody loved her old man.

59

Bright was furious that a deeply personal and traumatic event involving one of his SIOs was being splashed over the front page of a national newspaper to titillate their readership. The fact that it was happening in the middle of a two-hander – which itself was drawing global press attention – and was suggesting impropriety involving Stone and Oliver was objectionable. The Head of CID hadn't arrived at Middle Earth to moan or remonstrate with Stone.

He'd come to offer support.

'Keep your head down and make no comment if approached,' he said. 'I'll deal with English.'

'Good luck with that,' David said. 'Excuse the cynicism, guv. It took months to shake him off last time—'

'If he wants war, he'll get war.'

Rarely had David seen his boss this agitated. 'I appreciate your support, sir.'

'I will not have Oliver arriving home in the middle of a shitstorm unprepared. Give her the heads-up before her old man does. You concentrate on what you have to do and leave English to me. Got any restraints I can borrow? He's not going to like it.' Using forefinger and thumb, Bright spread the Venetian blinds on the internal window and peered into the MIR beyond. 'Look at this lot. You'd think they had sod all to do.' Letting go of the blinds, he turned to face David. 'I will not have this garbage derailing the investigation. Is that clear?'

'It won't, guv.'

'When's Frankie back?'

'Couple of days, maybe sooner.'

'She's making progress?'

'Always.' By no stretch of the imagination was that a dead

cert. Stone kept the faith with Frankie. 'I should have something to report later.'

'Glad to hear it. It's probably as well you're here and she's over there for the time being.'

David was angry. He didn't care if it showed. 'For the record, there's no truth in the rumour, guv.'

Bright threw him a disparaging look. 'When has the truth ever got in the way of a good story? There's more at stake than the investigation or your unblemished personnel record. I will not stand by and allow English to tarnish the reputations of detectives I have time for. I will crush this cockroach under my size tens to protect my department and the wider force, even if it means dragging him into court.'

Without another word, the Detective Chief Superintendent gathered up his belongings and stormed out. It didn't surprise David when his boss pulled up sharply outside his office door, scanning the curious faces of the Murder Investigation Team, finding Abbott's desk.

David knew what was coming.

'Dick, what's going on?' Bright barked.

Abbott looked confused. 'Nothing, sir.'

'That's what I thought.'

The head of CID didn't need to tell the MIT to get on with their work. Like wind-up toy soldiers, every detective and civilian in the room simultaneously began moving to the same drumbeat, reaching for phones, inputting data into HOLMES 2 – the second-generation Home Office Large Major Enquiry System – feeding the machine with completed actions. Mitch and Indira were knee-deep in paperwork. Still no hit on their missing person.

Not even close.

With Bright on the warpath, and a story circulating that they didn't understand, the MIT were understandably restless. Apart from Wells, Ben and Frankie, few people knew why David had left the Met. Not one to bare his soul, he'd kept it to himself. If not now, then later, his team would be googling everything English had ever written in order to get the lowdown on his history. David didn't blame them. It was in their nature to be curious. When the time was right, he'd tell them – assuming the man Bright had dubbed 'the cockroach' didn't do it first.

In the privacy of his office, David called Frankie to warn her. The line was engaged, so he called Anna. She told him that Frankie was on her way in. Emil had received a tip-off, a location where they might find Kristján and Eva. Finally, some good news for David to hang on to.

Bright would get his update after all.

60

The operation to trace Kristján and Eva had been well worked out by Frankie with the help of the major crimes team. When the DCI arrived at her office, the two consulted Google Earth and other maps. The target property was no more than a recreational hut on the outskirts of Hafnarfjörður. It was situated within a peaceful nature reserve and therefore unlisted. The name meant harbour fjord, according to Anna. It was a little over eighteen clicks from Reykjavík, twenty-five to thirty minutes by road according to Jacob, Eva's father. He'd been on the other end of the line for the past five minutes. Anna had put him on speaker so she could change into something more appropriate than a suit. Without batting an eyelid, ignoring Frankie like she wasn't in the room, the Icelandic DCI began to strip off.

'The cabin is inaccessible except by car,' Jacob said. 'I can show you.'

Frankie was shaking her head: *not a good idea*.

Anna zipped up her skinny jeans. 'No, Jacob. I'm sorry, but I can't allow it.'

'I insist,' he said. 'Eva will know I told you where they are. You have to give me the opportunity to explain—'

'That's precisely why you need to stay put.' Pulling on a sweater, ruining her hairdo in the process, Anna slipped on a pair of heavy-duty boots – and still the man begged to go along. 'Jacob, stop! This is going to be bad enough for Eva without you interfering. Detective Sergeant Oliver is keen to keep this as low key as possible. Trust me, these things are best left to us—'

'You won't hurt her?'

'No, of course not. As soon as we've located them, I'll call you.'

Accepting that, albeit unwillingly, Eva's father rang off.

Anna finished lacing her boots and stood upright. 'You ready?'

Frankie was already halfway out the door.

The police convoy set off at a pace, Anna and Frankie in the lead vehicle, three officers in two other cars, eight in total. Overkill, in Frankie's opinion. She kept her mouth shut. She'd offered to take the wheel, but Anna insisted. The DCI opted for a squad car, she knew where she was going, and the livery would pave the way if traffic slowed. Frankie stared out of the window, unable to imagine a traffic jam here.

Twenty minutes in, they left the main road. Anna issued an instruction over the radio for her team to kill their sirens and to wait for her stop signal. Her plan was to pull up short of the property and proceed on foot, a silent approach. Nothing was to jeopardise the element of surprise. The questioning of one definite murder suspect and a possible co-conspirator was a big deal in Iceland.

The wooden summer house was as dilapidated as Jacob had described it. Surrounded by wildflowers, it was no bigger than a shipping container. Painted black, it was one storey high with a corrugated iron roof and a weathered wrap-around balcony to raise the structure off of the moss-covered lava field. It had seen better days. Frankie was in love as she lay on the ground peering through a pair of binoculars.

She could spend time here.

Anna kept her voice low. 'I can't see anyone.'

'Me either,' Frankie said.

The radio crackled. 'In position. No rear exit.'

'One way in, one way out works for me,' Frankie said. 'Hold your positions. I'm going in.'

Anna looked at her, wary. 'Alone?'

'Yes alone.' Frankie made a crazy face. 'He's not a seven-foot two Viking who might rip my arms off. Guilty or innocent, he's a frightened kid who needs reassurance, not a tooled-up assault unit. Going in heavy-handed might spook him into doing something stupid.'

'That's what I mean. Eva is in there too.'

'You think he might take her hostage if he sees me? He won't. Trust me, I've seen the way he looks at her.'

'OK, yell if you need backup.'

'Just keep your lot out of sight.'

Jumping up, Frankie walked towards the timber hut. Stepping up onto the decking, she tapped on the door, dislodging a flake of peeling paint. Silence from within. No movement. There was someone inside. She could sense it. The potent smell of cannabis was a big fat clue. Maybe they hadn't heard her. She knocked again.

'Kristján, Eva, it's Frankie Oliver. Open up, please. We need to talk.'

Nothing.

She raised her voice. 'C'mon, you two. Stop buggering about. I know you're in there. I have questions. They need answering.' She half-expected them to come charging out of there and attempt to leg it. 'Look, you can talk to me or local police if you prefer. They're here too. In case you were wondering, that's not a threat. I've asked them to stand down for the time being. I know you'll do the right thing. Believe it or not, I'm trying to help you. I need you to tell me what you know, all of it.'

No answer.

She put her ear to the door.

There was movement inside and frantic whispers.

Frankie eyed a plant pot on the windowsill, its contents wilted long ago. A free-standing barbecue stood on the decking beneath it, a set of rusting tools hanging on hooks beside it: a fork and a set of tongs, relics from a happier time. She tried the window. The grey net curtain was too thick to see through. As she stepped sideways, Anna emerged from the trees. Frankie lifted a hand, a gesture to prevent her coming closer.

The DCI retreated.

The wonky old door handle seemed to grow in size the longer Frankie stared at it. With their phones off, Kristján and Eva had no way of knowing she'd turn up with or without her Icelandic colleagues. Instinctively, Frankie knew the cabin would be unlocked. The hut was so far off the beaten track, the likelihood of a stranger calling was equally remote. Something heavy, possibly metallic clattered to the floor. More whispering inside. Unsure of what was going on in there, Frankie decided to act. Glancing over her shoulder, she held up her hand, gesturing to the others to remain where they were. She was going in alone.

61

Abbott had arranged to rendezvous with his witness – the biker, Neil Richmond – at the Robin Hood, a pub off the old Military Road, around thirty-five miles from their Wallsend base. To get away from the depressing atmosphere in the office, and to build bridges with Dick, David pocketed his mobile, grabbed his car keys, then followed him out into the corridor and down the stairs in order to accompany him. Despite all good intentions on David's part, Dick didn't engage much on the journey west. With English on his mind, that suited the SIO to a T.

When they arrived at their destination, a red Ducati was in the car park, its owner easily spotted in the adjacent beer garden. He'd commandeered a picnic bench. Dressed in leather pants and a Dainese T-shirt that was wringing with sweat in a V-shape down the front, Richmond may as well have been waving a flag to attract their attention. A colour-coordinated jacket, helmet and gloves had been unceremoniously dumped on the benches at either side, a hint that the seats were taken. Most of the tables were full, the fine weather bringing everyone out for a ride in the countryside.

Abbott identified himself, introduced David, then took off to find three non-alcoholic drinks for them.

'Would you rather go inside?' Richmond asked.

'I'm fine out here.' David took off his jacket and tie, undoing the top button of his shirt. He nodded toward the Ducati. 'Nice wheels.'

'Thanks. You ride?'

'Not for a while.'

'Miss it?'

'What do you think?'

'Yeah, daft question.'

While Abbott was away, witness and investigator did what all bikers do. They discussed the UK's best roads, the most amazing scenery they'd seen on two wheels and yes, the inevitable close encounters with death. They had no common acquaintances. David's motorcycling days coincided with his career in the Metropolitan Police. In no time, the two strangers had formed an invisible bond.

Richmond lifted his sunglasses onto his head, wiping a thin film sweat from beneath his eyes. Though it was getting late, the temperature didn't seem to be falling any. He looked like he might expire at any moment. He was knackered. Since the school bell rang, he'd been out riding, he said.

Typical petrol head, David thought.

Richmond was not particularly tall. Not particularly young either, though with the means to treat himself, the attitude to live life to the full, irrespective of the danger. All sports were risky, some were deadly. David's parents had been killed climbing Glen Coe when he was six years old. Had it made him ultra-cautious? Not a bit. If anything, he'd gone the other way.

His career had certainly had its moments.

Other than looking out for his team, David had never considered the risk of anything he engaged in, though he was forced to slam the brakes on when Richmond began talking about the vehicle he'd seen and his near miss at Kielder.

'Hold on,' David said. 'We can't discuss that—'

'Isn't that why we're here?' Richmond glanced at his Ducati. 'Hey, I'm in no hurry. I just thought you might be. Is Abbott having a quick pint, do you reckon, or brewing his own beer in there? I'm clamming for a drink. Tap water will do.'

David turned his gaze to the rear door of the pub with no idea what was keeping Dick. 'I'm sorry, we'll have to wait. He was the original call-taker. It's important he's here.'

'In case I change my story?'

In the nick of time, Dick Abbott appeared, ending their discussion.

Waiting for him to join them was a bit more complicated than Richmond had suggested, though he wasn't too wide of the mark. Dick may not have been put forward for promotion, but he was nobody's fool. Having received the biker's information over the phone, he'd briefed the MIT verbally, without writing it down, realising that it might be crucial to the investigation. It was a good move. If Richmond's eyewitness testimony turned out to be pertinent to the case, a defence barrister might challenge any ambiguity between a contemporaneous note of a telephone conversation and a formal witness statement taken later. Stone and Abbott wanted the same thing, the option of writing down the information in one hit before Richmond added his signature.

'Pub's heaving . . .' Abbott swung his leg over the bench, placing three pints of fresh orange juice at the centre of the table, apologising for the delay. 'Didn't even have time for a piss.'

Four suntanned girls spilled out of the pub's rear door into the beer garden; one carrying her strappy sandals in one hand, a bottle of pink fizz and four glasses in the other, two mates following on behind. The last one to pass their table gave Richmond the eye, ignoring both detectives.

Seeing the exchange, Dick grinned.

Richmond gave him an eye-roll.

Dick laughed. 'Not even tempted?'

'You kidding? I have pupils older than her.'

'Must get myself some leathers,' Abbott joked.

'Get yourself some sense while you're at it,' David said bluntly.

If Abbott was trying to wind him up again, he was out of luck. English had beaten him to it. Anything Dick might say or do would pale by comparison. Ignoring him, David refocused on Richmond, asking him a series of questions, essentially going over the statement he'd already given over the phone.

The biker communicated with the fluency worthy of his English degree. When he finished speaking, Dick gave a nod to David, confirmation that the biker's recollection hadn't changed any. There was no point asking if the vehicle that almost mowed him down was diesel or petrol, or if it sounded like a bag of hammers as it shot by. With his helmet on, the only noise he'd have been aware of was his own engine and the blood rushing through his ears.

'Dick said you downloaded the headcam footage onto a thumb drive,' David said.

'Yeah, I brought this along so you could see what I've got.' Pulling an old MacBook Air from his backpack, he slid the thumb drive into the USB port, then pushed the computer across the table to David's side. 'Didn't think you'd want to view what I've got in a crowded pub. That's why I sat out here.'

'And there was me thinking it was to keep your eye on your Italian dream machine.'

Richmond beamed proudly, a hint of embarrassment, eyeing the Ducati as a father would a child. It might not have blond curly hair and big blue eyes, but the sports bike was beautiful, sleek and sophisticated. In design and performance, it was unrivalled, an opinion he'd shared with David while they waited for Abbott to reappear.

Abbott shuffled closer so he and David could view the footage together.

'It's not great,' David said. 'That's not to say our tech guys can't enhance it. I'm afraid I need the headcam too, Neil.'

Reluctantly, Richmond handed it over.

'It's an expensive piece of kit,' he said. 'Make sure you return it in one piece.'

Fifteen minutes later, before the signature ink was dry on his statement, all three stood up and shook hands. David had warmed to Richmond from the off. When you'd been a detective for as long as he had, you got a sense of who you could trust. In the short time they had known each other, the biker had come across as genuine and reliable. Abbott was right, if called to testify at court, he'd make an excellent eyewitness.

62

Calling out that she was coming in, Frankie turned the handle and pushed open the door. It swung inward, a wide arc, the sun flooding in with it, exposing the whole of the cabin's interior. She moved inside, leaving the door open to avoid panicking Kristján and Eva and to give Anna direct line of sight. There wasn't much furniture to speak of, four collapsible camping chairs, a small table covered in crap – cigarette ash mainly, sandwich crumbs, empty bottles. There was a blow-up double mattress at one end of the room, two rolled-up sleeping bags on top, a few items of clothing – and absolutely no place for the two kids to hide.

They were standing together in front of a small fire, totally busted, their faces pale and guilty. Frankie detected no fear in Kristján, just a shedload of distrust. Due to the dope she'd been smoking, Eva was totally chilled.

An object on the floor at their feet took Frankie's attention. Tarnished, possibly iron, hexagonal in shape, she didn't immediately recognise what it was. She wondered if this was what she'd heard clatter to the floor when she was standing outside a moment ago. Curious, she stooped down to pick it up. It was a calibration weight of 200 grams, the measurement recessed into the object. Turning it over, Frankie saw that it had been used as an ashtray for years.

The smell of weed almost knocked her out.

She raised her head, hard eyes on Eva. 'I never figured you for a fool. I thought you wanted to be a doctor.'

'I do.'

'Well, you're going the wrong way about it.'

Eva tipped her had back, a dirty look: *That's my business*.

'What do you think your dad would say if he knew about this?'

You didn't need to be a genius to see that the message had filtered through to Eva's addled brain. She leaned against Kristján, squeezing his arm so tightly it turned her knuckles white. She could hardly focus, let alone think or speak.

Frankie held up the ashtray. 'Good move to bin the roach ends in the fire. I wasn't joking when I told you that Icelandic police are outside. You realise you can kiss goodbye to your dream career if—'

'No!' Kristján cut her off. 'The dope is mine.'

'A simple blood test would prove you wrong,' Frankie said. 'Kristján, if you continue to lie to me, I will have you both arrested. Is that what you want to happen?' She paused, allowing the information to sink in. 'No, I didn't think so. I don't want to ruin Eva's potential to join the medical profession, or your plans either, so I suggest you both sit down and answer my questions truthfully.'

63

David received an email seconds before he and Abbott arrived at Middle Earth. As was always the case, whether or not the victim was identified, every forensic report began with a unique reference number to ensure that there was no accidental mishandling of information that might lead to a wrongful conviction. The document in his inbox related to the skeletal remains found by Kristján and Eva.

He didn't notice the security barrier lifting, allowing them into Northern Area Command HQ, but felt the vehicle decelerate and then stop.

He swore under his breath.

Misreading the situation, Abbott selected reverse gear. 'Sorry, guv. Didn't think you'd be going anywhere for a while.'

'I'm not.' As the car moved backwards, David looked up. Abbott had pulled up behind his vehicle, effectively blocking him in and was now trying to correct his mistake. They were talking at cross-purposes.

'As you were,' David said. 'I was talking to myself, not having a dig at you.'

'I'm happy to find another space.'

'No, leave it.'

Abbott pulled forward, killing the ignition.

He nodded toward the mobile in David's hand. 'Bad news?'

A nod. 'Hair sample lifted from the crucifix doesn't match our victim's DNA exactly.' David's mood improved as he read on. 'Actually, it's not as bad as it sounds. There's a familial match. Maybe the crucifix was an heirloom, as we thought. There the story ends. The profile isn't on our database.'

'Want me to run it through Interpol?'

'Yeah. We might get lucky.'

David opened the car door.

'Guv?' Abbott swivelled in his seat, his right arm resting on the top of the steering wheel. 'Before we go in, I want you to know that the guys are right behind you. They've all seen this drivel in press. Can't be easy to deal with, for you or Frankie, on top of everything else. I'd like to apologise for being a twat earlier. I had no idea what you were dealing with. Would a pint after work do it? I could murder a Tyneside Blonde.'

David laughed.

The beer did exist, brewed on the banks of the Tyne, though the joke was well past its sell-by date. 'You're on,' he said. It was good to see Abbott in a better frame of mine. 'On one condition . . . We don't talk about English.'

'Done.'

A second email arrived.

David checked his mobile. Another result, same sender, different victim. This one gave him pause for thought.

Dick noticed his hesitation. 'What's wrong?

'The Blonde will have to wait. Frankie raised an action to find the beer can Kristján alleged Scheving cut his finger on. The search team found it in a bush not far from where his body was pulled from the water. The blood found on the rim was usable DNA. A positive match. It seems Kristjánsson was telling the truth—'

'What else could he do?' Abbott mocked. 'The evidence was irrefutable. I wouldn't pin any medals on him. Guv, he lied through his back teeth about everything else, categorically denying Scheving's presence at the campsite on the night he died. You don't doubt his guilt, surely?'

'I dunno, Dick. It doesn't feel right.'

'In what way?'

'Why would a bunch of new graduates, with bright futures in front of them, lie to us because Kristján asked them to? He didn't strike me as someone with the capacity to exercise that level of power. Quite the opposite.'

'He could be playing you.'

David stared off into the middle distance, wondering if the lad was playing Frankie too. They had both interviewed their fair share of split personalities: mild-mannered on the one hand, ruthless on the other. Skilled liars all of them, until hard evidence forced them to alter their stories.

'Not one of the ten came clean at the first time of asking,' Abbott reminded him. 'I assume they have now?'

David nodded. 'Anna confirmed it.'

'There you go then. One of them took Scheving out.'

'Frankie's not convinced it was Kristján.'

'We have nothing on the others.'

'She thinks we're missing something.'

'Seriously?' Abbott's expression was scornful. 'What we're missing is a trick. How much evidence does she need? Scheving's blood was at the campsite *and* on Kristján's towel. Kristján's dabs are all over the camping equipment PolSA found dumped at Gordon's Wall. All ten of the happy campers legged it as soon as Mitch let them go. I could accept one or two of them cancelling their trip, but all of them? No, the only reason they'd decamp en masse is because they had something to fear. Kristján admitted asking them to lie. Does that sound like the actions of an innocent kid to you?'

'Just what I told her.' David felt the need to defend her even so. 'She's right to exercise caution. Nothing wrong with giving a suspect the benefit of the doubt. She'll come to the right decision when she's ready and not before.'

'What other explanation could there be? Her initial impression of Kristjánsson was a negative one. We talked about it. If she's changed her mind, she needs to change it back PDQ. If my opinion counts, Kristjánsson should be behind a cell door already. And, for the record, I'm not trying to score points, guv. I've known Frankie since she was a young 'un. I'd do anything for her, you know that. I'm not saying anything to you that I wouldn't be prepared to say to her face. She's not often wrong. I think she is this time.'

64

On the journey from Reykjavík to the isolated, rundown cabin, Frankie had switched off her phone to avoid interruptions. In an attempt to stop the inner narrative driving her insane, she'd employed a relaxation technique she'd learned years ago under hypnosis. Shutting her eyes, she'd taken deep breaths, imagined herself walking down a flight of stairs. At the bottom was a gate, a rubbish bin beside it. One by one, she dropped her worries into it: her fight with David; her heart-to-heart confession to Anna; all thoughts of her upcoming promotion; her grandfather's increasing memory loss; her fear of failure.

Even Joanna would be left behind on this trip.

As if by magic, the cotton wool inside her brain thinned out, like the early morning mist she'd encountered when she arrived at Kielder Water at the beginning of her investigation, allowing her the space to concentrate on one thing and one thing alone. She was now in the moment, facing two youngsters whose lives would irrevocably change depending on how they handled themselves in the coming hours.

She had to be careful with these two.

Kristján was making a brew. Eva was slumped in one of the camping chairs, dark glasses shading her eyes against the glare of the low sun. Frankie sat down opposite, her back to the door, not a stance she'd ordinarily take. It had been drummed into her to face the entrance in every situation, a position that gave her the upper hand, a prime location where she would spot trouble approaching. Today was the exception. Icelandic police had her in their sights.

A shrill whistle startled her.

She eyed the boiling kettle, Kristján standing beside it.

Maybe the threat was on the inside.

Removing the whistle from the spout, Kristján turned slowly, glancing over his shoulder to check on Eva. She looked sad, not frightened. He wished he could scoop her up in his arms and run. Oliver was no longer blocking the doorway, no longer standing, he noticed. She was, however, staring in his direction, a curious look on her face he couldn't readily identify. Turning his back on her, he glanced out of the window at the barren landscape. Was there really a surveillance team watching the hut, Detective Chief Inspector Jónsdóttir and her crew?

The big guns.

Or was Oliver bluffing, a way to get him to talk? He only had her word that someone was out there. Maybe she'd come alone. Kristján might be emotionally weak but he was physically fit. If he had a mind to, he could be out the door before she got to him.

Where the hell would he go?

That was the question he was asking himself. It was five kilometres to the nearest bus stop. Even if he reached the main road without being spotted, a roadblock could stop every form of transport heading into Reykjavík. Police would be watching his flat round the clock. He was unwelcome at his old man's house. He had no papers. He was trapped with limited options. That didn't mean there were none.

Frankie looked on as Kristján's right hand gripped the kettle like a vice. He didn't move for what seemed like ages. When he turned around, he must've been blinded by the steam that clouded his specs – the lenses were semi-opaque – and yet he appeared to be staring straight at her. All seeing. She couldn't read him and that freaked her out.

A ghost walked over her skin, a creeping sensation. Her scalp tightened. Breathing slowed. Heartbeat quickened. Despite the sun on her back, the temperature seemed to plummet to minus zero. She raised her arm, her fingers grazing an old injury to her forehead as she swept hair away from a sweaty brow.

The sensation caused a flashback.

Frankie ten years earlier. In uniform. A newly promoted custody sergeant. A police cell. A sinister expression on the face of a young man Kristján's age. He was staring too. Perfectly well behaved one minute. Cold and calculating the next. Dark eyes. Lights out. Perceptions skewed. She hadn't known at the time of his arrest that he'd been diagnosed as suffering from schizophrenia. He flipped, scaring her.

Scarring her.

Frankie brought her arm down.

Where was David when she needed him?

65

As well as clarifying exactly what biker Neil Richmond had and had not seen during his near-miss experience on the C200, taking time out with Abbott had helped clear the air. The detectives' informal review of the Scheving case in the car park at Middle Earth had given David reason to believe that one half of his double-hander might draw to a close before too long. His text to Frankie was short: **Beer can found. Blood analysed. Positive match. Report in your inbox!**

He waited.

No reply.

He sent another, more explicit than the first: **Update required.** He may as well have texted, *where the hell are you?*

Still no reply.

Frustrated, he accessed his contacts.

Anna's number rang out for a moment or two before the connection was made.

'Hi!' she said. 'How nice to hear from you so soon after your departure from our shores.' Her words didn't fit her tone.

He assumed she was busy or in a meeting, unable to talk.

'Excuse the interruption. I've been trying to contact Frankie. She's not replying to my texts and I wondered if you knew where she was—'

'You're making a habit of this, aren't you?' Anna didn't mince her words. 'In the spirit of international cooperation, I offered your force every assistance. Unless you know something I don't, I've not been demoted to Frankie's lapdog, or yours either. She's incommunicado. I'm sure she'll call you when she's able.'

Her abrupt manner surprised him. They were getting along

fine when she lifted him to the airport. 'Is there something bugging you, Anna?'

'You are. Why do men always expect women to be on the end of a phone?'

'I was worried—'

'Did Frankie ask you to worry?'

'No.'

'Do you reply immediately if you're busy?'

'No—'

'Well then, her phone is most likely switched off. I did tell you she was acting on a tip-off. She's still with the suspect.'

David wasn't sure he'd heard right. 'She?'

'You expect me to babysit her too?'

Shit! Frankie had gone in single-crewed.

'Clearly, she did not discuss her interview strategy with you.' Yawning, through sheer boredom at having nothing to do and irritated with the Englishman, Anna lifted her binoculars to her eyes. Frankie Oliver hadn't moved. She was still seated, facing Eva. As the college student wasn't speaking, Anna assumed that Frankie was. Though if that was the case, she wasn't one for hand gestures. She sat perfectly still, perhaps listening intently to Kristján's responses. She was definitely not writing them down. Perhaps recording them on her mobile, ignoring her boss on purpose. The young graduate was not in Anna's eyeline, though she'd seen him at the window a moment ago. 'I'm looking at her right now as it happens—'

'You're not with her?'

'Not physically, no. She asked me to give her some space. She's flying solo, David. It may interest you to know that everything has gone according to plan. No fuss. No arrest. Nice and easy.'

'No arrest?'

'The way she wanted it. I like her style. She's not going to jump until she's taken the suspect carefully through each and every piece of evidence and given him the opportunity to set the record straight. I'm sure you approve of that method.'

'Of course. Taking young people into custody should never be done lightly.'

'Then let her do her thing. She knows what she's doing. We're not on the clock. From what I can see, Kristján and Eva are eating out of her hand. This is Iceland. Everyone is chilled here.'

Kristján was jumpy. Acting odd. His hands shaking. He couldn't keep them still. Looking for signs that he might flip, Frankie had to remind herself that he was not the unfortunate young man she'd been thinking about a moment ago. A kid who, at the time of his arrest, was in fact experiencing a psychotic episode, hearing voices, fixated on the idea that the police were out to get him. His illness had brought him into contact with them on too many occasions for displaying behaviour likely to cause alarm and distress to others. He'd assaulted her, but the lad was ill. She couldn't let a negative experience throw her off course. She couldn't afford to show fear.

If that should ever happen, she may as well resign.

Frankie had come to find Kristján with the express intention of leaning on him until he came clean. That was still her mission. It would not be easy. He'd told so many lies, some of them convincing. They would be difficult to unravel. Aware of that, he may even have formed the impression that she was pissing in the wind. She knew different. As David had pointed out, she had her smoking gun. The hard evidence the MIT had uncovered was indisputable. It gave her a starting point. More than that, it gave her leverage.

The kid would discover that soon enough.

Kristján seemed to sense her growing confidence and it triggered an immediate reaction. Frankie recognised the fight or flight mechanism even before it had entered his head. He was displaying all the classic signs of anxiety – which made him highly unpredictable.

This was not good.

His eyes flicked to the open door, then beyond.

'Don't do it,' she said. 'You won't get ten metres.'

'I wasn't going to—'

'You were thinking about it.'

Eva raised her head to look at him: *were you?*

It was the first time the girl had moved since Frankie entered the cabin, the first time the two young lovers had looked at or spoken to one another. There could only be one reason for that. They had argued or one or both of them was in deep shit. When Eva turned to face Frankie, the DS expected her to do one of two things, deny that either of them had done anything wrong, or plead Kristján's case for bludgeoning a young man to death.

She did neither.

Frankie was ready to do her job.

She needed Kristján to explain the evidence away, piece by incriminating piece, in minute detail. The interview she was about to conduct couldn't happen any other way. It would be against everything she stood for to give a credible suspect an escape route. She couldn't lead a witness away from a potential life sentence. If he'd murdered Scheving, Kristján deserved to be punished. He was going to have to dig himself out of this one. If he decided to run, then so be it. He'd have to get past her first. How bad could it be if he overpowered her? She might have to take another one for the team, but she'd be fine. Anna had her back.

David heard the radio transmission as distinctly as if he'd been standing next to Anna. Spoken in Icelandic, it was incomprehensible, but he was used to auditory warnings. Like all emergency service personnel, he understood the language of urgency. It wasn't so hard to interpret cues that something major was going down. Though the male controller was calm, the intonation in his voice, the clipped dialogue, the speed at which he was transmitting messages to Anna, and vice versa, were all clues. Particularly telling was the pitch of her voice – a voice David knew and could compare with normal speech patterns.

'Anna, what's happening?'

She was breathless, as if she'd taken a punch to the gut. 'There's been a massive explosion—'

'Explosion? Where?'

'Not far from here. Multiple casualties. Suspected arson attack. All emergency personnel have been deployed.' She mentioned a place name he didn't recognise and would never be able to pronounce. 'I can't talk now.'

'Wait! What about Frankie?'

Anna was already gone.

David panicked.

The transmission was now muted where it had been clear. He imagined Anna on autopilot, slipping her device into her pocket as priorities changed. He could hear rustling. She'd forgotten to disconnect. She was running now, shouting orders, probably pulling her units out, telling everyone to fall back, redirecting some to the scene of the fire, others to hunt for the arsonist as directed by operational command. Events like these were unprecedented in a country proud of its low criminality.

David dry-heaved.

'Anna? ANNA!' Yelling at her was useless. If she couldn't hear him, she wouldn't answer. Not now, or ever. David heard further instructions. More voices. Other units joining the channel. Checking in. Moving out. All of them conveying a sense of urgency, an unfolding crisis their only priority, no one in any doubt that the imperative was to get a shift on. As they moved toward the danger, David imagined the danger moving towards Frankie.

'No!' He thumped his fist on the desk.

'Guv? You OK?'

Stone wiped his face with his hand. He had no words.

'What is it, guv?'

'Not now!'

The loudest voice in David's head was now British. It belonged to the detective standing in the open doorway, the DS who'd failed his promotion board, whose mouth was no longer moving, but hanging open.

When they had talked earlier, Dick had planted seeds of doubt in David's head. Now they began to grow; a warning that Kristjánsson was not only an accomplished liar but a Machiavellian-type character, astute and conniving, possibly unstable, who thought that the end justified the means. Add to that equation a propensity for violence that was off the scale, the distinct possibility that a detective had been left with little or no cover in Iceland, one unbearable scenario trumped all others. Northumbria Police could be shipping Frankie home in a box.

66

Every detective and civilian in the MIR had witnessed David's outburst. Yelling at anyone – never mind his Icelandic opposite number – was out of character. When Frankie's name was mentioned they were understandably worried. He had some explaining to do. Abbott thought he'd be better off doing it away from Middle Earth but David wasn't having that. He couldn't allow the MIT to end their shift with imaginations in overdrive.

Guesswork would drive them nuts.

Now in control, he kept his explanation light. 'Apologies, everyone. I overreacted, so if Dick is hoping to fill a vacancy he needn't hold his breath.' Nervous laughter, including from Abbott. 'I lost it, OK?' David lied. 'It's all this shit with English. I haven't time to explain it now. I will as soon as we put this case, or should I say cases, to bed. In the meantime, all I ask is that you don't believe everything you read in the papers.'

It was as good an excuse as any but all around the MIR faces were grim.

'When do you expect to hear from Iceland?' The question had come from a weary-looking Mitch. Frankie was his friend and mentor. She'd taught him everything he knew – and some – and made it fun along the way. He'd be completely devastated if anything untoward had befallen her. He wouldn't be alone.

She was more popular than overtime.

For the umpteenth time, David checked his mobile. Nothing new. He looked up, addressing them all. Using humour to hide his concerns hadn't worked. What he needed to do now was reassure them. 'I've put a call in to their incident room. Anna is an astute woman. Explosion or not, I'm sure she won't have left Frankie exposed. Anna said she's playing a blinder over there. Go home before your families no longer recognise you. Get some kip. We have an early start in the morning.'

For a moment, no one moved.

No one spoke.

Abbott chipped in with support. 'You heard the boss. As soon as we hear from Frankie, you'll be the first to know. By the way, not a word to her father. We don't want him worrying unnecessarily. Now, go on. Get out of here before we throw you out.'

David nodded his appreciation to Abbott, then sent Wells a text – **Our second office. Fifteen minutes?** – then put his phone away.

The squad were packing up now, tidying desks, shoving mobiles in pockets. Scooping up car keys, they bundled through the door, down the stairs and out of the building with David and Abbott bringing up the rear. There were rumblings of discontent on the way out. Frankie's dad was mentioned. There wasn't a detective alive who wanted to have that conversation with a man who'd already lost one daughter.

A reply from Wells: **See you there.**

David had one priority, to sink a few with Wells.

Frankie planned to keep it simple. To concentrate on Kristján, given that the evidence appeared to implicate him and him alone. She didn't dispute how he'd come across the barrel. Now she knew that the victim inside had been dead for thirty years before Kristján was even born, that was irrelevant. What she was after was information on Jón Scheving. A murder victim who had no one to speak for him. No one who gave a damn that he was stone cold in a freezer in the Newcastle morgue.

'Kristján, are you ready to talk to me?'

The lad's nod was slight, unconvincing. He handed Eva a mug of coffee and sat down.

Frankie turned her mobile on with the intention of recording the interview. Ordinarily, she'd have had a notetaker, a

DS or DC to write down responses contemporaneously so as not to interrupt the flow of questions and answers. Her device sprung to life with a deluge of notifications: emails, texts, missed calls and voice messages. All of them she discovered were from David.

Damn it!

Unable to ignore so many attempts to contact her, she stood up. 'I'll give you two a moment alone.' She moved towards the open door. Before she reached it, she turned. 'Kristján, I won't lie to you, you're in a lot of trouble. Do yourself a favour and think about that while I make a call.'

A flash of emotion in his eyes: anger, resentment, resignation? All three? Hard to tell. Frankie walked out onto the decking, hoping that he'd come to his senses. He was an intelligent lad. He must see how futile it was to lie to the police over an incident serious enough to take away his liberty for a very long time.

It wasn't a bad strategy to let him stew.

The chilly air made her shiver, though she was grateful for the midnight sun. So late and yet so light. The lava field was like a lunar landscape. She thought of texting Anna to have her crew stand down until she'd finished her interview, then decided against. There was little chance she'd get her way and – despite her doubts over guilt or innocence – every chance that Kristján might incriminate himself, at which point she'd have to stop the interview, have him formally cautioned, arrested and taken into custody.

Only Anna could do that.

Scrolling through her emails, Frankie clicked on one with the subject line: **Fwd: Beer can analysis. Submission date: Sunday, 23 June 2019. File number: D1/12897/19.** It had been sent to the SIO from the forensics lab. Confirmation of a definite match between blood taken from the can and Jón Scheving. Proof that Kristján had been truthful about something, albeit under immense pressure to do so from her boss. A second email contained the short statement of a witness, Neil Richmond, a motorcyclist who'd spotted a suspicious vehicle shortly after Maria Colman did. Finally, things were coming together for David – and for her too it seemed.

Right on cue, another text lit up the screen: **Still with us? I'm dying here. D x**

A kiss?

Frankie smiled at the informality. Her charismatic SIO was like a lot of Geordie men, a soft as clarts. At this hour, he'd probably had a beer or two. They were more friendly than most SIO/2ic pairings. It was nice to think that he cared. Quickly, she replied, giving no details he could argue with. Just enough information to keep him sweet. What else could she possibly say until after she'd spoken at length with Kristján and Eva? Frankie's dad was right. If those two came across, as she hoped they would, her unorthodox approach would be forgiven. Adding a kiss of her own, she pressed send.

Behind her, the old decking creaked.

The rotting wood beneath her feet moved very slightly as pressure was applied to the plank of wood she was standing on by someone heavier than she was. It was a creepy sensation. Silently, someone was moving towards her. Closer, then closer still. Quickly she scanned the landscape expecting, hoping, that Anna would see her reaction and show herself.

She didn't.

67

For a Tuesday night, Revolution was crowded. Wells had spread herself out in their usual booth. Only a fool would ask to join her. She'd eat most of the guys in there for breakfast. She had a pint waiting for David. As he walked towards her, he felt a slight vibration against his chest. Dejectedly, he checked the screen . . . About time. He'd never been so relieved to hear from anyone in his life. No call, just a short text from Frankie: **Apologies for the silence. Been off-grid looking for Kristján and Eva. Now located. A-OK this end. Anna has my back. x**

Anna has my back?

Christ! She didn't know.

He replied: **Utilise your backup. Do not, I repeat, do not—**

Deleting the text, he tried again: **Are they playing ball?**

He pressed the backspace key. The text disappeared. He couldn't do it. Frankie would wonder why he was asking and read between the lines. The question was bound to unnerve her. He couldn't afford that. Telling the squad that he was under stress and overreacting wasn't entirely fabricated, though he couldn't deny, even to himself, that he was preoccupied with English. Besides, Abbott could be wrong about the threat Kristjánsson posed. Frankie was an experienced copper. She could handle herself.

Couldn't she?

Frankie swung round to find Kristján standing there. Her heart almost stopped. Barefoot, he'd sneaked up behind her. He was staring at her, inscrutable. His eyes shifted across the lava field and back again. It occurred to her that he might be checking for local law enforcement. Ordinarily she could recognise the signs if suspects were about to do a runner . . . or worse.

She was about to find out.

Her confidence took a dive.

David had overheard some of her team gossiping in the bait room at Middle Earth, talking about the suspect, talking about her, some of the opinion that she'd lost the plot. He'd given her the heads-up, a warning that she was making herself unpopular. She'd shrugged it off, told him she didn't need him to draw her a picture, but now her mind was racing, adrenalin pumping through her veins.

Had she underestimated Kristjánsson?

Where the fuck was her backup?

'Sorry if I startled you,' he said.

'You didn't.' He had.

It had been a long, exhausting and emotional day. Frankie was strung out, far from home. Far from David. Had she made a mistake? Had he been right about Kristján all along? Had Dick and the rest of the MIT? Mitch was the only one who saw him as no threat, but as the evidence piled up, even he'd changed his mind recently. Was she too blind to see what was staring her in the face?

Was Emil's wobbly wheel about to come off?

Wells was stunned to learn that Frankie might be in grave danger, more concerned than she was letting on to David. As an investigative journalist, she'd stared death in the face herself, but not like this. She thought she'd seen him at his worst, but he was rigid on the seat opposite, face twisted in agony as he called Frankie's mobile, over and over with no response, terrified that he might lose another colleague, another friend, potentially more.

Wells had no words.

Since he'd arrived in the north, a broken man, she'd witnessed his relationship with Frankie blossom, professionally and personally. The detective sergeant had been his salvation. She'd seen into his soul. David had let her in, something Wells had never thought possible. Frankie had feelings for him Wells felt sure were reciprocated, though not yet acted upon by either one. The two women had joked about it over drinks. That conversation had taken place in this very bar, in this very booth, Frankie sitting where David now sat. She'd looked stunning that night and was in a great mood – tipsy, not blotto.

'He's a keeper, Frank. Too hot to be single and life's too fucking short—'

'And face a knock-back?' Frankie waggled a finger from side to side. 'Not going to happen. A career lasts thirty years, a lot longer than the average cop's love life. Divorce is an occupational hazard in our line of work and I'm not dumb enough to fall for it. David and I are mates. What we have is more important to me than a relationship with my boss—'

'Like hell! Who's talking marriage anyhow. Are you nuts?'

Frankie threw her head back, laughing.

'C'mon, what have you got to lose?'

No answer.

Wells placed her hands on either side of her face, her mouth formed into the letter O, feigning *The Scream*. 'Christ! You're not a virgin, are you?'

'No, but don't tell my old man!'

'Ha! Your secret is safe with me. I hope you realise that if you wait for David to make a move, you'll be past it.'

The smile slid off Frankie's face. 'I can't compete with a dead woman.'

Wells sighed, her eyes back on David.

Was history about to repeat itself?

68

On the wrap-around balcony in Hafnarfjörður, Frankie kept her cool. She was trying to second-guess what was going through Kristján's head and what she intended to do should he make his play. She wasn't sure she could take him if he went for her. That's when she saw it, the rusting BBQ fork, hanging on the wall, inches from his hand. As she studied him, he studied her, unblinking.

Despite the plunging temperature, a film of sweat seeped from her brow.

There was a faint whiff of smoke in the air, possibly from the wood burner inside, though none was coming from the cast-iron chimney overhead. Frankie thought that odd. Had Kristján come out to distract her, a diversionary tactic, while Eva set a fire to make an escape out the back? The rotten wood structure would burn through in minutes. With no rear exit, Anna's crew wouldn't be watching.

Kristján took a step forward and finally spoke. 'I really didn't mean to startle you,' he apologised. 'I thought you were on the phone.'

'Not anymore. What can I do for you?'

'We've run out of logs. Eva is cold. OK if I close the door? I didn't want to appear rude by shutting you out. I want to get the interview over with and take her home. I assume you've spoken to her father. He'll be worried.'

His attention once again shifted across the lava field.

Frankie followed his gaze and saw a plume of black smoke in the distance. 'What's that?'

He shrugged. 'Not sure. Are you coming in?'

Frankie relaxed, putting her unease down to exhaustion.

Escorting him inside, she invited him to sit and did likewise.

She got straight to it. 'I'm taping this interview . . .' She switched on her voice-memo app, placing her mobile on the table between them. 'If we're going to get you to Reykjavík tonight, we'd better get on with it. I need to know everything that went on the night you arrived in Kielder. You do understand why that is important?'

Kristján took a long deep breath. 'Yes.'

'Good Now listen carefully, both of you. You may not understand the relevance of my questions. You have to trust that I have a valid reason for asking them. Please answer everything I put to you.'

He answered with a nod.

Eva remained silent.

Frankie began with Kristján. 'I now know that some of what you've told me was untrue—'

He cut her off. 'I'm not guilty of any crime.'

'I hope that's the case.'

'It is, I swear.'

'OK, let's start again then, shall we? Initially, you denied that Scheving joined you at the campsite. You've now admitted that he did – as has Eva.' Frankie glanced at the girl, then at him. 'You told DCI Stone that Scheving was provoking Eva following an argument with her brother. Can either of you tell me what it was about?'

Kristján was shaking his head. 'I wasn't close enough to hear what was said.'

'Eva? Didn't you tell him later?'

'No, I didn't. It was none of his business.' She was pleading with Frankie to leave it there. 'The prick was hitting on me. He wanted to talk. I didn't. He was trying to get me on my own. Aron took offence. End of.'

Kristján corroborated what she was saying. 'Scheving was winding him up, inviting her to sit with him. Aron told him to back off.'

The most interesting part of what Frankie just witnessed

was that non-verbal plea from Eva to leave well alone, proof that Kristján didn't know about the assault upon her. And if he did know, then she hadn't been the one who told him. That appeal for confidentiality wouldn't show up on the tape. Frankie parked it for now and would record it when she wrote up the interview later.

She moved on, directing a comment to Kristján: 'I'd have thought that you'd be the one to square up to him if that was happening, rather than let her brother stick up for her.'

He didn't flinch. 'I told you, I didn't see it. I was looking the other way when I heard the commotion behind me. It was over by the time I turned around.'

So far, so good.

Frankie moved on. 'You gave a statement that Scheving cut his finger on a beer can that evening—'

'He did.'

'I believe you. Our search team recovered the can. It's been forensically examined, confirming what you told us.' The relief on Kristján's face was self-evident. 'You also said that Scheving left the campsite a short time afterwards. Is that also correct?'

The Icelanders were both nodding.

Kristján knew what was coming. She was going to ask the million-dollar question. If she believed his answer, he and Eva would be out of there. If not, Scheving's taunts would reach them from beyond the grave. Kristján felt Eva's tiny hand slide into his. He clasped it tightly, partly to stop it shaking, mostly to let her know that he had this covered. If he had his way, she'd be on her way home soon.

Frankie noticed a definite shift in their demeanour. They were both anticipating what she was about to ask. She decided not to play that game. For the first time in a long time, mostly due to her father's advice, she felt empowered, fully justified in interviewing these two together, convinced that she'd get a lot more out of them that way.

'Scheving wasn't the only person you saw that night though, was he?'

Kristján's eyes widened. 'He was, yes.'

Eva looked at him. 'She's talking about the vehicle in the forest.'

'Oh, that. Yes. Well, obviously someone was driving it. It was dark. We didn't actually see him.'

Frankie let his youthful arrogance ride. 'There are other eyewitnesses who saw a vehicle that night.' She looked at Eva. 'Please let Kristján answer my next question.' She switched focus again. 'Do you recall what time it was when you saw the vehicle and in which direction it was travelling?'

The answers he gave were similar to Eva's, including timing, give or take a few minutes. Was that part of their cover story, a way of throwing a stinger at police, an attempt to slow them down?

'This is very important, Kristján. Could you actually see the vehicle?'

'Only the headlights. It was travelling west.'

'Fast or slow?'

'Fast.'

'Did you see it return?'

'I heard it, not long after we all turned in. I couldn't swear that it was the same vehicle. It sounded like it. It was flying along; I know that much.'

So, there was a return journey. The vehicle had travelled west, then east, heading for Hawkhope. There were only two ways it could go from there, left to Falstone or right across the dam to Yarrow where the witness Maria Colman lived.

'What were your impressions of the vehicle? Can you describe the sound of it? I'm trying to get a handle on make, model or engine type. Was there anything distinctive about it?'

He took a moment to think. 'It wasn't new.'

'Makes you say that?'

'One of its lights was faulty.'

'Sounded like an SUV diesel vehicle to me,' Eva interrupted. 'My father owns one.'

Frankie remembered seeing a Ford Expedition parked on her parents' driveway. This was progress. It gave her the courage of her convictions to push on with the joint interview, even though David would disapprove.

'Was Scheving with you when you first saw the vehicle?' she asked.

'Yes,' Kristján said. 'He left straight after.'

Time to deliver the sucker punch. 'When did you next see him?'

'I didn't.'

'That's not true though, is it?' Frankie waited. 'Kristján, you're not helping either of us by telling lies. Stop pissing about. Don't you realise that I'm giving you the opportunity to set the record straight? The alternative is arrest, detention and possible extradition to face charges in the UK. I know a lot more about this enquiry than you think. And a damned sight more about you.'

'He's not lying. None of us saw Scheving again.' Eva met Frankie's gaze defiantly. 'You're picking on him because you see him as the leader of our group. He organised the fucking trip. That doesn't make him a criminal mastermind.'

'And yet he asked everyone to lie.' Frankie switched focus. 'Isn't that so, Kristján? And they all threw themselves off the cliff when you said jump.'

'I didn't kill anyone.'

'You've been questioned by police before though, haven't you?'

He looked accusingly at Eva.

She sent him a silent message: *I didn't tell her.*

69

'Finding your grandfather's body must have been awful for you.' The image of the old man's frozen corpse disturbed Frankie. 'I hate to dig up your past, but you were found out, Kristján. You weren't on the way home from school that day. When police realised that you weren't where you should've been, where you told them you'd been, how did you expect them to react? I'd have thought a lad of your intellect would have learned a valuable lesson. And yet here we are. You've lied again—'

He looked away.

'Nice one,' Eva said in his defence. 'Can't you see how upsetting this is for him? His father can barely look at him. Police poisoned his mind against him. How many more times do we have to tell you that we didn't want to be associated with Scheving? Some of us saw what happened to Kristján last time. Why do you think we lied when he asked us to? It's called loyalty—'

'Misplaced loyalty,' Frankie corrected her.

'This is persecution!' Eva spat the words out.

'No, Eva. Kristján brought this on himself, you all did. If you'd opened up, we wouldn't be having this conversation. Every violent death has to be investigated by police and coroner. Same goes with a sudden death. Local police had to be sure that his grandfather's death wasn't suspicious in any way. It's our job to ask questions. You must see that.'

Kristján turned to face her. 'I do and I've paid the price.'

Eva wasn't finished. 'Have you any idea what it's like having someone you love doubt you?'

'No,' Frankie said. 'I don't lie to those I care about. Honesty has its advantages.'

Kristján looked at Eva.

Frankie caught the distrust in both of them before they had time to hide it.

They had argued.

He wasn't supposed to know about the assault on Eva, though Frankie suspected he might. She wondered if Eva had her doubts about him and vice versa, not that they would ever admit it publicly. Having opened a deep wound, Frankie fully expected them to put the shutters up. Surprisingly, Kristján had more to say. He knew she wouldn't stop pushing until he told her everything.

'When I woke up that first morning, I went for a walk,' he said. 'I took my pictures and swam. Eva joined me. We found the barrel and called you. That was all true. When I returned to the campsite, the first thing I noticed was Scheving's tent. It was empty. I panicked.'

That was more like it. 'Why?'

'He'd been away for hours. He was off his face when he left us. With no compass to guide him back to camp, I thought he'd done us all a favour and lost himself in the forest. It occurred to me that he'd fallen into the water by accident or OD'd on the shit he was into. It scared the crap out of me. I knew that if he was found, dead or alive, you'd link him to us. Rather than face more police attention, I hid his tent. It was a stupid thing to do. I regret that now.'

Time to turn the screw. 'Is there anything else you'd like to tell me about that night?'

'Like what?' Eva was staring at Frankie, daggers for eyes. 'Do you seriously think that someone too weak to send Scheving packing is capable of murder? You're off your head—'

'Calm down,' Kristján snapped. 'You did!'

Eva blushed. 'I never accused you of anything—'

'As good as.'

'Don't yell at me! This is her fault, not mine. Can't you see, she's driving a wedge between us.'

'Eva, that's enough!' It suited Frankie that they were at each other's throats. She changed tack, ignoring the girl in favour of Kristján. 'You wanted Scheving out of the way, didn't you?'

'No, yes . . . not in the way you mean.'

Frankie crossed her arms, leaning back in the chair. 'My colleagues in the UK have a theory. They think you found out that he'd done something you couldn't live with, something you couldn't bear to let him get away with—'

'What are you on about?'

'I think you know.'

'Then arrest me.' Kristján shot out of his seat, hands balled into fists. 'I've had enough of this shit.' He grabbed his haversack. 'C'mon, Eva. We're leaving—'

'What about you, Eva?' Without moving her head, Frankie's eyes shifted to the girl. 'Did you kill Jón Scheving?'

'That's ridiculous!' Kristján defended her. 'She barely knew him. What possible reason would she have to kill him?'

The pressure proved too much for Eva.

Placing her hands over her ears, trying to kill the noise, big blobs of tears rolled down her cheeks, staining her face with mascara. Her sobbing stopped her boyfriend dead in his tracks. To look at him, Frankie couldn't believe he was faking it. If she was reading him right, he had no clue about the subtext.

'I'm so sorry, Kristján.' Eva caved. 'She knows.'

'Knows what?'

'I had motive.'

'What?'

Eva lost it then, a wail escaping from deep within. She told him about the assault by Scheving, blaming herself for bringing the police to his door, and for not confiding in him earlier. Leaning across, he embraced her, stroking her hair as she cried on his shoulder, trying to soothe her.

'Why didn't you tell me? I'd have got rid of him.'

Pulling away, she stared at him: *did you?*

Her reaction startled him. 'I didn't mean it like that. None of this is your fault, Eva. Detective Oliver is right. The only one to blame here is me. We wouldn't be in this mess if I'd come clean.'

'Now's your chance,' Frankie said.

He hesitated.

'Fuck's sake, Kristján. You're the prime suspect in a murder investigation. If you have more to give, however irrelevant it might seem to you, I want to hear it.' Frankie palmed her brow, feeling like a monster for having forced Eva's hand. And still he didn't speak. 'Fine!' She snatched up her phone. 'I've had enough of your bullshit. You're out of time.'

'No, please,' he pleaded. 'Noises in the forest woke me that night. I can only have been asleep a few minutes. I wasn't sure if it was wildlife or Scheving returning to the campsite. I heard a splash, I thought he'd fallen in, or one of my friends was taking a late-night swim. In our country, open-water swimming is a way of life.'

Finally!

Was this the barrel or Scheving going into the water? Frankie wondered. The person responsible for putting them there wouldn't be aware of an illegal campsite nearby. 'Did you investigate?'

'I tried. It was pitch-black. I found nothing.'

Eva's expression was blank, eyes front. Either this was the first she'd heard of his walkabout that night, she'd chosen to keep it a secret or he'd asked her not to reveal it. Was she responsible for that splash? If she knew anything, she wasn't about to share it.

Frankie refocused on Kristján. 'The splash you heard, was that after you saw the car?'

'Yes.'

'Think carefully. Was it before or after you heard it come back?'

'Before.'

'You're sure about that?'

'Positive.'

Such an innocent face.

It was easy to believe him, but was he giving Frankie the runaround? Holding his gaze, she went in for the kill with one last question she didn't really want to ask. 'Can you explain how Scheving's blood came to be on your towel?'

'What? That's impossible. It can't have been!' Comprehending the implication, yet baffled by it, his eyes found the floor. Eva turned to face him, a terrified expression. When he raised his head, his face was pale and gaunt, his attention firmly on Frankie. 'I can't answer that question. I have no explanation to give.'

70

Fresh off her flight, Frankie made her way through Glasgow airport's passport control and out into the main concourse with the intention of finding a taxi to take her to the city's central station. From there she'd hop on a train to Newcastle. With any luck, she'd make the two thirty and would be on Geordie soil by five. No sooner had the thought entered her head than her step faltered. David was standing beyond the barrier in the arrivals hall. With so much on his plate, this was unexpected, a nice surprise.

She walked on, a big smile developing.

Tired and strung out, he didn't return the gesture as the gap closed between them. He seemed conflicted. Dumbstruck. Unable to move. Unable to speak. Whatever had brought him here, whatever was on his mind, he wasn't ready to share it.

'Not even a hello?' She hadn't told him she was coming. 'How did you—'

'Anna told me.'

'Feeling guilty, was she?'

'What other choice did she have, Frank? That explosion trumped your operation. There were many casualties—'

'Yeah, I could have been one of them.'

'You can't have it both ways. If you choose to go in single-crewed, that's on you.'

Frankie kept her mouth shut. She'd left Iceland hoping that word wouldn't reach him that she was on her way home and, to be fair to Anna, she hadn't specifically asked her not to tell him that she'd broken ranks by talking to Kristján and Eva alone. That was a conversation for later.

'Miss me?' she said.

He took her bag. 'Missed your cheek. What's with the fat lip?'

'Scheving's father thought he'd rearrange my face.' Running the tip of her middle finger over the healing scar, she changed the subject. 'Can I buy you a coffee?'

He glanced at the nearest café. 'I'd rather get going. If we're quick about it, we'll miss the worst of the traffic and make the six o'clock briefing. If we have time, we can stop on the way.'

'Fine by me.'

'Unless you're desperate?'

She was. 'A hit of caffeine wouldn't go amiss.'

Searching his pocket for change, he held out an open hand, a few pound coins. 'Get yourself one to go.'

On the road, David asked for an update. Leaving out the fact that she'd ignored the rulebook, playing fast and loose with interview protocol – *like he didn't know exactly what she'd done* – Frankie filled him in on developments. He listened carefully as she spoke about the mystery vehicle the MIT were keen to identify, adding more eyewitness accounts, narrowing the time frame and the journey it may have taken through the forest and on to Kielder Village – assuming it was the same vehicle seen by other witnesses. Kristján and Eva were now in Reykjavík. Anna had been briefed. She'd retain their passports for the time being.

So far, so good.

David glanced into the passenger seat. 'You're satisfied that Kristján and Eva are innocent, because if that's the case, prepare yourself. The team think differently.'

'So you keep telling me. Look, pissing them off is the last thing I want, but it doesn't make them right.' Frankie swivelled in her seat to face him. 'Kristján gave a credible explanation on all points, bar one.'

'Which is?'

'I won't lie to you. He was stunned when I told him we'd found Scheving's blood on his towel.' She held up a hand, cutting off his objections. 'I know we have hard evidence against him. I also know that his bewilderment may have been a reaction to a nail in his coffin. I watched him like a hawk, David. The kid was scared stiff.'

'Of course he was—'

'No, he wasn't faking, neither was his reaction stereotypical. If he'd been guilty, he'd have fabricated a story to explain it away. He didn't even try. He just sat there, unable to comprehend what was going on.'

'And Eva?'

'Same. She thinks I'm a shit for picking on him.'

An angry blast of a horn made David pay attention to the road ahead. Traffic slowed. A potential problem outside of the car. It was the one inside that worried him most. Decelerating, he dropped a gear as the red brake lights up ahead became more intense, the cars in front swerving to avoid debris in the outside lane. He followed suit, changing lanes twice, destabilising the vehicle, apologising for throwing her around the car like a rag doll.

'Shit!' His eyes were on the rear-view mirror. 'That mess almost wiped out a biker.'

Frankie glanced over her right shoulder, relieved to see that it hadn't.

He caught her eye as she turned back. 'Sounds like you've made up your mind which way to jump—'

'I'm here without a prisoner,' she said boldly. 'In case you missed it, that was a big fat clue. If it turns out I've made an arse of myself, I'm sure you'll let me know. You obviously have reservations.'

'I trusted you when I left you in Iceland. And I trust you now.'

71

Frankie had expected condemnation, not acceptance. Last night, when Anna had finished dealing with the arson, she'd called to explain why she'd pulled out her troops, tipping her off that David had been on the blower, worried about her. He wasn't happy to learn that she'd gone in alone, less so when he realised that an emergency had given Anna no choice, leaving *her* with little cover. Was that the reason for his preoccupation when Frankie arrived, why he'd chosen not to mention it, leaving her to bring it up? Whoever coined the phrase drawing blood from a stone must have known him.

As the miles flew by, Frankie's farewell to Anna at the airport replayed in her head:

'Thanks for everything, Anna. You've been amazing and I'm proud to know you. You must come and visit me?'

'At Middle Earth? Will there be Hobbits?'

'I'm afraid not.' Frankie smiled. 'I meant at home, in Amble.'

'I'd love that.'

'Bring pastries.'

'I will! Good luck, Frankie.'

After she'd embraced Anna and watched her drive off, Frankie felt sad. It never ceased to amaze her how policing could bring two strangers together in a very short space of time. Having worked on many cross-border investigations, she'd felt this way before, only to lose touch, though she vowed not to allow this one to get away.

In Anna, she'd made a friend for life.

David's voice pulled her from her reverie.

'I spoke to Frank on the phone last night,' he said.

'Which one?'

'Your granddad. As you said, he was waiting for my call. I

wanted his take on the development of Kielder Water. He said the seventies were bleak but also uplifting—'

'Not if you were a resident of Plashetts—'

'True. He told me that the community stuck together, fighting to retain their homes. Many believed the reservoir would prove to be a costly white elephant. The march to progress won out in the end. I'm not saying it wasn't tough on those who had no choice but to accept it.'

'How did he seem to you?'

'Fine . . .' David pulled into the outside lane, accelerating. 'Why?'

'I'm worried about him. He's showing signs of dementia.'

'So will we at his age.'

'Not funny. Haven't you noticed him getting worse lately?'

'No, not really.'

'He is. He's perfectly lucid one minute, off on a tangent the next.'

'Isn't that an Oliver trait?'

Frankie threw him a dirty look.

'I don't think you have anything to worry about,' David reassured her. 'When you ask someone to cast their mind back fifty years, it's natural that they remember all sorts. Places they visited. People they knew.'

'Did he?'

'Yes. Ever heard of the mine called Seldom Seen?'

'No.'

'A pal of his worked there. Frank said the place name was a bit like you. Unless you wanted something, then he couldn't get rid of you.'

Now she laughed. 'I suppose we all stray off the subject now and then. You're not just saying that to make me feel better?'

'No, he enjoyed the craic and so did I.'

'Did he talk about my old man?'

'A lot. I probably know more about him than you do.'

'I doubt it.'

'Did you know he was into glam rock?'

She turned to look at him, eyes wide.

'Thought not. We forget our parents were young once.'

Frankie felt sad. Passing before their time, his parents would never get old.

He didn't dwell on it. 'How about your mum?'

She laughed. 'As a teenager, she was desperate to run away to Laurel Canyon in search of Crosby, Stills and Nash.'

'Did she make it?'

'No. Her dad wouldn't let her go. To this day, she never forgave him.' A pause. 'Bloody hell! Listen to us. What were we talking about?'

'I was about to move on to mispers,' David said. 'Your grandfather looked after his fair share in his day. Things were done differently then. The longer the disappearance, the higher up the scale the case would go until all enquiries were exhausted. Investigations were never closed.'

Frankie frowned. 'Isn't that what we do now?'

'With small children and the elderly perhaps. These days there's less consistency, a team approach. In your grandfather's time it was far more personal. Whoever took the first report continued to supervise the case. It was passed rota to rota, the physical file one officer's responsibility, twenty-four hours a day. Frank had it all to do: family liaison, interviewing known associates, writing up raised actions in longhand.' David glanced at her. 'Did you catch that documentary, *The Yorkshire Ripper Files*?'

'No, not yet.'

'There was that much paperwork, West York's Police had to shore up the floor. That's an extreme example. With state-of-the-art technology we have it easy compared to Frank.'

'Does he remember anyone fitting the profile of our guy?'

David shook his head. 'Nor any workforce accidents that might have accounted for a crushed arm.'

'Any significant fights on the construction site?'

'There were a fair few minor altercations, a case of handbags at ten paces, if that's not sexist—'

'It is. I should report you.'

'The least of my problems.' Before she had a chance to ask what he meant by that, he moved on. 'Asking Frank to recall events going back fifty years was always a long shot. He was delighted to help though. I told him the drinks are on us next time we meet.' His phone rang, interrupting the conversation. Frankie hadn't yet noticed the stack of newspapers on the rear seat. He'd have to tell her about English before they made it to Middle Earth. Pressing a button on his steering wheel, he clicked to answer hands-free. 'Hey, Mitch, what's up?'

'Indira found him, guv.'

72

David floored the accelerator, heading south. It was crunch time, the only opportunity he now had to fill Frankie in on English and his poison pen before they reached their base. He explained that Belinda Wells had tipped him off, warning him of what was likely to be published in the press, all of it libellous and potentially damaging, stuff neither of them wanted in the public domain.

'By us,' he said, 'I mean you and me, not her and me.'

'For a moment there you had me going.' Frankie's smile dissolved. 'She's hardly your type.'

He looked into the passenger seat. 'What would you know about my type?'

'Joking! Anyhow, what's it got to do with me?'

'Not a thing. I'm sorry, Frank. He's already put it out there. He's alleging a power imbalance, claiming that our relationship goes beyond the professional and flies in the face of our code of ethics. He has previous for it. That's exactly what he did after Jane's murder, blaming me for what happened to her, driving her crazy ex to kill her in a fit of jealousy. According to him, you and I are now an item.'

She pressed her lips together, stifling a grin. 'Like that's ever going to happen.'

'This is no joke, Frank. It's about as serious as it gets. Bright is up in arms. He knows there's nothing going on, but it reflects badly on the department, the wider force and us. It's damaging for me because I'm your supervision; for you, because you've just passed your promotion board and are on your way up. Camped out at Kielder, with nothing juicy to write about, English has trawled our social media, including Andrea's and Rae's, even your old man's. He has pictures of us together.'

'He's a slug. Who cares what he's saying?'

'If you sling mud . . .' David left the rest of the cliché unsaid.

'Yeah, yeah.' She waved away his concern.

'I know officers who'll believe it—'

'I know more who'll laugh in their faces.'

David pulled into the nearside lane. Frankie talked tough. She was worried though. He could see it in her eyes. 'You can't make light of this, Frank. It could have serious repercussions. Screwing your way to the top happens in every organisation, including ours. If you're male, you're one of the boys. If female, you're a slag. I can ride this out. You may not. This is a critical time in your career. You haven't yet been promoted and don't need that kind of smear on your character. If you don't believe me, see for yourself.'

Thumbing into the rear of the vehicle, he invited her to read the local and national headlines. A new one had appeared that morning: **THE DEEP: Northumbria SIO's refusal to go on record**

She swore as she skimmed the papers, each headline more damning than the one before. 'This is total garbage. We've done nothing to deserve this.'

'I'm sorry,' David said.

'For what?' She looked at him. 'It's not your fault.'

'Nor yours.'

'You think I give a shit about English? Think again.' She screwed up the copy and tossed it over her shoulder. 'We're squeaky clean. I'm not letting the cretin get away with this and nor should you. What have you done about it?'

'Zilch. Bright's dealing. He wants our focus on the job.'

The minute Stone and Oliver arrived from Glasgow, a brief conversation had taken place with DC Mitchell and PC Sharma. The SIO didn't ask for any further detail. To save time, he asked Mitch to address the squad immediately. The young officer hesitated. Even though he was a detective, Indi less senior – a temporary secondment to the squad – he'd insisted that she take the lead.

'She was the one who found our misper,' he explained.

David showed no hesitation. 'Let's do this.'

As they moved towards the door, Frankie smiled at Mitch. His gesture showed character. Her protégé was growing up. During her service, she'd witnessed detectives of all ranks take the credit for the efforts of others; some who'd signed their names to investigations they hadn't personally been involved in, including hers; some who'd stood on the necks of others in order to showboat in situations like these.

Mitch was bigger than that.

As the four entered the MIR from David's office, Frankie called the team to order. Detectives downed tools and paid attention. A hush descended on the room. The MIR was full to capacity, everyone ready for the big reveal. David, Frankie and Indira remained on their feet, the murder wall behind them, Mitch positioning himself at the front of the room, urging Indi on.

With all eyes turned in her direction, her expression was a mixture of excitement and nervousness. She spoke with the confidence of someone used to the limelight, the brevity of a more experienced officer, the forethought to include the detective who'd generously put her first.

'Mitch and I identified the victim by his fractured arm,' she said. 'His name is Clifford Charlton. And this is where it gets interesting. Adopted as a baby by one-time residents of Plashetts, he's of Italian descent. Formerly Luca Conti. Born 11 November 1947.'

'You've spoken to his adoptive parents?' David asked.

'No, guv. They've since passed away.'

'What's known of his natural parents?'

'Very little. Mitch and I were hoping to meet with the adoption agency, only no records exist. We suspect that it was an unofficial arrangement. A lot of that went on then. According to the file, Charlton-Conti was a loner when he went missing in 1976. The friends that were interviewed gave statements that he'd moved away shortly after construction crews moved in. He was unhappy for two reasons: he hated seeing his valley destroyed, and he was trying to trace his birth mother without success. Enquiries were made on that front. With no official records, nothing came of them.'

'Makes you wonder who didn't want her found.' Frankie glanced at Abbott. 'Any results on the hair sample from the crucifix?'

'Nothing positive. Interpol drew a blank.'

'Why doesn't that surprise me?' Frankie noticed that David was someplace else.

'We need help,' he said. 'And I know just where to get it.'

73

'Great job, you two . . .' David's comment drew a round of applause for Indira. The young aide blushed, receiving a gentle pat on the arm from Mitch as she took a seat beside him. With something important to share, the SIO moved on. 'Up to now, in respect of the barrel investigation, we've been concentrating on the development of Kielder Water, construction crews, how local people felt about having their homes destroyed. Theoretically, it wasn't a bad call. It seemed right for the location and Charlton-Conti's time of death, but there may be another explanation we haven't yet explored.'

The MIT were all ears.

'As I told Frankie on the way here, last night, I had a very interesting conversation with her grandfather.'

The whole squad knew Frank Oliver the first, a legend in his time.

As they stared at Frankie, she stared at David, question marks for eyebrows. 'Glam rock aside, unless I fell asleep, you didn't mention that anything of interest came up during his shuffle down Memory Lane—'

Pam's mouth fell open. 'Your granddad was into glam rock?'

'No, but my dad was . . .' Frankie pointed into the crowded room. 'Stop your sniggering. One word from any of you to my old man and you'll have me to answer to. I'm reserving that pleasure for myself. In fact, I've been waiting for such an opportunity my whole life.' Her comment provoked a further cackle of laughter. Resisting the temptation to join in, she apologised to David. 'You were saying, guv?'

'I happened to mention to your granddad that we'd found a crucifix and its Italian provenance. It set him off talking about the Second World War. Assuming you were paying attention at school, you probably know that Italian prisoners captured in the Middle East were brought to Britain in their droves from 1941 onwards, some to this area. They were used to alleviate labour shortages, particularly in agriculture. Food was a priority. Frank senior told me their clothing was marked to prevent escape. Otherwise they were given considerable freedom. Following the Italian surrender in 1943, thousands volunteered to work the land. Anyway, it brought to mind Professor Dawson's identification of farmland in the borders. Many camps remained active as hostels until around 1948, which happens to be only a year after our man Conti was born.'

'I don't understand,' Mitch said. 'Why were camps used as hostels?'

'To house farmworkers who chose to stay in the UK rather than accept repatriation,' David explained.

Mitch frowned. 'You mean by the men who were held in them as PoWs?'

The SIO nodded. 'Even during the war, they mixed with local people. You can't tell me that they didn't form close friendships. Sexual relationships.' He paused. 'If I'm reading this right, at least one young woman living in the area would've experienced the walk of shame. Find her, and you'll find Conti's birth mother.'

'Walk of shame?' Frankie bristled.

'I didn't put that very well,' David apologised. 'What I mean is, sex was frowned upon if you were single—'

'Yeah, well, intercourse isn't always consensual, especially in wartime. Name me a conflict where that wasn't a thing.' Frankie paused a beat, a thought occurring. 'For all we know, Conti's father may have taken revenge for what British soldiers did to Italian women.'

Indira Sharma agreed: 'There's a possible motive, right there, Sarge.'

'Why would a rape victim keep the baby?' Mitch asked.

'Because women do,' Indi said. 'For what it's worth, I agree with the boss. A walk of shame would happen either way, due to the stigma attached to unmarried mothers. My great aunt had a relationship with a GI during the war. She kept the baby and my great grandmother brought him up as her own. When the family attempted to trace the father, they met a brick wall. The US army didn't want to know.'

'Get on to the national archives and search for Conti,' Frankie said. 'If you find anything, let me know immediately.'

'Will do.' Indi stood up.

Mitch followed suit.

'No, let Indi handle it.' Frankie gestured for him to sit. 'While I was in Iceland, I uncovered some interesting information on the vehicle Maria Colman talked about. Locating that is as important than finding the birth mother. It may ID an offender. You all need to hear this.'

Mitch sat down.

Frankie looked for David's approval.

He gave her the nod to proceed.

Approaching two adjacent whiteboards pinned to the wall, she used a magnetic eraser to wipe them clean before picking up a marker pen from the tray beneath. Across the bottom of one board, she drew two parallel lines. 'Use your imaginations, girls and boys. This is Kielder dam, a distance of three quarters of a mile across.'

On the north side of the dam, she wrote the place name Yarrow, drawing two vertical lines representing the C200, adding the location of Kielder Village at the top. On the south side of the dam, she wrote Hawkhope, drawing vertical lines she marked as the Lakeside Way and, further up, the Belling peninsula where Kristján and his mates had set up camp.

'Now then . . .' She scribbled specific details as she spoke. 'X marks the spot. This is the campsite. At midnight, Kristján, Eva and their friends saw an unidentified vehicle heading west towards Belling at a fast pace on the access road from Hawk-hope, here.' She pointed to the location. 'They described this as a possible SUV, quote, "not new" unquote. A diesel vehicle with one faulty light. At around 0015 hours, Kristján thinks he heard the same vehicle returning, travelling east at speed.'

'Did any of the others hear it?' As receiver, Pam questioned everything.

'No. Everyone else was pissed. They probably crashed out the minute they all turned in.' Frankie waited for Pam to finish taking a note and lift her head. 'OK to carry on?'

A nod, and a reminder from Pam. 'We've since ruled out a forestry vehicle.'

'Yes, and that's important. So, Maria Colman lives here.' Frankie pointed at Yarrow on her diagram. 'At around the same time, she saw a vehicle she couldn't name, though she also thought was a diesel. It was old, noisy, belching exhaust fumes, being driven at breakneck speed. She couldn't be more specific on time. I mean, how long after midnight it was. With me so far?'

Everyone was nodding.

'Then there was Neil Richmond, the final eyewitness. He arrived at Kielder Village at around 2315 hours, only to find that he had no means to pay for gas. His wife delivered some' – Frankie used her fingers as inverted commas – 'around an hour later, so at approximately 0015. He filled up and took off, travelling east, and was almost written off by a vehicle coming the other way. No lights on. Motorcyclists by their very nature are observant. Their lives depend on it. Fortunately, he was wearing a headcam. The footage is now being examined.' Frankie found Abbott in the room. 'Dick, I assume they haven't come back to us?'

'Not yet,' he said.

'Well, having seen the terrain at night, there's no doubt in my mind that the driver, assuming this is the vehicle used to transport the barrel, would have no choice but to use his lights on a pitch-black access road through the forest. At that late hour, under cover of darkness, he or she might have been under the impression that they wouldn't be spotted, ditto on the road across the dam.'

'Thank God he was,' someone muttered. 'Or we'd be nowhere.'

'I suspect there was a fourth eyewitness, over and above Kristjánsson, Colman and Richmond.' Frankie paused for breath. 'I don't think our Icelandic visitors murdered Scheving. I know many of you disagree with me, but I reckon the mystery driver is our man, for both incidents. I think he was seen by Scheving and was forced to silence him.'

'He had a hell of a night then.' Dick couldn't help himself. 'Sorry, I think you're wrong.'

'Noted.' Frankie stood tall, waiting a beat. When no one else argued, she carried on. 'At first I thought that the driver switched off his lights once he reached the C200 to hide a faulty headlight that might be remembered. That doesn't add up though.'

'Why not?' Mitch asked.

'Because it too is unlit. We know that from when the guv'nor and I visited the Observatory. The conclusion I came to was that the headlights weren't switched off until the driver approached Kielder Village, just before he encountered Richmond on his bike, so maybe he's a local man, someone who knew there were private homes there with CCTV. If he was covered in Scheving's blood, he wouldn't want it on tape, would he?' Frankie scanned the room. 'So, what do we think? Is this one vehicle or three?'

'One,' Pam said. 'We should merge them with a question mark.'

'Anyone disagree?'

There were no dissenters.

'David?'

'The timing fits. The driver didn't figure on a group of rough campers violating forest rules, nor encountering a motorcyclist at that time of night. Pam, alert the house-to-house team with details of the vehicle, dodgy lights and exhaust, and lean on the tech team while you're at it. We need an ID on that vehicle ASAP. In the meantime, at the earliest opportunity, we need to speak to Richmond's wife. Kielder village is nine miles from the dam, a drive of around twelve minutes. She must also have seen the vehicle as she drove home. Dick, you're in charge here. Frankie, you're coming with me.'

74

Convening a press conference required careful planning and liaison with the media team beforehand, never more so than while working a double-hander as high profile as the investigations Stone and Oliver were currently dealing with. The MIT had worked day and night searching for the mystery vehicle. With little progress to show for their efforts, morale had plummeted. The barrel case had, if not ground to a halt, then lost its momentum. Everyone knew it, including them.

With no national or international disasters to keep the press busy, hashtag #thedeep continued to dominate, especially but not exclusively on social media. David and Frankie were understandably nervous as they sat down in an empty meeting room to discuss strategy and write a press release.

He wanted no interruptions.

Placing a mug of tea on the table for each of them, Frankie linked her hands behind her head and studied him. Aware that in an hour from now he'd be the public face of the Northumbria force, he'd made an effort to perform that function suitably dressed. In a formal navy suit, white shirt and striped tie, he looked the part. She felt shabby by comparison. He'd been uncharacteristically quiet all morning and that worried her.

Setting his papers down, he whipped a ballpoint pen from his breast pocket.

'Do you have a plan or are we winging it?' Frankie said.

The irony was lost on him. 'That's why we're here.'

'I was joking, David.'

He had his serious face on. 'The upside is, with Scheving's father banged up, his mother deceased, ditto Charlton-Conti's adoptive parents, at least we don't have to experience another gut-wrenching televised appeal for witnesses to come forward by distraught relatives. We have positive news to share. An ID for both victims is a good start. I'm hoping it'll keep the press happy for now.' He stretched his arms toward the ceiling, eyeing her across the desk, rolling his head from side to side to ease his aching neck. 'There are things we don't want made public. I don't intend mentioning the mystery vehicle. That'll tip off the driver that we're on to him. He'll either torch it and go to ground, or hide it where it can't be found.'

'Will you take questions from the floor?'

'Of course.'

'And if English is there?'

'Then he's there.' David blew out a breath. 'Blimey! It's like an oven in here.'

It wasn't as bad as he was making out. If Stone had a temperature, it had nothing to do with what he was wearing. The witch hunt they were experiencing was getting him down. Frankie suggested he lose the suit.

'Yeah,' he said. 'Feels like a uniform.'

Pushing his chair away from the table, he stood up, taking his jacket off as he walked toward the window. On the wall next to it was a line of hooks. An abandoned hanger was dangling from one of them. He hung up his jacket, loosened his tie and undid the top button of his shirt. Pushing open the window, he turned to face her, his expression changing as he saw the look on her face.

He spread his hands. 'What?'

'Aren't you worried about English asking awkward questions?'

'He wouldn't dare.'

'I wouldn't be so sure—'

'Then I might answer, I might not.'

'That's assuming he got through the door.'

'Look, if you'd rather not come, that's fine with me.'

'And miss the opportunity to see the whites of his eyes?'

Frankie grinned. 'You have as much chance of keeping me away as playing for the Toon.' David was a lifelong supporter of Newcastle United Football Club. Like any other kid in the area, male or female, as a youngster he'd dreamed of playing on the hallowed turf of St James's Park. 'Besides, I've never met a snake before. I'd like to introduce myself in person—'

'Keep it professional, Frank. I don't want you running off at the mouth and finding yourself in the spotlight tomorrow.'

'Me?' She put a hand to her chest. 'I'll be the epitome of cool, guv.'

'You'd better be.'

Fifteen minutes later, with his press release in good shape, David got up, retrieved his jacket and put it on. 'If there are any tricky questions, defer to me.'

'Don't worry, I'll keep it shut.' She watched him do up the top button of his shirt, then got up and walked towards him. 'Come here, your tie's not straight.' She adjusted the knot. 'Stand still, man. That's better, can't have you going in there looking like a bag of shite, can we?'

His smile reached his eyes. 'When did you turn into your mother?'

'When I took the job as your 2ic.' Smoothing down his lapels, Frankie could smell his expensive aftershave and stepped away. 'All done. You ready?'

'As I'll ever be. Actually, I have an idea. I need to make a call. See you in the conference room.'

Frankie turned to go.

'Frank?'

She glanced over her shoulder. 'Yeah?'

'Whatever I say in there, go with it.'

75

Frankie watched David enter the packed conference room. He kept his focus on his destination, rather than face the volley of camera flashes from TV and newspaper journalists gathered there. He sat down in the centre of a long table, the force logo behind him, an overly large microphone in front and one on either side. Frankie took a seat on his right, a nod to a member of the media team who was sitting on his left ready to kick off proceedings.

'Shall we begin?' she asked.

David gave an almost imperceptible nod.

She tapped her microphone. 'Ladies and gentlemen, thank you for attending this morning's conference. For those who don't know me, I'm Sinead Byrne, Media and Communications Manager. To my right is Senior Investigating Officer, Detective Chief Inspector David Stone, Northumbria Murder Investigation Team. To his right, his second-in-command, Detective Sergeant Frances Oliver.' There wasn't one among those assembled who didn't know exactly who was seated out front. The detectives' faces had been on many a front page in the past few days, on and off duty, together and separately. 'You know the drill. The SIO will make a short statement. Please let him finish, then we'll take questions from the floor.' Byrne held up a press pack. 'You should all have one of these. If you don't, see me afterwards.'

Leaning in, Frankie whispered, 'There'll be a stampede.'

David dropped his head. If he looked at her, she'd see that he counted himself among those attracted to Sinead. From the attention she was receiving, anyone would think she was a supermodel on a catwalk. She was going through the motions professionally, in the soft, low-pitched and very appealing Irish accent she was famous for among the rank and file. If she asked the press to strip off and bare their arses in public, they would oblige.

She was still speaking. 'Please identify yourselves before fielding a question and switch all mobiles to silent now. Thank you.'

David squinted as more flashes went off. 'Good morning, everyone. I asked you here to update you on developments on two bodies found in close proximity to one another in rural Northumberland, specifically at Kielder Water, on Saturday the twenty-second of June. Post-mortem results confirm that they both died in suspicious circumstances. My team have now identified the skeletal remains of the first victim as Clifford Charlton, one-time resident of Plashetts, which, as you know, no longer exists. His date of birth is eleventh November 1947. His birth name was Luca Conti and he was reported missing in 1976.'

'Adam English.' He gave the name of his tabloid. 'What kept you?'

Sinead leaned into her microphone, about to ask English what part of 'let him finish' he'd failed to understand.

David cut her off. 'This conference will end if there are any more interruptions.' He carried on as if the waste of space had never opened his big mouth. 'We're interested in tracing past and present relatives of Luca Conti. We'd like to talk to anyone who might have information to give us about his disappearance or his adoption, which we've been led to believe happened soon after his birth.'

David waited a beat, a quick glance at his statement, a chance for journalists to catch up.

'The second body is that of an Icelandic national, Jón Scheving, a man we have reason to believe was rough camping on the banks of the reservoir, very close to the scene of the first discovery. Several people in the area at the time have been helping with our enquiries. We're asking anyone we've not yet spoken to, who was in the area between 2300 hours on Friday the twenty-first of June and 0700 hours on Saturday the twenty-second of June, to get in touch, whether or not they saw any suspicious activity.'

As he shuffled his notes, David exchanged a look with Frankie, a sign that he was about to throw a spanner in the works. He leaned in, turning his head away from the micro-phone, whispered 'hold your bottle', and then raised his voice to the waiting crowd. 'We're particularly interested in any vehicles that may have been in the vicinity during the time parameters I just mentioned. We know that there was a motor-cycle in the area. I'd like anyone who saw it to come forward.'

At that moment, his plan fell neatly into place. Now Frankie understood what he was up to, why it was necessary to make that call, and who to. He'd done it brilliantly with a magician's sleight of hand. It was a good move, not strictly by the book, but that didn't bother her. David's endgame was to flush out the offender.

76

As several hands went up, Frankie glanced out of the window. In the car park below, she noticed an unfamiliar black Tesla Model S in David's designated parking spot, the sun glinting off its bonnet. Her gaze shifted as the rear door to the conference room swung open. Bright crept in, closing it quietly behind him so as not to draw attention to himself, a nod in her direction. He'd obviously seen the 'live' broadcast, arriving in the nick of time for the Q&A. Scanning the room, he immediately homed in on English, whose raised hand was being ignored by the SIO.

A smirk flooded Frankie's face. Now Bright was here, just about anything could happen. Waiting for the fun to start, she pulled out her phone and typed a message to Dick Abbott:

Would you do me a favour?

Name it.

Surreptitiously, beneath the tabletop, she typed her request.

'Belinda, did you have a question?' David was saying.

Hearing the name, Frankie hit send and looked up.

Wells was flanked by David's nephew on one side, English on the other. Frankie half-expected her to elbow the latter in the ribs for all the trouble he was causing, except she stood head and shoulders above him. Such a jab would likely knock his teeth out.

'I have two,' she said. 'If I may.'

'Go ahead.'

'Charlton is a very common name, Conti less so. Are we, to coin a phrase, talking Italian? And, if so, have you spoken to his adoptive parents?'

'In relation to your first question, that is a line of enquiry we're following. Sadly, his British adoptive parents have since passed away, though we're in the process of tracing any relatives he may have in the UK and Italy.'

David's nephew had his hand up too.

David felt a mixture of guilt and sadness. They had been like passing ships at home, with hardly time to grab a bite to eat together, let alone have a proper conversation. He'd have to up his game as surrogate parent, at least make it up to him when things died down.

He gave Ben the nod.

'Ben Stone, *North East Times*. You mentioned that the bodies were found close together. Does that mean these incidents are linked?'

David shook his head. 'Not at this stage, though the investigations are being run in parallel with one another.'

'Can you share cause of death on either victim?'

'Not at the moment, no. And that's two questions.' David pointed at a journalist he knew before anyone accused him of favouritism. There had been more than enough accusations in the papers this week.

The man he'd invited to speak ID'd himself. 'Sean Simpson, *Evening Chronicle*. I believe you and DS Oliver recently travelled to Iceland. Do you have a suspect there?'

David sidestepped the question. 'We've spoken to a number of individuals: the victim's relatives, witnesses and local police.'

'Do you have anyone in custody?'

'No.'

'Sounds like a jolly at the expense of the British taxpayer,' English interrupted. 'No wonder questions have been raised about your conduct, Detective Chief Inspector. Is there any substance to the rumour that you and DS Oliver are about to be removed from this murder investigation?'

David answered with a question of his own. 'Says who?'

Bright called out, 'Perhaps I could answer that for you, Mr English.'

The journalist looked over his shoulder. 'And you are?'

'If you'd done your homework, you'd know. For the record, Northumbria Police have every confidence in DCI Stone and DS Oliver. Our legal team are presently examining your bogus allegations. They'll be in touch with your editor-in-chief in due course. You'd better warn him to get his chequebook out and practise his zeros. Your slanderous accusations are going to cost.'

English eyeballed Bright, challenging his authority.

Fiercely loyal, Frankie wanted to wipe the smirk off his fat face. She looked on as the two men locked horns, allegations and rebuttals continuing for several minutes from both sides. Never in Northumbria's history had Bright been involved in such a public slanging match. Aware that it had been captured on TV, English was in no hurry to back down.

Byrne stood up. 'Ladies and gentlemen, this conference is now over.'

There was a rush for the door.

Wells walked towards Frankie, stopping briefly on her way out. She didn't say anything. Her attention was drawn to the other side of the room where Byrne and Bright were deep in conversation, their heads so close they were almost touching. Turning to face Frankie, Wells leaned in, dropping her voice to a whisper. 'Is the detective super in a relationship?'

'With Sinead?' Frankie laughed. 'No.'

'Good, I rather like him.'

'Tough. He's taken.'

There was genuine disappointment on Wells' face. 'Well, if you're no use to me as a matchmaker, is there anything Ben and I can do for you?'

Frankie shook her head. 'We're fine.'

'You look like shit.'

'Bugger off and insult someone else, why don't you?'

'Actually, there is one thing.' David edged his way into the conversation. 'When our appeal for witnesses goes live this evening, our guys are going to be stretched. Is there any chance you can spare Ben to search your newspaper's archives?'

'Looking for what?' he said.

'PoW camps in the Kielder area—'

'Ah . . .' Belinda studied him.

'What did I miss?' Ben asked.

Wells glared at him. 'Think about it.'

The penny dropped. 'You're looking for Conti's father?'

A nod from his uncle. 'That's highly confidential, until I say otherwise.'

'Noted,' Ben moved off, waving at Frankie before he disappeared from view.

'I swear that kid gets more handsome every day,' Frankie said to David as a text arrived. 'Shame your brother got all the looks.' She checked her mobile. The text was from Abbott. **Sorted!** He'd added a raised thumb emoji.

She was out of her seat before David had the chance to ask what she'd been up to, striding across the room, heading for the snake. 'Mr English, so nice to meet you in person.' She proffered a hand. He didn't take it. 'Suit yourself.'

'DS Oliver.' David arrived at her shoulder.

She turned to face him.

'I'd like a word,' he said.

'Now?'

'Yes, now.'

'Shame. Mr English and I were just getting acquainted. Keep your enemies close, guv. Isn't that what you taught me?' She eyeballed the journalist. 'You're a piece of work. No, cancel that. You're a piece of shit. We deal with guys like you every day. Mark my words, you *will* live to regret your actions. You have no idea what I'm capable of when riled. Ask anyone.'

'Believe me, I haven't even started yet.'

'Me either.' Frankie stood tall, all five feet nowt of her. 'What did my guv'nor ever do to you, anyhow?'

The journalist didn't respond.

'That's what I thought. I wouldn't call him boring exactly,

but he's hardly newsworthy. No offence, guv.' She switched her focus to English. 'I'm much more up your street. I've done things that would make your eyes bleed. Feel free to pick up your shit shovel and start digging.'

English eyeballed Stone. 'She's funny. I can see the attraction.'

Taking hold of her upper arm, David pulled her to one side. 'Seriously? Are we doing this now? Step away, Frank.' He flicked his head toward the door, urging her to leave well alone. 'Go! We don't want any trouble.'

'Trouble?' Bright had arrived. 'What's going on?'

English taunted them. 'A lover's tiff, by the looks of it.'

'Hey, man! You should see us at home.' Frankie switched her focus to Bright. 'Morning, sir. I'd love to stay and chat, but DCI Stone and I have work to do. I'm only here to give our guest the bad news.'

'It won't look good if you arrest me,' English said. 'Just saying.'

'You'd better get your walking boots on. It's quite a hike to Kielder. I'm afraid your vehicle is being towed away. It was parked in a designated bay in a zone restricted for police personnel.' She tutted loudly, cocking a thumb toward the window. 'It seems someone got upset around the time you decided to rubbish us on TV.' Frankie glanced at David, feigning suspicion by narrowing her eyes. 'Wasn't you, was it, guv?'

English raced to the window to find his beloved Tesla being uplifted. A split second later, the low-loader carrying it moved off. Behind him, Bright high-fived Frankie.

David laughed.

The journalist swung round, his face red and sweaty. 'This is fucking outrageous.'

'Perfect timing, if you ask me.' Bright glanced at his watch. 'Your deadline looks doubtful. If you make it, I'm Detective Chief Superintendent Philip Bright, one L, not two.'

'Call your dogs off.'

'No can do,' Bright said. 'Fixing this is in your own hands.

You'll be looking over your shoulder for the rest of your natural if you persist in your quest to bring shame on any officer under my command. Think on it.' Taking a few steps forward, he stuck his head through the open window, looking down at Abbott in the car park, directing operations, a satisfied expression on his face. Bright checked out the vehicle registration: ENG115H. 'Love the plate,' he said. 'Shame the numbers are illegally spaced.' When he turned around, the journalist was already gone.

77

Tynemouth beach, Stone and Oliver's second office, was full of holidaymakers. Just minutes from their base, it was the place they favoured whenever they wanted a breath of air, a chance to recharge their batteries or have a private conversation. Ordinarily, they just walked, bouncing ideas off one another, trying to make sense of what they did and didn't know. Like any jigsaw, there was only one way the pieces would fit together.

Out of the car, ignoring the crowded promenade, they made their way down the ramp onto the sand. The tide was out, a few surfers in colourful wetsuits in the distance; a few kids paddling at the water's edge; no swimmers. Even in summer, the North Sea was cold enough for penguins.

Just thinking of a dip gave Frankie goosebumps.

They turned left, heading in an easterly direction, warm sun on their backs. After about five minutes, much of it in silent contemplation, Frankie kicked off her shoes, tied the laces together and slung them over her shoulder. David had binned his suit in favour of jeans and a polo shirt. As he slipped on his shades, she could see herself reflected in them.

'I have to ask you something,' he said.

'Sounds ominous.' Frankie stopped walking and turned to face him. 'If it's about Abbott's involvement in shafting English, leave him out of it. I take full responsibility.'

'It's not. However, since you brought Dick up, I'd like to know if he's given you earache lately—'

'Not especially, why?'

'Just asking.'

'For a copper, you're a terrible liar. Does this have anything to do with him mouthing off at the briefing while I was away?' She gave a wry smile. 'Yeah, I heard about it. Pam told me.'

David didn't answer.

'I hope you put him in his place. I gather he was well out of order.'

'I did and he was. That's not why I'm asking.'

Frankie frowned. 'Is it because he disagrees with me over who's responsible for Scheving's death? He's entitled.'

'Nice of you to be so understanding.' Frankie ruffled the hair of a springer spaniel who'd run up to say hello, a smile to its owner before resuming their chat. 'When Dick had a go in the MIR, didn't it occur to you that he was kicking out at someone he cares about? Don't we all do that from time to time? You can forgive him a little resentment, surely. He's disappointed—'

'Yeah, I get that—'

'Well, thank your lucky stars it's him and not me. If the roles were reversed, I'd have been a right pain in the arse.' She smiled, trying to lift his mood. 'Dick had a lot riding on his promotion board. You've not met his wife, have you?'

David was shaking his head.

'She's high-maintenance, knocking him out of the park in terms of ambition. His ego has taken a dive, that's all. Give him a break. He'll come around.'

'You think so?'

'I know so.'

'Fair enough.'

'You might at least try and sound convinced.'

He flicked his head. 'C'mon, let's walk.'

Frankie hung back, tipping her head, allowing the warm wind to kiss her face. She could taste sea salt on her lips as she looked out over the sparkling water, watching the rise and fall of the tide. It calmed her, as it always did, rushing inland, washing over her bare feet. Something was off with her boss and she thought she knew what it was.

He called out, tapping his watch.

She moved towards him. 'Be honest, your concern isn't about Dick the person, is it? It's about his take on the investigation, the fact that he's making waves for me? Or are you wavering, edging towards his perspective? If that's it, just say so. I'm big enough to take it.' She had to find a way to convince him that Dick wasn't the only one acting weird. 'Fuck's sake, David. You need to start trusting me.'

'I do!'

'Do you? I mean *really* trust me. You've made all the right noises, but I'm not feeling it, so stop fence-sitting and make your mind up. I need your full support, not some half-arsed attempt. If that's too hard for you, then throw me under the bus and go with the majority point of view. Just don't blame me if you end up with egg on your face.'

A moment of intense emotion passed between them.

'Look,' she said. 'Every one of those kids was interviewed by you and Emil. Anna even had a go at them. There was no evidence against any of them except Kristján. I re-interviewed Aron before I left Iceland. Until the misunderstanding at the barrel site, he claims he had no idea that Eva was keen on Kristján and vice versa. It was only when she went into hysterics after he decked her boyfriend that he put two and two together. He regrets overacting when he heard her scream and has apologised for it.'

'Did you manage to get anything out of him regarding the assault on her?'

'Aron? No, I couldn't ask him outright, could I? Not without breaking a confidence. I didn't get the impression that he knew about it.'

David raised an eyebrow. 'Why would he admit it? It gives him motive.'

'As you keep reminding me, all the evidence points at Kristján. He coughed to hiding the tent and gave a credible explanation for doing so. You're not seriously suggesting they're in it together?'

'The thought had crossed my mind.'

'No shit.' Frankie looked away.

'Was Aron OK with her seeing Kristján?'

'Seems so. Why?'

'Just curious.'

'They were in the same class at school, though not that close. Aron described him as a loner. Too serious for his liking. A teacher's pet with few friends. When police questioned him about his grandfather's death – and before you ask, Aron brought it up, I didn't – he said the other kids laughed because he's such a weed.'

'He's not a weed now.'

78

They had been going in circles. Tired and frustrated, David threw his leg over a driftwood log. Eyeing the horizon, he sat down, shoving up so Frankie could join him. As she did so, he scanned the beach, glad to be away from the claustrophobia of the office, grateful for the opportunity to set the record straight. Abbott was making out that Frankie was seeing only what she wanted to see. Dick's morale was on the floor, his pride bruised. It was as simple as that.

Any SIO had to remain open to all suggestions, allowing his or her detective mind to do the job it was designed for. David couldn't allow indecision to overwhelm him to the point where he lost the ability for critical thinking. As certain as Dick was that Scheving's killer was an Icelandic national, Frankie was adamant that he or she was not. The seesaw effect of these opposing opinions was driving David mad.

'That was a big sigh.'

He turned to look at her. 'Yeah, well, I didn't come here to talk about Dick.'

'Oh?' She made a smiley face. 'Did you bring a picnic?'

'Be serious. I'd like to talk about Charlton-Conti, specifically the circumstances surrounding his death—'

'What's there to talk about?'

'One fatal blow, Collingwood said, not a frenzied attack. With no organs to examine, she can't say for sure that the injuries he suffered weren't worse. Leaving that aside for a second, I've been trying to second-guess what type of offender we're looking at. Who in God's name would kill, bury a body and dig it up almost forty years later, at great risk, shifting it to a watery grave?'

'Makes little sense to me.'

'OK, then let's go back to basics. The barrel was weighed down. Not enough to submerge it beneath the waterline. I've racked my brains and come up with only one scenario—'

'Which is?'

'That Kielder reservoir means something to the victim, the perpetrator, or both. Getting inside the offender's head is the key to unlocking this investigation. What do we normally do when a person dies?'

'Conti didn't just die—'

'Humour me a second.'

'We bury them, as the killer did.'

'Exactly. In his case, assuming it was a he, to hide a crime. What would you or I do under normal circumstances?'

Frankie took a moment to think it through. 'Mark the grave with a headstone.'

'And in the case of a cremation?'

'Set them on fire? Is there a point to this?'

'Shut up and listen. And afterwards?'

'Did I suddenly wander into the *Mastermind* studio? If so, I'd like to choose my own specialist subject and it wouldn't be *The Undertaker's Daughter* by Kate Mayfield *or* Sara Blaedel.' Frankie spread her hands, a gesture of frustration. 'In answer to your question, I don't know . . . Commission a plaque in a garden of remembrance, if I could afford it—'

'And if you couldn't?'

'That's all I got. You lost me.'

'C'mon, you're on the right track.'

Frankie scratched her head. 'Scatter their ashes at a place that holds some meaning for the deceased?' Her eyes widened. 'Ohmygod! It's an act of contrition. He's not only sorry, he's bringing the body home.'

'Bingo. We need to think about his psychological makeup. What drove him then, what's driving him now—'

'An SUV with dodgy lights,' she carped. 'Pity we can't find it.'

'Yeah, it would help.'

Frankie's expression darkened. She was no longer looking at him. Her head was bowed, her focus on the sand. David could see the wheels turning and sensed that, having processed the information, she'd landed on some detail that might be important and probably was. He could spot a lightbulb moment from fifty yards.

She oozed confidence as she turned to face him. 'Fancy playing *The Generation Game* instead?'

Now he wasn't following.

'Conti was reported missing in 1976,' she said. 'That's thirty-eight years ago. When I was studying for my promotion board, I looked up the Office for National Statistics in case they threw me a low-baller. Did you know that forty-five per cent of males convicted of murder in England and Wales are between the ages of twenty-five and forty-five?'

'No.'

'Neither did I. For women, it's thirty-five plus. Chances are, our offender is in that age range. For argument's sake, if we figure on thirty-five, that would make our offender, male or female, around seventy-three years of age by now. Empty, an oak barrel weighs a hundred and twenty pounds. Weighed down, a lot more. No one that age could lift it. I think it's the son or daughter of a killer returning Conti to his birthplace.'

79

The MIT were flat out when Stone and Oliver arrived at Middle Earth next morning. The appeal for information was working. Telephone lines were hot, every detective and civilian on the phone, taking statements to feed into HOLMES. There was the occasional oddball caller but, in the main, the public response had been open and above board. The majority claimed to have knowledge of the Charlton family. In this part of the world, it was a common name. Detectives were aware that it could lead nowhere. In a largescale murder investigation, that was a given. Interestingly, three callers recollected seeing a motorcycle in Kielder Village. Abbott was understandably upbeat, directing operations.

Frankie gave him a wide berth as Pam wandered up to speak to her.

'Richmond's wife finally returned our call,' she said. 'You were right, Frank. She did pass a couple of vehicles on the C200 after dropping off petrol for her husband. However, all had their lights on and she doesn't remember details. I gather she was full of hell, keen to return to her bed.'

'Damn it.' Frankie sighed. 'Did the house-to-house team come up with anything?'

'Yes and no. We put together a comprehensive list of all types of utility vehicles registered in Kielder Village. That's not saying much. Just about everyone drives one in rural Northumberland. Every householder in the village, whether or not they drive, was re-interviewed. None of those we checked out so far has dodgy lights.'

'That doesn't mean our man hasn't had it fixed.'

'CSIs examined every vehicle. They found nothing

suspicious that fits the bill. Keep the faith, Frank. We still have a few vehicles left to trace.'

'Any that don't appear on the DVLA radar?'

'Funny you should mention that,' Pam said. 'Mitch drew up a proforma for the uniformed division, ensuring that every resident was asked the same set of questions. During their enquiries, three came to light. You know how these things go – *Farmer Giles has two, but one is old; so-and-so's brother up the road owns one, though it's off the road; my cousin sold his recently.* I'll let you know if it comes to anything.'

'Thanks, Pam. Did Indira find anything on Conti?'

'Not yet.'

Frankie's mobile rang. 'I'll have to take this. It's the tech team.'

'Fingers crossed they found something on Richmond's headcam.'

Frankie walked away, lifting the device to her ear. 'Oliver.'

'It's Vikram. You got a minute?'

'Stop teasing. Do I run or walk?'

'Either way, you need to get down here.'

Hope reigned. Frankie found David in his office, feet up on his desk, his mobile wedged between ear and shoulder, a pen in his right hand, a pad on his knee. He looked up from scribbling a note and met her gaze. He seemed more upbeat than she'd seen him in ages, more inclined to believe that solving the old case might find Scheving's killer. He nodded, inviting her to sit, mouthing the word: sorry.

She remained standing, using her hands as winders.

He got the message. 'Sorry to cut you off, Ben. Frankie needs me, I've got to go.' A pause. 'Yeah, see you later. I'll bring take-away . . .' David rolled his eyes at Frankie. 'Dude, my budget is screwed. It's the *only* way I can pay you . . . Yeah, I'll tell her. Thank Belinda for me.' He hung up, sat up, his focus on Frankie. 'What is it?'

'Tech team want to see us.'

'Positive news?'

'Think so . . . . Hope so.' She eyed the mobile in his hand. 'What did Ben want?'

'He found PoW camps scattered right across the region: Gosforth, Ponteland, Wooler, Blyth, one at a caravan site at Amble not far from your place—'

'Nothing local?'

'There was one at Byrness, Camp 667, only thirteen miles as the crow flies through the Kielder Forest Drive, as we now know it. No problem for army vehicles shipping PoWs to work during the war. More importantly, it's only fifteen miles up the A68 to Jedburgh, where Professor Dawson thinks Luca's body may have been buried.' David consulted his handwritten notes. 'The camp remained open until 1948 so it also fits the time-line. What's more, only one Italian prisoner listed there bears the surname Conti. Flavio Conti – could be Luca's father—'

'You want me to put Mitch and Indira on it?' She took in his nod. 'Before or after we meet with the tech team?'

'Do it now! I'll meet you outside in two.'

'On my way.' She turned to go.

'Frank?'

'Yeah.' She swung round.

'Conti may not have been a military man. According to your granddad, civilians were interned on grounds of nationality alone. If he was a soldier, I'd like to know if he was fit or wounded when he arrived in Britain, if he worked outside of the camp and where. I have no idea how detailed archived material is. If any personal items are listed in Conti's possessions on arrival, I'd like to know about them too.'

80

Vikram Chandra looked up as Stone and Oliver entered his office, raising his reading glasses onto the top of his head, a big smile on his face. He was super fit, eyes brimming with health, late thirties with a fabulous head of jet-black hair and a wicked sense of humour. To call him good at his job would be an insult. He was universally accepted as the best analyst in the country. Though David rated him highly, there was only so much anyone could do to identify a vehicle moving at speed.

The digital exhibit he'd submitted for examination was, to the untrained eye, little more than a split-second smudge of movement taken in bad light on Richmond's headcam. The vibration of a motorcycle in transit further complicated matters. At best, the footage was jumpy, at worst indecipherable. More worrying, it was the only hard evidence available to the MIT. As such, there was a lot riding on Vik's ability to enhance it. Whether the level of intensification would have any evidential value in the long run was debatable.

With that troubling thought lingering, David sat down, hoping the analyst's efforts would reveal some detail of the utility vehicle he was so desperate to trace, no matter how small. He apologised for the poor quality of the exhibit.

Vik waved away his concern. 'Nothing floats my boat more than a challenge, guv. Believe it or not, I've seen a lot worse—'

Frankie pulled a face. 'Hand over the registration then and we'll be off—'

'That I can't do, even with the expensive toys I have at my disposal.' He was equipped with the most cutting-edge technology on the market, forensic enhancement tools and intelligence software that was highly effective in the fight against crime. His dark eyes flitted from Stone to Oliver, where they rested a moment. 'Would I be right in thinking it's an old vehicle you're looking for?'

Her expression was inscrutable.

For fear that it would reach the press, at David's insistence, no one outside of the MIT had been passed this information. For that reason, the exhibit was merely marked with a reference number and general description: Headcam recovered from witness Neil Richmond.

'Stop me if I get warm,' Vik said. 'As you already know, vehicle age ID was introduced in 2001/2 with a 51 plate. The vehicle you're looking for predates that. It has a (T) prefix which ran from the beginning of March to the end of August, 99. I can't see the rest of it, sorry—'

Frankie spread her hands in frustration. 'You dragged us down here and that's all you've got?'

'I never said that—'

'Didn't you? How else can we interpret "we can't see the rest of it"?'

'Patience, Frank. I may not have the full plate but I'm far from finished.' He didn't wait for an apology. The mood she was in, he wouldn't get one. Like everyone in the wider force and beyond, he'd seen the slanderous allegations circulating in the press about her relationship with Stone and didn't believe a word of it. 'I managed to scale up the footage to a much higher resolution.' Pulling his keyboard closer, he typed a command and hit return, his attention shifting to a point over their shoulders. 'Take a look.'

The detectives turned. A single photographic still had been uploaded on a wall-mounted smart TV. David got up and moved closer, peering closely at the enhanced image. What Vik had done with it was nothing short of a miracle. He swung round. 'I don't know what to say, except bloody well done.'

'Not bad, is it?' the analyst said proudly.

'Not bad?' Frankie was also on her feet, dead impressed. 'Vik, it's amazing.'

'Is it a Mitsubishi?' David asked.

'Good guess,' Vik said. 'We thought so too at first.'

David spoke without turning around. 'You've changed your mind?'

Vik hit the keys again, eyeing his monitor. The image changed to one showing three SUVs side by side: a Mitsubishi L200, a Toyota Hilux and a Ford Ranger. This was replicated on the TV Stone and Oliver were looking at. 'Can you see how the Mitsubishi's rear passenger window is more stylised?'

'Yeah,' Frankie said. 'It's slightly kicked up at the rear, rounded almost.'

'Correct.' Vik split the screen, showing the enhanced headcam exhibit on one side, the three SUVs on the other. 'I consulted with colleagues and industry experts. Collectively, we were of the same mind. What you're looking for is a twenty-year-old, first-generation, dark-coloured Ford Ranger pickup.'

Simultaneously, Stone and Oliver agreed.

'Can we see it in motion?' Frankie asked.

'Certainly.' Vik hit his keyboard one final time. 'Blink and you'll miss it, so keep your eyes peeled.' He glanced at his wide-eyed groupies. 'You ready?'

'Go for it,' David said.

The still image disappeared, replaced by a short, enhanced, video clip. Checking again that he had their full attention, Vik pressed play, this time focusing on the TV screen rather than his desktop monitor. For a second or two, all Stone and Oliver could see was tarmac illuminated by a single headlight. Then, suddenly, the Ford Ranger emerged out of the darkness. The headcam flicked away as Richmond veered off to the side to avoid a head-on collision. His was a narrow escape.

81

It had been months since Frankie had caught up with Vikram, let alone used his technical expertise in the course of an investigation she was involved in. They were big mates, hanging out together when they were state zero. They weren't often off duty at the same time. To show her appreciation, she high-fived him before dragging herself away from his secret hideaway, a big smile on her face as she turned and waved goodbye through the window. Leaving with far more detail on the SUV than she dared dream of going in, she kept a tight hold on the statements he'd obtained from the industry experts he'd talked about, plus a thumb drive containing an interactive digital brochure on the Ranger pickup the Ford Motor Company had been good enough to supply. It was not, and never had been, available to the general public.

Her buoyant mood evaporated as she entered the corridor.

Looking both ways, she found a couple of uniforms, one male, one female, deep in conversation outside a locker room. David was nowhere to be seen. He'd gone on ahead, keen to share Vik's findings with the MIT.

He could've waited.

Should have.

She set off at a pace, bursting through the double doors, hoping to catch him before he reached the MIR. They had important stuff to talk about. Fortunately, Bright had waylaid him in the stairwell, giving her a chance to collar him. She felt deflated and surplus to requirements. Their new lead had already been delivered to the man in charge of Northumbria CID . . .

'Good to know,' she heard him say as she walked up behind him.

'Yeah, terrific job, guv.' From behind Bright's back, Frankie gave David a hacky look: Aren't you the hero?

Bright swung round. 'There you are! Brilliant work, both of you. You might get Brownie points for this if you play your cards right—'

'Give mine to Chandra,' Frankie said. 'The man is nothing short of a genius.'

'That's very generous—'

'Credit where it's due.'

'I'm needed at Forth Banks. I'll call on him before I leave.'

'He'll appreciate that, sir.' Frankie smiled broadly. 'Thank you.'

Bright told Stone to keep his head down. 'You too, Frank. Don't be handing English any more ammunition. Your dad might be first in the queue to punch his lights out, but we could do without any more negative publicity about you. This is an important moment in your career. Make the most of it.'

'Sir.' It didn't feel important.

Satisfied, he walked away.

David was about to do the same.

'Wait! David, can I have a word?' Opening the door to an empty office, Frankie asked him to step inside, wanting to say her piece before briefing the team. Curious, he perched on the edge of a desk, leaving the only available seat for her. She didn't take it. The recently redecorated room was covered in a film of dust, the floor still protected by polythene sheeting, the smell of cheap paint lingering.

Closing the door, she turned to face him. 'This new lead is bound to throw the investigation wide open.'

'I hope so, it's a major breakthrough.' David studied her for a moment. 'Am I missing something? If you don't mind me saying so, you seem underwhelmed—'

'No.'

'So why the smacked-arse face? We're all agreed that if we find the vehicle, we'll find the offender.'

'We might be a step closer to identifying our target, but we have a shedload to get through before we throw absolutely everything at it. The guy from the Ford Motor Company told Vik that most pickup trucks were bought as light commercial vehicles. When they arrived in the UK, they were predicted to be the next best thing. They failed to meet expectations, accounting for less than two per cent of the market share—'

'That'll help, not hinder us.'

'Yes, but it'll take ages to trace and interview the owners, nationally and locally. We simply don't have the manpower to handle it. Shouldn't we at least acknowledge the fact that the T-plate on the pickup could be dodgy, put there to throw us off the scent?'

'We can't help that. A vehicle ID is a good start. If the plate bothers you so much, why don't you ask Vik if he can improve on what he gave us—'

'Seriously?' She gave a pointed look. 'You don't want much, do you?'

'No harm in asking. He might identify an accessory that makes it stand out.'

'He can't. I asked him already. He said there was no after-market upgrade that he could see. In short, it's bog-standard, no nudge-bars, side-plates or fancy lights.'

'Then we'll have to work with what we have.'

'Then you'll have to cough up for overtime.'

'Frankie, relax. That's my problem, not yours. The ACC is giving Bright earache. He told me so. He's been ordered to do whatever it takes to come out of this with Northumbria's repu-tation intact, including his and ours. Budgetary constraints are no longer an issue. That means we re-interview everyone – and I mean everyone.'

82

While David was updating the Media and Communications Manager, Frankie made use of his office so she wouldn't be disturbed by the MIT. She logged onto HOLMES to see if anyone owning a Ford Ranger had come up in the Conti or Scheving murder investigations. None had. She checked the vehicle index to see if anyone in the force area had come to police notice with one of those vehicles. There were a dozen, none registered within the search parameters David had decided upon. Collecting them from the printer, she sat down, sifting through them, twirling a lock of hair round her forefinger.

David wandered in.

He seemed relaxed after seeing Sinead.

Frankie made a move to vacate his chair.

'As you were . . .' Gesturing for her to remain seated, he scooped up his laptop and sat down near the open window. 'I have some admin to take care of. How far have you got with the target vehicle?'

'Not very.' She held up the printout. 'I found twelve possibles on the vehicle index.' The A4 sheet hit his desk, a list that would grow and grow by close of play. There was nothing surer. She was about to check the PNC when a depressing thought stopped her. 'Does *Auto Trader* still exist?'

'Digital only.' He gave a cheeky smile. 'You looking for new wheels?'

'I wish. It occurred to me that whoever dumped the barrel might want to get rid.'

'It's worth a punt.' He opened his laptop, ending their exchange.

Leaving him to it, Frankie resumed work, bringing up Safari, a quick search for the motor magazine. The page loaded with a search box and an invitation: **Find your perfect car.** Entering the postcode for Kielder Water & Forest Park, together with the make of the target vehicle, her mood plummeted as the number indicator displayed over fifty thousand Fords for sale.

'Shit!' This was not looking good.

Using the drop-down menu, she scrolled up, searching for the exact model she was after. Her heart sank. In brackets, next to it, was a number larger than she'd hoped for. She swore under her breath and spoke as if David knew what she was talking about, which of course he didn't.

'This is exactly what I was getting at,' she said.

'What is?' He stopped typing, peering over the top of his specs.

'*Auto Trader.*' She pointed at the monitor. 'This month's issue has 1780 Rangers in the system.'

He winced. 'How many on a T-plate locally?'

She consulted the page again. There was an option to choose the distance from her location. She selected 'within thirty miles' and let out another sigh. 'Twenty-nine.'

'They'll do for starters.'

'Yeah, well I'm going to need help. OK to raise an action with Pam?'

'Fill your boots. Make sure she allocates it to Dick.'

Abbott was made for the job. He was savvy, lightning fast, understood the need to cover all the angles. Where vehicle enquiries were concerned, there was nothing he didn't know. These types of assignments could be tricky. They required intense concentration, cross-checking and follow-up. Even on official documentation, vehicles were often listed with the wrong colour, the wrong model. People moved and didn't notify the DVLA of a change of address. By no means was the system foolproof.

David looked up. 'Was there something else, Frank?'

'I understand your choice, but Dick might not like it. What

I mean is, it's a bit of a climb-down. He was acting up while we were in Iceland, deputising as your—'

'Tough. This is a team game, Frank. He knows the area better than anyone else and spent time in the motor vehicle squad when we had one. In terms of colour, I want every Ford included in the trawl, light or dark. The one we're looking for is almost twenty years old. It could've been resprayed and never recorded as such with the DVLA.'

Frankie picked up her pen and scrawled a note for the receiver:

URGENT ACTION: Allocate to DS ABBOTT. All T-reg Ford Rangers to be checked on the DVLA, as per SIO search parameters, to include all vehicles registered north of the River Tyne and within a 30-mile radius of Kielder to take in the Scottish border region.

DS Oliver

Timing and dating the note, she got up and left the room. Pam was at her desk in conversation with Charlie, the office manager, an old soldier with receding hair and a face that only a mother could love. The two were the best of friends and worked closely together. Frankie hung around until Pam got wise that she wanted a word on the QT.

When Charlie moved away, Frankie explained that Vik had identified the target vehicle. Handing Pam the action, she waited for her to read it. 'By all means alert Dick. I need him on it as soon as, but keep it quiet from the rest for the time being.'

Pam asked, 'Why the secrecy?'

'The boss intends to raise it at the evening briefing. He wants to make it clear that the information goes no further. We're in enough shit with the press. Bright's had enough. He wants to come out of this squeaky clean and so do we. This lead is our keepy-back, the one we hope will turn the investigation around.'

'Understood. Leave it with me.'

Frankie walked away satisfied that she'd say nowt and that Abbott would give it his all.

As she re-entered David's office, she thought about a car her father once owned. It had extra lights, wide wheels and nudge-bars, front and rear, until there was a public outcry because they were dangerous to pedestrians. He'd removed them. Such factory-fitted accessories would appear on the DVLA vehicle spec. These anomalies were things Abbott wouldn't miss and why it was vital to give the job to an experienced human who could differentiate between the information being spat out of the system and the reality on the ground. Every tiny detail had to be cross-referenced. That's why vehicle enquiries generate so many jobs.

'You OK?' David asked.

'Yes, all done.' She sat down.

'Why the big sigh?'

'If I'd been responsible for dumping the barrel, offing Scheving or both, I'd be disposing of the evidence, wouldn't you?'

'Probably.' He gave her an odd look. 'You're linking these investigations? I thought that was my job.'

'I'm not ruling it out.' Frankie back-pedalled. 'Sorry, I don't mean to tread on your toes.'

'Relax, I was teasing.'

'Oh.' She refocused. 'It worries me that the offender has had time to torch the vehicle or sell it on. There are literally thousands of motorists driving around with no tax or insurance, in some cases no licence, and getting away with it. Who'd stop them? We're thin on the ground in the sticks. I hope to God the offender hasn't scrapped it.'

'If that's the case, Dick is our man. Relax, you know what he's like for dotting the Is and crossing the Ts. He'll have every vehicle double and triple-checked. If one has dropped off the radar recently, he'll find out where it was disposed of and by whom. He'll follow the paper-trail to prove it's no longer on the road and find the registered keeper. You have to trust him.'

What other choice did she have?

83

Pam Bond was loitering at Abbott's desk when Frankie entered the MIR fifteen minutes later. Dick had his back to her, but she could tell he was about to shoot the messenger. Double O Seven shoved a piece of paper at his chest as if she were serving a summons. It fell to the floor. Dick wasn't overjoyed with his new assignment. Concerned that he was lashing out at the receiver, Frankie picked up her pace and headed over there.

'You dropped something.' She pointed at the floor.

Dick picked it up and glared at her. 'You're kidding, right?'

''Fraid not, it's an important action.'

'Is it bollocks! It's grunt work and you know it.' He crossed his arms, a sour expression on his face, making no attempt to apologise to her or Pam. 'Oh, I get it. This is payback for disagreeing with you over Kristjánsson, right? A blind man on a galloping horse could spot that he's your man. If I'm right, your promotion is screwed.'

'Excuse me?'

He threw the action on his desk. 'Forget it.'

'No, let's not.' Frankie turned her head. 'Pam, give us a moment.' She may as well have said, sling your hook. As the receiver moved away sharpish, Frankie was aware of other detectives' eyes upon her. They had been watching the row unfold. Wondering whose side they were on, she eyeballed Abbott. 'If you're going to be a twat, let's have the gloves off someplace else.'

'I'm not.'

'Good, because you're getting right on my tits. You got a problem with the action? Take it up with the guv'nor. I don't give a shit either way. He gave you this because where vehicle enquiries are concerned there's nowt you don't know. It needs doing and it needs doing now.' She acted like nothing untoward had happened between them. In the pressure cooker environment of a major incident room, people disagreed, though usually more politely. Dick had said his piece and so had she. His mood would be over in a flash. She handed him the list she'd made in David's office. 'That'll get you started. I hope we're not too late. The age of that Ranger worries me.'

'Why?'

'It's hardly a cherished motor, is it? The older they get, the less important they become. A newer car would have monetary value. It would be insured for a high sum and covered by expensive roadside warranty. None of that is the case with a twenty-year-old banger. Can't be worth much, can it? Even less to someone covering their tracks. I'm concerned that it may already be crushed in a scrapyard looking like a metal version of SpongeBob SquarePants.'

'You're not selling it to me.' Abbott didn't crack a smile but he did climb down. 'I'll do it . . . on one condition. No, make that two . . .'

Frankie knew he'd cave. 'You'll do it because I asked nicely, but by all means name your price.'

'You don't interfere and . . .' He stressed the word and. 'You find me a cupboard so I can take myself away from this lot. It's like Euston station in here.'

'Done.' She smiled broadly. 'I'm sick of your ugly mug anyhow.'

'Am I excused from the briefing?'

'You're excused from life until the big reveal.'

He grimaced. 'Don't hold your breath.'

Their spat was over.

In many ways, Dick was the big brother she'd never had and always dreamed of. Guiding her from a young age, protecting her, shielding her from those who'd given her grief over the years. The person she could rely on to pull her up when times were tough. She was happy to return the favour. They had shared some dark times and also a lot of laughs. They enjoyed a camaraderie hard to come by, even by police standards.

'Frank?' he called out.

She retraced her steps, delivering a warning. 'There are no more concessions.'

'I'm not asking for any. Before I shoot off, have you got time for a quick handover? If I'm disappearing, you should know that I might be on to something. Pam collared me before I had a chance to share.'

'Oh?' Intrigued, Frankie pulled up a chair and sat down.

'Do you know the Pheasant Inn?'

'At Stannersburn?' She took in his nod. 'Yes, why?'

'About half an hour ago, I took a call from a lass called Stacey Grainger. She works behind the bar. Last night, she overheard a punter she knows only as Tony telling one of her regulars that he'd seen a motorcyclist on the night before the barrel was found. He got the timing right but was sketchy on location. He told her that we were trying to trace a biker in connection with two deaths.'

'Two?' Frankie's heart leapt. 'He definitely said two?'

'His exact words, according to my source. She claims she can spot a liar from a mile away, as most barmaids can. She thought he sounded off. I've since spoken to a Mr Mason, the regular she mentioned, and he thought so too. I checked in with our contact at Crimestoppers and spoke personally to the three callers who responded to Stone's appeal for witnesses who might have seen or heard a motorcycle. None of them is called Tony.'

Dick didn't need to draw her a picture. Frankie was way ahead of him. He thought Tony was the guy they were hoping to flush out, the reason David had mentioned the motorcycle at the press conference. A question arrived in Frankie's head: why had Tony linked two deaths when the police hadn't? There could only be one reason for it. She stood up, walked round to Dick's side of the desk. Placing a hand on either side of his face, she kissed his forehead.

The man was a legend.

84

The Pheasant Inn was set back off the C200, close to Kielder Water. Covered in a verdant wall of Virginia creeper, it was nestled in an idyllic spot in the heart of the Northumbrian countryside, the perfect choice for those looking to explore what the county had to offer. Inside, the bar was cosy and welcoming. The smell of food being enjoyed by its customers made Stone's mouth water the minute he stepped through the door. He hadn't eaten for hours.

That was not why he'd come.

The young woman behind the bar gave him a knowing smile of recognition as he approached. She'd obviously seen his appeal for witnesses on TV. They had spoken briefly on the telephone, shortly after Frankie had burst into his office giving him the heads-up on Dick's revelation. That short conversation led the SIO to believe that she'd make an excellent witness. He'd set off to meet her in the hope that she might give a good description of the punter she believed had made stuff up.

'DCI Stone?' Her smile lit up the room. 'I'm Stacey Grainger, in case you hadn't worked that out.'

'Good to meet you, Stacey.' David thumbed to his right. 'This is my colleague, DS Oliver.'

'Can I get you anything before we sit?'

David scanned the pumps. 'Pint of Jakehead for me, thanks. Frankie?'

'A tonic with a bit of ice would be lovely.'

As Stacey pulled his pint, David leaned on the bar watching her. She was mid-twenties, small in stature. She had great skin, dark eyes, short spiky hair, tinted purple at the front. Her casual vest showed off super fit arms, a swimmer or rower perhaps, someone with a gym membership. He hoped her memory was equally in good shape. Like Dick and Frankie, David found it odd that the punter she'd rung in about – Tony, assuming that was his real name – had linked two incidents when he had been careful during the press conference to stress that they were entirely separate.

Was this man trying to put the blame on Neil Richmond, deflecting it from himself? Having met the biker, David was as sure as he could be that he wasn't involved. If he had been, why make contact with the MIT? Why hand over his head-cam? As the SIO, David could have compelled him to do it, except he'd be nowhere if Richmond hadn't taken the initiative to come forward. The biker had gone along with his ploy to draw out a dangerous, unpredictable offender. His motivation was genuine – to assist the police.

So, was Frankie's hunch right? Had Jón Scheving seen the barrel going into the water and been taken out? A case of wrong time, wrong place? A damage limitation exercise by someone desperate to cover his tracks? High on a cocktail of drink and drugs, the Icelander would not have been in a position to defend himself.

'Penny for them.'

David looked up.

Stacey was staring at him, wiping her hands on a beer towel advertising Wylam Brewery, a local firm. She picked up her drink and walked round the counter, asking the detectives to follow. She led them through a small archway to a table in the far corner of the next room. She'd placed a 'Reserved' sign on it. David noticed there was one on the tables either side. Instinctively, he knew that no diners would claim them. This was an astute young woman he was facing.

85

On the way through the archway, Frankie caught sight of an old brick on the mantelpiece with PLASHETTS stamped into it in capital letters, a poignant reminder that the village once existed. The walls of the pub were adorned with a number of framed photographs of the mining community who'd lost their homes to make way for Kielder Water. The residents had not been forgotten by the owners of the coaching inn.

David gave the witness a few moments to get settled, making small talk, trying to put her at ease before the interview began. It was important to establish how familiar she was with the clientele.

'Have you worked here long?' he asked.

Stacey took a sip of her drink. 'Two years, give or take.'

'You like it?'

'Yeah, I do. To be honest, outside of hospitality, there's little employment around here. I still live at home. My mum makes sure my expensive English degree isn't wasted. I write through the day, spend my evenings here. It's a perfect combination – and the owners are good to me.'

A non-verbal nudge from Frankie to David: we haven't got all day.

Receiving the message, he focused on the witness. 'As I told you on the phone, it's vital we trace the man you rang in about. Ideally, we'd like a physical description. Anything you can recall that might help us identify him. Hair and eye colour. Approximate age. Distinguishing features, that kind of thing.'

'He was a big bloke. Mid to late thirties. Not in the front of the queue when looks were handed out. Six three or there-abouts.' Stacey glanced at Frankie, who was taking notes. 'Am I going too fast?'

'No, I'll stop you if I need to recap. Was he dark or fair?'

'Dark. A smattering of grey at the sides.'

'Eyes?'

'Blue, maybe grey, I'm not sure.'

Frankie watched David twist his puzzle ring around his little finger, considering where to go next. She concentrated on their witness. 'Hands, face and clothing tell a lot about someone, Stacey. If the guy you saw had gnarled hands, that speaks volumes. If he was immaculately dressed, with manicured nails and a pale complexion, that says something entirely different. Looking at you, for example, I'm betting you're a Megan Rapinoe fan.'

'Busted!' Stacey laughed. 'Is there a woman alive who isn't?'

Frankie smiled. 'It's a good look, one I'd never carry off.'

'Against regulations?'

'Something like that.'

'The guy was the outdoorsy type. Powerful physique. He wore jeans and a black T-shirt. No logo. He had rough hands. Could've been a manual labourer, farmer or forestry worker. We get a lot of those in here. Oh, and he had quite a tan. Don't think he'd ever heard of sunblock.'

'Working or middle class?'

Stacey shrugged. 'He wasn't landed gentry, if that's what you mean. He spoke with a local accent, broad Northumbrian, not posh—'

David cut her off. 'On the phone, you said he wasn't local.'

'No, what I said was he wasn't *a* local – as in, to this pub, this immediate area. When you live in a place like this you know everybody and they know you. We're inundated with strangers on a normal week. More so this week. Most are here to witness the absurdity going on at the reservoir. The guy you're looking for falls in between, neither local nor stranger. I've seen him maybe two or three times.'

'Including last night?'

'Yes.'

Assuming Tony was the man they were looking for, Frankie wondered if his previous visits were to recce the place, deciding where to dump the barrel and the best time to do it. Had he been across the dam in the dead of night? Why Belling peninsula? Why not somewhere closer to the C200? A place that offered a quicker, more direct escape route. David's voice interrupted her thoughts . . .

'What was he like when he first walked in,' he asked. 'Presumably, you give every punter the once-over when they arrive—'

Stacey smiled. 'It's second nature, right? I never know who'll come through that door. I've met some interesting folks working in bars . . . and some I wish I hadn't.'

'Like this guy Tony?'

A nod. 'I guess it's the same for you guys. You develop a sixth sense—'

'If you know what's good for you,' Frankie said.

'He wasn't looking around when he came in. I'd have noticed if he had been. Nor did he appear nervous. Preoccupied maybe. He ordered a double Clynelish with ice and remained at the bar on a stool.'

'Is there a pattern to when he comes in? If we can work out the exact time and day of the week, we have a better chance of tracing him.' David meant mounting a surveillance operation, though he didn't voice it. 'Anything you can tell us would be helpful.'

'I only work weekday evenings so that narrows it down a little. I think on each occasion it was a Wednesday, as it was last night. I can't swear to it.'

Frankie made a note to check out if any local clubs met on a Wednesday. The witness was smart, articulate. She was helping a lot. 'Any idea where he lives?'

'I never asked and he never said. A lot do, just to strike up a conversation.'

David scratched his head. 'So, he didn't say why he was in the area?'

Stacey shook her head. 'Some punters are chatty, others just read the papers, drink up and leave. He was one of those. I'd get more comment from a pint glass. The guy had nothing to say—'

'Do you mean shy or unsociable?' Frankie interrupted.

'I'm not a psychologist.'

'Give us your best guess.'

'He was miserable, brooding, the type with stuff on his mind and nothing on his lips. When customers are like that, it's best to leave them be.'

'If he was so uncommunicative, how do you know his name?' David's was a good question.

'My brother is called Tony. I overheard someone call him that on his first visit. It stuck, I guess. Can't for the life of me remember who spoke to him. This time around, he didn't say two words until Bill came in.'

'Mr Mason?'

Stacey nodded.

'One of my detectives has already spoken to him,' David told her.

'Yeah, I know. He was in here earlier. Anyway, he was the only one this guy Tony spoke to. He didn't approach anyone else and they didn't approach him. He seemed to know the pub though.'

Frankie looked up from her notes. 'Makes you say that?'

'Dunno, he just seemed comfortable, like he'd been here before, maybe before my time. I asked the owners if they knew him. They thought he looked familiar, but we get a lot of folks in here. As you can see, this place isn't very big. It's hard not to engage, if you know what I mean. As I said, your guy managed it. I served him and that was it.'

'Food and drink?'

'Drinks only. He was knocking back whisky like there's no tomorrow.'

'How did he pay?'

'Cash.'

David frowned, disappointed. 'Did he make any phone calls? I'm sorry to ask so many questions. It all helps to build an image.'

'No calls. People who don't want to talk usually play on their phones. Not him. I don't recall seeing one either.' Stacey pointed at their empty glasses. 'Can I get either of you another?'

'No, we're good, thanks. Almost done.' David asked Frankie if there was anything he'd missed.

She focused on Stacey. 'How long did he spend here?'

'Half an hour, maybe less. I got the impression he was waiting for someone. I figured it might be a woman, maybe someone else's woman—'

'What gave you that impression?'

'His mood. I wondered if he'd been stood up. He brightened up when Bill arrived. Bill sat at the bar, as he always does. We were talking about something and nothing when this guy butts in, completely out of the blue, telling us that your lot were interested in a motorcyclist for the deaths across the road.'

Frankie lifted her pen. 'Is that so strange? Surely everyone who's been in lately has talked about what's going on at Kielder.'

'Locals are sick of hearing about it. No offence, but they can't get shifted for press and police.'

'None taken. Are you certain you weren't discussing the investigation?'

'No. As I said, Bill and I were in general conversation. I was aware of the guy looking our way, like he was trying to edge his way in. A lot of lonely people do that. They want someone to talk to. Your guy wasn't like that. At one point it occurred to me that it might not have been a woman he was waiting for. Bill is overtly gay and lovely with it. As soon as this guy opened his mouth, I realised I was wrong.'

'What do you mean?' David asked.

'He wasn't interested in Bill. All he wanted to talk about was seeing the motorcycle and how significant it was to a double-murder investigation. There was no prelude to it.'

'Is that why he'd come in, do you think? To drop it into the conversation?'

'That's exactly the impression I got. It was bizarre. My bullshit detector shot off the scale. I'm sure he was stringing us a line. Shortly afterwards, he finished his whisky and left.' Stacey paused momentarily. 'I never get to see the evening news because my shift starts at six. It's how I relax when I get home.' She looked at David. 'When I saw you on TV, I decided to get in touch.'

'You did right.' Frankie thanked her.

'That's what Detective Sergeant Abbott said.' Stacey glanced at her watch. 'Look, I'm sorry, I have to go before I'm fired—'

'One last question,' David said. 'Any idea how the guy got here?'

'He wasn't walking, I know that much.'

'How come?' Frankie asked.

'Guys put their keys on the bar.' She looked at David apologetically. 'I hate to stereotype men but they use them like miniature status symbols. Hey, look at me! I've got a shiny new motor. There was one in late last night, full of hell as it happens. God's gift to womankind, big drinker, drives a Tesla, not that I was remotely impressed . . .' Stacey hadn't noticed the look of satisfaction that passed between the detectives. 'Talking of remote, Tony didn't have one.'

Frankie's eyes widened. 'There was no fob?'

Stacey shook her head. 'Not as we know it.'

David exchanged a knowing look with Frankie.

Since T-plates, car keys had evolved.

86

Stacey Grainger said the drinks were on the house, a kind offer David refused. If he didn't pay, he didn't drink. He loathed cops who were on the take, accepting freebies at every opportunity and told her so, adding his thanks. 'If you see Tony again, please call me, day or night.' He handed her a twenty note and his contact details. 'Please bear in mind that the man we've been discussing may be an oddball, entirely innocent of any wrongdoing, of no interest to us whatsoever. The opposite may also be true, in which case your intervention may prove invaluable to us.' He finished with some sound advice: 'If you see him, don't go out of your way to engage him in conversation. I don't want to tip him off, nor do I want you to put yourself at risk.'

With his warning ringing in her ears, Frankie held on to her emotions until they were outside the inn, walking towards her vehicle. In the relentless sunshine, their eyes met briefly across the roof of her car. A moment of deep joy. Despite what he'd said to Stacey Grainger, neither detective thought that the man she'd brought to their attention was just a weirdo. It looked like their plan to draw an offender out of the shadows had worked.

Slipping on her sunglasses, Frankie opened the doors and climbed in.

You could fry eggs on the leather seats.

Pulling her belt across her chest, she fired up the engine and turned the aircon on full blast. Reversing out of her spot, she floored the accelerator, sending a plume of brown dust high into the air as they joined the main road.

Scooping her notes off the dash, David flicked through them, then called the MIR and asked for Pam, putting his mobile on speaker as he waited for her to pick up. When she did, the incident room sounded busy. On top of the usual ringing phones and overworked printers, they heard excited conversations they weren't properly able to interpret.

Keeping her eyes on the road, Frankie stated the obvious. 'Something's happened.'

'No shit.'

Pam came on the line. 'Guv, what can I do for you?'

'You can tell me what's going on, for starters.'

'Mitch and Indira struck gold. They found Flavio Conti's records.'

'Yes!' Frankie eased off the gas.

'That's great news,' David said. 'Frank and I just left Stannersburn. Should be with you in an hour. In the meantime' – he glanced at Frankie's notes – 'we don't have a surname for Tony but I'll email his description. Circulate it to the team. Have it checked against PDF data on males we currently have in the system.'

Personal Descriptive Forms had been completed on every individual interviewed in connection with the investigation, whether they had come via the house-to-house team, from officers engaged on vehicle enquiries or members of the public providing witness statements. These forms contained personal details: physical descriptions, vehicles owned and previous convictions where they existed. A search of HOLMES 2 would flag up any similarities.

Buzzing now, David couldn't wait to reach Middle Earth.

Using his ID to gain entry to the MIR, David pushed open the door. Frankie followed him in. It was hotter than a sauna in there despite open windows and cooling fans. They had no sooner crossed the threshold than Mitch and Indira collared them. Heat and Mitch didn't get on. Dark patches of sweat were visible around the armpits of his navy shirt. By comparison, Indi was the epitome of cool. She might just have stepped out of a refrigerator. The most noticeable thing about her was a pair of weary eyes.

Frankie congratulated them both.

'Thanks,' they said at the same time.

Mitch handed the SIO a number of photocopied documents.

He sifted through them with Frankie breathing down his neck, then looked up. 'You got all of this without a warrant?'

'Yes, it's in the public domain.'

'Impressive.'

'That's what I said.' Indi blushed. She'd embarrassed herself.

Making nothing of it, David turned to Mitch. 'You happy to take the floor at the briefing? It'll save time.'

'Yes, guv.'

'I want digital images of these on the murder wall in twenty minutes and the team summoned, all except Abbott. We need him to stay on the vehicle enquiries.' He handed the documents back. 'Might be an idea to get yourself a fresh shirt. Borrow one if necessary. The Chief Super is on his way down. He'll kick your arse if he sees you like that.'

The team already knew the news about Flavio Conti. Mitch didn't need to repeat it. With the MIT looking on, he uploaded the first of the images he'd shown the DCI on his way in. It was a PoW Index Card from Byrness Camp, a photo-ID – two photographs of Conti, one front-facing, one to the side, like police mugshots. The card contained useful information. Conti was a lance corporal, born 8 May 1927. The document included full identification, hair and eye colour, complexion, his height recorded at five ten. A counterfoil gave his place of birth as Bergamo, a city in the alpine region of Lombardy; Frankie knew it was north-east of Milan in northern Italy.

'As you can see,' Mitch said. 'The index card is signed and dated on the eleventh of November 1944, exactly three years to the day before his son Luca was born.'

'How can we be sure it's our guy?' Charlie said. 'For all we know, Flavio Conti could be the equivalent of John Smith.'

Detectives and civilians chuckled.

'We thought you'd ask that,' Indira said.

'Maybe this will convince you.' Tapping on the keyboard of his laptop, Mitch brought up the next page of his presentation, a split screen. Two black-and-white images, side by side.

Charlie scratched his head. 'So, he grew his hair and sometimes cracks a smile. What does that prove? I asked about his name, ya divvy. Pay attention, lad.'

More laughter.

'Don't take the piss, Charlie. Get your specs on and look closer.' Frankie had seen what he hadn't. If Dick had been there, he'd have seen it too. She felt a lump of pride rise in her throat. Mitch, her protégé, was kicking it out of the park.

She gave Mitch the nod to continue.

'On the left is Flavio Conti's front-facing image copied from the PoW Index Card Indi and I found in the Second World War archives,' he explained. 'The one on the right is Luca Conti, taken from his missing persons file.'

'Christ!' Pam said. 'They're almost identical.'

Someone behind Mitch began a slow handclap.

He swung round.

'Top drawer.' Bright cupped a hand to his ear. 'What was that you said, Charlie?'

87

David picked up his toast, eyeing Ben across their tiny breakfast table. It was 7 a.m.. Another belter of a day forecast, a good one in prospect for both of them. For David, it was business as usual; for his nephew, the editing and submission of an article on deaths in British jails. David had read the piece. It was damn good, well researched, with no extraneous content that might turn off readers. Ben had interviewed key figures in the HM Prisons and Probation Service as well as the families of those who'd lost loved ones.

David was immensely proud of him.

Since his father's death three years ago, he'd turned his life around. Luke, David's brother, wouldn't recognise him now. Every day, his son was growing in stature, gaining in confidence under the tutelage of Belinda Wells. She'd taught him never to trust a source without corroboration from another, that leads didn't simply fall into place where investigative journalism was concerned. Like the police, reporters had to seek them out by following the clues, linking strands of evidence together. Only in the police, they had to do it with their heads chopped off, sacrificing a social life, even on a sunny weekend.

'So, what's next?' Ben asked.

David stopped chewing. 'For you or me?'

Ben sliced the top off his boiled egg. 'Is that a loaded question?'

'I was just wondering if you'd had more thoughts on joining the force?'

'Look, if you're going to object—'

'Did I say that?'

'You didn't have to—'

'Chill out, man. If that's what you want, I have no intention of standing in your way. You have a strong work ethic. You've proved yourself capable of chasing a story. I think you'd make a good detective . . .' David poured more coffee. 'Or a snout. You'd be good at that too.'

Ben grinned. 'Cut the careers advice and tell me what you're leading up to. What do you want, Dave?'

'At the moment, nothing. I'll let you know if that changes. Thanks to you, we found Flavio Conti. I'm convinced that the key to his son's death is somehow linked to his birth. I need to find his mother, which means investigating the work his father carried out during his internment at Byrness Camp. Pinpointing exactly where he was deployed is proving more difficult than we imagined.'

'I can do that for you,' Ben said. 'As you keep reminding me, difficult doesn't mean mission impossible.' He tapped on his article. 'I'll have to finish this first. It shouldn't take that long.'

'Thanks, but I put Mitch and Indira on it. They're knee-deep in archival material as we speak. The problem is, the records are incomplete.' David wouldn't dwell on what ifs.

Ben asked: 'How's Frankie doing?'

'Trying to keep up morale. The team are on their knees, her included.' David glanced through the window at nothing in particular.

Ben studied him like a worried father would a son.

Sensing his gaze, David turned to look at him. 'If Frankie is right about Kristjánsson's innocence, this case could make her, even before she's officially promoted.'

'And if she's wrong?'

'Then she'll have to live with it.'

88

At seven thirty on the dot, Dick Abbott drove to the small shop around the corner from his house, parking outside. A yawn escaped his mouth as he yanked on the hand brake. He took a deep breath. There was a time when five hours' sleep would be enough to keep him going. Not anymore. The half-bottle of Scotch he'd downed when he got in late from work hadn't helped. He'd woken with a massive hangover a couple of paracetamols and two cups of coffee wouldn't shift. A self-administered breathalyser had shown him to be over the drink-drive limit.

He felt like shit.

He looked like shit.

Thank Christ for shades.

To hide bloodshot eyes, he grabbed his from the sun-visor. Slipping them on, he got out and locked the car. Moving away from the vehicle, he lit a cigarette, trying to shrug off the feeling of guilt. He ought to have taken a taxi, or called Frankie, asking for a lift. He'd done so before with the excuse that his motor was playing up. Except, last time she'd told him to get his act in gear.

Next time you hang one on, take a rest day.

To hell with that.

This morning, despite his self-imposed headache, he had reasons to be cheerful. Last night, he'd bitten the bullet, levelling with his wife over his failed attempt to qualify for promotion. Linn had taken it better than expected. She'd told him to forget it and move on. If she was disappointed, it didn't show on her face as she went to bed. Now the pressure was off at home, his head was where it should be, fully focused on his new assignment. The vehicle enquiry had gone well. He'd narrowed down a list of Ford Rangers for further investigation. At the SIO's request, he hoped to finalise it by lunchtime. Who could blame him for engaging in a private celebration?

Binning his fag down the drain, he walked across the street.

The bell rang as he opened the shop door. 'Morning, Kim.'

The young woman behind the counter glanced at her watch. 'Couldn't you sleep? If you fancy doing a round, our paperboy slept in. Third time this week. I'll murder the little sod when he shows his face.'

'Careful. Threats to kill was a criminal offence last time I looked.'

She grinned.

Grabbing a carton of fresh milk from the freezer and a packet of extra-strong mints, Dick selected his usual newspaper from the stand. He was about to approach the counter when, in his peripheral vision, the headline of another tabloid caught his eye, resulting in a double-take. His stomach took a dive as he stooped to pick it up. He speed-read the text, then turned the page where the article continued.

He couldn't believe what he was seeing.

'You going to pay for them or just read them for free?' Kim said. 'If you were fifteen, I'd be clipping your ear.'

He looked up.

She was staring at him, hands on hips. 'What's wrong? Your hands are shaking.'

Dick threw some cash on the counter. Before she could ring it in and collect his change, he was gone, on a mission to warn Frankie.

The line was engaged.

He sent a text. **Call me, NOW!**

89

Frankie had almost reached Middle Earth. A few moments ago, she'd answered a call without thinking, assuming it was David. He often called on his way into work to discuss the shape of their day. Instead, a woman's loud voice filled the car. Her name was Tessa Haynes. For the past few minutes, she'd been giving Frankie what for. She couldn't get a word in edgeways. Haynes hadn't stopped for breath. She'd been questioned about a vehicle she claimed she didn't own. Given her agitated state, Frankie thought she'd better let her get it off her chest.

Suddenly, there was silence.

Bliss.

'Hello?' Haynes said. 'Are you there?'

Bugger. 'What kind of vehicle are we talking about?'

'An old Ford. I told the officer that it's not my car. It's my son's—'

The security barrier lifted as Frankie drove towards it. 'How did you get this number?'

'Does it matter?'

'It does to me. This is a dedicated line and I need to keep it open.'

'Don't you dare hang up on me.'

Negotiating the car park, Frankie couldn't see a parking spot and had to go around. What was this, Tesco? 'Calm down please, madam.'

'No, *you* calm down. I've never been questioned by your lot in my life and I don't intend to start now.'

Frankie could feel her patience waning. One minute she was enjoying her drive from the coast, singing along to Ingrid Andress' 'Lady Like' on Spotify, the next she was listening to a crazy woman whose voice could shatter glass.

This was not how she liked to start her day.

'Who gave you this number?'

'He did.'

'He who?' This was getting silly.

'Are you taking the piss? How the hell should I know?'

'Mind your language or I'm hanging up.'

'I apologise. I'm just frustrated.'

That made two of them. 'If you were talking to one of my colleagues, he'd have identified himself.'

'He probably did. Who remembers a random name?'

Frankie would never forget hers. 'Well, whoever it was, it was a mistake. *He* had no authority.' She suspected that 'he' might be Abbott. Was he on to something? She'd soon know. They had a meeting planned at eight before the troops arrived and the MIR got busy.

'You're a cop, aren't you?' Haynes was saying.

'I'm a detective, yes.' Frankie was about to double park when a traffic officer vacated a space near the security barrier. She shot into it, before anyone else could, giving him the thumbs up through the window.

Haynes yelled: 'It's. Not. My. Car. It's my son's. He's away at university. I've told him to change the bloody address. He's taken no notice. He won't and he hasn't. His insurance is cheaper from my postcode, apparently. I don't want the police at my door. Sort it out.' She hung up.

Abbott spied Frankie from a hundred yards away. She was leaning against the bonnet of her car, her legs crossed at the ankle, arms crossed over her chest, in no hurry to go inside. She didn't look happy. Assuming she'd seen the headline, he pulled up beside her, leaving his newspapers on the rear passenger seat. He climbed out, full of hell, almost taking the door off its hinges as he slammed it shut.

'Frankie, I'm so sorry.'

'Not as sorry as I am. Why did you give her my number?'

'What?'

'Haynes.'

He had no idea what she was on about. 'Who the hell is Haynes?'

'The woman who just burst my eardrums, presumably someone on your list.'

'I don't think so.' Abbott spread his hands. 'Whatever she told you, it has nowt to do with me.'

'Have you been drinking?' She glared at him. 'You smell like a distillery. Look, I know things have been tough for you lately. If you have a problem, I need to know about it. I can only help if you talk to me.'

'I had a few last night, not this morning. What do you take me for? Look, can we not do this now?' He nodded to his vehicle. 'Get in.'

'Excuse me?'

'I said get in.'

90

In the car, Frankie turned to face him. Another media outlet, this one national, had picked up on the story English was peddling and run with it. Dick grabbed the newspaper from the rear seat, handing it over. The front page screamed a falsehood: **IN CHARGE & OUT OF CONTROL: a covert affair**. If that wasn't bad enough, the article beneath was worse, two photographs on the next page mind-blowing. They seemed to support the ridiculous headline. The first captured Frankie smoothing down Stone's lapels, making sure he looked his best for the press conference. It could have won a Mr & Mrs competition. They were smiling at one another.

Frankie glanced up at the window where they had been standing at the time, her mouth drying up. Her eyes moved to the conference room, reversing the process. In her head, she was looking down at the very spot where a Tesla belonging to English had been uplifted, causing him the inconvenience of retrieving it from the police pound. 'Jesus! What have I done?' She wiped her face with her hands. 'The boss warned me not to wind the bastard up.'

'Frank—'

'Don't! I made this mess. He'll never forgive me.'

'Yes, he will. It'll blow over.'

'Will it? I don't think so.'

She glanced at the tabloid. The second image was even more damning than the first. Tynemouth beach. Sun-drenched. The same couple perched on a log, laughing together, waves breaking on the sand behind them, like a fucking holiday snap. The past few days scrolled before her eyes. Top of that list, a homemade card propped up against a bottle of champagne. David had placed it on her parent's mantelpiece to celebrate a promising future, an upcoming promotion that might now be in doubt.

She felt the blood drain from her face. 'How could I have been so stupid?'

'Shit!' Abbott was looking over her shoulder.

'What?' She didn't turn around.

'Chief Super. Keep your head down.'

She slid down in her seat. 'Has he seen us?'

'No, he turned left.'

'Get going. If he asks, you haven't seen me.'

Frankie changed cars. Nudging her vehicle forward to get a view of Bright, she waited until he entered the building, then drove through the barrier at speed, calling Stone. She had a grovelling apology to make. There was no time like the present. David answered immediately, a cheery hello. Road noise confirmed that he was mobile, probably on the A19 southbound, the quickest route to Northern Area Command HQ.

'Hey, Frank. On my way with croissants—'

'We need to talk.'

'Can it wait? I'm minutes away.'

'No.' 'This is a conversation we need to have in private. Meet me at Silverlink by the Porsche Centre.' Already heading in that direction, she hung up before he asked any awkward questions, reaching the rendezvous before him.

He arrived within minutes, a curious expression on his face as he drove by. Parking his vehicle in front of hers, he got out, walking towards her, a bakery bag in his hand, a big smile she knew wouldn't last.

His mobile rang as he approached.

'Don't answer that, it's Bright.'

91

Having used the rear entrance, Abbott was at his desk chewing a mouthful of extra-strong mints when Bright charged into the MIR. He made straight for Stone's office, making such a forceful entry that the door crashed against the interior wall as it swung open, making a large dint in the plasterboard. He stepped back, scanning the room, then made a beeline for the most senior detective he could find, which happened to be Dick.

'Where are they?' he said, like Abbott knew the answer.

Abbott swallowed the mint he was chewing. 'Sir?'

'Stone and Oliver. Where are they?'

'Maybe caught in traffic? Anything I can help—'

'Don't give me that bullshit. Oliver's car was parked next to yours when I drove in. Get her on the phone, now!'

Dick made the call. 'She's not picking up, guv.'

'You have three seconds to find them if you want to keep your job.'

David was beside himself, trying not to show it as he moved along the noisy corridor towards the Detective Chief Superintendent's office. He stopped outside the door waiting for Frankie to catch up. The sign facing him seemed to get larger and more forbidding the more he looked at it. Raising his arm, he knocked in the vain hope that Bright had calmed down. Abbott said he'd never seen him so angry. Frankie's face was ashen. She'd fallen over herself to apologise. The damage was done. Nothing they could do but take what was coming – which may or not include their removal from the investigation or even the MIT.

'Let me do the talking,' he said quietly.

'Like hell. This is all my fault.'

He glared at her. 'That wasn't a request.'

'Fine!' she whispered.

A muffled, commanding voice reached them through the door. 'Come!'

David rolled his head, loosening the tension in his neck. Turning the handle, he pushed the door open, stepping inside with Frankie on his heels. The most senior detective in the Northumbria force didn't look up as they approached his desk and stood side by side like two four-year-olds summoned to the headmaster's office for launching paper aeroplanes in class. A capital offence where David went to school.

'Sir, you wanted to see us?'

Bright was seething, his teeth clenched tightly. His jaw resembled the edge of the Grim Reaper's scythe. He shook the tabloid in their faces, exposing the photographs. 'Are you fucking insane? These images are timed and dated. Explain to me how, when the rest of the squad were working round the clock, you dipshits found the time to play sandcastles.'

David glanced at Frankie.

She bit her lip, resisting the temptation to say what was on her mind. She had a tendency to use humour and now was not the time.

'I asked you a question, Stone.'

David's answer fell on deaf ears.

The row went on for a good twenty minutes, Bright reiterating what he'd said when Adam English took a very public swipe at Stone and Oliver in print, a blemish against the wider force that their guv'nor had taken personally. He had every right to be furious. He'd shielded them from the worst of it. With the help of the force's legal team, he'd taken it on his own shoulders to deal with the fallout so they could focus on the investigation. That support was now like egg on his face.

Never in his career had David felt so guilty.

Wells' voice entered his head.

When she'd warned him that English was in town, it had shaken him to the core. He'd declined her offer of a bed for the night because the snake might have him under surveillance. Knowing the capability of his adversary should have been a big red flag. A powerful tool in the fight to follow. And yet he'd taken his eye off the ball. Jane, his late colleague, would have kicked his arse for it.

Bright was yelling now. 'Give me one good reason why I shouldn't can you—'

'Because we're almost there, guv.' It was the first time Frankie had opened her mouth. 'Because—'

David cut her off. 'Guv, as I already said, we were on an official break—'

'The boss is right,' Frankie said. 'This is not what it looks like.'

'What DS Oliver is saying—'

'I can hear what she's saying Stone, I'm not deaf.'

David knew that Frankie wasn't about to fold. She was in danger of saying something they might both regret. It didn't take long to arrive . . .

'The beach is a bolthole, less pressurised—'

'Is it?'

Frankie gave a nod. 'It's a tip I got from a writer friend of mine. Whenever he gets stuck, he takes himself out of his environment. It really works. Isn't there somewhere you go to work through complex cases?'

'Are you taking the piss? As it happens, I do have somewhere. It's called the incident room.' Bright turned his head slowly, fixing on the SIO. 'So, this is a regular thing, Stone? Maybe you'd like to rewrite the murder investigation manual. An ice-cream briefing sounds like fun.' He scowled 'It. Stops. Now!' He waved the newspaper again. 'Do you really think anyone reading this shit will give you the benefit of the doubt?'

'It's tit for tat, sir.'

'He's right,' Frankie said defiantly. 'English is spinning a pack of lies. I took away his big boy's toy. He's levelling the score. For the record, I take full responsibility. David warned me not to aggravate him. Take me off the case, by all means, but leave him on it. This post-mortem may be making you feel better, but it's dead time for us. No pun intended. We're making excellent progress and, with respect, we have a shedload of work to do.'

'Listen to her, Stone. She's out of control. I will *not* tolerate insubordination.' His laser eyes found their target. 'Frankie, you're standing on very thin ice. Let me give you a piece of advice. If you ever channel Kate Daniels again, I will remove you. One I can cope with. Two will give me a coronary.'

Frankie stifled a grin. Kate Daniels was a DCI in charge of another Murder Investigation Team, the most revered SIO on the force bar none. 'I'll take that as a compliment, guv.'

David cringed inwardly, expecting a backlash for her impertinence.

Surprisingly, Bright said nothing.

Frankie stepped back over the invisible line. 'Guv, I'm no angel, I accept that. The boss has given you an explanation. You must know that we'd never discredit the force intentionally. If you're willing to accept that, along with our profound apologies, we'd like to go now.' Bright opened his mouth to speak. She got in first with four magic words guaranteed to stop him in his tracks. 'There's been a development.' She paused to let them sink in. 'Mitch found out that Flavio Conti was deployed to work in Jedburgh, just fifteen miles from Byrness PoW Camp, which coincides with Professor Dawson's findings. We're one step away from an arrest. If you remove one or both of us, English wins.'

92

Stone and Oliver were told to get the hell out of Bright's office. They scarpered before he had a chance to change his mind. David blew out a breath, closing the door quietly behind him. Wiping his sweaty hands on his trousers, he set off along the corridor towards the MIR with Frankie by his side, grateful that he still had a job. How long that would last would depend on results.

He glanced at Frankie. 'When precisely did you get that update from Mitch?'

She didn't look at him.

'You didn't, did you?'

'It's better you don't know.'

'Jesus!' He stopped walking, grabbing her arm to slow her down. 'If Bright gets wind of this, he'll take your warrant card, you know that, right?'

'The first bit was true . . .' She winced, waggling her hand from side to side – a fifty-fifty gesture. 'I may have overstated the second. Mitch is meeting someone he thinks might be able to confirm Conti's deployment—'

'"He thinks"?'

'Relax, it wasn't a complete fabrication.' She held up crossed fingers, an expression bordering on panic she was trying and failing to hide. 'Mitch will be super quick, Bright none the wiser.'

'And if he bumps into Mitch?'

'He won't. I banned him from base until he brings us what we need.'

It took a nervous two days for Mitch to find the proof and corroborate it. The hiatus wasn't wasted. Work had begun in earnest on tracing Ford Rangers with a 1999 (T) prefix. Abbott had come up with seventy-six vehicles within the area parameters David had laid down, an unsurprising number given the rural locality.

A team of detectives, assisted by uniformed personnel, had worked twelve-hour shifts, checking each and every one, ruling them in or out of the investigation as enquiries were completed. Out in the case of Tessa Haynes, whose son had since been spoken to and advised to inform the DVLA of a change of address or face the consequences. It was tough going, an operation that drained resources, human and financial. Finally, the MIT were down to the last ten. On that front, they were closing in.

Mitch and Indira were giving an update on High Barns Farm where Flavio Conti had been put to work during and after the Second World War. As always, they had done their homework. They were in conference with the Stone and Oliver in the SIO's office. Having skipped their lunch, they had brought treats.

'High Barns is made up of arable and pastureland,' Indi said.

Frankie asked, 'Did you consult with the Land Registry like I asked?'

A nod. Indi popped a last bite of a Twirl in her mouth, rubbed her hands together to get rid of any debris, then passed David and Frankie an A4 sheet she had balanced on her knee. She leaned forward. 'As you can see, during the time Flavio was deployed to work there, the deeds of High Barns show the owner as Mr Graeme Latimer. In 1980, ownership passed to his son, Ross Latimer. On *his* death last year, the property was inherited by the present owner, Scott Latimer.'

A dig from Frankie. 'Did none of these men have daughters?'

'You're assuming the farm was passed down the male line,' Mitch said. 'That's what we thought at first, only we checked the will bequest. Scott Latimer is the nephew, not the son of Ross.' He paused a beat. 'Guess where he's from?'

93

'Plashetts?'

'Close enough,' Mitch said. 'Actually, Falstone.'

A rush of adrenalin lifted the hairs on Frankie's bare arms. Her heart was racing as she stared wide-eyed at Mitch. 'Are you absolutely sure?'

'Positive. Scott Latimer was born in December 1980, eighteen months, give or take, before Kielder Water was officially opened. His father was born and brought up in the village.' Knowing how significant this was, Mitch could hardly contain himself. 'Sarge, Scott Latimer is also on Dick's list. And that's not all . . .' He turned to Indi, who looked set to burst. 'Go on, your turn.'

'Latimer is already in the system,' she said excitedly. 'He was interviewed during the house-to-house. I checked his PDF. He was driving a piece-of-shit Renault, not an old Ford Ranger, but he fits the description of the guy who was mouthing off about a motorbike to Stacey Grainger in the Pheasant Inn.'

'Whoa, wait a minute,' David said. 'I don't understand. How come he was interviewed if he lives in Jedburgh? I didn't authorise such a wide house-to-house sweep. Who submitted the PDF?'

'PC Sara Gallagher. She works out of Hexham.'

'Get her in here,' Frankie said. 'I need to speak to her.'

'I did that already,' Mitch said. 'Latimer happened to be in the area, visiting his aunt, when Gallagher was doing her rounds. Fortunately, she had the wherewithal to include everyone and anyone she came across. She doesn't know it yet, but her actions may well have unlocked the case.'

'I still need to see her,' Frankie said. 'Sort it for me. Who's the aunt?'

'Ruth, same surname.'

David said, 'So Ruth is Ross's wife?'

'No, guv. She and Ross were cousins. Their fathers were brothers. Indi prepared a family tree.' He handed over a second A4 sheet. 'As you can see, her father married twice. Scott is the child of her half-brother, John.'

David took a moment to recap, counting on his fingers, starting with his thumb. 'Scott Latimer has local ties. He's in the system. He fits the physical description of a man who I firmly believe was giving himself an out by pointing the finger at the biker, Neil Richmond. He's on Dick's list and now he's on mine. Five out of five. Are we all agreed that he's a credible suspect?'

'If he isn't, I don't know who is,' Mitch said.

'Absolutely,' Frankie said.

Indira was nodding enthusiastically.

David let go of his little finger, his focus on Mitch and Indira. 'You two, stand down. You deserve a break. Be ready to travel within the hour. Thanks to Gallagher, we know what vehicle Latimer was driving when he visited his aunt. We have reason to believe he also owns a Ford Ranger. If that's the case, his neighbours will have seen it.'

David paused a beat.

'If we're canvassing adjacent farms for information, I need to alert Police Scotland that we're making enquiries across the border. I'll work on it and let you have a proforma before you leave. Frankie, log on to Google Earth. Take a look at High Barns. When you've done that, speak to Gallagher. Find out what Ruth is like. You and I need to pay her a visit.'

94

Frankie logged on to further her research and check access roads to High Barns Farm. The camera zoomed in over a patchwork of fields of different colours, a large farmhouse, two barns and several outbuildings. The access road was to the south. The camera swung round slowly 360 degrees. There were four vehicles parked in the farmyard, two tractors and two cars, neither of which looked like the flatbed Ranger she was looking for. She scribbled down the map reference shown at the bottom of the screen and the date that the image was taken: 12 May 2015.

Logging off, she picked up the phone and called Hexham police station. A civilian answered. Frankie introduced herself by name and rank. 'I need to speak with PC Gallagher.'

'Just a moment, I'll see if she's available.' Frankie heard the tapping of keys. 'Sergeant Oliver? I'm sorry, Gallagher is state zero.'

'Give me her home number then. It's urgent.'

'I'll verify your number and call you.' Standard protocol.

Frankie waited patiently. David was scribbling away, preparing the proforma. Seconds later, her mobile rang. Satisfied that she was legit, the civilian clerk gave the number she was after and rang off.

Frankie redialled.

The phone rang out for several seconds.

'Hello?' A yawn. 'Whoever this is, please go away.'

'Wake up, Sara. It's DS Oliver, Murder Investigation Team.'

'Oh. Sorry, Sarge. Can you hold on?'

'Make it quick.'

Frankie heard the phone go down on a hard surface, a bit of whispering going on. Gallagher had company. She was probably putting some distance between them. The click of a door closing.

'Right, Sarge. How can I help?'

'You already have. I'll not go into it now. All I can say is, it won't be forgotten, by me or my guv'nor. I need information on Ruth Latimer, a woman you interviewed during the Falstone house-to-house. You remember her?'

Gallagher confirmed that she did.

'What's she like?'

'Lovely.'

'That's not what I'm after. Flaky or sensible?'

'The latter. She didn't flinch when I rocked up at her door. She was serenely calm, smart, well-spoken, in excellent shape physically and mentally.'

'That's better. And her nephew, Scott?'

'In a hurry.'

'Meaning?'

'He had somewhere to go, Sarge. Couldn't understand why I wanted his details when he didn't live in Falstone. Is he involved in the Kielder incident?' Frankie was about to sidestep the question when Gallagher continued: 'That would surprise me, if I'm honest. When I explained why I needed to take down his details, he cooperated fully.'

Frankie was on the back foot. 'Nothing struck you as odd about him?'

'No. He was shy, a nice bloke.'

'Good to talk to you, Sara. I'll call you if I need any more. Get yourself to bed.'

'Ha! Have a good day, Sarge.'

The line went dead.

Gallagher's description didn't sound like the man Frankie had conjured up in her head following her meeting with barmaid Stacey Grainger. The thought prompted questions. Had Latimer lied to Gallagher about the vehicles he owned? Was Abbott's list out of date? Was it possible that Latimer had sold the Ranger on, the new keeper failing to register his or her address? The old key fob Grainger had seen on the counter of the Pheasant Inn would suggest not.

Frankie sat back, considering.

Latimer was involved somehow. She didn't know how and wouldn't know for sure until the team canvassed the farms near his home and reported in. Though he was too young to have been responsible for the death of Luca Conti, she strongly suspected that he'd dumped the barrel into Kielder Water. Another question bubbled to the surface like Scheving's last breath: If Latimer hadn't killed him, then who had?

95

Frankie's mobile rang, startling her. Anna Jónsdóttir's name appeared on the home screen. Unsettling, given the Northumbria detective's last thought. She stared at the device, then at David, wondering why his counterpart would be calling in the middle of a double-hander. Anna would know how swamped they were. What the hell did she want? Unless . . .

'You going to answer that?' David didn't look up. 'I'm trying to concentrate.'

'Sorry, I was miles away.'

Now he raised his head. 'Everything all right?'

'Yeah. Why shouldn't it be?'

'You seem uptight. That usually means you're telling porkies.' He glanced at the mobile advancing across her desk.

Avoiding eye contact, Frankie took the call. 'Hey, Anna. I was just thinking about you.' In hindsight, that was a stupid thing to say with David earwigging. Frankie was struggling to keep her composure, desperate to talk, though not with him in the room. 'You'll have to be quick though. The boss and I are heading out soon.'

'Chasing a lead?'

'Potentially.'

'Me too . . . in relation to your case as it happens.'

Her words struck Frankie dumb. There was only one investigation Anna could be talking about. She'd had no involvement in the other. Frankie's faith in Kristjánsson's innocence had been questioned by every detective in the MIT. Had Anna joined them in that view? Had *she* missed some vital piece of evidence that the Icelandic DCI had since found?

That depressing thought produced a flashback.

Frankie was standing with pathologist Beth Collinwood

on the shore of Kielder Water examining exhibits: a rock, a camera, a wet towel. Three separate evidence bags. The last item contained traces of Scheving's blood. Blood that Kristján was unable to explain away. Had she made the wrong call?

Anna's voice broke her mind-trip. 'Frankie? Are you still there? Would you rather I call back?'

'No, go ahead.'

Having heard one half of the conversation, more importantly the tone of it, David stopped what he was doing. He gestured for her to put the phone on speaker. Frankie feigned misunderstanding. He wasn't buying it. He marched across the room and did it for her. He was standing over her, as concerned as she was . . . almost.

He said, 'Anna, is this a private conversation or can anyone join?'

'Well, it's work-related. It seems my collaboration with British law enforcement will go on longer than anticipated.'

'Oh?'

Panic seized Frankie's throat and gave it a squeeze.

David clocked her reaction. 'Is that why my 2ic is acting weird?'

'I don't know. Maybe you should ask her. I was about to give her the heads-up on something she asked me to do before she left the country. A team of CSIs have taken Scheving's flat apart. Squirrelled beneath the floorboards they found a stash of records: dates, times, locations, amounts of money, flight details. I'm sending everything through to Frankie now. I'm just letting you know that it's on its way. I was going to copy in the SCDEA, but I thought your golden girl might like to notify them.' She was referring to the Scottish Crime and Drug Enforcement Agency.

Frankie's relief was instant. It soon gave way to anger for panicking like a child in the dark. She found her voice. 'You deserve the credit, Anna. Thank you, we appreciate the intelligence.'

Keen to get going, David tapped his watch.

Frankie nodded.

Anna spoke again. 'And that's not all.'

'Hold on a second.' Frankie met David's gaze. 'If you want to head down, I'll catch you up.'

He shook his head. 'I'll wait.'

'I won't keep you long,' Anna interrupted. 'I had an illuminating conversation with Jón Scheving's psychologist. She told me that he was referred by the hospital following a serious suicide attempt, the first of many. He was messed up, trying to put his drug habit behind him. On her advice, he stopped visiting his father and had been receiving death threats from the prison, and not only from his old man.'

'That's appalling,' Frankie said. 'Whatever happened to confine, secure and rehabilitate? Óli needs to up his game.' She explained to David that Óli was Head of Security at Hólmsheiði Prison.

'A complaint is on its way to the governor as we speak,' Anna said. 'Anyway, Jón was deteriorating rapidly, racked with guilt over the assault on Eva, wanting to make recompense for what he did. He was off his head when he attacked her, disgusted by his behaviour, given what happened to his mother.'

'That explains the artwork in his flat.'

'Yes. The psychologist suggested that he write down his feelings. He wrote to Eva, apologising for the crime, but the letter was never sent.'

'Why?'

'He hand-delivered the letter but didn't turn up for a follow-up appointment. The psychologist sent it to me.' Anna paused. 'Brace yourself, it makes grim reading.'

Frankie knew it would upset Eva. What victim would want to hear from a perpetrator? What purpose would it serve except to offload guilt? Try as she might to hold that line, compassion overrode her ill-feeling toward Jón Scheving. Hearing about his plight was bad. Reading the letter would be a whole lot worse. He never stood a chance. She couldn't imagine what living hell his life must've been.

'That's it from me,' Anna said. 'Oh, by the way, I'm seeing Kristjánsson tomorrow.'

Frankie's heart almost leapt from her chest, seeds of doubt returning. 'For what purpose?'

'I'll get back to you on that.'

96

Mitch had been on the blower. He and Indira were on their way up. Frankie Oliver was going nowhere for the time being. She waited, eyes on her boss. There were a lot of reasons why she wanted to bring the double-hander to a close. Victims Luca Conti and Jón Scheving deserved justice. That was and always had been her battle cry.

Nothing else mattered – except, this time it did.

Because of her, David was in trouble. English had rubbished his reputation and hers. As far as she was concerned, he could take his fabricated headlines and shove them up his arse. Wrapping up these cases would rip the wind from his sails. If the opportunity to take a pop at them was removed, the journalist would likely pick on someone else. Anyone who'd sell his seedy tabloid was fair game.

Frankie wasn't finished with him yet.

A knock at the door.

Abbott, Mitchell and Indira entered.

David swivelled his chair to face them, instructing them on how he wanted the canvassing operation to play out across the Scottish border, handing them each an A4 sheet. 'There are just three farms bordering Latimer's land. Take one each. Keep it low key. Treat it like you're doing a sweep of all farms.'

'What excuse do we give?' Indi asked.

'You're working on reports of stolen vehicles from farms on our side of the border. Not strictly true. Don't let that stop you. Keep it casual. Ask what vehicles they have, what their neighbours have. Don't go pointing fingers. On no account are any of you to go near High Barns. If Latimer is our guy, we can't afford to tip him off. Any problems, give me a shout. Frankie, you ready?'

The woman who opened the door was around five eight with cotton wool hair tied in a long plait that was hanging over her right shoulder, a few stray hairs softening her face. Sharp eyes were framed by gold-rimmed specs. She wore a loose smock shirt and black cropped pants. Her hands were covered in flour and she had a speck of white powder on her left cheek. She looked much younger than her eighty-nine years.

'Ruth Latimer?'

'Yes.'

'I'm Detective Sergeant Frankie Oliver and this is my boss, Detective Chief Inspector David Stone. We're following up on enquiries made by PC Gallagher in relation to two separate incidents on the shores of Kielder Water.'

'And they've led to me?'

'We think you may be able to help us, yes.' Frankie pointed into the hallway. 'May we come in?'

Ruth Latimer stepped inside, leading the detectives into a large, uncluttered living room. Two rooms knocked into one. It was light and airy with modern furniture. Clean lines. Fresh paint. Contemporary artwork that looked expensive. She offered them homemade lemonade which they declined.

'I'm having one. It's unbearably hot out there.'

'More so in the kitchen, I imagine.' Frankie pointed at her hands.

The woman laughed. 'I'm not baking, Detective. This is chalk, not flour.'

Frankie felt guilty for making assumptions. 'You're an artist?'

'Amateur, not professional. I prefer to use my fingers than a brush or paint knife. Excuse me a moment while I wash it off. The dust gets everywhere.' She disappeared, returning with a tray, three glasses and a jug of cloudy liquid. She set it down on a side table, pouring a glass for herself. 'If you change your minds, help yourselves.'

They all sat down.

David had asked Frankie to take the lead. Her first impression of the potential, possibly crucial witness, mirrored Gallagher's. Ruth Latimer was unruffled, intelligent, articulate. Still, these were unchartered waters. Frankie was about to embark on an interview that might tear the woman's life apart. In such circumstances, there was no telling how she might react. Frankie felt no need to go around the houses. Still, she intended to do everything in her power to make it as painless as possible. She had her suspicions about what had happened here.

97

Frankie stared into the eyes of a teenager, a boy she suspected was around fourteen years old when the image was taken. She recognised him from a photograph Mitch had secured of Scott Latimer, who she believed was responsible for dumping the barrel and the brutal murder of an Icelandic national. The boy was tall, well built. Ruth had her arm around him. They were smiling into the camera, a happy snap.

A second image confirmed his identity. He was now fully grown, an adult standing beside Kielder Water. There were tell-tale signs in the background that made Frankie's her heart race, reinforcing her belief that she was closing on her target. Few sections of the reservoir were fenced off. This one was. The backdrop identified the location as the north shore, close to the Wave Chamber where Scheving had met his death, less than half a mile from the Belling peninsula.

Such an innocent image.

A damning one, nevertheless.

David had seen it too. He sent Frankie a non-verbal message to push on.

She pointed at the photographs. 'Is that your son?'

Ruth gave a warm smile. 'As good as. He's my nephew.'

'You have no children of your own?' Having looked into it, Frankie already knew the answer.

'Sadly, no.' The light faded from the octogenarian's eyes.

Frankie let it go. She'd have to return to the subject and wasn't looking forward to it. 'I believe you've lived in the area for some time.'

'All my life. I'm afraid to say that like the rest of my genera-tion I'm rather parochial in attitude. The rest of the world has passed me by, pretty much.'

'You can't improve on perfection.' Frankie smiled. 'This is a beautiful spot.'

'Indeed.' The smile was returned.

'Ruth – may I call you that?'

'That is my name.'

Frankie sat forward, elbows on her knees, hands clasped loosely in front of her. 'This may seem like an odd request. I'd like you to cast your mind back to the mid-seventies. Were you aware of a young man going missing around that time?'

'Everyone was. His parents were beside themselves.'

'That would be Mr and Mrs Charlton?'

'Yes, I didn't know them that well. They were, to use that awful phrase, incomers. Less connected than those of us who were born and bred here. From memory, they kept themselves to themselves when they were here—'

'"When they were here?"' David queried.

'They travelled a lot, Detective Chief Inspector. Falstone was their second home. It stood empty for much of the year and fell into disrepair. It caused a lot of resentment locally, I remember that much.' Ruth's expression darkened. 'Probably why my father wasn't keen on the family.'

Frankie could think of another reason.

'Nevertheless, there was a community-led search organised by the rector of St Peter's,' Ruth continued. 'The young man's name was Clifford, wasn't it?'

Frankie glanced around the room, noting the absence of a TV. It was obvious to her that Ruth Latimer hadn't seen the press conference where David had named Clifford Charlton, giving out his date of birth and the name he was born with. Had he done so, this witness would have been in pieces. There was something to be said for ignoring the news.

'Were you involved in the search?'

'No, my father was sick. I was playing nursemaid.'

Sick had more than one connotation.

'To be honest, the police were less concerned for Clifford's welfare than his parents were. He'd inherited their wanderlust and had taken off before, though on previous occasions he'd kept in touch. That's what convinced them that he'd come to harm when he disappeared without a trace. They've since passed away. Unsurprising. Word is, it broke them.' Ruth looked forlorn. Melancholy had set in. 'I don't suppose you ever get over something like that.' She focused on Stone. 'Is it Clifford's body you found at Kielder?'

Stone hadn't said a word throughout the interview.

He didn't answer.

Frankie turned her head, the better to see him. His silence was no avoidance tactic. He seemed not to have heard the question. His attention was on the window over Ruth's shoulder. He's seen something Frankie hadn't. A split second later, an SUV came into view. It slowed, almost to a stop, then took off at speed, tyres squealing as the tread skidded on the hot tarmac, the wheels attempting to gain traction. Scott Latimer was the driver.

98

As he got in the car, David snatched his radio off the dash, using his call sign: 'Mike 7125 to Control. Assistance required. Falstone. Anyone in the area? Suspect on the move. I repeat, suspect on the move—'

Control: 'Stand by. All available units, proceed to Falstone and await instructions.' There was a short break in transmission. 'Control to 7125: Backup on way.'

A Traffic officer responded immediately. 'Tango 5285: Bellingham. Standing by.'

David pressed to transmit: 'Tango 5285, proceed Tarset Tyne Bridge and hold for further instruction.'

'Roger.'

David heard her siren before he'd even finished speaking. She was familiar, one of Andrea's Traffic crew. As mad as a box of frogs but nevertheless competent. He imagined her, foot to the floor, other units racing to the location. She'd make it to Lanehead in less than three minutes. 'Control: any patrol cars in the area? I want a roadblock at the eastern end of the C200.'

Ruth had heard the racket outside. Commotions of this sort were rare in Falstone, a peaceful village with a population of around two hundred and fifty. Not having turned quickly enough to see her nephew drive away – and finding it odd that Stone had got up and left so abruptly – she asked again if the identity of one of Frankie's victims was the missing man Clifford Charlton.

'Not that it has anything to do with me,' she added. 'Whoever it is, it's terribly sad.'

Aware that her last sentence was about to become a personal reality, Frankie took her time formulating her response.

'Clifford may once have been a missing person,' she began. 'He's now a murder victim. In order to find out what happened to him, I need to investigate his life. His whole life. I think you can help with that.'

'Me?' Ruth frowned. 'Other than what I've already told you, I'm struggling to see how. Unless you have more to tell me.'

There was plenty, none of it good. 'Did you ever meet Clifford?'

'As a young child perhaps, but he was at boarding school, then university. I can't remember meeting him in later life.'

'Did you know he was adopted?'

'I had no idea. Why would I? As I said, our families weren't close.' Ruth looked away.

Frankie had seen a flicker of alarm before she answered. It was time to level with her. 'DCI Stone and I have unequivocal proof that one of our victims had Italian connections. During the Second World War, his father worked at High Barns, a farm now owned by your nephew, Scott Latimer.'

Stone was in hot pursuit. 'Mike 7125. Target heading south. Shilling Pot. Driving a white Renault Captur. Registration mark: November. Lima. Six. Eight. Alpha. Foxtrot. Golf. All units, stand by.' He had no choice but to follow the target vehicle. Had Latimer been unaware that police were on to him, things might have been different. A surveillance detail would have sufficed. That was no longer an option. Having spotted David through the window of Ruth's cottage, Latimer was now a fugitive fleeing justice. If he wasn't caught, he'd go to ground.

'Mike 1089 . . .' *Abbott's call sign.* 'Heading your way, guv.'

'Update required.'

Abbott: 'Neighbouring farms confirm suspect owns a Ford Ranger.'

Stone: 'Understood. What's your position?'

Abbott: 'Approaching Kielder village from the west.'

Stone: 'Find a location and stop. I'll update if he's coming your way.'

Abbott: 'There's a narrow bridge east of me, guv. I'll park up and decamp.'

Latimer had two choices out of Falstone. He'd made the right one. SUV or not, only a fool would take the minor road to Hawkhope and across the Kielder dam. Too risky. In not taking that route, he'd made it easy for the SIO. With police at either end of the C200, his target had nowhere to go.

Ruth flushed slightly. As soon as Frankie mentioned High Barns, she saw cracks appearing. There was a difficult road ahead. Questions that would likely break the old lady's spirit, transporting her to a place she'd rather not go.

This was going to hurt.

'Did you visit the farm during the conflict?'

'Yes, I spent a lot of time there as a girl.'

'Helping your uncle?'

'Yes. I'm not following—'

'I'm sorry, I think you are. Look, if there was any other way of saying this, believe me I'd use it. Clifford Charlton's given name was Luca Conti. He's the son of Flavio Conti.' The eyes of Frankie's witness filled with tears. She knew the name. 'Ruth, was Luca *your* son?'

99

'Mike 7125. All units. Target vehicle has turned right. Now westbound on Shilling Pot.' Shilling Pot was a short stretch of the C200, less than fifteen hundred metres long, famous as the only street of that name in the UK. 'Passing Kielder dam,' David continued. 'Traffic heavy both ways.'

'5285, standing by at Lanehead.'

'Received,' David said. '1089, you in position?'

'Affirmative.' Dick had blocked off the bridge.

Up ahead, Latimer was flying, David on his tail. So far, so good. Then the worst thing that could happen, did. A slow-moving Land Rover with trailer attached moved onto the road in front of him, the driver oblivious to his presence. Forced to brake hard, David slammed the heel of his hand on the horn, an elongated and angry blast, a swear word to go with it. With neither blue light nor siren, he had no other way of warning the driver to pull over.

Ruth began hyperventilating. Frankie helped her up, moving her into the garden for some air, grabbing a box of tissues from the kitchen counter on the way out. They sat down, Frankie in two minds whether to call an ambulance or the local GP. She had a duty of care to keep the old lady safe, an obligation to get help if it were needed. Ruth was having none of it. Breathing easier now, she begged Frankie not to make a fuss. Probably terrified that her neighbours would want to know why the cops were at her door asking questions.

She had a point.

Placing a hand gently on hers, Frankie did her best to comfort her, wondering how David was faring in the hunt for Scott Latimer. If anyone could catch him, he could.

The Land Rover had taken no avoiding action. If anything, he'd slowed down, making it impossible for David to pass. As far as the driver was concerned, the SIO was a boy racer engaged in hot pursuit of an equally dangerous opponent on a peaceful stretch of road with no thought for other road users, most of whom were holiday motorists, caravanners, campers and walkers. Latimer had probably worked out that he had eight miles to cover. He'd be hoping he could make it to Scotland before police could stop him.

He could think again.

'Tango 7003: Anything I can do?' Andrea had joined the hunt.

David changed down, flashing his lights at the driver in front.

Andrea spoke again, the epitome of calm as always. 'Tango 7003: en route to your location. Please respond.'

'Welcome aboard,' David said. 'ETA?'

Andrea: 'Five minutes.'

'Make it four. All units, I have the eyeball. Target weaving in and out of traffic. Causing distress to other road users.'

'7003: Patrol officers now covering Tarset Bridge. Tango 5285 following me with backup. Westbound civilian vehicles now stationary until we put this to bed.'

'Appreciate the heads-up,' David said. 'Passing Tower Knowe Visitor's Centre. Shit!'

Andrea: 'What's happening?'

Stone: 'Near miss. He's flying.'

A beat of time. 'Emergency vehicles informed, guv.'

'Good call, Tango 7003. We might need them.'

Despite the baking sun, Ruth Latimer's hands were like ice. Half an hour ago, she was out in her peaceful garden getting creative, leaving her artwork propped up on an easel as she left to answer the door. Now, she was distraught, her head in her hands, sobbing for a lost love. A lost child.

She looked up. 'I'm so sorry, Sergeant Oliver.'

'Take your time, Ruth. Deep breaths. That's it. You've had a nasty shock. I'm the one who should be apologising. Intruding on private lives is the worst part of my job. It was never my intention to upset you.' Frankie would have given anything not to. 'I know only too well what it does to have personal issues raked over by strangers. I hope you understand why I had to ask.'

'I do.' Ruth dried her eyes, the speck of chalk gone from her cheek. 'That's sounded heartfelt. You have personal experience?'

'I've had my fair share of tragedy—'

'The reason you do what you do?'

'Yes.' Frankie said without hesitation. 'There's no rush. We can stop now. I can call again when you're feeling up to it.'

'No.' Ruth sat up straight, her emotions in check. 'I'd rather get it over with. I've not spoken about this since I was seventeen.'

100

'Mike 7125. Target driving erratically. Excessive speed – eighty and climbing. Using both sides of the road. Vehicles having to take avoiding action. I have no opportunity to pass or stop. Unable to take him. Maintain your positions.'

'Tango 7003. Closing on you.'

If David knew Andrea, she'd be there in seconds.

There was nothing to match the adrenalin rush of a car chase. His excitement was marginal compared with his fear for other road users. He had a call to make. Pull off or continue the pursuit. He dropped his visor. The sun was low in the sky, shining directly in his eyes. It would be the same for Latimer.

An added hazard.

'7125: Passing Bull Crag peninsula. No change otherwise. Shit! No, wait. Westbound traffic ahead of me slowing. Hold for an update.' Long pause in transmission as David craned his neck to see what was happening. 'As you were, Control. Motorists responding to flashing lights. Pulling over, allowing us to pass. A few stragglers. I still have the eyeball.'

Abbott: '1089. Change of plan, guv. I've taken up position west of Bakethin Reservoir. Quarter mile south of the bridge to prevent target vehicle from leaving the C200 onto Kielder Forest Drive and making it onto the A68.'

Stone: 'Received. Stand clear.'

Abbott: 'No one is getting past us, guv. Found myself a lumberjack. Logging truck almost in position.'

'Yeehaw!' Tango 7003 laughed. 'Let them truckers roll, 10-4.'

David bloody loved Andrea. She was unflappable. Nothing fazed her.

He heard her siren as she approached.

She spoke again, her mind firmly on the job. '7125: I see

you. I'll take it from here. By my calculation, there should be a gap soon. Once the target realises he has no escape, he might double back. Watch yourself.'

Ruth wiped her face again, ready to say more. 'Flavio was a wonderful young man. We fell in love and I became pregnant. My father was furious. When Luca was born, he made me put him up for adoption . . .' She let the sentence trail off, unable to go on. The woman was inconsolable.

'You didn't have any contact with the Charltons over it?'

'No.' Her expression hardened. 'I had no idea my baby's adoptive parents had any connection with the area. I was told the opposite. My father said he'd been placed with a good family in the south. He wouldn't even allow me to register the birth.'

'He arranged the adoption?'

A nod. 'I asked if I might receive photographs as Luca grew up. He said they would upset me. What he meant was they would upset him. He was an authoritarian. Very strict. I'd brought shame on our family. He wasn't having that. As far as he was concerned, I was fraternising with the enemy. He banned me from seeing Flavio.'

'Was your father a farmer too?'

'An aircraft engineer.'

Frankie didn't react. Ruth's answer had brought to mind the cable ties Beth Collingwood had found in the barrel, specifically her comment that they were developed for use in the aeronautical industry – though she didn't mention it. 'We found a very unusual crucifix with Luca's body. It's a unique piece of jewellery. Very old. Do you have knowledge of such an item?'

'Flavio gave it to me.' Ruth got up suddenly, disappearing into the house.

Fearing that she might be about to collapse, Frankie followed her in.

'Mike 7125: Eastbound lane clear. Go!'

Tango 7003 screamed past him, closing on the target. No thumbs up as she flew by. Andrea's eyes were like lasers, firmly on the target. Total concentration. One purpose in mind. '7003: I have the eyeball, thank you. I'll take the commentary from here. Travelling north-west on the C200. Blues and twos engaged. Police stop sign illuminated. Suspect vehicle exceeding the speed limit. Seventy-five, seventy-eight mph. 7125, keep your distance.'

'Received.' David slowed, pulling into the middle of the road to get a better view, eyes scanning every dirt junction on his left, aware of a concentration of tourist attractions, every one of them representing a tragedy waiting to happen. Now Andrea was making a noise, hikers were moving off both sides of the road, many of them youngsters. A horrible thought occurred. 'Tango 7003, be advised, you're closing on Hawkhirst Scout Centre.'

'Noted. Passing it now. Clear signs on the road, Control. Target vehicle ignoring them. Still in pursuit. Five hundred yards and closing. No change from the driver.' There was a short pause. 'Control, I can see him looking in his rear-view mirror. He's aware of police vehicle following. Making no attempt to pull in or slow down.'

'Control: copy that.'

101

Frankie called out. 'Ruth, are you OK?'

'In the living room.'

Frankie found her taking a leather-clad box from an old oak chest. Setting it down on the dining table, she opened it up, removing a faded black-and-white close-up of herself as a seventeen-year-old. She handed it to Frankie. As a young woman, Ruth was fair, beautiful, the crucifix around her neck.

Frankie looked up. 'May I borrow this?'

Ruth was reluctant to part with it. 'It's the only one I have.'

'I promise to return it.'

The old lady gave a nod, then dipped her hand into the box a second time, selecting another photo which she also passed to Frankie. 'This is Flavio.'

'He's very handsome.' Frankie asked her to sit down and waited until she'd done so, before removing a photocopy from her bag. It was the split image Mitch had shared with the MIT: Flavio Conti's PoW ID on one side; on the other, the photograph contained in Luca Conti's misper file. She handed it over. 'As you can see, your son was the double of his father.'

Ruth stared at the image, hot tears streaming down her face.

'I'd like you to keep it,' Frankie said. 'I'll arrange a proper copy as soon as I'm able.'

'Thank you. This is so precious.'

The reservoir was on the right, an expanse of shimmering water surrounded by forest, a clear blue sky, many sailing boats, a sight that would normally lift David's spirits. Not today. Today, they represented great danger. The chase was taking place where the C200 was precariously close to the shoreline. If Latimer had a mind to, with split-second timing on his part, a deliberate and determined nudge to the Traffic car and Andrea would end up in the drink.

As she shot across a bridge, David breathed a sigh of relief. The hazardous stretch was behind her.

'Tango 7003: I'm now overtaking and level with suspect vehicle. He's looking at me through his window. I'm indicating that he should pull in. No response. He's looking straight front now, ignoring me. Approaching Matthew's Linn. Car park on the right. Withdrawing behind him. Retaining position. Still displaying stop sign. No reaction.'

'Control: Roger that.'

Moving out of his lane, David straddled the centre of the east–west carriageways, content that Andrea had everything under control. He was an advanced police driver. She took it to another level. Dick, Mitch and Indi would take care of Latimer when his road ran out.

'Tango 7003: Retaining safe distance from behind. I have no intention of getting in front of him, Control. Aware of civilian vehicles on adjacent forest road tracks. Pursuit ongoing.'

Frankie sat down, putting herself at eye-level with Ruth. The old lady was choked, holding the photocopy to her chest as if it might fly away. There were still questions Frankie wanted answers to. It felt improper to ask, but unavoidable if she was to gain a clearer picture of what happened next. It didn't sit well with her.

She pushed on. 'Did you ever see Flavio after giving birth?'

Ruth shook her head. 'I was grounded for months. When I was finally allowed out, my uncle told me he'd gone home to Italy heartbroken. My father had warned him off, forbidding him to come near me. My uncle stuck up for me. They fell out over it.'

Frankie thought there was more to it than that. 'Did you ever hear from Flavio?'

Ruth shook her head again. If any letters came, I never received them.'

'I'm sure he wrote.' Frankie hoped he had.

'That's kind of you, Sergeant Oliver. If he had, he'd have sent mail to my uncle who would have found a way to get it to me. That's the kind of person he was.'

'There's a mention on the missing person file that Luca – Clifford as he was then – moved away and then returned to the area. I think I know why. He'd been trying to find you, Ruth. He didn't stand a chance. There were no birth records. The adoption wasn't official. I think he'd been asking questions, maybe happened on the wrong person and was murdered as a result.'

Ruth met her gaze. 'And you think that person was my father?'

'Do you?'

She looked out the window, lost in her memories. Ruth locked eyes with Frankie. 'He ripped that crucifix from my neck. I found it in his desk. The day he took my baby, I hid it in his blanket.'

She knew. And now her father was dead, the only way the MIT would prove it was if CSIs were able, with Professor Dawson's help, to establish that he'd buried the body on his brother's farm. Frankie was now certain that Ruth's late uncle wasn't the killer. Her father had motive. He'd gone to great lengths to separate mother and child. He'd arranged an illegal adoption. He had access to cable ties. He was the last person to want his daughter to be found. Unravelling these family secrets was bringing the investigation to a close.

102

David kept his distance, eyes scanning both sides of the road. Frankie would be wondering what was going on. She could guess. Latimer wouldn't have run if he'd been innocent. There was no doubt that he was responsible for dumping the barrel, but what of Jón Scheving? David forced himself to concentrate on the Traffic car ahead. Andrea had the target covered, her primary concern to ensure that no one got hurt in the process of stopping him. In the hands of a desperate man, a vehicle was potentially a fatal weapon. Latimer had no intention of giving up, though he hadn't and wasn't ramming the police vehicle.

That could change.

'Tango 7003: Target driving at excessive speed. Seventy-five in a sixty limit. Ignoring instructions to pull over. Driving dangerously. Making no attempt to deviate or cause damage to my vehicle . . . OK, we're on, Control. Roadblock visible ahead. He's seen it! Stop, stop, stop, 7125. He's looking for somewhere to turn around. Control, if this happens I'll take decisive action and make a hard stop.'

Ruth glanced at Frankie. 'When was Luca killed?'

'The missing person report was filed in 1976.'

It was a moment of unmitigated sorrow for the old lady.

'Ruth?'

She turned to look at Frankie. 'That explains so much.'

'How so?'

Ruth took a deep breath. 'That year, my father had . . . an episode, a mental breakdown if you will. It was completely out of the blue. He spent some time in hospital and never fully recovered. I nursed him until he committed suicide in 1980.'

'Oh, I'm so sorry.'

'I wish I felt the same way.' The old lady's tone was harder than before. 'He ruined my life. Unmarried, with no siblings, I inherited this house when he died. I searched every inch for papers documenting Luca's adoption. I found nothing. Forgive me for saying so, but I have no sympathy for him. I lived in agony for years.'

'Is there someone you'd like me to call?'

'That's very kind. You get off. I'll call Scott.'

David slowed, moved out to get a better view. Lots of parked vehicles. The logging truck spanning the road. A rat in a drain-pipe wouldn't get through the small gap on either side. From a safe distance, Abbott was attempting to flag Latimer down. No chance. Andrea would be forced to stop him.

David was ready to help if necessary.

'Tango 7003: There's a forest track on the left. Trees on either side. No opportunity for suspect to leave the road. I have a clear view. Yes, he's stop, stop, stop! Cancel that, Control. He's attempting a U-turn . . .'

There was no need for David to brace for impact.

He was out of his car, running towards her.

Having done this many times, Andrea timed the hit per-fectly. 'Tango 7003: Control, I've stopped my vehicle to contain the situation. Hard stop. I repeat, hard stop. Slight damage to my vehicle. Renault Captur will require a front-end lift.' A wry smile from Andrea as she climbed out of her car. Job done. She lifted her radio. 'Control: 7125 now on scene. Suspect is out of his vehicle. No attempt to resist arrest. No ambulance required. All units, stand down.'

103

A debrief was underway in the SIO's office, Inspector Andrea McGovern in attendance, even though moving traffic violations would be low down the pecking order, giving way to the more substantive offences on the custody record. Frankie took the lead, updating them on her productive but very sad interview with the suspect's aunt. Strung out, exhausted by the emotional ground they had covered, Frankie continued: 'Ruth described Scott Latimer as a loving, caring nephew—'

A knock at the door interrupted her, mid-flow.

Abbott entered. 'Processed and in a cell, guv.'

'Take the weight off,' David said. 'How was he on the way in?'

'Talkative.' Abbott pulled up a chair, nicking a biscuit as he sat down. 'More than once I had to tell him to keep his gob shut.'

'You think he'll cough?' Frankie asked.

'For moving the body? Yeah, no question.' Abbott bit into his cookie.

David caught Frankie's anxiety before she had time to hide it. Pretending not to notice, he glanced at Abbott, debating whether or not he was having a dig at her, deliberately framing his answer to throw doubt on the suspect's involvement in Scheving's murder, or if he was stating the case as he saw it.

'Latimer told the custody sergeant he'd cooperate fully,' Abbott said. 'He also declined a solicitor. Not many prigs do that.'

'Prigs? Do me a favour!' Andrea threw him a disparaging look. 'He's a farmer with no form, not so much as three points on his licence. An a-typical offender, if you ask me. Otherwise he'd have been knocking seven bells out of me on the C200. For Christ's sake, the guy held his hands up.'

An hour later, in possession of all the facts, David ordered an immediate search of High Barns Farm. Other than agricultural machinery and quad bikes, no vehicles had been found. An ongoing search of the farmhouse by CSI had harvested some interesting documents that had been photocopied and forwarded on to him, supporting Ruth's claim that her father might have been, probably was, responsible for the death of her illegally adopted child. Searching the surrounding farmland would prove more difficult, a deposition site much harder to find. It would take hours. Hours they didn't have.

It was time to make a move on Latimer.

He'd been in his cell for long enough.

David stood up. 'Ready, Frank?'

Ready might be overstating it.

104

Stone reiterated the caution to Latimer. He was well out of his comfort zone, evidently unfamiliar with a police interview. A big man, just as barmaid Stacey Grainger and PC Sara Gallagher had described him. A gentle giant with a swarthy complexion, kind eyes and the mild manner of a man who'd spent more time with animals than he did with humans. He seemed resigned to his fate.

David suspected that he wasn't a 'bad' man in the true sense of the word. Not like some of the evil low-lives he'd had the misfortune to come across and whose criminal records were longer than his arm. The conundrum raised by Latimer's uncharacteristic behaviour had him scratching his head. He was content to go slowly and had asked Frankie to chip in whenever she felt it was necessary.

First, a piece of well-meaning advice: 'Mr Latimer, I urge you to accept legal counsel. You're facing the most serious charges, including a count of murder—'

'I didn't murder anyone, Mr Stone. You have to believe—'

'Let me finish, please. You'll have every opportunity to explain yourself in due course. I repeat, one count of murder, one of failing to report and register a death, concealment and disposal of a body, a number of moving traffic offences and failing to stop for a police officer when required to do so. Do you understand?'

'Yes, sir.'

David crossed his arms, a glance at a flimsy file lying open before him. 'During our investigation into two separate incidents at Kielder Water, a number of witnesses came forward with information about a particular vehicle they had seen just before midnight on Friday, the twenty-first of June and in the early hours of Saturday, twenty-second of June. We have evidence that identifies that vehicle as a Ford Ranger. Do you own such a vehicle?'

A nod. 'Yes.'

'Where is that vehicle now?'

A resigned expression. 'Parked up at the Hexham Mart.'

Scribbling down his response, Frankie intervened: 'Mr Latimer, on Saturday the twenty-second of June, the body of a murder victim was found. We have since identified the remains as Luca Conti, a man also known as Clifford Charlton who went missing in 1976. We know you didn't harm him. He died before you were born. As you already know, this afternoon your aunt, Ruth Latimer, has been helping with our enquiries. She filled me in on a lot of family history.'

Latimer's mouth turned down. 'Is she OK?'

'She is . . .'

Stone was hoping that was still the case. Without her nephew to support her, Ruth was on her own and would struggle.

Frankie leaned forward, passing an A4 sheet across the table. 'For the tape, I'm showing the suspect a copy of exhibit JT1. Mr Latimer, this was found by crime scene investigators in a bureau at your farmhouse. Can you explain what it is?' A beat of time passed. 'For the tape, the suspect is nodding.'

'It wasn't hidden . . .'

'I didn't say it was.'

Inhaling deeply, Latimer wiped a sweaty hand across his face, his nails ingrained with muck. 'It's a letter written in 1976 by my great uncle, Graeme Latimer, to his brother John. I believe it was originally sealed in an envelope and never sent. It has been in my family for almost four decades, though I was unaware of it until last year.'

'John Latimer is the father of your aunt, Ruth?' Frankie asked.

'Yes.'

'Would it be fair to say that Ruth was closer to her Uncle Graeme than she was to her father?'

'It seems so, reading between the lines.'

'What does the letter say, exactly?'

Latimer sighed. 'Look, you've obviously read it. Do we have to do this?'

'I'm afraid we do,' Stone confirmed. 'I can see how distressing it is for you. This is your chance to set the record straight. Take your time. We have all night. I'm sure you want this over with as much as we do.'

Latimer said, 'Graeme was pleading with John to come clean for having murdered Luca Conti.'

'Luca Conti being your aunt's only child,' Frankie said. 'A child taken from her soon after he was born?'

A nod. 'John was caught burying his body at High Barns.'

'Caught by whom?' Stone asked.

'His brother, Graeme. He'd seen lights. Gone out thinking he'd find a poacher.'

'Did he inform the police?' The SIO already knew he hadn't.

Latimer confirmed it. 'No, though it weighed heavily on his conscience. Up to that point he and John had been close. There's reference to an argument. John asking too much. He'd used emotional blackmail, telling Graeme that it would destroy Ruth if he turned him in.'

Frankie asked: 'Did Graeme know that police were investigating Luca's disappearance?'

Latimer nodded. 'That's what prompted the letter.'

'I take it John refused to come clean?'

'Yes.'

'Go on.'

'When Graeme died, his son, Ross, inherited the farm.'

'And presumably the letter,' Stone said, just to be clear.

'Yes. Realising that his father had concealed a murder, he kept it to himself. Last year, he was diagnosed with stage 4 cancer. With no children of his own to inherit the farm, no realistic expectation of survival and with Ruth being the age she is, he called to tell me that the land would pass to me. My late father is John's son from a second marriage, Ruth's younger half-brother. As you can imagine, I was grateful for Ross's generosity. Since I was a kid, Ruth has always taken care of me. Having the farm meant that I could return the favour.' His bottom lip began to quiver.

Frankie locked eyes with the suspect. 'Let me guess. There were conditions attached.'

'Exactly that . . .' Latimer cleared his throat, more upset the longer the interview continued. 'Ross asked me up to High Barns. He was very ill by then. He told me what had happened to Ruth during the war, about the baby's adoption and that his father's brother had done something dreadful. Up to that point, I had no idea about any of this. He demanded that I put things right.'

'So, in your wisdom, you exhumed Luca's remains?' Stone said. 'Why in God's name didn't you tell Ruth and contact the police? Luca's body could have been returned to his mother legally, for a proper burial.'

'I'd promised my uncle that I'd carry out his instruction, as ridiculous as it sounds in hindsight.'

Frankie shook her head. 'As commendable as family loyalty is, you could've said no.'

'Believe it or not Sergeant Oliver, I was trying to do the right thing.'

Frankie's expression was one of incredulity.

Stone felt that he too might have felt sorry for the guy had it not been for the small matter of Scheving's death – assuming Latimer was responsible. With a niggling doubt gnawing on the inside of his brain, David pushed an A4 pad and pen towards the suspect. 'Start drawing. I want to know where on your farm Luca's body was buried, then we'll take a break.'

105

Latimer was possibly the most cooperative suspect the SIO had ever come across. Stone was in a good mood, even though he still had to find the physical evidence to prove the case before resuming the interview, this time with Scheving in mind. Before he even reached the MIR, David was on the phone to the search team coordinator with important information he knew would make his day, his week, possibly his whole year – certainly his evening. That's if he ever got through.

Stone was about to hang up when a male voice came on the line.

'Dave, if you're asking for an update, you're out of luck, mate. My guys are still searching barns and outbuildings.'

'They haven't got to the fools and horses yet?' David grinned at Frankie. On account of his first name, the coordinator's handle throughout the force was Trotter. It had been so since the day he joined up. Assuming his best south-east London accent, David drew out the words as he spoke. 'You're not the only one working, Rodney.'

Laughing, Frankie pushed open the door to the MIR.

'The suspect came across?' Trotter said. 'What did he do, draw you a map?'

'You just answered your own question.' David caught Abbott's eye, raising a hand, indicating five minutes, while maintaining his conversation with Trotter. 'I have the coordinates of the burial site. I'll send them across in a mo. It's quicker if I talk you through it. As you leave the road and drive up to the farmhouse, on the right-hand side there's a four-acre field with a clump of Scots pine on the southern border.'

'Yeah, I see it. I'm there now.'

'This is your lucky night, mate. Latimer indicated a spot to the east side of the trees at the bottom of the pasture. He says you'll see the grave because he's had no time to conceal it. Your overtime is already approved.'

'You're all heart,' Trotter said.

'Heavy date?'

'No. There's a bloody big bull in the field.'

106

David sent the map to Trotter, then made some notes on his interview with Latimer. Two minutes later, hearing footsteps approaching, he looked up expecting to find Frankie. Abbott stuck his head round the door and was beckoned in. He had a steaming mug of coffee in his hand. He didn't sit and David didn't invite him to.

'What's on your mind?'

'Thought you could do with this.' Abbott put the mug down.

'That was your in. Now tell me what you *really* want—'

Abbott hesitated. 'Guv, for the record, I hope Frankie is right about Kristjánsson but, with respect, I know her better than you do. She's struggling—'

'She told you that, did she?'

'No, but I can sense it. I thought you should be aware.'

'Noted.' Now David understood why he'd come. 'How was it in the viewing room?'

Busted, Abbott dropped the pretence. 'Unsettling . . . for all of us.'

David knew that he'd have watched every second of Latimer's interview. 'Why's that then?'

'I should have thought that was obvious. Doesn't it worry you that Latimer protested his innocence on the murder charge?'

'Not a whole lot, no. He's facing life imprisonment. You'd be hard pushed to find a suspect who wasn't in denial under those circumstances.'

'I don't believe he did it.'

'So you said . . . countless times.' Abbott was beginning to piss David off. 'Don't beat yourself up over it. I don't expect you to agree with Frankie on every investigation. So, keep pushing, keep challenging. Blind trust gets us nowhere. If nothing else, that interview with Latimer should've taught you that loyalty is an admirable but overrated quality that can backfire spectacularly.' If Dick was playing mind games he'd picked the wrong opponent. David cast his fishing line . . . 'No need to panic, is there? Between us, we have this double-hander covered. Should Frankie turn out to be wrong, we have all the hard evidence we need to put Kristjánsson away.'

'Guv, for the record, I wasn't trying to undermine her earlier.'

'I'm pleased to hear it, because subverting the efforts of anyone on this team is inadvisable. If you're genuinely sorry for having done so, it's her you should be telling, not me. I'm sure she'll appreciate it.'

'That's it, I can't find her.'

'She's around.'

'Well, if I knocked her confidence earlier, I'd like the opportunity to put that right.'

Time to reel him in. 'Aren't you still doing that?'

'Guv?'

'You breeze in here, telling me that she's in a bad place, then have the gall to offer a half-arsed apology for putting her there. Get off the fence, Dick. From where I'm standing, it looks like she was right all along. If that is the case – and it's a big if at the moment – it's a significant accomplishment. What were you hoping for? A massive flop so you could ride in, rectify it, and say I told you so?'

'No, guv.'

'Good, because while you're entitled to express an opinion you've gone about it the wrong way. You've disappointed me and made it hard for her.'

'That's why I'm here, guv.'

'Is it? Why am I not convinced?'

Abbott didn't answer.

'You can go,' David said.

Shamefaced, the DS turned away.

David spoke again before he reached the door. 'Actually, if you do see her, give her some space. She'll be planning her interview strategy. Scheving's case is hers. When we go back in, I want her focus on Latimer, not on you.'

'Yes, guv.'

David drew a line under his interference. 'I have a job for you. Get someone up to High Barns to assist the search team. Trotter has an unwelcome visitor.' He explained about the bull. 'And talk to the CSIs. See how they're doing. Now . . . the suspect needs a break and so do I. Make sure he gets refreshments. I'm not convinced Latimer will be as cooperative second time around.'

107

One down, one to go. David held the door open as Frankie re-entered the interview room. Whatever Abbott's opinion on her state of mind, she looked supremely confident, ready to take the Scheving case to Latimer. She sat down facing him. During the break, he'd changed his mind about legal representation. His brief, April Goodwin, was already seated, a woman of indeterminate age, sharp eyes, high cheekbones. She was dressed in a formal navy suit and crisp white shirt.

David formed the impression that she'd spent the day in court.

A vibration in his breast pocket. He slipped his mobile out, surreptitiously checking the screen. A message from DCI Anna Jónsdóttir: **Call me.** It sounded urgent. He couldn't deal with it now. Did he even want to? Putting the phone away, he took the seat opposite Goodwin, a memory stirring: Kristjánsson appearing through the trees on Kielder's north shore, avoiding eye contact, Frankie voicing her misgivings:

Looks a bit shifty, don't you think?

David was rigid in his seat, head pounding, only vaguely aware of the recorder being switched on. He managed to identify himself when required to do so for the tape. Introductions complete, Frankie launched straight in, her voice pulling him from a daydream more akin to a nightmare than any he'd experienced.

'Mr Latimer, you were very cooperative this morning with regard to an incident involving Luca Conte and the disposal of his remains at Kielder Water – and for that we thank you. A transcript of that interview will be made available to your solicitor, Ms Goodwin.' She didn't mention cable ties, though they had been found. 'A search of your property and the land at High Barns Farm is ongoing.'

David was finding it hard to concentrate.

Anna's text had provoked a sense of unease, questions piling up. Why had the Icelandic DCI decided to pay Kristjánsson a visit at this late stage of the investigation?

Why so guarded on the nature of it?

Moreover, why the urgency of her text?

Why text him and not Frankie?

Oliver had made up her mind that Kristjánsson was innocent, in spite of hard evidence to the contrary, Scheving's blood on his towel providing a direct link between suspect and murder victim, the final nail in his coffin, some might say. The uncertainty over how it got there had been worrying David.

Had Abbott been right all along?

Clocking his anxiety, Frankie faltered in her delivery.

David could feel the tension coming off her.

It seemed like an age before she spoke again. 'Mr Latimer, earlier today you stated that you didn't murder anyone. Tell me what you meant.'

Latimer glanced at his solicitor.

Stone held his breath.

Goodwin nodded.

The atmosphere in the room was tense.

Latimer hesitated, undoubtedly distressed. 'When I was disposing of the barrel in the reservoir, I was aware of someone or something approaching through the woods. I thought it might be a deer, then this guy appeared from nowhere. He was waving his arms around, mouthing off in a foreign language. At first, I thought he needed help. I didn't understand what he was saying.'

David relaxed.

This was Scheving – no doubt about it.

Stone couldn't remember who'd said that man's whole body records his emotional thinking but it was undeniable. Latimer was showing signs of distress, his breathing laboured, the muscle beneath his left eye twitching. His posture was stiff and he was unable to keep still. Frankie's body language was equally visible. She was in control, the embodiment of calm. Motionless, she never took her eyes off the suspect.

These non-verbal clues gave much away.

Frankie didn't need the handwritten notes David knew were in the file in front of her. She would have memorised them and knew exactly what she was doing. 'Was this before or after you deposited the barrel?'

Latimer cleared his throat. 'After.'

'How long after?' When he didn't speak, she said, 'You were seen by this man, weren't you? Is that why you killed him, to cover up your crime?'

'No, it wasn't like that!'

David saw where she was heading: crunch time had arrived.

Frankie homed in on her suspect. 'OK, explain how it was then.'

'He came at me like a man possessed. He was off his head. He came at me again and again with a knife. It was like a horror movie. The third time, I picked up a piece of wood and hit him.'

'Where did you hit him?'

'What?'

'Which part of his body?'

Latimer glanced at his brief.

Again, Goodwin nodded. Money for old rope. She hadn't opened her mouth once.

'He lunged at me. I stepped aside and lashed out, striking his head as he fell forward. He wouldn't stay down and came at me again with the knife, so I hit him a second time.' Latimer's eyes were haunted, as if he'd relived the incident a thousand times.

108

Frankie took a moment.

He was off his head.

Those five words corroborated Kristjánsson's account and that of his Icelandic friends. High on drugs and alcohol, in possession of a weapon, Jón Scheving had behaved in a threatening manner at the campsite and was undoubtedly in a foul mood when he left, having fallen out with everyone.

Frankie imagined him skulking away after being shunned by Eva, her brother and the rest of their group. At her behest, Anna and Emil had re-interviewed nine of 'the ten' on this very point, reporting back that each and every one of them had supported Kristján's assertion that his back was turned during the altercation; he didn't show up until it was all over.

As Frankie reviewed the evidence in her mind, two scenarios presented themselves. One: alone, drugged up and wounded by such a public rejection, Scheving heads off into the forest in what 'the ten' described as a foul mood, and takes out his rage on a stranger. Two: he finds a place to end his morbid existence, shoots up, is spooked by Latimer and lashes out, coming off worse.

This second theory was a distinct possibility.

Prolonged drug use had triggered toxic psychosis in Scheving before, including paranoia. Demonic hallucinations were well documented in his medical history. If Latimer surprised him in the forest in the early hours, frightened him even, there was no telling what he was capable of.

Her eyes flew back to the file in front of her. Inside was a copy of the heart-breaking letter Scheving had hand-delivered months earlier to his psychotherapist – bizarrely, another letter that was never sent, this to a victim rather than a perpetrator.

Eva, I know you don't want to hear from me after what I did. I can't imagine how much you hate me as you read this – if you read it. I've been told that you might refuse, but I had to write, not to clear my conscience, to make excuses or beg forgiveness, but I've thought of nothing else since I attacked you. Knowing what I've done, apologising, won't ever make up for it, I know that. I've done many bad things I'm not proud of, but what I did to you was far worse. I'd rather kill myself than put another girl through it. My mother was murdered by an animal like me. I was there. I saw it. I see it every time I close my eyes. I have taken every kind of drug to blot it out but it's still there. By the time you read this I may already be dead. It's what I deserve. What I crave. I'm sorry.

Jón

Those gut-wrenching words from such a young man in the prime of his life would stay with Frankie for a very long time. Her eyes shifted to Latimer. 'How was the man when you left him?'

'I didn't wait to find out. I legged it to my SUV and drove away. I meant to stop, not kill him, I swear.'

Frankie wanted more. 'What did he look like? Describe him to me.'

'I can't. It was dark. No moon. I was terrified.'

Frankie dropped her head on one side. 'How did you know he had a knife if there was no moon?'

'I'd switched off my headlights in case I was seen. My torch was lying on the ground, the only available light. I saw a rounded blade and panicked. I honestly thought he was going to kill me.'

That made sense too. Kristján had described the knife as long and curved 'Well there we have a problem,' Frankie said. 'We found no weapon at the scene—'

Latimer sobbed, 'I took it, along with the lump of wood I hit him with. You'll find them in the Ranger.'

'Think very carefully before you answer,' Frankie said. 'Did you push him into the reservoir?'

'No!'

'Are you sure about that? You seem very distressed.'

'What do you expect? You're trying to pin a murder on me! It wasn't like that. Everything I've said is true.'

Frankie glanced at Goodwin. 'The victim was alive when he went in.'

'No, I swear, that's not how it was.' Latimer's tic had returned. 'I, I just wanted to get out of there. The guy . . . he was unconscious on the ground when I left him. Please, Sergeant Oliver, you have to believe me. He wasn't going to stop. It was him or me.'

109

Latimer was escorted to a cell protesting his innocence. It was hard to watch a man with no form, who'd shown genuine remorse and cooperated fully, face the prospect of imprisonment. Frankie felt no sense of victory, only profound sadness. She was exhausted. In need of sleep. She gathered up the file, a glance at David as she stood up. There was no laudatory expression in his eyes. Quite the opposite. He was tense, acting as if there was unfinished business.

She couldn't fathom it.

He pushed past her, leaving her affronted in the interview room.

Goodwin spoke. 'Nice to meet you, Detective Sergeant Oliver. This is clearly a case of self-defence. I'd be grateful for full disclosure as soon as you can manage it. I have much to discuss with my client.' As they left the room, she scanned the corridor, eyes on Stone's back. 'Please pass on my thanks to your SIO. He's obviously a busy man.'

Frankie answered with a nod.

Goodwin was having a dig. David had shown disrespect to a fellow criminal justice professional. He'd left without a word to either woman. He was now moving at speed, on the phone, without a backward glance. Probably trying to find out if the Ranger had been uplifted and if any weapons had been found. Even as the thought passed through her head, Frankie knew she was kidding herself.

There was more to it than that.

What had she missed?

The call Stone was making continued to ring out. He sat down, tapping his fingers impatiently on his desk. Finally, it was picked up. He was talking before his Icelandic equivalent had even said her name. 'Anna, apologies for the delayed response. Your text came in just as Frankie and I were about to interview a suspect in the Scheving case.'

'How did it go?'

'Almost there.' Technically they were. 'Unless you're about to throw a last-minute spanner in the works—'

'No, but I have been building bridges,' she joked.

'Meaning?'

'In the interest of thoroughness, I took Kristján to see his father. The least I could do, given that your intervention, or should I say Frankie's, made matters ten times worse between them. I'm pleased to report that it went well. They're not there yet, but they've come to an accommodation. Lads of his age need a role model. The reason you care for Ben, right?'

'Right.' David was watching the door. Frankie would be there any second. 'Anna, sorry to rush you. I'm up to my eyes here. No disrespect, but I don't have time to play happy families. You implied the call was urgent.'

'It is. I have important information for you.'

'Go on.'

'Kristján ran after me as I left. He was very emotional, grateful for my mediation. Now he has it back, or close to it, he doesn't want to risk losing his relationship with his father and decided to come clean—'

'About what?' David braced himself.

'He knows how Scheving's blood got on his towel.'

'What?'

'You heard me right the first time, David. That first night at Kielder, he couldn't settle. He heard a cry and left the campsite to investigate, a detail he omitted to tell you when interviewed. He came across Scheving lying passed out on the ground. Thinking he'd OD'd, he checked for a pulse. Jón was still breathing so he left him to sleep it off. Next morning, Kristján noticed blood on his hands. He went for a swim to wash it off. Having already admitted to hiding Scheving's tent, when Frankie mentioned the towel, he panicked.'

110

'Has Anna taken a formal statement?' Frankie's expression was downbeat.

'Yes.' David studied her. 'I know what you're thinking. Did Scheving manage to drag himself to his feet and fall into the water accidentally or was he given a shove? Either way, we'll never prove it—'

'I hate loose ends.'

'Me too, but no mystery is ever fully resolved and not every collar feels like a victory. There are always unanswered questions. Hang on to what the pathologist said. Irrespective of the drowning, the brain injuries would almost certainly have been fatal.'

'Still.'

'OK, then ask yourself why, when Kristjánsson has no clue that we have someone in custody, he'd add to his statement and implicate himself in a murder? Wouldn't happen. You were right to trust your guts. Latimer's admission of what he did and how he did it – striking two blows to the back of the head – squares with Scheving's injuries. We'll soon have the weapon to prove it beyond reasonable doubt. Let's face it, a murder charge won't stick. A half-decent barrister will make a case for self-defence, and rightly so, in my opinion. Congratulations, you did a great job. Take the credit and move on.'

There had been many lows during the case. More than once, Frankie had reached crisis point, unable to decide if Kristján was innocent or playing her. She'd stepped over the line, broken the rules for reasons she felt were fair and just. Any lingering doubts were behind her now, evaporating like the mist over Kielder Water on the morning the investigation began.

She'd passed her promotion board, taken care of Scheving's side of the double-hander and stood up for what she believed in, risking alienation from the MIT. Having said all that, she'd benefited from being out of her comfort zone.

The coming week was illuminating. At High Barns Farm, crime scene investigators had spent many days preserving evidence from the house and the land. Professor Lorna Dawson's expert analysis of samples taken from the burial site proved conclusively that Luca Conti's body had indeed been buried there – evidence that would stand up in court when the time came. Latimer had been charged with a long list of offences and been remanded in custody to await trial, his Ford Ranger having been recovered from Hexham Mart. Scheving's knife had been found, along with a bloodstained piece of wood, just as Latimer said it would be.

There were often times when police officers had to break hearts in order to detect murders. Ruth Latimer was a case in point, though Stone and Oliver were able to balance that out by giving her something precious in return for helping them. When she answered the door at her home in Falstone, she was surprised to see them standing on the doorstep. She appeared to be doing OK.

They sat in the garden drinking lemonade.

Frankie informed Ruth that due to the age and condition of Luca's remains, his body would be released for burial quite soon. Ruth thanked her, consoled by the knowledge that she'd be able to bury her son and visit a graveside in due course.

'I've made arrangements for him to be laid to rest in St Peter's churchyard. I may not have had him with me in life, but you've made it possible for us to be together in death.' She gave a half-smile. 'Not that I'm planning on going anywhere anytime soon. A long time ago, I reserved a double plot in the hope that I might one day find him. Thanks to my nephew, I did.' Sadness filled her eyes. 'May I ask where Scott is now?'

'On remand in Durham Prison,' Frankie said. 'I'll let you know the trial date as soon as it's been set.'

Ruth nodded. 'I'll be in court to support him and be here for him when he gets out.'

'We can help with visits when you feel up to it,' Stone said.

'Detective Inspector, I may be ancient, but I can assure you that I'm perfectly capable of using the internet and finding my way to Durham on the bus.'

Frankie pressed her lips together. 'That's you told, guv.'

'Is that what you came to tell me?' Ruth asked.

'No, we came to give you this.'

Frankie handed her one of two parcels she took from her bag, then waited expectantly for Ruth to open it. Inside were two framed photographs – one of her son, Luca; the other of her former lover, Flavio – the images Frankie had shared with her on her previous visit. Both had been professionally restored.

Tears filled Ruth's eyes as she looked up at her. 'I will never be able to repay you.'

'Don't thank me.' Frankie nodded toward Stone. 'My guv'nor paid for the digital enhancements.'

Ruth reached out, put a hand on David's and squeezed it. She had no words.

'We'd also like you to have these.' Frankie gave her the second parcel. It contained a bound volume of letters crime scene investigators had found in the attic at High Barns, over a hundred and fifty of them. 'We'll let you have the originals and the crucifix as soon as the court case is over,' Frankie said. 'Flavio wrote to you every week for three years. We hope it brings you some comfort knowing that.'

111

Just off an evening flight from Belfast a week later, Bright received a party reminder as he woke his mobile on arrival at Newcastle International Airport terminal. He'd been friends with Frank and Julie Oliver for a very long time. They were begging him to turn up to Frankie's big night. He was exhausted, in two minds whether to go. A second text, this one from his wife, was the clincher:

Raid the freezer for supper. Staying over with mum. x

With Ellen out, there was no danger of Bright going home to an empty house and a TV dinner when Frankie's mum was providing a banquet to celebrate her daughter's departure from the MIT. Bright could almost taste the delicious homemade pies. Moreover, it would give him his first opportunity to shake hands with the only female detective capable of giving another one of his protégés a run for her money. Kate Daniels would be looking over her shoulder before long. Hopping in a cab, he told the driver to take him directly to the police club.

Only Frankie could be late to her own promotion do. Her eyes widened as she entered the club. It had nothing to do with the balloons and streamers, or the round of applause she received as she walked in. Flares, platform shoes and glitter were the order of the day – a glam rock theme. The whole team were there, along with every single member of her family: her grandparents, mum and dad, Andrea and Rae. Anna Jónsdóttir had flown over from Iceland to join them. It was great to see her again.

The celebration had been going on for a good few hours, getting more and more raucous by the minute. Frankie was excited at what the future held, but sad too. She loved each and every one of them and hoped it wouldn't be long before she re-joined the Murder Investigation Team.

Abbott arrived at her shoulder. He'd had far too many. 'They seem pally,' he said, pointing toward the far side of the room. Anna and Vikram were standing at the bar, deep in conversation.

'Have you and Anna been introduced?'

'Not yet.'

'You'll like her. She's great.'

'Vikram thinks so too, by the looks.' Dick smiled. 'You having fun?'

'Yeah. Shame Linn couldn't join us.'

'Her loss.' Dick said. 'Have you *any* idea how proud I am of you?'

'Stop it! I'm wearing mascara.'

'I noticed.'

Frankie gave him a hug and hung on, their difference of opinion over the Scheving case a distant memory. He'd got over his injured pride and apologised for doubting her. As he staggered away, she slumped down on the seat beside her grandfather.

'You're busted, Granddad.'

'Is this fancy dress, Frances? No one told me.'

'Me either. Don't worry about it.' She took his glass. 'Let me get you a refill.'

112

As she approached the bar, she felt terribly sad that her grandfather couldn't remember spilling the beans on her father's music choices. There were times that ignorance was definitely bliss. Andrea was leaning against the counter when she arrived, a big grin on her face.

Frankie gave her the side-eye. 'What did I miss?'

'Not a thing.'

'Stop teasing.'

Andrea turned to face her, placing her elbow on the bar. She leaned in and said quietly, 'You know that job you asked me to do?'

Frankie placed the palm of her hand on her chest. 'Me? You must be mistaken. I have absolutely no idea what you're on about.'

'Whatever.' Her sister-in-law was enjoying this.

Frankie couldn't help herself. 'It's done?'

'And dusted.' Andrea paused, making her wait. 'A few days ago, I received an anonymous tip-off that Adam English was tanked up at the Pheasant Inn. I cannot imagine how they got my number.'

Frankie grinned. 'You didn't—'

'Relax, I sent a colleague. Tango 5285, the one David thinks is as mad as a box of frogs. She laid in wait, then followed the Tesla for two miles before pulling it over. English refused to blow into the bag and was arrested. Turns out he was three times over the limit.'

'Outstanding!'

'He appeared in court this morning. His brief argued against a totting-up ban on grounds of exceptional hardship, but he's used that excuse before. It didn't wash with the magistrates, so he changed tack, said his client would submit to a drink-drive rehabilitation course. That didn't work either. With nine points on his licence, English was disqualified for three years. You should've seen his face—'

They high-fived.

Frankie asked, 'Does David know?'

Andrea nodded.

'What did he say?'

'Not much, but then I told him the rest.'

'What do you mean?'

'It gets better.' Andrea bit her bottom lip. 'An angry outburst from the dock added a charge of contempt, two weeks' imprisonment and a fine of two grand. Northern adjudicators don't appreciate being yelled at by flash southerners with loud mouths. Bet that won't appear in the rag he works for.'

113

More guests were arriving off late shift, Ben and Wells following them in. Frankie's father gave Belinda a peck on both cheeks as she shimmied towards him, ready to party. Frankie waved at her, then glanced back at Andrea, still buzzing with the knowledge that English would be sleeping in a cell while she was out celebrating, then remembered why she had two drinks in her hand. When she returned to where her grandfather was sitting, he was gone. She looked around and couldn't see him in the crowd.

'Don't panic, Inspector. He's with your mum.'

Frankie swung round.

David was standing there.

'Has anyone told you what a complete and utter tit you look in that?' Frankie wasn't talking about the sparkly jacket, a red Bowie T-shirt underneath, but the mullet wig he was wearing. 'Actually, it suits you.'

'I'm going to miss you, Frank.'

'Yeah? Well, keep working on that vacancy.'

'It's yours as soon as I can make it happen.'

They held each other's gaze for a long while.

Frankie's heart was full, but there was an empty feeling in the pit of her stomach. She'd miss him too. 'You do realise that you're the reason I want to stay in the madhouse? I'd hate to leave without you knowing that.'

There, she'd finally said it.

She formed the impression that he already knew.

She was floating on the ceiling looking down on herself, an out-of-body experience. He was stone-cold sober and looking deep into her eyes, *really* looking. Was she reading him right?

She hoped so. There was no awkwardness. No regrets. No shop talk either. They had done enough of that.

'Will I get to see you?' she said.

'For sure . . .' He smiled at her like only he could. 'I still owe you a show and a curry.'

'I'd like that,' was the only thing she could think of to say.

A beat of time, another intense moment.

His attention shifted to a point behind her. 'Your dad wants you.'

She necked her wine, not wanting to break the spell. 'He can wait—'

'I don't think so somehow.'

She was dragged away protesting. Clearly, she didn't want to dance to Mott the Hoople's 'All the Young Dudes'.

Quarter to midnight.

Rubbish at goodbyes, David decided to slip away before Frankie noticed he was gone. As he searched his pocket for keys, in two minds whether to find her before he left, a voice reached him from behind, part of a conversation that made his hackles rise.

He glanced over his shoulder.

The comment wasn't a poke, one officer to another, the usual disrespectful banter over a couple of pints. It was a piss-take at someone else's expense. A snide remark from a half-cut retired detective too fond of a free bar; one of those occasions when no one was listening, when backs were turned, leaving the boring git talking to a newbie too polite to tell him to get lost.

The words that spilled from his mouth set Stone thinking about an unsolved case he was desperate to crack, one that had been put aside awaiting new leads. Had he heard right? It wouldn't be the first time a throwaway remark in a social setting had reopened an investigation that had been left to lie on file. Coppers sharing anecdotal stories over a beer often picked up intelligence from one another and ran with it.

In his head, David was joining dots.

What he'd picked up could disappear like a puff of smoke. If it didn't, he'd be lost without his most valuable asset working alongside him. Unable to assist in the investigation would drive Frankie insane. She was heading for new horizons, a posting that would keep her fully occupied, another chance to prove herself. She'd be among new colleagues, part of a uniform shift, no on-call duty to drag her down. With time on her hands, she'd be having fun, having a life, showing everyone what she was made of. They would fall for her, like he had.

That thought would keep him awake tonight.

His eyes flicked across the room.

Frankie threw her head back, laughing at something Dick had whispered in her ear. The two detectives were surrounded by a team who liked nothing better than to let off steam. Her eyes were on fire. She was brimming over with happiness. David thought about the 'moment' they had just shared. Whatever it was, he couldn't spoil it by telling her what he'd overheard. If he did, there would literally be murder on the dance floor.

A potential breakthrough in a cold case was no longer her problem.

Not so for David – he'd be all over it by morning.

Acknowledgments

Many thanks to my outgoing editor Francesca Pathak who helped shape Black Fell – and to my new editor, Sam Eades, whose enthusiasm for this book and our future working relationship is infectious. Grateful thanks must also go to my freelance copy-editor Anne O'Brien and everyone at Orion and elsewhere who made this book come alive . . .

One of these is Professor Lorna Dawson of the James Hutton Institute, Head of Soil Forensics, aka 'the soil sleuth' whose expertise in that field of analysis helped immensely.

To friends and fellow authors, Lilja Sigurdardóttir and Yrsa Sigurdardóttir (no relation) who were kind enough to help me out when Covid put paid to a fact-checking research trip to Iceland during the writing process. Any geographical errors in the text are my own.

To neighbour and biker, Neil Richmond, who appears in this book as himself, along with his wife, Kathryn. A long time ago, over a glass of wine, I promised Neil he'd make an appearance in print one day. Years later, he reminded me and . . . well, what was I to do? Black Fell provided the perfect opportunity to put him on the page and shut him up.

Thanks as always to literary agent Oli Munson, top bloke and very definitely considered part of my extended family, even though he's a Spurs supporter.

A big high-five to my brilliant family: Paul, Kate, Max and Frankie; Chris, Jodie, Daisy and Finn; and my partner, Mo, to whom this book is dedicated. You are the best.

Credits

Mari Hannah and Orion Fiction would like to thank everyone at Orion who worked on the publication of *Black Fell* in the UK.

Editorial
Sam Eades
Sahil Javed

Copy editor
Anne O'Brien

Proof reader
Laura Gerrard

Audio
Paul Stark
Jake Alderson

Contracts
Anne Goddard
Dan Herron
Ellie Bowker

Design
Tomas Almeida
Joanna Ridley

Editorial Management
Charlie Panayiotou
Jane Hughes
Bartley Shaw

Finance
Jasdip Nandra
Nick Gibson
Sue Baker

Marketing
Lucy Cameron

Production
Ruth Sharvell

Publicity
Alainna Hadjigeorgiou

Sales
Jen Wilson
Esther Waters
Victoria Laws
Tolu
Rachael Hum
Ellie Kyrke-Smith
Sinead White
Georgina Cutler

Operations
Jo Jacobs
Sharon Willis

Discover Mari's latest lead character
Detective Chief Inspector Kate Daniels

Read on for an exclusive extract from new
Kate Daniels thriller

THE LONGEST GOODBYE

Prologue

Before the phone rang, Kate Daniels' shitty day was like any other in the murder incident room, until Pete Brooks came on the line. Normally cool in a crisis, the control room operator seemed rattled. There was a lot of background noise too. She knew instantly that a major operation was in full swing; a manhunt he called it: PolSA, a firearms team, dog section, the works.

Finally, he managed to get the news out.

'Officer down, guv. Shot in the back.'

Kate felt sick.

An injury to any colleague, on or off duty, was a tragedy. This one was as serious as they came. Potentially life changing. Kate's stomach took a dive, convinced that he was about to tell her that the officer concerned was one of hers . . . before he told her that it wasn't. The duty Senior Investigation Officer had been called out.

So why was Pete calling if she wasn't required?

'It's Georgina, boss . . . I'm so sorry.'

He was sorry?

What the hell did that mean?

Sorry was something you said if you bumped into a stranger, accidentally knocking them sideways; sorry was a word people used when they had been unkind to a loved one and wanted to make nice; sorry was an overused coverall for bad behaviour, a throwaway comment that followed a minor mistake, a meaningless sentiment. Why was he sorry? He hadn't pulled the trigger.

Paralysed by his words, Kate's mind raced through all the possible outcomes, none of them good. Georgina had to live.

She had to. That improbable hope died in her heart as the controller spoke again.

'She didn't make it, boss.'

*

Death is something we all face. It was a constant in Kate's life, but Pete's words took her breath way. Ceasing to exist was final. The end of the line. No going back. That's it. End of. There was nothing else.

Racing to the scene with coordinates for Rothbury riverside, she called for an update. There was none. Forty-five minutes later, in an area flooded with police activity, she pulled up sharp, got out of her vehicle and climbed into full forensic kit. Terrified of what came next, she sucked in a breath, wiped her face with her hands, then slammed the tailgate of her Audi shut.

All eyes turned in her direction.

A uniformed officer pointed her in the right direction. With a sense of urgency, she moved towards the River Coquet. Woods fringed the water's edge, a pretty path she'd walked a million times with Georgina, though never for exercise.

They got enough of that at work.

Though now she was running along a dirt track. It was then she saw it, if not the crime scene, a deposition sight, a white crime scene tent erected to keep prying eyes at bay, hers included. Lifting the tape surrounding the inner cordon, she was immediately confronted with a problem.

The Senior Investigating Officer, DCI Gordon Curtis, tried to block her way. 'What are you doing here?'

'Minding my own business.'

'Get the hell out of my crime scene.'

Ignoring his request, Kate stepped aside.

He grabbed her arm.

She glanced at his hand, them at him, a hostile expression. 'Get the fuck off or you'll regret it.' She shrugged herself free.

He didn't try to stop her.

She approached the tent, her heart kicking a whole in her ribcage by the time she reached it. She stood there, adrenaline pumping, a cold sweat forming on her brow. She was in danger here. Professionally, not physically. Protocol dictated that she turn around and return to base.

She couldn't do it . . .

She wouldn't . . .

Some things were more important than regulations. Pure desperation was driving to her to see for herself that those who'd found the body were not guilty of mistaken identity. Wanting it to be true didn't make it so. An officer had been murdered. If not Georgina, then another colleague whose family would suffer.

The last few steps felt like a mile.

And still Kate clung to the hope that an error had been made.

Opening the flap, she stepped inside, in no doubt that she was breaking every rule. She was past caring. Even though she knew what to expect, it was a shock to view the body of a much-loved colleague lying face down on the ground, arms splayed out, a dark patch of blood across her back. Kate knew instantly that it was Georgina. She'd entered the wood, alone and unprotected, with no police issue radio on which to call for help.

A sitting duck for anyone who'd do her harm.

Pathologist, Sue Morrisey, was on her knees, in the middle of her examination, recording her initial impressions that the SIO should've been there to witness. Pausing the recording, she glanced over her shoulder, her blue eyes managing to convey sorrow and compassion non-verbally through the narrow slit between cap and mask. She looked at the body, then at Kate, an expression the detective chief inspector interpreted as confusion over who would oversee the investigation.

'Are you taking over, Kate?'

'No . . . I had to come.'

The pathologist's nod was almost imperceptible. 'I hate to ask, but would you mind helping me turn her over? Curtis stepped out. I don't know why—'

'Well, it wouldn't be for police work, would it?' Taking a pair of gloves from her pocket, Kate pulled them on.

'Ready?' Sue said.

Kate was not ready. How could she be? This was Georgina, daughter to Molly, wife to Nico, mother to Charlotte and Oscar, all of whom she knew personally, a family whose lives were about to implode.

For them and for Kate, life would never be the same.

On autopilot, her eyes scanned the scene to see what it would tell her, drifting to a point two yards from Georgina's body – to something that did not belong to her. Kate imagined a female inspector, shocked and out of breath, crouching down, checking for signs of life, instinctively removing her hat before doing so, forgetting to collect it when the pathologist arrived. The hat lay upturned on the ground, the cap badge upside down, symbolising a fallen colleague.

It was the small things that got to you.

A tear fell from Kate's eye.

She wiped it away.

'Kate?'

'Sorry . . .' She cleared her throat. 'Where do you want me?'

Sue noticed Kate's chest rising and falling heavily, evidence that she was under immense stress, mentally unprepared to carry out her request. 'Nowhere. I don't know what I was thinking. Step out. I'd be grateful if you could find Curtis for me.'

'No . . . please,' Kate begged. 'I'd rather it was me.'

Sue hesitated, then gave a nod. 'Georgina would want that.'

It took all Kate's resolve not to bawl. She wanted to gather Georgina up in her arms and take her home to her family, for no other reason than to avoid what was coming, a post-mortem, identification, trauma for all involved. Sue would be as gentle in her handling of Georgina's lifeless body as any doctor would a live patient. Still, Kate the friend, not the detective, wanted to spare her that indignity.

Restarting her recording, and with Kate's help, Sue rolled Georgina over, noting that there were no other injuries on the body as far as she could tell . . . 'There's mud on her uniform trousers, a lot of it, ingrained, more than I'd expect to see if the victim had fallen, clear evidence that she'd been kneeling when shot.'

Kate was broken.

This wasn't murder, it was an execution.

1

Three years later

Jackson's emotions were all over the place as the vehicle he was travelling in approached the city centre. The journey south had been a blast: a short stop for a Big Mac, a crateful of Ouseburn Porter to wash it down with, a welcome home gift his mother called "Mobile Happy Hour". Only in Newcastle would you find four grown-ups wearing Santa hats without a hint of embarrassment.

The miles had flown by.

As the car drove down the hill toward the Tyne, there was a lull in conversation. In the distance, the arch of the Millennium Bridge changed to the colour purple. Jackson's gaze shifted to the slow-moving, inky black water beneath, the cityscape beyond reflected on the surface, a mirror image underlined by a thin slither of light from the underside of the pedestrian walkway. He'd never been able to put into words his attachment to his birthplace, except to say that a vice closed around his chest every time he left, a feeling that was even more profound when he returned. After a three-year absence, all he'd dreamt of for weeks was this moment.

He felt deeply touched being there.

Raising his mobile, he zoomed in, capturing the image of the iconic bridge, marking his return to home soil. The Quayside was rammed tonight, everyone having a lush time as they sang and danced drunkenly in both directions, from one of the many nightspots on either side of the river.

In a few minutes he'd be joining them.

'Good to be home, son?'

The question had come from Jacob, the best chauffer in the business, his mother's driver for as long as Jackson could remember, ferrying him to and from school until he was old enough to go by himself. Unable to speak, he nodded at the sympathetic eyes looking at him through the rear-view mirror.

Picking up on what had become a friendly staring contest, his brother Lee gave his Jackson's arm a solid squeeze, slurring his words as he spoke. 'Comin' unstuck again, young 'un?'

Jackson looked away, embarrassed. 'Does my head in every time.'

'Hey! We've all been there, haven't we guys?' Neither man in the front answered, or if they did, Lee didn't seem hear them. He was too busy yanking the ring-pulls off two more beers, shoving one in Jackson's hand, clinking cans. 'Get your crying over with. We're local heroes going home, right?' He put an arm around Jackson's neck, pulling him into a tight hug that felt like an arm lock, adding his voice to Chris Rea's *Driving Home for Christmas* as it bled into the car from the radio.

Jackson pulled away.

Lee mumbled into the ear of the front seat passenger: 'Get what I asked for?'

Tony hadn't said a lot since their journey began. He'd allowed Jacob to entertain the brothers in the rear on what was and had been going on in the party city locals called The Toon. Jacob was comedy gold, Tony the exact opposite. He couldn't crack a smile if his life depended on it.

His mother's money man was a hard man to read, mild-mannered one minute, ruthless the next. Reaching into his breast pocket, he retrieved a folded envelope, passing it into the rear without a backward glance.

Lee handed it to Jackson.

'What's this?' he asked.

'An early pressy, from me to you. And while we're on the subject, I have another surprise for you. We're not going back to Spain. When the New Year arrives, we're staying put—'

'But, I thought mam said—'

Lee pointed at the envelope. 'Get it open, man.'

Intrigued, with Lee breathing down his neck, Jackson slid a finger under the flap to get at the contents, two match day tickets in the posh seats – Newcastle United home game at Christmas – every Geordie's dream. When he looked up, the tears were back. As gifts go, this was right up there.

He fist-bumped his brother.

'Game on!' he said.

STONE & OLIVER SERIES

THE LOST
Alex arrives home from holiday to find that her ten-year-old son Daniel has disappeared. It's the first case together for Northumbria CID officers David Stone and Frankie Oliver. But as the investigation unfolds, they realise the family's betrayal goes deeper than anyone suspected. This isn't just a missing persons case. Stone and Oliver are hunting a killer.

THE INSIDER
When the body of a young woman is found by a Northumberland railway line, it's a baptism of fire for detective duo DCI David Stone and DS Frankie Oliver. The case is tough by anyone's standards, but Stone is convinced that there's a leak in his team – someone is giving the killer a head start on the investigation. These women are being targeted for a reason. And the next target is close to home...

THE SCANDAL
When *Herald* court reporter, Chris Adams, is found stabbed to death in Newcastle with no eyewitnesses, the MIT are stumped. Adams was working on a scoop that would make his name. But what was the story he was investigating? And who was trying to cover it up? When a link to a missing woman is uncovered, the investigation turns on its head. The exposé has put more than Adams' life in danger. And it's not over yet.

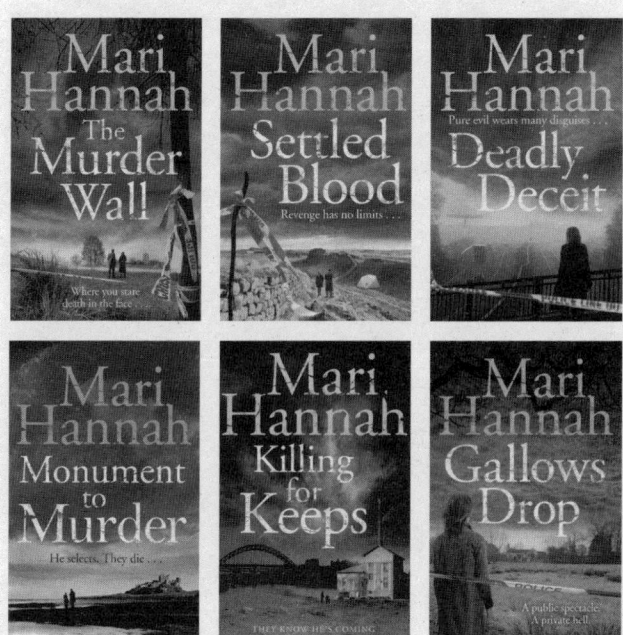

HER LAST REQUEST

'Involving, sophisticated, intelligent and suspenseful
– everything a great crime thriller should be'
LEE CHILD

'A gripping, twisty police procedural – fans of the
Kate Daniels series will love this one'
SHARI LAPENA

'Compelling, page-turning suspense. Kate Daniels
is a character to cherish, and Mari is a
writer at the very top of her game'
STEVE CAVANAGH